Typeset by Robert Newland, Edited by Jonathan Downes
Cover design and Layout by Mark North
Photographs by Robert Newland, Mark North and Jonathan North

<small>Using Microsoft Word 2000, Microsoft , Publisher 2000, Adobe Photoshop CS.</small>

First published in Great Britain by CFZ Press 2007

**CFZ Press
Myrtle Cottage
Woolsery
Bideford
North Devon
EX39 5QR**

© CFZ MMVII

All rights reserved. Without limiting the rights under copyright reserved above, no part of this publication may be reproduced, stored in or introduced into a retrieval system, or transmitted, in any form of by any means (electronic, mechanical, photocopying, recording or otherwise), without the prior written permission of both the copyright owners and the publishers of this book.

ISBN: 978-1-905723-15-7

CONTENTS

FOREWORD BY JONATHAN DOWNES	5
INTRODUCTION	9
HAUNTERS OF THE BYWAYS	11
MURDERER'S LANE & THE GIBBET PIT	27
THE VILLAGE OF THE DEAD	31
LEGIONS OF THE DOWNS	37
GHOSTLY GOINGS ON	47
HAUNTING BEYOND THE GRAVE	63
THE DEMON JUDGE OF DORCHESTER	69
THE LEGACY AND CURSE OF BETTISCOMBE MANOR	73
THINGS THAT GO BUMP! IN THE NIGHT	91
MUSIC BARROWS & FAIRY FOLK	105
LOATHERS OF CHRISTIANITY	117
SPECTRAL LIGHTS	121
BRING OUT YOUR DEAD	129
THE WISHING WELL OF LOVE & DOOM	135

DORSET'S DEVIL	143
WORK-A-DAY WITCHERY	147
PINS & NEEDLES	153
PROTECTIVE WITCH CHARMS	155
DIANA THE MOON GODDESS & THE MAGIC CIRCLE	161
THE RIDING OF THE WITCH	163
THE WITCH'S MIZ-MAZE	169
THE BELL THEIVES	171
MAGICAL JUSTICE	175
THE PILLAR & THE CONJUROR	179
MEGALITHS & MONOLITHS ON THE MOVE	183
THE DEVIL'S HELLSTONES	185
THE DEVIL'S HUNTING GROUND	191
MYSTERIOUS CREATURES	197
STRANGE PHENOMENA	239
BIBLIOGRAPHY	265
ACKNOWLEDGEMENTS	267
INDEX	269

FOREWORD

by Jonathan Downes

Francis James Child (1825–1896), was an American scholar. Much of his life was devoted to the comparative study of British vernacular ballads. He accumulated, in the university library at Harvard, one of the largest folklore collections in existence, studied both manuscript and printed sources, and carried his investigations into the ballads of languages other than English, meanwhile giving a sedulous but conservative hearing to popular versions that were then still surviving.

I first 'met' Child through a book called *'The Drifters'* by James Michener, which in many ways was a proscribed text for the hippy generation. The 'Child Ballads' as they are known, are a reoccurring motif in the book, and act as a background to fictionalised retellings of the socio political struggles of the late sixties.

This got me interested in folksongs as a subject in itself, and over the years I collected a number of examples of the peculiar evolution which happens to something that is basically an oral tradition, rather than a written screed. In 1978 a bloke called Andy Cameron had a hit single with a song called *"Ally's Tartan Army"*, which included the following lyrics:

"We're on the march with Ally's Army/We're going to the Argentine/And we'll really shake them up, when we win the World Cup/Because Scotland is the greatest football team."

Ally was, by the way, the Scotland World Cup team manager or something like that. But I digress. Some years later I was given a CD of Irish rebel songs, which included a song called *"God Bless Ireland"*, which had exactly the same tune. Since then I have found that it is a country and western song and a Methodist hymn, and it would not surprise me at all to find that there are several other versions.

I have often wondered which song was the original. The tune is simple, and easily learned, lending itself to a marching song, a hymn, or a children's rhyming song. I would be unsurprised to learn that it had been a marching song for one (or both) sides in the English Civil War, and would not be completely gob smacked to learn that a version of it had been sung by the Roman Legions!

Mark North, one of the authors of this present volume, has been a friend of mine for well over a decade, but it was only when putting the final touches to this book, that I recognised the similarities between him (and his co-author), and the largely forgotten Professor Child.

Folklore is an arcane study at the best of times, and it is one that covers a very wide range of subject matter. At one end of the spectrum you have simple stories, handed down from parent to child over successive generations, acquiring more embellishments each time it is passed on. These stories - in many ways - are like the folksongs I described earlier, and there are many books which contain a smattering of such tales.

But this book is different. Like Professor Child, Mark and Robert have trekked across their native county of Dorset, not only collecting folktales, but attempting in many cases to investigate the truth behind these otherwise amorphous legends. They have - equally importantly - provided an enormous photographic archive of the places and people named in the tales, and have eventually produced a volume of almost encyclopaedic scope.

They should be commended for their diligence and hard work in preserving these tales which - to my knowledge at least - have never been collected together in this form, for future generations.

Well done lads.

Jon Downes
(Director, CFZ)
The Centre for Fortean Zoology,
Devon
May 2007

'All these, however, were mere terrors of the night, phantoms of the mind that walk in darkness;'

Washington Irving: *The Legend of Sleepy Hollow*, 1819

INTRODUCTION

Sunshine sparkling on streams, sheep and cows grazing peacefully among endless rolling hills, whispering waves breaking on beautiful beaches, picture postcard villages and cream teas. This is Dorset. But there is another side to Dorset, a side dark with mystery and folklore, of half remembered fireside tales, of peculiar customs and strange beliefs.

Step into folklore and you will enter into a world of superstition and wonder, of dark enchantments and of dreadful horrors. Great riches and extreme poverty, curious encounters, fantastic fortunes as well as sadness and loss. Spellbinding magic, intoxicating thrills, foul deeds, death and destruction alongside humour, joy and laughter, love, and tragedy. It is far richer than one could ever believe. It will amuse you, intrigue you, captivate you, and draw you in without you realising it. Where before a simple crossroads or clump of trees were nothing out of the ordinary, in this world of folklore ones perception alters and becomes animated, so that they are no longer just places in the landscape, but the actual haunt of a ghost or spectre, or indeed, a place of symbolic meaning where once something incredible happened. In the world of folklore, a common museum exhibit like a dried cat, or witch bottle suddenly takes on a greater significance, it is no longer just a dusty object in a glass cabinet, but an actual magic charm to protect against evil. The world of folklore is vast and mysterious and sometimes contradictory, yet it is all around us waiting to be discovered, and when it yields its secrets, it leads us back to an older rustic culture, back to a world that our forefathers experienced day to day.

In this fast-paced, modern, scientific-age, it is of course safe to laugh at such fanciful folklore, but when the grey mist veils the downs and the winds roar at night, when Dorset is alive with hidden torment, then perhaps you are more likely to think a little more seriously about such things. Many of us are guilty of an odd kind of double-thinking. We might deny the existence of ghosts and the like, but how many of us would care to spend the night alone in a haunted place. Is anyone wise or brave enough to say that these incredible folktales have not, at least, a grain of truth in them? For this is Dark Dorset!

RESTLESS BYWAYS

Ancient byways with secrets untold,
Their hidden torment begins to unfold,
Their twists and scars are there to see,
Their dark past holds the key.

The wind's haunting melody gives a clue,
The trees close in engulfing the light,
Dread begins to fill my soul
As the chill air begins to bite.

The dead reach out across the void,
Embracing a shudder of fear,
Make haste! Make haste!
Away from.

Those dark and dismal lanes where restless spirits wander,
Spectres, ghosts and apparitions dwell,

And ghastly phantom funeral processions
Haunt to the chime of the midnight bell.

Robert Newland

HAUNTERS OF THE BYWAYS

If you should but venture beyond Dorset's main roads, along the narrow winding lanes, you will soon come upon one of the many remote quiet villages of the county where you can escape the hustle and bustle of modern life.

In the past, few people travelled to such isolated places, especially at night. Those that *did* would make haste to the nearest inn for a drink, and a bed to gain refuge from the terrors of the night. Still, there *were* people who braved the late hours to travel on the open road.

When Dorchester was but a small market town, three brothers settled down all snug by the crackling log fire of an old Dorchester inn. Outside, the pale moon cast down its silvery light, and the chill wind blew the last leaves of autumn against the windowpane.

"It's a cold night," said the landlord. *"Especially for such as dance outdoors."* A criminal had been hanged earlier that day, a mile and a half down the road, at an isolated spot called 'Monkey's Jump.'

The elder of the three brothers looked out of the window. *"Wouldn't care to be in such a lonely place tonight."*

"Nor I," agreed the second brother. *"A night such as this is best left to the dead!"* The youngest brother laughed, and scoffed at his elder siblings. *"Hark at that, landlord, my brothers are afraid of the dark!"*

"We're not afraid," protested the elder. *"We are just as fearless as you, but a wise man knows when to leave some things well alone."* The youngest then proceeded to jest and mock his brothers' cowardice, and boasted of how much braver he was than they.

Then an old man who had been quietly listening in the corner piped up. *"Why don't you show us all how fearless you are, by offering that poor soul who swings a hot bowl of soup to warm his heart."*

The young man quickly drank down his beer, and without a second thought agreed to the challenge. The landlord brought from the kitchen a bowl of hot steaming broth, and placed it on the table in front of the young brother. He couldn't back down now.

With only the uneasy thoughts of the hanged criminal to keep him company, he pursued his way west along High West Street, carefully carrying the hot bowl of soup. Soon he left the town behind. Ahead of him was nothing but a dark lonely road, and the dejection of the unknown. Eventually, in the far distance, he could see the gallows silhouetted in the night sky, and the dead man dangling from it. As he approached closer to the gallows, an inexplicable fear suddenly began to take hold. Never had the young man felt so melancholy, and the nearer he approached the gloomy gallows, the more dismal he became.

It was the very hour of midnight when he finally reached his destination, and there the grisly sight of the dead man greeted him; his bulging, bloodshot eyes gazed down at him, and his plump, black, tongue, engorged with blood, protruded from his gaping mouth. The eerie creak of the corpse swinging in the breeze suddenly made the young man feel quite sick, and sent a shiver down his spine, but he had come this far, and he was determined to see the challenge through.

He held up the bowl of broth to the dead man. *"Here sir, I have brought some hot soup to warm you!"* Suddenly a dismal groan passed the dead man's lips, and a ghastly croaking voice replied. *"Blow it, it's too hot!"* Instantly waves of horror swept over the young man, and in sheer terror he dropped the bowl of soup, and fled screaming. He ran without stopping all the way back to the comfort of the inn, and to the wisdom of the living.

The young man had indeed proved how fearless he was, but it came at the hefty price of fear itself, the very thing he claimed he was without. Fear, they say, can lead a man to drink; it's no wonder then that many a ghostly tale has been told over a pint, yet often it is the name of the public house itself that begins the story.

Until recently, Halstock had an inn called, *The Quiet Woman*, with a sign outside depicting a headless woman. Though the pub has sadly gone, the gruesome tale it commemorated still haunts the village to this day.

In the seventh century a baby girl called Juthware (pronounced *Uth-are*), was born in the village, but it was a difficult birth, and her mother died leaving her to be brought up by Benna, the girl's father.

St. Judith, as depicted on *The Quiet Woman* Inn sign

Benna looked after his daughter as best as he could, but what the girl needed was a mother, and in time he relinquished his loss by taking another wife.

This second wife was a Welsh woman called Goneril, who was also a widow, and had - by her former husband - a son called Bana. All was well at first, but as the years passed, Goneril began to despise her step-daughter, for not only was she beautiful, but she was a devoted Christian, often fasting and doing penance for her sins.

Many pilgrims and wayfarers travelled the roads, and would often seek shelter at Juthware's father's house. Benna was a good, but sick, man, and remembering the kindness of his first wife was always keen to show hospitality. And so while they ate, Juthware would pass among them with drinking horns of wine and ale, and listen to their wonderful stories of Our Lord's birth and life.

The Quiet Woman Inn, Halstock

When Benna died, Juthware followed her father's example of hospitality. This angered Goneril, who could not stand her stepdaughter's good qualities any longer, and so she contrived a plan to be rid of her.

Goneril's chance came one morning, when Juthware came to her complaining of chest pains. She told Juthware to rub some cheese onto her chest and stomach, first thing in the morning and last thing at night, and the pains would go.

When Goneril saw Juthware doing this, she went secretly into the wood, and there slaughtered a lamb, and left it for the wolves. The next morning she went to her son, and told him that Juthware had given birth to a child in the wood, and had fed it to the wolves. However, Bana would not believe her, so she took him into the wood and showed him the remains of the bloodied carcass. But still Bana would not believe it, so she brought Juthware to the wood and ordered her to remove her vest. Bana examined the garment and found the stains of motherhood.

In a fit of rage, he drew his sword, and cut Juthware's head clean off. Goneril's face was triumphant, but as she revelled in her step-daughter's death, to her horror, Juthware's severed head called to her body. It jerked, and rising slowly to its feet, gathered the head, and moved - with measured mechanical steps - down the hill, and along the lane to the church, and there placed her head on the altar before finally dying. Soon after, Juthware became known as Saint Juthware, and a shrine was dedicated to her at the place of her martyrdom.

But the gruesome tale doesn't end there, for at one o'clock in the morning on All Saints Day

(1st November), Saint Juthware's ghost is said to return to repeat the incident. She is said to be seen carrying her head in the lane leading to Abbots Hill, alias Judith Hill.

Perhaps one of the most terrifying experiences that can be imagined, is the sight of a person - apparently alive - but without a head! Headless hauntings are not uncommon in Dorset.

At Loders, near Bridport, a headless coachman has been seen haunting Yellow Lane on foot going towards Waddon Hill. The legend says that he is searching for his head after it was decapitated by a tree branch.

The seventeenth and eighteenth centuries were a great era for the horse-drawn carriage, but the narrow winding tracks and roads that were used as coaching routes were treacherous, and therefore accidents were common. However, even in the best of conditions, the roads were at the mercy of robbers and highwaymen. A coach was once held up, and robbed, by highwaymen, at Coach Lane Gate, near Hambury Farm, West Lulworth. The driver was killed, and beheaded with a sword, and ever since the lane has been haunted by the phantom coach and its headless driver.

Kingston Russell House, on the Dorchester to Bridport Road, is haunted by a phantom coach drawn by four headless horses, driven by a headless coachman, carrying four headless passengers, and even sporting a headless footman! On certain unspecified nights, the coach is said to drive up to the door, stop for a short time, and then drive away again. This haunting may seem like a work of fiction, but the coach has been seen many times. In 1988 an elderly lady attending a folklore lecture at Sherborne, claimed to those assembled there that she had seen the phantom coach back in the early 1920's when she was a young girl.

The drive leading up to Kingston Russell House is said to be haunted by a phantom coach drawn by four headless horses, driven by a headless coachman

There is a phantom coach with a pair of headless horses near Handley Cross, which - according to *Ghosts and Legends of the Dorset Countryside* by Edward Waring (1977), was seen in the 1930's, by a Mr. Elliott of Upwood. The coach and horses came thundering over Oakley Down, from the Cranborne direction, and vanished upon reaching the Salisbury road.

But not all such ghosts appear decapitated. A spectral coach where the driver and horses have retained their cervical vertebrae intact, is said to appear along the stretch of Roman road between Bradford Peverell and Muckleford. It is said that a coach being driven from Bradford Peverell to Muckleford once overturned into a bog by the roadside, and the driver and horse were killed. Before the 1950's, the story of the phantom coach was so firmly impressed in the minds of the Muckleford residents, that the children were sent to Stratton School along the main road, for fear of seeing the ghostly coach at the spot where the accident happened.

Another phantom coach that suffered a similar fate, haunts the road that leads from Holnest towards Broke Wood. The coach is said to be heard clattering along the road, and as it approaches the second bridge called Hunter's Bridge, it appears and careers off the bridge and crashes into the stream.

Trent Barrow Pond, at the foot of Carlock Hill, is reputed to be bottomless. It is here that a coach and horses with passengers careered off the road never to be seen again. However, on moonlit nights along the stretch of road known as Ham Lane adjacent to the pond, the eerie sound of galloping horses and ghostly cries can be heard.

At Wool, beside the mediaeval bridge over the River Frome, there is a Jacobean manor house called Woolbridge House. The manor was once owned by the famous Turbevilles family, upon whom Thomas Hardy based his book *Tess of the D'Urbervilles* (1891). It is from Woolbridge House, that a ghostly coach-and-four has been seen driving out into the gloomy evening twilight towards Bere Regis, where the former Turberville mansion was once sited. The coach is alleged to forecast doom, and can only be seen by the direct descendents of the Turbervilles family.

The Internet can be a wonderful resource for folklorists, but - sadly - details are often vague. One incident involving the Turberville coach, comes from the Holmebridge House website (www.holmebridgehouse.co.uk) and tells a story allegedly recalled by a clergyman from Wool, who "many years ago" once invited a gentleman from Wiltshire to stay with him. His visitor, who arrived late on a dark night in December, had driven from Wareham in his carriage. When he reached the clergyman's house he asked whether any of the neighbouring gentry had a coach and four.

"Why no", replied his host. *"No-one in the whole neighbourhood has a coach-and-four in these days"*.

"Well, somebody must have", said the Wiltshire gentleman. *"Because, when coming to you in my carriage, I saw an old fashioned four-in-hand with out-riders being driven at a great rate. To whom does it belong?"*

The terrifying spectral Turberville Coach thunders over the bridge at Woolbridge Manor

The Parson looked at him curiously. *"No-one round here has such a coach"*, he said. *"you surely must have seen the Turberville coach. But there's an old story connected with it, that no-one possibly can see this Turberville coach, unless he has the family blood in his veins."*

"In the reign of James I my ancestor, Phillip, married Margaret Turberville, niece of the old Squire of Woolbridge," replied the guest to his host's astonishment.

In R. Thurston Hopkins's *Thomas Hardy's Dorset* (1922), the author meets a local thatcher who is known as the 'Old Gover' and discusses about the legend of the phantom coach.

> *Then I asked Gover about the Turberville ghost which we are told haunts this lane, and which is the subject of an allusion in Hardy's Tess of the D'Urbervilles. His keen old face became serious at once. No ghosts or goblins had troubled him, he said, but John Rawless and another chap saw as plain as could be a funeral going along from Woolbridge House to Bere Regis, and they heard the priest singing in front of the coffin, but they could not understand what he did say. There was a cattle gate across the road in those days and Rawles ran to open it, but before he could get there the coffin had passed through the gate and it had all vanished: He had often heard tell of people who had seen ghosts, and he would not be put about if he did see one himself.*

"So you have not seen the blood-stained family coach of the Turbervilles?", I inquired.

"No, I never see that," said Gover, shaking his head, *"nor never heard of it."*

"Then , as it is a tale that every child should know," I said, "I will tell you now, and you shall believe it or no, precisely as you choose. Once upon a time there was a Turberville who deserves to be remembered and to be called, so to speak, the limb of the 'old 'un' himself, for he spent all his days in wickedness, and went roaring to the devil as fast as all his vices could send him. I have heard it said that he snapped his fingers in the face of a good parson who came to see him on his death-bed, saying he did not wish to talk balderdash, or to hear it, and bade him clear out and send up his servant with fighting-cooks and a bottle of brandy. Gradually all the drinking and vice, which had besieged his soul for so long, swept him into a state of temporary madness and he murdered a friend while they were riding to Woolbridge House in the family coach. The friend he struck down had Turberville blood in his veins too, so you may be certain the blame was not all on one side. Ever since the evil night the coach with the demon horses dragging it sways and rocks along the road between Wool and Bere, and the murderer rushes after it, moaning and wringing his hands, but never naving the fortune to catch it up. The spectacle of the haunted coach cannot be seen by the ordinary wayfarer; it is only to be seen by persons in which blood of the Turberville is mixed."

"Ah!" nodded old Gover, "I don't hold with that story. If so be as that 'ere Turberville who murdered t'other hev a-gone up above, 'tain't likely as how he'll be wishful to go rowstering after that ripping great coach on a dalled bad road like this." And then he shook his bony finger in my face and added: "And if the dowl have a-got hold on 'im he won't be able to go gallyvanting about - he'll be kept there!"

Since then the Turberville coach has been seen in 1885, in 1900 and more recently in the 1960s, by a bus driver who mistook it for a real coach. This is not an isolated occurrence because another spectral coach-and-four is said to haunt the road between Stoke Abbott and Beaminster.

There is a mourning coach at Lytchett Matravers, which was witnessed on more than one occasion. Children used to say the phantom coach, decorated as for a funeral, came out from the holly trees, and went up and down the road at Huntick Hill. The coach was seen around 1900, by a man walking home late one night. He heard a clattering of horse's hooves coming up behind him and turning around saw what he described as the most beautiful sight he had ever seen. The mourning coach, brilliantly lit up and drawn by two horses, went past him and up the road before turning around and passing him again, but there was no sign of a driver. Prior to that, in the early nineteenth century, a Mr Billy Bartlett saw the coach and following behind it a procession of ghostly mourners carrying lighted tapers. Dorset's only other known phantom mourning coach is said to haunt outside the foreboding Bettiscombe Manor.*

* 'Bettiscombe Manor.' See chapter:' The Curse and Legacy of Bettiscombe Manor'.

Before the twentieth century, it was usually only the wealthy who could afford the hire of a mourning coach for a loved one's funeral. The poor had to make do without such luxury and therefore had only the use of pallbearers on foot to carry the coffin to the place of burial.

At the village of Marnhull, a phantom funeral is supposed to be seen at midnight, crossing Sackmore Lane, from Fillymead to Dunford going towards a legendary battlefield near Todber, where in 1870 a vast number of human bones were uncovered. No mourners are seen to follow the pallbearers, who have their faces hidden beneath the pall. The same funeral also haunts Grove Field, near Nash Court.

Another frightening funeral procession was actually once seen in the mid nineteenth century at a place near Culpepper's Dish, not far from the hamlet of Briantspuddle. A woman who was returning home with a bundle of kindling, was resting by the wayside when she suddenly heard the sound of tramping feet, and then looking along the lane saw four headless men appear carrying a coffin. The terrified woman promptly fled the scene leaving her bundle behind, and nothing and no-one could persuade her ever to return and collect it.

A ghostly funeral procession haunts this lane near Culpepper's Dish

More ghostly funeral processions are said to haunt the following places:

- Three Gates just above Colepay Cottage, on the Broadwindsor to Drimpton road;
- On the Lytchett Minster to Poole road, where four headless bearers carrying a coffin disappear into a hedge;
- On the stroke of midnight in Milborne St. Andrew;
- In the dark sunken lane known as The Cutting between Powerstock and West Milton;

At midnight, at Shipton Gorge near Bridport, a phantom funeral procession with four headless pallbearers haunts a place called Gadger's Hole, between Kennon Hill and St. Catherine's Cross, and is said to be seen heading towards the village.

A funeral procession, with six headless pallbearers haunts Ruscombe Lane from Powerstock to North Poorton.

One particularly strange haunting, is that of a mysterious ghostly coffin that has been seen several times lying in the B3078 road, a mile north of Wimborne. It is said to appear near an old barn where a man committed suicide. He was buried - according to custom - with a stake through his heart, at a crossroads* about one mile to the north on the parish boundary between Colehill and Hinton Parva. A similar ghostly coffin was seen by a motorist lying in the road near Gillingham. Reports from the nineteenth century mention how a coffin fell from its horse-drawn hearse at the very same spot.

A ghostly severed hand is said to terrorise the village of Pimperne. According to William Chafin in his *Anecdotes and History of Cranbourn* [sic] *Chase*, (1818). On the 16th December 1780, Chettle Common, in Bursey-stool Walk, was the scene of a serious fracas between a gang of poachers, and some gamekeepers. The poachers were all armed with deadly weapons called swindgels (resembling the flails used to thresh corn). They attacked the gamekeepers, who only had sticks and short hangers† to defend themselves. The leader of the poaching gang, a Sergeant of the Dragoons named Blandford, struck the first blow, which broke a gamekeeper's kneecap instantly, putting him out of the chase. Another keeper received a heavy blow from a swindgel, which broke three ribs, and which later caused his death.

The remaining keepers, with their hangers at the ready, closed in upon their opponents, and in all the commotion Blandford had one of his hands severed from his arm just above the wrist, and fell in agony to the ground; and the others were dreadfully cut and wounded. They all surrendered, and were taken to Dorchester Assizes, where they were condemned to be transported for seven years. But in consideration of their great suffering from their wounds, the Judge commuted the punishment to confinement in gaol for an indefinite term.

After many years they were released, and Blandford opened a shop in London, where he eventually died. As for his severed hand, it was buried with full military honours in St. Peter's cemetery, Pimperne. Yet, since its burial, the lanes around Pimperne are haunted by the hand, which is seen dripping with blood, inching its way along the ground, in search of the arm to which it had once been attached. The hand has often been seen at *Bloody Shard Gate* some distance away.

Ghosts often haunt boundaries, such as crossroads, gates, and even bridges. This is because a boundary is an `in-between place`, always in a transitional state, like midnight. *'The Witching Hour'*, is between one day and another, and as such these thresholds serve as possible doorways to the world of the dead.

Daggers Gate,‡ West Lulworth, is allegedly haunted by the ghost of a witch who was found dead nearby and then buried at the gate.

---

* *'Crossroads.'* It was customary to bury the bodies of suicides, criminals and suspected vampires at crossroads, the reason being that the ghost of the deceased would be confused by the choice of roads and would be unable to find its way home. The custom of burial of suicides at crossroads in Britain was abolished in 1823.

† *'Hangers.'* the landsman's equivalent to the cutlass. The hanger was developed from hunting swords and was the standard weapon of the infantryman (along with the musket).

‡ *'Daggers Gate.'* See chapter, 'Work-a-day Witchery'.

A severed hand, that was buried in St. Peter's cemetery, Pimperne.
It is said to haunt the lanes around the village in search of the arm to which it had once been attached. The hand has often been seen at Bloody Shard Gate some distance away.

About two miles west of Evershot, is a junction called Red Post. The unusual name derives from the English Civil War, when a post of Parliamentarian soldiers was ambushed by a band of Royalists. Ever since, the junction has since been considered a bad place, and someone passing at night may hear the blood curdling war cries and screams of battle.

The bridge by Corfe Castle is haunted by the headless ghost of a woman, dressed in a long white nightgown. She has been seen several times, the most recent on the 4th July 1967, by a local man, who was driving home at two o'clock in the morning, when the apparition drifted across the road in front of him.

Winters Lane, Portesham, the ghost of a headless man has been seen sitting on a farm gate by the roadside and illogically, heard whistling!

The road that leads south from Horton, East Dorset, is reported to have two ghosts. A young boy clad in seventeenth century Stuart style dress who is said to cross the road, and then vanish. The other, the ghost of a nun believed to be from the Benedictine abbey that was situated at Horton.

Another unknown ghost is that of a weeping young girl dressed in black, seen haunting the eerie sunken lane to the north of St. John the Baptist church at Symondsbury. In 1984 Mrs Addams of Bridport mistook the girl for a living person. When asked why she was crying, the young girl promptly vanished!

St. Andrew's, Kinson. The cemetery is haunted by a headless ghost of a young woman

Graveyards are often thought to be haunted places, but few cemeteries boast a *real* ghost. However, the headless ghost of a young woman haunts the churchyard of St. Andrew's, Kinson, near Bournemouth. According to Stephen Newland in his *Weird and Wonderful Tales of Dorset* (1982), a woman's skull with a marlinspike* embedded in it was found nearby, some years ago. It is not known who she was, but one explanation may be that she was murdered after betraying a smuggler to the Revenue men.

---

* *Marlinspike is a tool that is used for splicing rope. It can be a tapered metal pin or carved of wood*

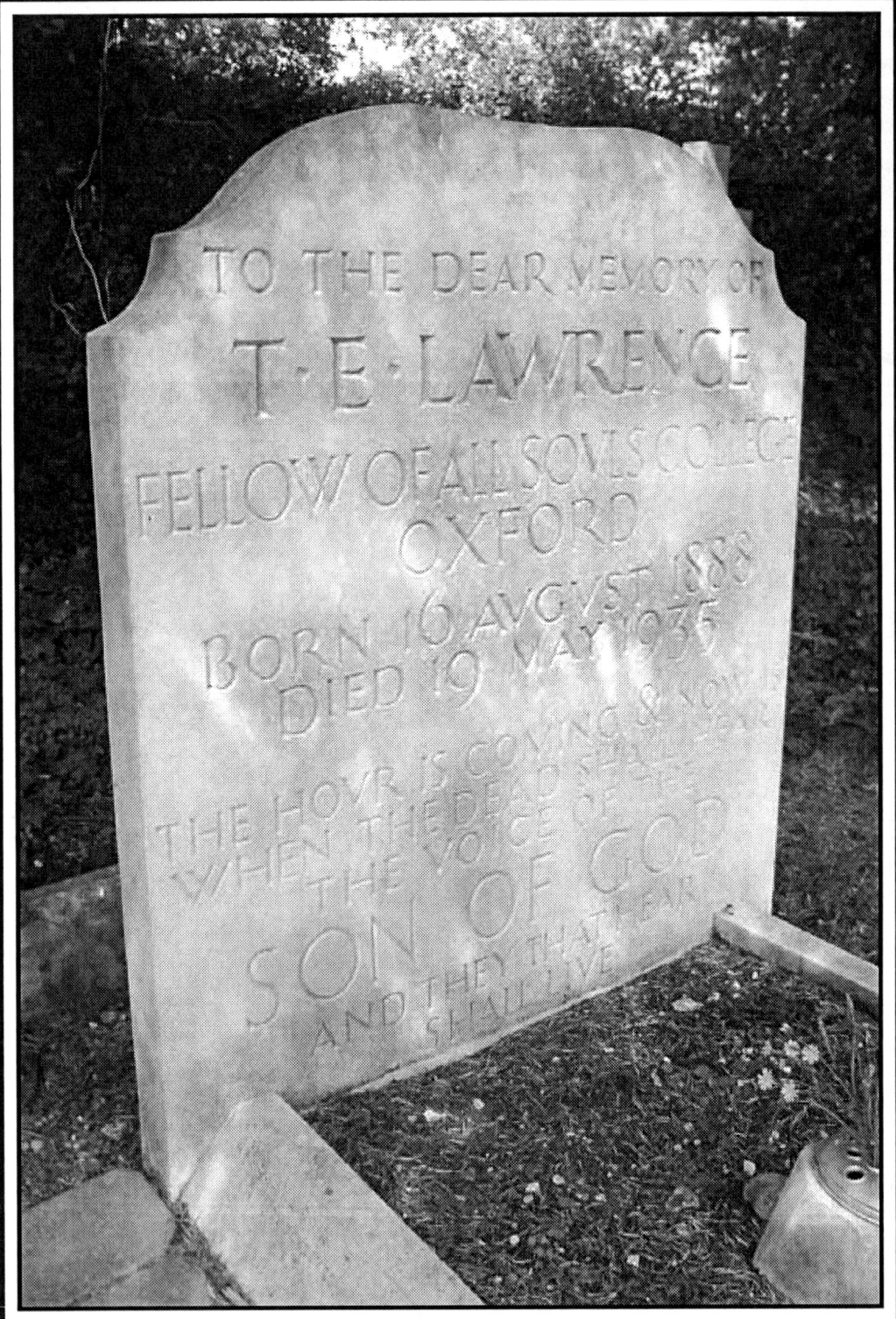

T. E. Lawrence's body lies buried at Moreton cemetery

A wreath placed by a tree, which was planted near the roadside in memorial where Lawrence had his motorcycle accident

No-one can say for certain who - or what - these ghosts really are, or indeed the mystery that lies behind their deaths. However, there is one road ghost that is known by name, and whose identity is in no doubt. This is probably the most famous of all Dorset's 'haunters of the by-way'; Colonel Thomas Edward Lawrence, a.k.a 'Lawrence of Arabia' war hero, archaeologist, and author *, who was involved in fatal motorcycle accident on 13th May 1935.

On that ill-fated day, Lawrence was riding back to his home at Clouds Hill from Bovington Camp, on his favourite motorcycle the *Brough Superior* (which he nick-named *'Boa'*, short for *'Boanerges'*, the *'sons of thunder'* in Greek mythology) when he came upon two errand boys, riding bicycles hidden from his view. As he came upon them at great speed, he swerved violently to avoid them. Losing control of his motorcycle, Lawrence was thrown over the handlebars, receiving severe injuries to the brain. His physical strength was so great, that he lay unconscious for nearly five days before he died of congestion of the lungs and heart failure.

The evidence at the inquest revealed a curious contradiction. Corporal Catchpole of the Royal Army Ordnance Corps. was standing about a hundred yards from the road, near Clouds Hill, when he saw Lawrence on his motor-cycle - travelling at about fifty or sixty miles an hour - pass a black private car going in the opposite direction, just before he heard the crash. The two boys, whose evidence at times was confused, had no memory of a car passing them.

Lawrence was laid to rest in St. Nicholas Church cemetery, Moreton, on May 21st 1935, and a memorial plaque was later erected by the roadside to mark the spot in which he fell. Since his death, the sound of his roaring motorcycle has been heard by farmers just prior to sunrise. But reports say that the noise abruptly ceases before anything is seen.

---

* *Lawrence of Arabia. Lieutenant-Colonel* **Thomas Edward Lawrence**, *CB, DSO (August 16, 1888 – May 19, 1935), known professionally as* **T.E. Lawrence** *and, later,* **T.E. Shaw**, *but most famously as* **"Lawrence of Arabia,"** *gained international renown for his role as a British liaison officer during the Arab Revolt of 1916-18. Lawrence's public image was due in part to U.S. traveller and journalist Lowell Thomas' sensationalised reportage of the Revolt, as well as to Lawrence's autobiographical account, Seven Pillars of Wisdom. (From Wikipedia, the free encyclopedia).*

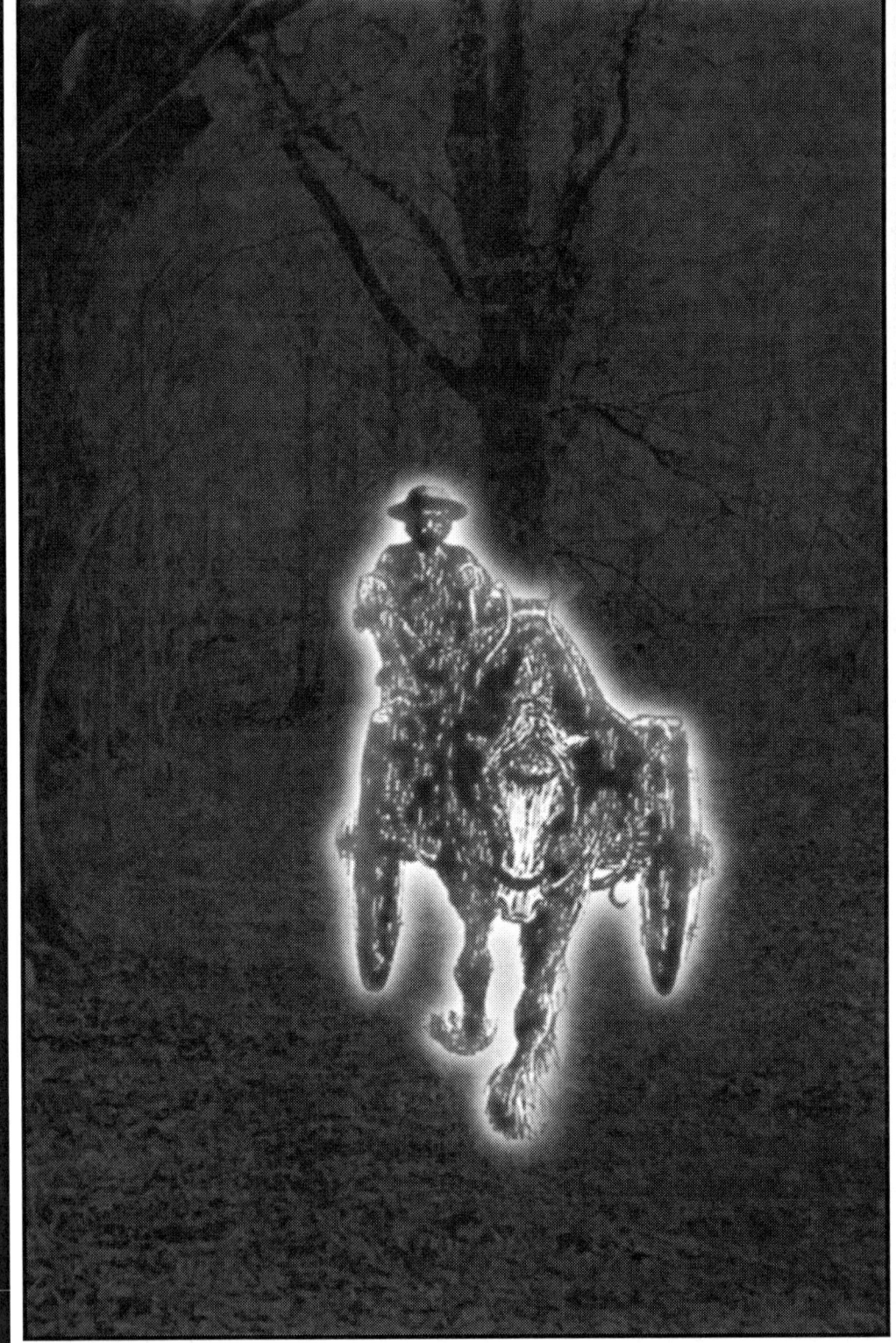

MURDERER'S LANE
& THE GIBBET PIT

Nestled at the foot of Bubb Down Hill lies the sleep little village of Melbury Bubb. With only one road in and out, it is indeed a remote and hidden spot, but even this village with all its unique charm, has its own dark tale to tell

On the night of 10th November 1694, the peace was shattered by a most violent and brutal murder. The victim, a farmer by the name of Thomas Baker, was on his way home from Dorchester market after a successful day's trading. When coming over Bubb Down Hill along the old drove, he was attacked by two assailants. Without warning, Thomas Baker was pulled from his cart and pinned to the ground. As he struggled to get free, a large rock was slammed down hard upon his head, smashing his skull wide open. As Thomas Baker lay dying, the two villains searched his pockets for money, but the money was actually in the two saddlebags slung over the back of his horse - which in all the commotion, had galloped off homewards along the rutted track. The two murderers fled empty handed into the darkness.

The horse carried on down the track, skirting the flank of Bubb Down Hill, before finally reaching the farm where the Baker family eagerly awaited their father's return. However, when they saw only the horse and cart, Jimmy and Mary Anne - Thomas Baker's son and daughter - grabbed a lantern each, and went in search of their father. They retraced the horse's route back along the track, where eventually they found the lifeless body. It was plainly obvious that he had been murdered; the victim of a bungled robbery; but as there were no witnesses or clues to the crime, no-one was brought to justice.

The A'corn Inn at Evershot

*And they heard the cry, from the branches high,
Of the hungry carrion crows.*

John Leyden: *Lord Soulis*

Seven years passed, and the two murderers were in the *Acorn Inn* at Evershot, where they were overheard by the landlord arguing about the killing. They were caught that very evening, and after spending the night incarcerated at the village lockup, they were taken to Dorchester Assizes where they were convicted and sentenced.

Their punishment: to be taken back to the place where they had committed the grisly crime, and to be gibbeted alive - hung suspended in the air, and left to die in irons or chains, for the sake of example, and there to be left until carrion-crows had picked their bones clean! It was made known that no-one was to help the criminals in their distress. Indeed to do so was a criminal offence in itself. And so it was done. The doomed men were clamped in an iron cage that had been made by the Evershot smithy, and hung from the branch of a tree adjacent to an old chalk pit and left to die.

A day or so after, a woman by the name of Martha Spigot was returning from Yeovil when she came upon the two dying men. *"Water, Mother. Water for the love of Heaven"*, they groaned. Water she had none, but taking pity on the dying men, she reached up and pushed a tallow candle into each of their mouths. Martha was caught in the act, and was taken into custody, and later punished with seven years imprisonment at Dorchester gaol.

The two villains corpses were left gibbeted for many months, and when the maggots and crows had removed every piece of rotting flesh, their bones were disposed of. So none would forget this dreadful incident, the old drove was named *Murderer's Lane,* and the place where the two murderers were gibbeted became known as *The Gibbet Pit.*

Thomas Baker's grave with its well weathered, broken headstone upon which the much faded inscription reads:

HERE LEITH
THE BODY OF THOMAS BAKER
ELIVS (alias) WILLIAM WHO WAS
BABEROVSLY MVRDERED ON
BVBDOWNE HILL NOVEM 10
1694

can still be found to this day in the cemetery of St. Mary the Virgin Church, Melbury Bubb, but it is said his spirit does not rest, for Thomas Baker's ghost has been seen haunting Murderer's Lane.

Murderer's Lane where the young Mary Pitcher encountered the ghost of Thomas Baker

In an article by G. W. Greening featured in the *Dorset Year Book 1949-50*, Mary Ellen Pitcher (neé Bowditch) of Evershot, described how she once witnessed Thomas Baker's ghostly horse and cart. The sighting took place on one damp and foggy November night in 1866, when she was a girl of seven. Young Mary and her parents were walking along Murderer's Lane towards Melbury Bubb, when they heard the distant breathing of a horse. Along the track they saw come around a bend, the faint glimmer of lanterns, and heard the approaching creak of cartwheels. *"Stand aside in the ditch 'n let Thomas Baker's horse and cart go past"*, said her father, *"I've a zid it before"*. Mary and her mother stood to one side while her father stood the other. Mrs Pitcher said she felt so frightened that she shut her eyes and did not open them until the apparition had gone. Sadly, shortly after telling this intriguing story, Mrs Pitcher died, aged ninety.

THE VILLAGE OF THE DEAD

A long Dorset's Purbeck coastline, between Kimmeridge Bay and Lulworth Cove, is the mysterious village of Tyneham.

The Second World War made it necessary for the British Army to extend their existing training area and on 19th December 1943 the inhabitants of Tyneham were evacuated, and were never allowed to return. Before leaving, they left a note pinned to the church door. It read:

> *'Please treat the church and houses with care;*
> *We have given up our homes where many of us have*
> *lived for generations to help win the War to keep men free.*
> *We will return one day and thank you for treating the village kindly.'*

These words must have fallen on deaf ears, for the buildings are today derelict, lying in ruins, and only those buried in the churchyard remain.

Amongst the ruins of abandoned village of Tyneham, still stands St Mary's Church

The school and church were later restored to serve as a kind of memorial to what is now a village of the dead. Even so, the village of Tyneham still has a few ghostly residents.

Reported in the *Bournemouth Daily Echo*, 25th February 2003, a ghostly figure was photographed through a window of one of the derelict cottages. Christopher Grist, who took the photograph, didn't give it another thought until the film was later developed, and his partner asked if he had manipulated the image on a computer. He said that he hadn't, but noticed immediately what she was implying. There looking through the window, between the trees, was an image of what appeared to be a figure of a man. *"I'm sceptical myself,"* he said, *"but there's definitely something there."* Others who have seen the photograph can make out a shape thought to be a figure wearing a helmet. *"It's a bit unnerving,"* he said. "It looks like a man in a grey coat with a flat cap on". Could it be a ghost? Or could it be a simple trick of the light upon the foliage?

Christopher took another photograph of the trees through the same window just a few seconds before taking the photograph of the spectre. On that one there was no weird shadow or outline of a figure. Christopher later went back to Tyneham to check out the area and see if there was any foliage or anything else which might explain the eerie shape. "There wasn't", he said.

Could the mysterious phantom be a soldier from the Second World War? Or could it be the ghost of another deceased resident? In the late eighteenth century a young dairy maid named Jane Gilbert committed suicide by hanging herself in one of the cowsheds of Baltington Farm (pronounced *Backington*) after her beloved had left her to seek a new life in London. Because there were no crossroads available in the village for the customary burial of a suicide victim, she was buried high up on the ridge on the parish boundary between Tyneham and Steeple. At midnight poor Jane was laid in her grave; naked, without the dignity of a coffin, and - because the villagers feared that her corpse might wander as a vampire - a stake was driven through her heart, before her lonely grave was covered in.

Balington Farm - The scene of a tragic suicide

THE MEMORIAL OF MAIDEN'S GRAVE

Alas, Alas poor sorrowful Oak tree,
Did it hurt when they carved that coffin into thee?
Did you bleed a tremendous loss?
Like the blessed Saviour upon the cross.
Were they hard to swallow? The bones that fed your roots,
Was it bitter? The sap that drove your shoots.
Do you remember young love's broken dream?
And Baltington Farm and the silent scream,
And the short journey from life to death,
And the sudden jolt that ceased the breath!
Did you weep for the young dairy maid?
When in lonely earthen grave was laid,
And at the stake, driven, cracking through her breast,
So to prevent a possible vampire nest.
Did you weep? Did you cry?
Did you wonder why?
All long ago, or so it might seem,
Forgotten memorial of young love's broken dream.

Robert Newland

Maiden's Grave Gate

The site of the Coffin Tree in 2006,
Insert: drawing of the Coffin Tree as it appeared in the 1930's

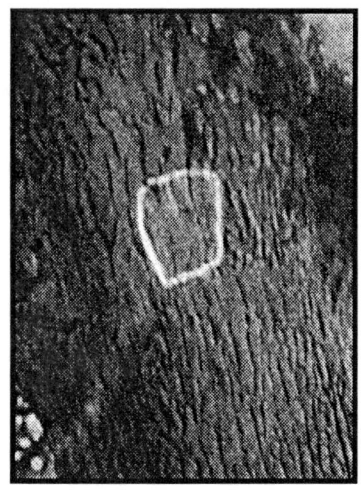

The carved coffin

So none would ever forget this sad tragedy the place of Jane's burial was named *Maiden's Grave Gate*, and to add further to the memory, some four hundred yards away beside the road leading down to Tyneham there was carved upon the north side of an old oak tree the outline of a coffin. The tree soon became known as the *Coffin Tree*, but, alas, the tree - like the rest of Tyneham - has been hit hard by the ravages of time. This once important landmark, and piece of Tyneham's history, now lies a fallen and forgotten limbless trunk decaying by the road side.

There are many such wayside graves in the British Isles, the most famous of which is *Mary Jay's Grave* sometimes called *Kitty Jay's Grave* on Dartmoor in Devon. It is interesting to note that the tale of Jay's Grave has remarkable similarities to Dorset's *Maiden's Grave*. Both were young dairymaids, both hanged themselves in a cowshed, and both incidents happened at about the same time. However, unlike *Maiden's Grave*, the Devon tragedy has touched innumerable hearts for Jay's grave is never without flowers. It has been widely written about and has appeared on numerous television and radio programmes, and more recently, folk singer Seth Lakeman composed a song, called *Kitty Jay*, in her memory.

Another story of a girl who suffered a similar fate to that of Jane Gilbert can be found in the north Dorset village of Dewlish, at a place called *Betsey Caine's Corner*. According to the story told by Mr. Edward Parsons in Chris Ellis and Andy Owens *Haunted Dorset* (2004), in the early nineteenth century, a local girl called Betsey Caine, hung herself in a farmhouse in the village, it was presumed the reason for this was because she was pregnant. The girls body was buried under the wood at what has become known as *Betsey Caine's Corner*, which is situated on the road to Milborne St. Andrew. Mr. Parsons grandfather is alleged to have seen Betsey's ghost sitting on a gate.

Just a short walk from Tyneham, along an unmade road, is Worbarrow Bay. There, during the seventeenth century, a smuggler was startled by a group of revenue men. Escaping along the beach, he found himself facing a wall of unclimbable rock, and had no choice but to wade out into the sea, where in the still water he was stoned to death. It is said that his screams can still be heard on the nights of the waning moon.

The spectral screams of a smuggler are heard at Worbarrow Bay

LEGIONS OF THE DOWNS

Visioning on the vacant air
Helmed legionaries, who proudly rear
The Eagle, as they pace again
The Roman Road.

Thomas Hardy: *The Roman Road*

The undulating grassy slopes of the downs were cultivated by the Celts more than two thousand years ago, and are perhaps the most prominent feature of the Dorset countryside. Apart from their use in early farming, the downs have also played a vital role in links with prehistoric settlements; notably the Ridgeway, which spans from West Dorset to the Purbecks. When the Romans invaded in 43A.D, they used their expertise to create long stretches of road, replacing and improving some of the county's ancient trackways. Many of these roads still exist today, such as the Dorchester to Weymouth (A354) and Badbury to Salisbury roads.

The memories of past civilizations continue to haunt roads - and other areas - around the ancient downland, even appearing in the form of spectral armies in full battle-armour retracing their march along familiar routes. The first recorded account of a phantom army in Dorset was on the 29th June 1662. It was recorded in *Prodigies in Somerset and Dorset, 1661-2* reprinted in *The Somerset and Dorset Notes and Queries, 1894.* So the story goes, when travelling along the stretch of road between Winterborne Abbas and Dorchester, two holy men; a reverend and one of the king's chaplains, witnessed upon the hill adjacent to the road what appeared to be a magnificent troop of mounted horsemen with colours blazon. The two men were amazed at this sight, and made haste in order to get ahead of the procession, so they could meet up with them. Arriving at Dorchester, they waited for them to appear, but were disappointed after a long wait to find no sign of the cavalry's arrival.

On questioning some of the townsfolk they were told that there were no such horsemen riding by that day. So did the two men have a momentary glimpse of the past? This may well have been the case, as the old Roman road from Dorchester to Eggardon is a place where a phantom Roman Legion, and many supernatural and inexplicable events have occurred.

Sixteen years later, in 1678, the town of Wareham was alerted by the threat of invasion! This story of the assault on the town, was retold to the Reverend John Hutchins (the eighteenth century author of *History and Antiquities of Dorset*), by Thomas Bolt who was born and raised in Wareham twenty-one years after the incident.

Reverend John Hutchins

The Windswept down at Grange Hill, Creech, where the spectral army was encountered

When news of the invasion reached Wareham,
the bridge at the south entrance of the town was barricaded

His account begins as the residents of Wareham had always told it. One cold December night, several thousands of armed men were seen marching along the Ridgeway from Flower's Barrow to Grange Hill, by Captain John Lawrence, the owner of Creech Grange. At the same time, his brother - plus four clay-cutters making their way home after finishing a day's work - also saw the phantom army.

A great noise and clashing of arms was heard by residents of the local hamlets and cottages, who quickly abandoned their supper and homes to warn the neighbouring town of Wareham of the forthcoming invasion. When news reached Wareham, the bridge at the south entrance of the town was barricaded, and the boats all drawn to the north side of the River Frome to prevent the invaders from entering the town. Even the local militia was quickly summoned to the town to lay in wait for the advancing army, but as the hours ebbed away, no sign of the mysterious invaders arrived, leaving the townsfolk terrified and shaken by this whole affair.

Hutchins notes that after this event, Captain Lawrence and his brother went to London to testify their oath before a council, of the mysterious manifestation at Grange Hill. Hutchins also remarks that if Captain Lawrence's family affections had not been recognised by the government, then he and his brother would have been severely punished, as the country was still engulfed in a wave of hysteria generated by the so called *'Oates's Plot.'** Yet Hutchins discredits the eyewitness accounts as mere mirages caused by rolling fog upon the downs, which can cause the most familiar shapes like rocks, trees, and ruined buildings, to take upon any form that one might imagine.

Printed in the 1968 edition of the *Somerset and Dorset Notes and Queries*, there is an interesting letter, written by Lady Jane Culliford (neéLawrence) to her husband, who then in turn, passed it on to the Lord Treasurer of Danby in 1678. She discusses the same eyewitness accounts of the appearance of a great number of horsemen and foot soldiers on Grange Hill.

Lady Culliford then explains to her husband about the written oaths sent to London, and gives her thoughts that if the apparitions were seen by one or two men, then they could have been

---

'Oates Plot or Popish Plot.' A story invented by Titus Oates and Israel Tonge in 1678 of the existence of a plot conspired by English Roman Catholics to assassinate King Charles II, burn down London and to slaughter all Protestants, thus placing his Roman Catholic brother James, on the throne.

deceived due to failing eyesight But for eight or ten to have seen the *same* phantoms between two risings of Grange Hill, where bushes and trees are scarce, and so exposed that a crow may be seen at a great distance, seems impossible to explain.

She also makes clear in her letter, that the first to encounter the phantom army are the four clay-cutters returning home. They are the very same men who informed her son (Capt. John Lawrence) and her daughter, who joined with others to witness the legion marching upon the downs of Grange Hill just before the sun began to set.

After Lady Culliford expresses her concerns for her children's safety, she signs-off, and dates the letter 17th September 1678, which is interesting as this slightly differs from Thomas Bolt's account of the apparitions being observed one night in December. It may be that Thomas Bolt was told the tale inaccurately, as it was many years after the sightings of the spectral army at Grange Hill.

Claims of encounters with spectral armies upon the Purbeck Downs continued into the 20th century. A mother and son were walking one afternoon on the headland above the sheltered cove known as Chapman's Pool near Worth Matravers, when her son claimed he saw Roman soldiers, but she could see nothing. However, his descriptions of the legionnaires were so detailed, that he could define the metal fringes on the soldiers' tunics. The last known reported sighting of the Purbeck phantom army appeared in 1970, to an elderly woman who saw the legion marching over Knowle Hill at Church Knowle.

Ghosts of Roman Soldiers have been seen at Chapman's Pool near Worth Matravers

It has been claimed that the same phantom legion at Flower's Barrow has also been seen to march west towards Bindon Hill, on numerous occasions during times of national crisis.

In the *Dorset Year Book* 1959-60. One such incident allegedly happened to a man living in the Lulworth area early in the Second World War when the threat of a German invasion caused much concern to many inhabitants of coastal areas. One August evening in 1940, the man in question was making his way by foot along an old disused dirt track upon the Ridgeway to his observation post, when he became suddenly aware of the sound of *something* in front of him. Drawing closer the sound grew louder, and the man soon recognised the distinct sound of a regiment on the march. He quickly moved to one side to allow them to pass only to find, he could not see anything which was responsible for the noise. He stood amazed on the verge for many minutes as the invisible legion passed. He swore that he heard the chinking of metal upon metal, and the occasional muffled cough, which he continued to hear until the sound faded into the distance.

Later that week he told a couple of local residents of his ghostly encounter. The elderly man only gave a nod in recognition while the other told him that night, *"the Legions were on the march."*

Similar stories of Roman soldiers in vast numbers appearing at times when Britain was in its hour of need, come from:

- Old Priest's Track to Swanage;
- A352, Sherborne to Dorchester Road;
- Abbotsbury Hill; and the disused stretch of Roman road that runs parallel to the A354 at Ridgeway Hill, between Dorchester and Weymouth.
- The A354 road to Dorchester close to Winterborne Monkton, has also been another place where these spectres have been seen.

Approximately a mile east of the old disused Roman road at Ridgeway Hill, between Weymouth and Dorchester, is the area known locally as *Came Down*. In the late Summer of 1918, Mrs F. Carré decided to take a trip to the Ridgeway by taking the train to Upwey Halt. When she arrived, she took her dog for a wander upon the grassed downs of the golf links, which were always deserted during the First World War.

She found one of the many barrows upon the down, and sat down to admire the view, while her dog went off to explore a nearby coppice. Looking over the patchwork countryside, she was suddenly aware of voices singing in the distance. She presumed they were soldiers, as they had a certain rhythm that she recognised, as soldiers often sang as they marched past her house on the High Road in Weymouth. She did not pay much attention to this until the singing came closer. She described the singing more like *"glad sonorous chants with long sentences, beginning in low tones increasing to higher notes and then abruptly ending with a loud shout."* Then followed the crashing of metal upon metal, which intensified as the sound drew nearer, and nearer. She suddenly raised herself quickly to her feet to see what could be responsible for this terrific noise, and realized that the language they were singing in was

A phantom army of Roman soldiers is supposed to appear marching along the old solitary Roman Road on the Ridgeway that runs parallel with the Dorchester Road leading to Weymouth

A strange ghostly warrior with a hideous scarred face haunts the area around the ancient hillfort of Badbury Rings, near Wimborne at night

Latin! The sound abruptly ceased. Confused, she panned the horizon, but the soldiers were nowhere to be found.

Other similar experiences can be found at Badbury Rings, near Wimborne Minster, the ancient hillfort, which was captured by the Second Augustan Legion under Vespasian in 43A.D. It is also claimed that this was the site of *Mons Badon,* the great battle in which the legendary King Arthur claimed victory over the Anglo Saxons in 518A.D, and where he killed at least a hundred and sixty men single-handed. It is no surprise to hear, that at midnight King Arthur and his spectral knights return to haunt the battlefield.

According to Jeremey Harte in his *Cuckoo Pounds and Singing Barrows,* 1986, In 1970, an organised archaeological expedition of students camped within the Rings, experienced a legend which - for them - turned into reality. One night, the students were abruptly awoken by the sounds of marching and clashing metal, accompanied by shouts of military orders, in a language they did not recognise. In blind panic they quickly abandoned their camp. The terrors at Badbury Rings continued towards the end of the 1970's, with particular reports of a strange ghostly warrior with a hideous scarred face haunting the area at night. According to veteran folklorist Peter Underwood, he was last seen in 1977.

It is not just lonely, isolated areas which are haunted by ghostly armies. Strange as it may seem, phantom legions have been known to appear in our modern suburban homes.

About four miles south of Badbury Rings - on the edge of Poole - can be found, the village of Corfe Mullen. The village is cut in two by the course of an old Roman road that linked Hamworthy with Badbury. Secret Dorset, Peter Underwood 1995 It was here during the Summer of 1993, that terrified residents of the aptly named *Roman Heights Estate* reported seeing phantom Roman soldiers. Witnesses claimed to experience much ghostly activity on the estate, including distinct sounds of soldiers marching, metal clinking, and the sound of men's voices conversing in a strange language. Many occupants living in different properties on the estate, also witnessed the manifestation of Roman centurions walking through the solid walls of houses, and out into the streets.

The track that later became the Roman road that runs through Corfe Mullen, is thought to be the route which the Roman general, Vespasian and his legions used after landing at Holes Bay, Hamworthy, to attack Badbury; the first of twenty hillforts to be captured by the invaders. The course of the road running through - or near - houses, may explain why the phantom soldiers appear to walk through walls.

Ghosts often follow the routes they once trod, ignoring any later constructions, thus, ghosts appear to glide through walls or climb stairs that no longer exist.

The many phantom armies of Dorset - as we have seen in previous pages - all share a close association with ancient earthworks. This would suggest these hauntings are the results of violent battles. One such bloody battle that claimed a large loss of life, was the siege of Maiden Castle, near Dorchester - Britain's largest stronghold at the time - which was captured, like so many other hillforts, by Vespasian and the Roman Second Augustan Legion in 43A.D. A ghostly appearance of this scene was sighted in the early 1980's, by a woman walk-

Do ghosts tread the ramparts of the ancient hillfort of Maiden Castle, near Dorchester?

The Second Augustan Legion re-enactment at Maiden Castle

ing the ramparts late one evening. She was startled to see a group of Roman soldiers marching within the central enclosure. Her companion saw nothing, but it became apparent that she was obviously very frightened by what she had seen, and quickly left the site.

Two miles north of Maiden Castle is the county town, Dorchester. It was this town that was first established by the Roman invaders after they defeated the tribe of the 'Durotriges' at Maiden Castle. Durnovaria, as it was later named by the inhabitants, first evolved round a military camp becoming later an administrative centre when the legions left.

For public entertainment the people would attend the earth bank enclosure south of Dorchester known as Maumbury Rings. This was a former prehistoric henge that was adapted by the Romans as an ampitheatre for games and gladiatorial combats. It is this unique archaeological site which has given rise to a tradition that on certain days of the year, if anyone falls asleep while resting upon the turfed banks of the rings, they can glimpse the phantom Roman legionnaires of the past and see them engaging in mock combat.

From a Sketch taken from Old England: A Pictorial Museum by Charles Knight (1845). The amphitheatre is at Mambury Rings, a stone age site not far from Dorchester.

Ghostly Roman soldiers are known to stray from their comrades in arms. On 13th October 1969, twelve boys from Guy's Marsh Borstal* near Shaftesbury, and two adult supervisors set up a working camp within the wooded confines of Thorncombe Woods at Higher Bockhampton just outside Dorchester. It was during this Autumn evening, that a boy from the borstal came rushing into the camp terrified of a ghostly figure he had seen in the trees. The boy described this apparition as a man dressed in a toga and wearing a helmet, armed with a sword

In the United Kingdom, a borstal was a juvenile detention centre or reformatory, an institution of the criminal justice system, intended to reform delinquent male youths aged between about 16 and 21.

The site of the old Roman Road in Thorncombe Woods at Higher Bockhampton, where a ghost of a Roman soldier was seen

and shield. Intrigued by this ghostly encounter the rest of the boys and the two supervisors went back to the area of the sighting, and were amazed to see the ghostly figure, still there floating silently some feet above the woodland floor. One of the supervisors decided to approach the figure with a torch, but as he did so the apparition suddenly disappeared.

It is interesting to note that when the party from Guy's Marsh Borstal established their camp at Thorncombe Woods, they were unaware that the camp was sited upon the course of the old Roman road that ran from Dorchester to Badbury. This is the reason why the Roman soldier appeared to float, as he must have been standing at the original level of the Roman road.

Stories of people claiming to have encountered these silent sentinels can be found in other parts of the county, including Nottington Corner along the A345 to Weymouth and at the hillforts Hambledon Hill, Hod Hill and Dudsbury Camp.

The Tudor built Whitecliff House at Woodhouse Hill, Studland, is said to be built on the site of a Roman villa, and on certain nights, a Roman captain is seen in the company of a British maiden walking within the grounds of the house.

Even in the Roman military town of Durnovaria (Dorchester) upon the high earthen rampart known as Colliton Walk, a ghostly figure resembling a Roman centurion is said to patrol the area at midnight when the moon is on the wane.

GHOSTLY GOINGS ON

Any historic building - whether a grand stately home, or a rustic cottage, will at most times appear perfectly normal to the casual visitor; few would consider it as being in any sense 'spooky'. Looks can be deceiving, however, as people who have lived there may tell.

In the early part of the nineteenth century, the owner of the grand manor house at Stalbridge, decided to let a friend and her family of young children make use of it for the Christmas season, on condition that they should do whatever the old house-keeper required of them.

When the lady and her family arrived, they were met by the housekeeper at the door. After welcoming the family, she gave them a conducted tour of the building starting in the main hall. She gave specific instructions that on no account should anyone be present in the main hall at the stroke of five o'clock in the evening.

The hauntings at Stalbridge House

Not questioning the housekeeper, the family agreed to her unusual request, which for sometime was observed, except for one occasion when the lady had some children visit the manor house during the afternoon, to play with her own offspring. As the evening drew on, the lady had the visiting children taken home. After saying goodbye to them, she found herself on her own in the dimly lit main hall of the house. Everything appeared normal, except for the usual noises that seemed to bring the house alive; the creaking of ancient timbers, and the eerie sound of the wind, which hummed almost into melody as it moved under gaps in the doors and windows. Then suddenly the clock in the main hall struck five.

Startled by the chime, she noticed that the air began to chill all around her, and a distant sound of muttering could distinctly be heard. Turning to look up, and straining her ears towards the direction of the sound, she stared in terror, as a figure of a woman engulfed in flames burst straight through the door of one of the first floor bedrooms. The apparition glided across the floor, illuminating the landing in an ethereal light, and could be heard mumbling to herself, *"I have done it. I have done it,"* before disappearing into the next room. The lady who stood and watched this spectral vision in awe, quickly rushed upstairs to the two rooms from which the figure had emerged, and then vanished, only to find that both were locked.

Curiosity overcoming her fear, the lady returned to the main hall at five o'clock the next evening only to witness a repeat of this ghostly activity for a second time. Now thoroughly convinced that it was *not* her imagination running wild, the lady quickly made plans to return with her children to their home in London. On the way home, she took the opportunity of calling upon the owner of Stalbridge Manor to explain the cause of her sudden departure, and to find out what caused the haunting. On listening to her story, the owner who knew of the incident only too well, began to tell her the grim tale that would soon explain her ghostly experience.

Some years previously, the house had been occupied by a widowed mother and her only son. On one particular day, the son came to his mother, and told her that he had fallen in love with the gamekeeper's daughter. The mother, outraged by such foolish talk, strictly forbade him from ever mentioning the affair again. Time passed, and the son decided to tell his mother that he was going to marry the girl. The mother was very close to her son, and objected to such a ridiculous proposal, refusing to give her blessing on such a marriage. However, after some months, the wedding between the son and the gamekeeper's daughter *did* take place, in spite of the mother's intolerance to her son's marriage. She then banned the couple from ever entering the manor house again.

It wasn't until many months after the wedding, that the mother began to show remorse towards her son and his new wife, and decided to allow them to live with her at the manor. They returned to Stalbridge, and at first all went well until one evening, on returning from a days hunting, the son came back to find his mother in a distressed state. She told him the tragic news that his wife had burnt to death!

The mother explained how his wife had entered her dressing room to change for dinner, and stood beside the fireplace, when suddenly she was engulfed in flames. She had accidentally trailed her long dress into the hearth setting herself on fire.

He accepted the tragic tale of his wife's death without question for many years, until he heard the wicked truth from his dying mother. When she lay on her deathbed, she confessed the dreadful crime she had committed. It had been *she* who had deliberately pushed his wife into the fire.

"She deliberately pushed her into the fire."

It is no surprise to discover how after the death of the murderess, the manor was haunted by her spirit appearing every day at five o'clock in the evening (the time at which the crime was committed) as a frail figure exclaiming her own guilt, wrapped by the immortal flaming coils of her sin.

The ancient, ten-foot high, grey stone wall that surrounds the parkland for five miles, is the only reminder of times past. The once great seventeenth century Jacobean style manor house which stood within Stalbridge Park was sadly demolished in 1822, taking with it the resident ghost. But all is not lost, as two stout pillars, which support the gates, are each surmounted with a furious lion head. It is these stone ornaments that have given rise to another local legend. When St. Mary's church bells ring, or when the clock strikes midnight, the lions descend to drink at a pool that lies just inside the gates, while on Hallowe'en they take to rampaging the streets of the village.

Peter Underwood, investigator of psychic phenomena, once said that *"Britain has more ghosts per square mile than any other country,"* and there may well be some truth in this, especially when you consider the amount of ghost stories that have been collected and reported in this particular county over the years. Whilst it is accepted that many reported ghostly encounters are - at the worst - total fabrications, and - at best - good yarns that have passed into legend, one is left with an impressive number of authenticated accounts which are at least somewhat believable. If one even isolates all the genuine stories with natural explanations, there still remains a large amount for which there is no rational explanation.

It is most often the case where a ghost is said to haunt a building, that there has been a dramatic or tragic tale attached to a person's life or death within - or outside - the house. But what ghosts really *are* is another question entirely, which has puzzled mankind for centuries. While there have been many differing theories trying to explain the existence of ghosts, some stories defy explanation. The most widely regarded possibility, is that ghosts are spirits of the dead that can - under certain conditions - return to this mortal plane. But another popular theory among researchers is that when there has been a period of extreme emotional and physical stress an enormous output of electrical energy is distributed by the brain. These high emotional energy surges are somehow trapped in a specific place in the building, and are occasionally retrieved as sounds or projected images. Known as `The Stone Tape` theory, this might possibly explain why so many ghost sightings are related to murder and violence.

However, the general subject of ghosts covers a wide range of different psychic phenomena.

One example of this are Doubles or Co-walkers. These are what we *perceive* as ghosts but which appear even though the person is seen as a ghost is in fact still alive - these ghostly forms may appear in the exact likeness of an individual person to give a warning of their impending fate. The German term *Doppelgänger* is often applied to such apparitions. But other disembodied ghosts of the living, such as *Wraiths* and *Fetches*,* commonly appear to distant friends and relations at the very moment or near to death of those they represent.

Built in 1505 by Sir Thomas Trenchard, the Tudor Manor House at Wolfeton, near Dorchester, remained the great home of the Trenchard family until the end of the eighteenth century.

---

*'Fetch.' Hence fetch light and fetch candle. – See Spectral Lights.

Wolfeton Manor, near Dorchester

It was at Wolfeton House during the latter half of the seventeenth century, that an incident involving a *Fetch* took place, when *another* Sir Thomas Trenchard, an assize judge, decided to invite guests for dinner one evening. No sooner had they sat down to eat, when the sober Sir Thomas, whose face had been quite happy throughout the day, suddenly changed to a twisted expression of terror, as he turned to look at his wife who was seated opposite him on the end of the long great refectory table. Pausing for a moment, eyes still firmly fixed upon his wife, he abruptly stood up and ordered that his carriage should be made ready and also that his marshal should be summoned to accompany him. This sudden change in Sir Thomas left his family and guests bemused, as - without any reason - he left the house in his carriage for Dorchester.

While travelling, with his faithful marshal seated beside him, Sir Thomas began to explain to him of his unexpected and inappropriate departure from Wolfeton. He related how when he sat down for dinner, he distinctly saw standing behind Lady Trenchard's chair, an exact likeness of his wife. But what startled him most of all, was that this grotesque *Fetch* of his wife was standing with her head under one arm, with streams of blood flowing from the stump of her neck.

The marshal tried to reassure Sir Thomas Trenchard that he was just tired, and had imagined the strange vision. Just then a messenger on horseback from Wolfeton House forced the carriage to stop. The breathless messenger informed Sir Thomas of the tragic news that Lady

Trenchard was dead. The marshal asked the messenger how she had died, he replied her Ladyship had just committed suicide by cutting her own throat. Thus the fetch's vision of her death was fulfilled.

Following that tragic day, Lady Trenchard's headless ghost dressed in grey, walks the three rooms into which the Great Chamber was divided, and also in the room where the suicide occurred.

Other hauntings of Wolfeton House include an unidentified male member of the Trenchard family, who has been seen driving a ghostly coach and horses up the main staircase, replaying a dangerous feat by which he is said to have won a wager when he was alive. A ghost of a Catholic priest also haunts the gatehouse in which he was held captive until taken to Dorchester to be hung, drawn, and quartered.

In the past, suicide was often regarded an unpardonable sin, and it was widely believed that a person's spirit was damned to remain on this earth for all eternity. Their bodies were often buried at crossroads, parish boundaries, outside the cemetery, or on the north side of a church cemetery, as it is an area often cast in shadow and deemed suitable for restless souls.

Stories of suicide ghosts are very common amongst hauntings in Dorset homes. Eastbury House, Tarrant Gunville holds one such strange and curious tale.

Construction of the magnificent Eastbury House, was started in 1718 under the guidance of George Dodington. Unfortunately the house was never fully completed, as two years later

The entrance to the once magnificent Eastbury House at Tarrant Gunville

Dodington died, leaving the estate to his twenty-nine year old eccentric nephew George Bubb.

The son of a Weymouth pharmacist, the now distinguished and wealthy George Bubb, Dodington, set his sights on completing the construction of the unfinished house, which his uncle had started. During his forty-two years of occupying Eastbury, he spent a large amount of his fortune on alterations and embellishments to the building. At a cost of a hundred and forty thousand pounds it was completed in 1738. According to the Rev. John Hutchins, it was, *'One of the grandest and most superb in the county and indeed the kingdom'*.

Dodington employed the services of a steward by the name of William Doggett, during Eastbury House's construction. This surprised the villagers, because he was renowned throughout the district as a dishonest thief who would steal to make money at his employer's expense.

Known to many as *'Old Doggett'*, he was a man instantly recognisable by his knee breeches tied with yellow silk ribbon.

With Old Doggett now managing the estate, George Bubb Dodington spent most of his days in London where he became an ambitious member of parliament renowned for his political chicanery. Later in life he was given the title of Lord Melcombe a year before his death in 1762, and it is alleged that several years before his death he frequented Buckinghamshire, where he became a 'Monk of Medmenham' at Sir Francis Dashwood's notorious *Hell-Fire Club.**

Whilst Dodington was away attending to his civic duties, Old Doggett remained at Eastbury, where in an effort to avoid becoming bankrupt, fraudulently sold off his master's building materials.

The master always announced his return, so Old Doggett always had sufficient time to find and repay the stolen money.

One day without warning, George Bubb Dodington *did* return unexpectedly. News got to Old Doggett that his master had been seen standing beside the Blandford road just after disembarking from the London Mail Coach, and that he was on his way home. He panicked, as all about him lay the evidence of his mismanagement and illegal dealings. It was already too late

---

**'Hell-Fire Club.'* The Hellfire Club was the popular name for an exclusive English club that met irregularly from 1746 to around 1763, run by Sir Francis Dashwood. During the time of the club's operation, they were commonly thought to hold notorious, orgiastic and Satanic meetings at Medmenham Abbey, beside the Thames and later at West Wycombe Caves.

The term was not invented by the 1750 club; they first met to celebrate an earlier club founded in 1720 by Charles Edward. Other clubs using the name were set up throughout the 18th century.

The club was founded by Sir Francis Dashwood after he returned from his Grand Tour of Europe. According to the 1779 book Nocturnal Revels, on the Grand Tour he had visited various religious seminaries, "founded, as it were, in direct contradiction to Nature and Reason; on his return to England, [he] thought that a burlesque Institution in the name of St Francis, would mark the absurdity of such Societies; and in lieu of the austerities and abstemiousness there practised, substitute convivial gaiety, unrestrained hilarity, and social felicity."

In the late nineteenth century a gruesome discovery was made at St. Mary's Church, Tarrant Gunville

to cover his tracks. He thought his work and life was finished at Eastbury, and went into the library and shot himself.

After his death, it was believed that if you happen to be at the Eastbury Park Gates at midnight, you would see a ghostly figure wearing a wig and knee breeches tied with yellow silk ribbon, awaiting to be collected by a coach-and-four complete with headless coachman and horses, only to be taken to the house to re-enact his own suicide. It was also said that in the library where the deed was committed, there could be found a bloodstain that only disappeared when all but one wing of the house was taken down piecemeal in the 1780's by Earl Temple, who was unable to maintain the property.

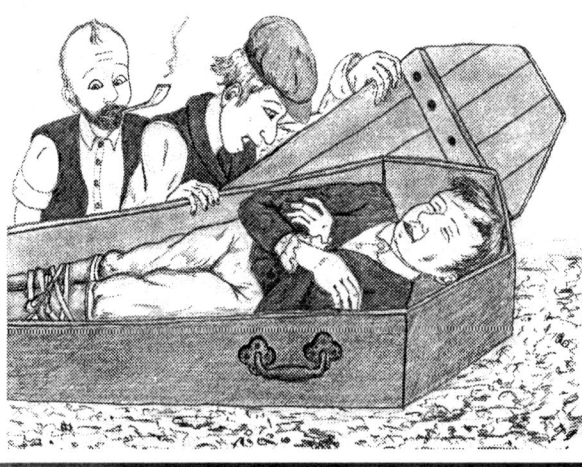

But the story is far from over, as when St. Mary's, the parish church of Tarrant Gunville was rebuilt, with exception of the tower in 1845, workmen exhumed an incorruptible corpse of a man with his legs bound together with ribbons of yellow silk. Stories circulated that the body was Old Doggett and at midnight he would emerge from his grave as some kind of ghoul or vampire to prey upon the innocent villagers, in order to drink their blood and consume their flesh as they lay in their beds asleep.

It was widely considered in the past by some people that animals could not become ghosts, because they did not possess a soul. But there are many stories of hauntings that *do* include animal ghosts, most notably the spectral black dogs.

One of the famous haunted houses in the county has to be Athelhampton Hall, near Puddletown. Open to the public seven months of the year, it is perhaps one of the most beautiful examples of fifteenth century domestic architecture in England. And it remains so despite a disastrous fire that swept through the East Wing in November 1992.

One of Dorset's most famous haunted buildings - Athelhampton Hall

When entering this grand Tudor house via the vestibule, it is easy to feel the presence of something watching you. This is no surprise, as seated upon a pedestal above the main arch of the vestibule is a stone carving of a crowned ape tethered to a chain, and sitting with a solemn expression upon its face.

For just over five hundred years, since it was built by Sir William Martyn in 1483, the massive battlemented house has been the home of the Martyn family. It is reputed the Martyn's kept apes as pets, which is why they adopted them into their coat of arms. Apart from being a emblem, it is also said that a ghost of an ape is known to haunt the house. This may have given rise to the Martyn family motto: *'He who looks at Martyn's ape, Martyn's ape shall look at him'.*

The tragic legend that is often used as an explanation for this ghost, began when a young lady of the Martyn family was jilted by a lover, and decided to commit suicide. The girl fled through a secret door in the oak panelling of the Great Chamber, closely followed by her pet, a tame ape.

*'He who looks at Martyn's ape,
Martyn's ape shall look at him'.*

The stone ape seated upon a pedestal above the main arch
of the vestibule at Athelhampton Hall

She ran up a hidden staircase, and closed the door to her chamber where she killed herself. Unfortunately, the ape was trapped on the staircase, where the poor creature remained, and eventually starved to death. Though the ape's ghost has never been seen, it can be heard on quiet nights scratching desperately for a way out.

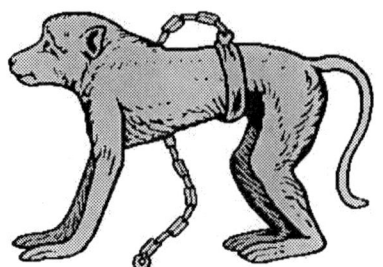

But the phantom ape is far from alone in haunting Athelhampton Hall. .

A pair of duellists also haunt the Great Chamber. They once interrupted a woman guest who was reading. Annoyed at being disturbed by such an outburst, she asked the two young men to stop, but they both ignored her and fought on. The woman pulled continuously at the bell rope to summon one of the servants, but no-one arrived. So she returned to her chair. The duel continued until one was cut across the arm and they both left the room. When the lady told the owner of his unruly guests, he replied rather puzzled. *"I can't understand what you are talking about as you have met all the guests who are staying here, at tea."* Who the duellists are is not known, but they are believed to date back to the Civil War when Athelhampton had Royalist connections. Other ghosts include a ghostly cooper who taps industriously at the barrels in the Wine Cellar, which can be accessed via a secret panel on the right hand side of the fireplace in the Great Hall

The ghost of a grey lady passes through the walls of the East Wing from the landing to the State and Yellow Bedrooms. She was witnessed by a housemaid, who noticed her sitting in a chair of one of the rooms. Thinking she was a visitor, she told her politely that it was getting late and the house was soon to be closed to the public. The grey figure then rose, and to the amazement of the housemaid, disappeared through the wooden panelling. The housekeeper also witnessed the apparition sitting in the same room, and described her as wearing, 'a rather full, plain dress, and a gauzy sort of head-dress, then she gradually faded away.'

The final ghost to be seen at Athelhampton is that of the Black Priest. This sighting was also seen in daylight by another housemaid who was aware of footsteps behind her. The housemaid turned to see a distinct figure, which she described as a 'hooded monk, dressed in black, standing outside the bathroom door.' It is possible this was the ghost of a Catholic priest of the Martyn family.

Ghostly sounds of plainsong and chanting were heard on numerous occasions in the late Nineteenth Century emanating from the Elizabethan manor house at Purse Caundle. This began when a staircase was removed from the manor because of a so-called 'fairy.' A hidden well was revealed where - legend said - a child had accidentally fallen to its death, to linger on as a ghost or fairy haunting the ladies of the house. The spirit was soon laid to rest when a priest was brought in to perform an exorcism.

The manor is also the site of a pack of ghostly hunting dogs, which can be heard baying on the bowling green at Purse Caundle on Christmas Eve, New Year's Eve, and Midsummer Eve. The pack are said to date back to the thirteenth century when John Aleyn lived at Purse

Caundle Manor, which was once a hunting lodge for King John (1166 – 1216).

Plumber Manor, Sturminster Newton, has a similar phantom pack of hounds. Legend has it that when the Lord of the Manor was attending to the hounds, he disappeared, never to be seen again. It was thought he was torn to pieces while trying to separate two fighting dogs, and only his thumbs were recovered. Following this, his ghost has been sighted rushing out of the house closely pursued by the hounds and sound of hunting horns.

Most of the hauntings that have been mentioned have either been contributed to by tales of violence or sadness, but this is not the case with all. Some ghosts appear to revisit their home, or a special place, that held happy memories for them when they were alive.

Sherborne Castle, which lies close to the former Old Castle, was built by Sir Walter Raleigh in 1594, and was the only residence in which he found peace and happiness. It is perhaps for this reason that his spirit returns to the castle every year on the eve of the feast of St. Michael, (29th September) and of his execution at London in 1618, after his arrest and imprisonment in the Tower of London as a conspirator against King James I. Sir Walter Raleigh's ghost is said to walk beneath the trees in the castle grounds before sitting on the stone seat named after him. It was here in his former life that he would smoke the tobacco that he was famed for introducing to England.

Another ghost who returns to his former home is a monk of Forde Abbey. It is thought this apparition is of Thomas Chard, the last Abbot of Forde Abbey, at the time of the dissolution of the monasteries in the sixteenth century. His ghost is reputed to walk along *Monk's Walk* and also in the abbey's Refectory, before sitting at the great table.

Sandford Orcas near Sherborne, the impressive Tudor Manor House, built in 1540 by Edward Knowles, became the subject of much interest and debate amongst the public and media during the 1960's and 1970's due to its multiple hauntings, which to some even rivalled the infamous Borley Rectory, in Essex for the title of *'the most haunted house in England'*.

The fanciful ghost stories and tales that were told then have since passed into legend, but for the Claridge family who lived there at the time, the experiences were all too real.

Their first encounter with the supernatural occurred in 1965, when Colonel and Mrs Claridge leased the manor from the Medlycott family. In that year they became aware of mysterious sounds of heavy footsteps, voices, and whispers, rapping on doors, and beautiful music playing, which seemed to emanate from a room above the gatehouse. Poltergeist activity followed, with the movement of furniture, picture frames, and the opening of windows.

The Claridges encountered many different types of ghosts during their occupation of the manor. The first to become visible to them appeared in 1965 in the doorway in the lower courtyard. The same year, they witnessed the form of a lady in red ascend the main staircase from the Great Hall and disappear through the closed door of the Solarium. Mrs Claridge described the ghost as a "dear old lady, with white hair wearing a hand-painted red silk dress of the Georgian times."

On other occasions, the Red Lady is only heard coming up the stairs, by the rustle of her silk dress. Another phantom, a little girl dressed in black Victorian dress, has been seen at times, standing sadly at the foot of the same staircase.

Another phantom woman was seen by the Claridge's son-in-law, who noticed a woman in Elizabethan costume, walking from the manor house towards the courtyard, from his bedroom window one night.

It was not long before reports began to appear in local and national newspapers. Former employees supported the claims by giving their own accounts on the strange experiences they had during their time at the house.

This was soon followed by a team of psychic investigators lead by Benson Herbert from the Paraphysical Laboratory at Downton, Wiltshire. They were invited by the Claridges to spend a few nights at the haunted manor house in 1966. Their investigations verified five independent ghosts. Benson Herbert later added that *'a prima facie case has been made out for the house being haunted'*.

Perhaps the most terrifying apparition encountered by the team at Sandford Orcas was the ghost known as the 'Stinking Man.' This repulsive phantom could be heard between the hours of ten and eleven o'clock at night by the unearthly sound he made, as if bodies were being dragged around the house, and once from the servants quarters he was heard tapping on the door five or six times. The ghastly thing about this ghost is the stench of decaying flesh that he leaves in his wake.

It was in the small bedroom of the nursery wing, that a former kitchen maid of the manor saw the ghost suddenly appear at the foot of the bed swaying from side to side. She described: "'His form was outlined against the window. He stood tall, in evening dress and his face appeared evil". The apparition stood staring at her for a while before disappearing. The following evening the maid was in the great hall when she became aware of the presence again. "It was just as if someone was there compelling me to look at them, and yet I could see no-one. I felt unable to move," she said.

It is thought this evil spectre was once a depraved footman or valet, who in his lifetime was known to rape the young maids of the house, and it is for this reason he targets only virgin girls.

According to Rodney Legg in his investigations into the hauntings for the *Dorset Magazine*. In order to test this, two women, *allegedly virgins*, were brought to the house by Benson Herbert, to spend the whole night in the small bedroom as part of an experiment arranged by the Paraphysical Laboratory to try and entice the spirit from hiding. At nine o'clock the following morning, the two women emerged from the locked room in a terrible state; they both independently described the apparition as a seven-foot tall man, dressed in Georgian period costume. The whole affair smacks of more innocent times. The thought that any contemporary parapsychologist would even *dare* to ask whether their colleagues were *virgo intacts* (and not expect either a lawsuit, or a punch in the mouth) is too stupid for words.

Colonel Claridge's daughter, Mrs Georgina Richards, also once spent the night in that small bedroom and was awoken by invisible hands clutching round her throat. She felt herself dragged to the edge of the bed, and then hurled to the floor. For about two hours she struggled furiously with her unseen attacker, until she managed to escape and run from the room. From that day she refused to enter the manor house after dark.

The beautiful, but sinister, manor house at Sandford Orcas

Viewing the exterior of the house, one might notice the similarity in decorative stonework to that of Athelhampton Hall. This is no surprise, as Sandford Orcas is connected with Athelhampton by marriage between the Knoyle and Martyn families. There is little wonder then that the stone carvings of the Martyn's Apes, which perch high on the gable ends of Sandford Orcas Manor, gave rise to a legend by a former footman and house-keeper, who were afraid of them, complaining that they would laugh and move in the moonlight.

On the East Wing of the manor can be found the attractive arched gatehouse. It was apparently here in the early part of the eighteenth century, a former tenant-farmer decided to commit suicide by hanging himself from a pulley. Ever after his spirit has been seen walking in the garden, lurking in the stables, and often appears passing the kitchen window between three and four o'clock in the afternoon.

It was one warm July day in 1966 around half-past three in the afternoon that the ghost of the farmer was captured on film by Colonel Claridge's daughter, Georgina Richards. Mrs Richards took the photograph of her son David, the pet dog, and Mrs Jean Briggs, in the confines of the manor's garden, and no-one else was present at the time it was taken. But when the photograph was developed, Georgina was surprised to discover what appeared to be a figure of a man wearing a white smock, standing in a stone archway behind the dog's head. The only conclusion the Claridge's could come to was that this was the ghost of the farmer who had committed suicide all those years ago.

Soon other photographs were taken on different occasions, purporting to show at least six of the manor's ghosts. They included a Franciscan Monk, and an Elizabethan woman.

When the house was open to the public, visitors intrigued by the hauntings would come to Sandford Orcas hoping to have their *own* spiritual encounters. On one occasion, two ladies from London were startled by an old lady who, before disappearing, was sitting in a chair at the end of the bed. The two ladies told Colonel Claridge what they had seen. He later found that the description matched the exact resemblance to a woman's portrait that hung in a room that wasn't normally on view to the public. On another occasion, a man who looked in terror as he entered the principal bedroom, to witness a grisly re-enactment of a murder taking place on the huge four-poster bed. Needless to say he didn't stay long to tour the rest of the house. The Claridges knew all too well what the gentleman had witnessed, for in that room two murders were committed, and they *too* had witnessed them on occasion, for the room was where the Claridges retired to sleep.

One morning in December 1970, at four o'clock, the Colonel awoke to find a pair of hands putting a monk's habit over his face as though to smother him. He promptly shouted at the thing and it disappeared. This is thought to be the ghost of a renegade priest who is known to have murdered his master by smothering him with his habit.

Similarly at two o'clock one July morning, the Colonel was sleeping in the antique four-poster bed, when he awoke with a sense of horror, and as his eyes adjusted to the dark, he became aware of the outline of a man glaring down at him with a look of hatred in his glistening white eyes. Then all at once the hunched figure vanished into the darkness, only to appear again on each of the succeeding seven nights.

The visitations ceased until the following July, and then occurred again at the same time for another seven consecutive nights. Colonel Claridge believes what he had seen during the week was the frightful *Moorish** black servant. Centuries ago he is reputed to have murdered his sleeping master in that very bed by garrotting him with a length of wire, only to return to the scene of the crime after his own death as a ghost.

The hauntings persisted even more in this bedroom as on the 5th October 1971, at half past seven, the Colonel was startled by the appearance of three cowled monks walking from the entrance of the bedroom to the door by the bed. The Colonel called his wife, and watched as another three monks followed. Before they all eventually disappeared, the Colonel's dog apparently attacked one of the monks in the doorway.

---

*'*Moorish.*' *Of or pertaining to the Moors. Also the name for Urdū or Hindustānī language.*

Directly behind the four-poster bed, there is a secret passage where a body of a boy is thought to be buried. This boy was a naval cadet, who at the age of fourteen, entered Dartmouth Naval College, but within two years of his absence from Sandford Orcas, was brought back to the manor as a prisoner after supposedly murdering a fellow cadet. It is said that as punishment for his crime, he was imprisoned in a room in the servants' wing where he remained, driven insane by the confines of his cell, until his death at the age of twenty-seven. His body was taken from the room, and walled up by his mother in the secret passage.

In 1979, Sir Christopher Medlycott, who leased the manor to the Claridge family once commented about the hauntings. "I don't believe it is haunted at all, as our family have lived there for forty-four years, and never heard or saw anything". And when questioned about the walled up naval cadet, Sir Christopher Medlycott replied that this was absolutely ridiculous as it could not have possibly happened, due to the fact that his parents were living there at the time.

The years passed at Sandford Orcas, and more and more ghosts have joined the already extended list of hauntings inside and outside. One was the ghost of a dog named Toby who died in 1900, and revisits the Great Hall on the 15th September each year.

In the Dining Room, which was once part of the Kitchens of the house, a man dressed in a black hat and cloak is often seen looking across the room in the direction of the windows. There is an old lady in a mackintosh who comes in at the small garden gate, crosses the courtyard only to disappear into the gate leading to the nursery wing. By the mid 1970's the ghost sightings, which started as a mere handful now reached such epidemic proportions that the hauntings at Sandford Orcas began to be taken less and less seriously. Even the stories of the Colonel were becoming contradictory, with inaccurate and contradictory details such as times, dates, and historical facts.

It could be that some of these hauntings were indeed made up for the purpose of bringing in the paying public, but on the other hand, it could be that Sandford Orcas serves as some kind of ghost magnet or portal where the dead can converge to haunt beyond the grave.

St. Mary's Church, Beaminster

HAUNTING BEYOND THE GRAVE

The visitation of a boy's ghost in the town of Beaminster, in the early part of the eighteenth century, became the focus of an unsolved murder mystery. The original account came from the *Gentleman's Magazine* of 1774, reprinted by J. S. Udal in *Dorsetshire Folklore* (1922).

This encounter with the supernatural happened at a Beaminster school, which was held every Saturday in the gallery of the parish church of St. Mary, to which there is a distinct entrance leading from the churchyard. It was here on the 27th June 1728, after a day's tuition, that the schoolmaster, John Guppy, dismissed the boys as usual. However, twelve of them stayed, loitering in the churchyard, playing with a ball.

That Saturday, at twelve o'clock noon, four of the boys decided to leave the game and return to the school in search of some pens, as one of the boys still had the key, and hadn't, as yet, returned it to the parish clerk. Upon entering the church, they were startled by a noise that sounded like the striking of brass pans. Quickly, without hesitation, they ran back to the others, who were still playing, to tell them what they had heard. After some discussion, they came to the conclusion that someone was hiding in there in order to frighten them, so - with courage - all twelve returned to the church once again to find the practical joker. But the search was in vain and no-one was found.

It was as they passed the stairs that led to the churchyard, the boys suddenly heard a second noise of heavy footsteps tramping up the stairs. Terrified they fled round the church, passing the belfry, when suddenly they heard the spectral voice of someone preaching, followed by the sound of a congregation singing psalms, which lasted for only a few minutes.

Once again the boys resumed their game like nothing had happened, until one of them went back to the school for his book. On reaching the school, he was shocked to discover - lying six feet before him on a writing desk - the apparition of a white coffin, with its brass nails, and a piece of tape (or gartering) attached to one of the handles. The boy cried out, and quickly ran back to his friends - bruising himself as he fell down the stairs - to tell them what he had seen. The other boys all rushed to the school, where they converged on the door, pushing and shoving, to get a good view of this strange sight. Most of them saw the white coffin, but as the doorway was so narrow, only five of the twelve nearest the front saw the distinct apparition of their friend John Daniel, who had been dead for the past seven weeks, sitting some distance from the coffin. The first to recognise the apparition was John Daniel's half-brother Issac, who cried out:

"There sits our John, with such a coat on as I have" (in the lifetime of the deceased boy, the half-brothers were usually clothed alike) *"and with a pen in his hand, and a book before him, and a coffin by him. I'll throw a stone at him."* The other boys tried to stop him, but he threw it anyway, and in doing so said. *"Take it."* Whereupon the apparition and coffin promptly dis-

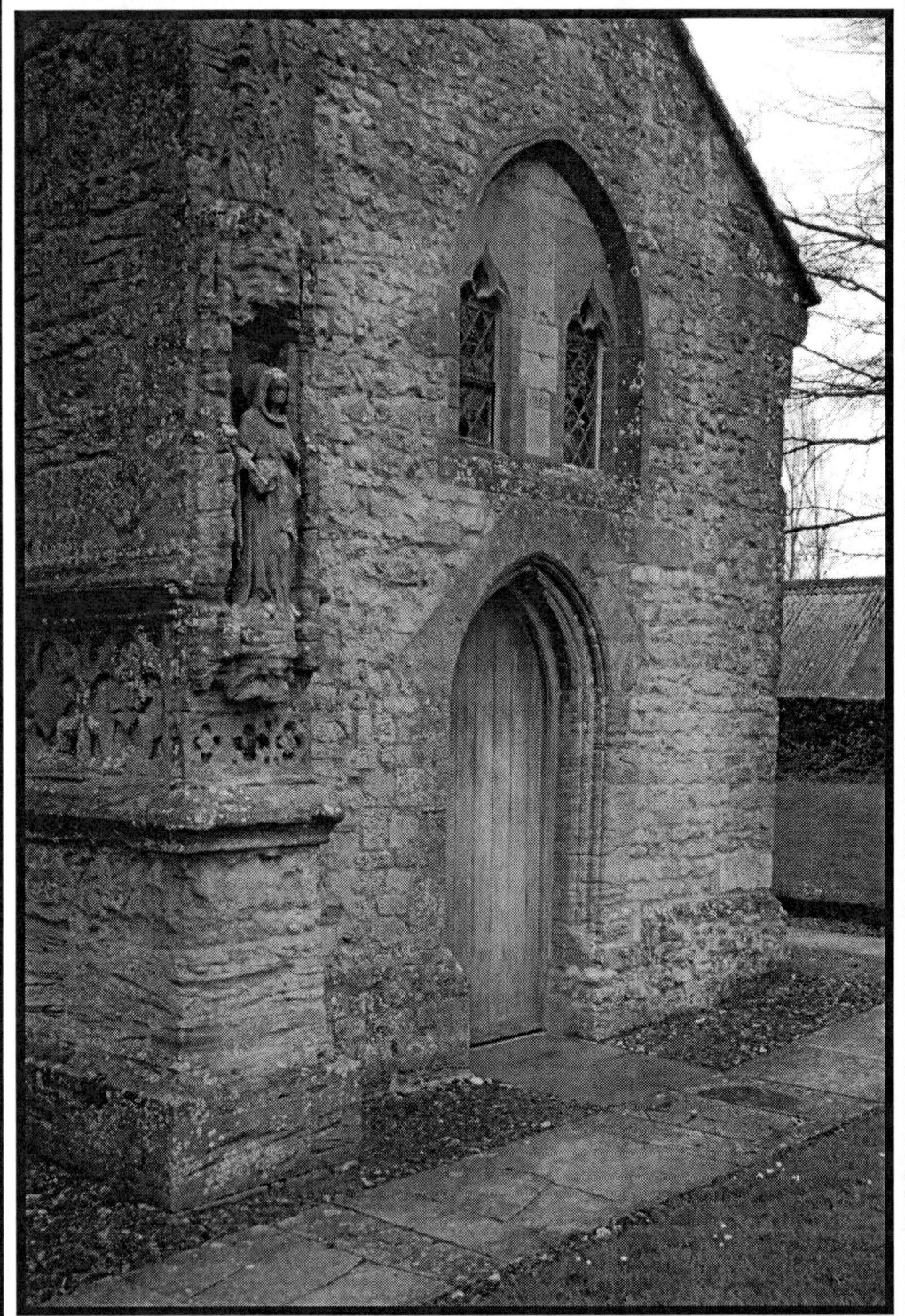

The entrance to what was then Beaminster School

appeared, leaving the church in darkness for two to three minutes.

Once word got around the town about the haunting at St. Mary's, it caused quite a stir. The deceased boy's relatives approached the Justice of the Peace, Colonel Broadrepp of Mapperton Manor, who requested that the twelve boys involved in the incident, whose ages ranged from nine to twelve, were brought to him.

The Colonel questioned only eight of the group of boys, who each gave detailed accounts about the ghostly visitation. Their description of the ghostly coffin, even down to the type of hinges, tallied exactly with the coffin in which John Daniel's body had been buried. However, one of the older boys, who was twelve years of age, never knew John Daniel as he had entered the school *after* John's death. He gave such an accurate description of John Daniel, that he observed something else that the other boys failed to notice; a white cloth or rag bound around one of John's hands. Apparently a woman who was later questioned, and who had prepared John's corpse for burial, admitted that she had taken a white cloth from the boy's hand, having been put on a week or four days before his death as a dressing.

The body of fourteen year old John Daniel had been found a month earlier in unusual circumstances, on a small island of sand and gravel in a field two hundred and twenty yards west of his stepmother's home at Knowle. His body was later buried in St. Mary's churchyard on Saturday 1st June 1728, without even a coroner's inquest, on the grounds of his stepmother, Elizabeth Daniel (neė Stodgell), saying that the boy had been subject to fits.

After the interrogation of the boys, John Daniel's body was immediately exhumed, and a coroner's inquest was held; the verdict returned to the effect that the boy had indeed been strangled.

The verdict seemed to rest mainly on the depositions of two elderly women who told the inquest how they discovered a *black list** around the neck of the boy's corpse a couple of days after he was found.

The joiner who put the body into the coffin, noticed the shroud was not put on in the usual way, but had been cut into two pieces - one laid under, the other over - the corpse. A chirurgeon† who was present with the jury, could not possibly affirm any dislocation of the neck.

Suspicions pointed to John's stepmother as the murderer, but due to the lack of evidence she was never convicted of the crime. It would appear that after the inquest into the murder of John Daniel, the perpetrator was never caught, and the case pursued no further, leaving this violent crime permanently unsolved, though the warrant for an arrest still remains on file at the county archivist's office in Dorchester.

Meanwhile the hauntings at St. Mary's persisted six weeks after the first initial sighting, with the appearance of a spectral figure, witnessed by two members of the congregation attending a Wednesday service at the church.

---

* *'Black list.'* A band of bruising.
† *'Chirurgeon.'* One whose profession is to cure bodily diseases and injuries by manual operation; a surgeon.

The names of the 24 jurors at Daniel's inquest are unknown, but 38 names are on this Coroners warrant. The 20 men and 18 women listed would presumably have been witnesses including many names that appear in the ghost story. The warrant, including a narrative of the incident at Beaminster is kept at the Dorset County Record Office.

The first to see the spectre was a servant girl of fourteen, who was said to have been," *of very good repute for veracity.*" She was kneeling behind her master in the gallery, when she noticed a woman open the door adjoining the stairs, and look towards the part of the gallery used for schooling. According to the girl, the woman was thin of stature with a pale complexion, wearing a sombre or dark coloured gown, with a flowered neckerchief and a straw hat.

Thinking that the woman wished to speak with her master, the girl discreetly tapped his shoulder to gain his attention.

The master had a child seriously ill at home, and instantly thought the woman was a messenger bringing news of his child's condition. Hastily he rushed down the stairs from the gallery in pursuit of the woman, when the door unexpectedly slammed before him with a loud bang, startling both the minister and the rest of the congregation. The master rushed out into the churchyard to find no sign of the woman. He searched in vain around the church to no avail, and was left mystified how anyone could move out of the churchyard in only a split second, and just simply disappear.

When people heard about the incident, they instantly believed the woman was undoubtedly the ghost of John Daniel's mother Hannah Daniel, who had died when he was born in October 1714, as the girl's descriptions were so accurate for someone who had been just a baby at the time of Hannah's death.

Three centuries have passed, and the memory of John Daniel refuses to be dead and buried, for apparitions seen in the early hours of a morning in late August 1998, have re-opened interest in the murder mystery.

Located about three quarters of a mile southwest of Beaminster near Knowle Farm, can be found a private walled burial ground known as *Daniel's Knowle*. It is here that the grave of James Daniel, a lawyer of Beaminster, is buried. It was at the age of seventy-four that James joined the Monmouth Rebellion fighting at the battle of Sedgemoor on the 8th July 1685. After the terrible defeat, he fled like many others from the battlefield. Though many of his comrades were captured, James Daniel managed to reach his Beaminster home, where he remained in hiding. Being a man of considerable influence, a substantial reward was offered for his capture.

James thought it unwise to remain in the town with the Bloody Assizes already in operation, and fled once again from the king's forces. The fugitive Daniel eventually found refuge in a barn at Knowle, where he hid amongst some threshed straw. Unsuccessfully searching his abode, the king's soldiers gathered information of his possible whereabouts, and made their way to the barn at Knowle. They raided the barn, thrusting their bayonets into the loose straw, but miraculously they missed Daniel. Once the soldiers had departed, he went home where he remained in hiding again until the persecution of the rebels had subsided.

James Daniel came out of hiding, and he lived to the great age of one hundred. On his death in 1711, according to Daniel's wishes he instructed the barn at Knowle to be removed, so it could become a private cemetery for his remains, and those of his descendants, at the very place where he believed God had saved him.

It was near this family cemetery, that a ghostly encounter was witnessed by Peter Beer, who farms at Knowle Farm. Mr Beer went out at 4.45 a.m. to check on one of his cows which was expected to calve in a field near the burial ground. As he approached the pregnant cow, he discovered that it had already began to give birth, so, to see the animal more clearly, he switched on his powerful torch. To his amazement, as he panned the beam of light towards the cow, he saw two spectral figures standing close by watching.

Mr Beer told the *Bridport News* on 28th August 1998. *"I picked her out to be a woman because she was wearing a sort of long white gown and the boy had a dark outfit"*. The shocked farmer was only standing ten paces away when the woman glanced back at him. *"She had pink eyes!"* quoted Mr Beer.

When the cow finished calving it stood up and walked out of the way, while the two ghostly apparitions made their way to the cemetery, where he heard the distinct opening and closing of the graveyard gates. At this moment, Mr Beer quickly rushed back to the farmhouse quite shaken by the ordeal. Later that morning he returned to the site to put his mind at ease, and to find out if there was a grave of a woman and child in the private cemetery. He was able to make out one inscription of a couple and a child on one of the eroded gravestones.

The Beer family have only lived at Knowle Farm since 1997, and knew nothing of the Daniel family, nor of the 1728 ghostly incident at St. Mary's, until they heard the stories from a descendant of the family - Robert Willoughby, who approached Beaminster Town Council for help with restoration of the family cemetery. It has been thought that the sighting witnessed by Mr Beer *could* be connected with the murdered boy John Daniel, and his mother Hannah, as it is possible that John may lie in the graveyard. However, it could also be linked to another story of a boy, once found hanged in the farmhouse; this may explain the mysterious happenings encountered by the Beer family while living in the farmhouse - the sound of footsteps on the landing, lights mysteriously found switched on in unoccupied rooms, and doors opening of their own accord. But whatever the case may be, the strange phenomena surrounding Knowle Farm and *Daniel's Knowle* cemetery will forever be a mystery.

THE DEMON JUDGE OF DORCHESTER

In the year of 1685 a shadow fell across Dorset in the guise of bloody rebellion, and in the days that followed true horror swept the land. For that autumn the dreadful sight and smell of rotting human body parts, hung up along the main highways, and in the towns, was a gruesome reality.

All this stomach wrenching horror came about due to the death of King Charles II, who was succeeded by his Catholic brother, James, the Duke of York - King James II. But Charles had an illegitimate son, James the Duke of Monmouth, who was a Protestant.

On 11th June 1685 the Duke of Monmouth landed at Lyme Regis with about eighty followers. After a short prayer his soldiers cried out. *"A Monmouth! A Monmouth! And the Protestant religion!"* These words were soon to echo across the West Country, for he marched onwards to Taunton, in Somerset, Devon, and back into Dorset, gathering support for his claim to the throne.

His army grew from town to town recruiting men from the farms, and the revolt soon became known as *The Pitchfork Rebellion.* Word soon reached King James II that his nephew the Duke was on the move with a vast number of men heading east, so James II sent an army commanded by Lord Faversham to crush the revolt before it got out of hand.

On the 6th July the two armies clashed at the Battle of Sedgemoor, and though Monmouth's army fought bravely, they were no match for the highly trained troops of The King. Monmouth's army fled the battlefield, and the Duke ran for his life. The next morning he was captured near Horton Heath, eight miles south of the hamlet of Woodyates, disguised as a farm labourer, hiding in a ditch at a spot now known as *Monmouth's Ash.* He was taken to London and promptly tried for treason, and was finally beheaded on Tower Hill on the 15th July 1685.

Understandably, King James II did not wish for any more repeat performances of the rebellion, so he selected the most cold blooded and ruthless of all the country's judges to deal with the remaining survivors of Monmouth's army. The Denbighshire born, thirty-seven year old, Judge George Jeffreys was chosen for the job as he was noted for his swiftness in dealing out justice and his merciless sentences.

Judge Jeffreys travelled from court to court, Winchester, Taunton, Dorchester, etc, where, in all, some 1400 prisoners were brought before him. The court hearings soon became known as *The Bloody Assizes,* for in total some 300 men were unpleasantly put to death by being hung drawn and quartered. Their body parts were hung up, displayed around the towns, and along the roads as a stark warning for anyone plotting against the king.

Around 800 men were sentenced for transportation to the colonies as slaves, of which many succumbed to sickness on the journey and were thrown overboard to feed the sharks. The rest were either pardoned or kept in custody.

Judge Jeffreys opened the Bloody Assizes at Dorchester on the 5th September 1685 at the Antelope Hotel in an oak-panelled room known as 'The Oak Room.' He was staying nearby at a house in High West Street, (now a restaurant, but still known as his lodgings to this day) and made his way to and from the court hearings by way of a secret passage so that jeering, angry crowds could not see him.

One evening after dealing out a day's harsh justice, Jeffreys was at his lodgings when it was made known to him there was a young girl outside in the street wishing to speak with him. The girl was sent for, and Jeffreys listened to all what she had to say. She begged for her elder brother to be spared the death sentence he had been given that day. Jeffreys made it clear that he would do so on one condition - she would have to spend the night with him in his bed. The girl reluctantly agreed.

Judge Jeffreys' Lodgings - now a restaurant in Dorchester

Early the next morning while Jeffreys lay asleep, the girl slipped out of bed and prepared to go home. The room was dark and in order to see to dress, she drew the curtains. To her sheer horror on the other side of High West Street she saw her beloved brother's lifeless body hanging from the neck by a *Bridport Dagger*. One can only imagine what she must have felt by being used and betrayed by the outrageous Jeffreys, but no doubt she left the room heartbroken.

By the time the court had moved on, Judge Jeffreys had sentenced 74 men to death, condemned 175 men to transportation, 9 were fined or whipped, and 55 were pardoned.

The Bloody Assizes opened at Lyme Regis on 11th September 1685. The next day twelve men were executed on the beach west of the Cobb, and their body parts were spiked up along the railings around the church. Two of the men's heads were impaled on the iron gates of the great house in Broad Street, now known as Chatham House. It was here that Jeffreys was said to have dined on the night before the executions. Ever after his ghost has been seen carrying a bloody bone in the house, and gnawing upon it outside in the street.

The Duke of Monmouth's ghost is also said to haunt Dorset. He is supposed to be seen (still attached to his head) at night, riding upon a white horse along the road from Lyme Regis to Uplyme. It was by this road that he left Lyme Regis at the start of this doomed rebellion.

The following statement comes from Jeffreys' Prescript to the Sheriff of the county showing the brutality of punishment:

"These are, therefore, to will and require of you, immediately on sight hereof, to erect a gallows in the most public place to hang the said traytors on, and that you provide halters to hang them with, a sufficient number of faggots to burn the bowels, and a furnace or cauldron to boil their heads and quarters, and salt to boil them with, half a bushel to each traytor, and tar to tar them with, and a sufficient number of spears and poles to fix and place their heads and quarters; and that you warn the owners of four oxen to be ready with dray and wain, and the said four oxen, at the time hereafter mentioned for execution, and you yourselves, together with a guard of forty able men at the least, to be present by eight o'clock of the morning to be aiding and assisting me or my deputy to see the said rebels executed. You are also to provide an axe and a cleaver for the quartering the said rebels."

BRIDPORT DAGGER

Once, the town of Bridport saw its greatest prosperity as a net and rope manufacturer for both the fishing industry and navy. It was also where hangman's rope was made. It was customary to say that anyone who had been hanged, had been 'Stabbed by a Bridport Dagger.'

THE LEGACY AND CURSE OF BETTISCOMBE MANOR

Many people are not familiar with the literary works of Francis Marion Crawford, and now much of it is little read or out of print. He was born in Italy in 1854, of American parents, and was educated at Heidelberg, Rome, and Harvard. Through the 1880s and 1890s he continued to travel extensively, and his novels and stories reflect a variety of exotic settings. Crawford wrote more than forty romance and adventure novels and popular histories, enjoying great success and appeal in the United States and the rest of the world. However, he is probably best remembered for his collection of ghost stories. It was the story of the *The Screaming Skull* originally published in *The Evening Standard* volume of strange stories and later, after Crawford's death in 1909, *Wandering Ghosts* published in 1911, was to become Crawford's landmark horror story, and which has appeared in numerous anthologies.

Francis Marion Crawford

The story of *The Screaming Skull* is one of the longest of his ghost stories. Set in Cornwall in a fictitious village of Tredcombe, the tale concerns a human skull that - as the title states - periodically screams, and a retired naval captain, Charles Braddock, who may have been indirectly responsible for the death of the skull's original owner. The tension is emphasised by the narration being a first-person monologue by the captain, to a visiting friend, as the events occur. Crawford waits to the end, with the death of the retired naval captain to quote the fictitious *Penraddon News* reporting a coroner's jury at Penraddon returning a verdict of death by murder *"by the hands or teeth of some person unknown."*

Only then does Crawford admit in a footnote that the story is based on the legendary Bettiscombe skull.

> [*Note.* — Students of ghost lore and haunted houses will find the foundation of the foregoing story in the legends about a skull which is still preserved in the farm-house called Bettiscombe Manor, situated, I believe, on the Dorsetshire coast.]

It is this footnote that makes perhaps the story even more chilling - no flimsy, floating things in the night as one might expect of hauntings, but actually based on something that is very real and exists. So what is it that makes the legend of the Skull at Bettiscombe fascinating to inspire Crawford in penning his famous ghost story?

The poster for the 1958 American film 'The Screaming Skull' Though it is never credited, the film is based on Francis Marion Crawford's classic horror short story

From annals of folklore, an intriguing aspect of this symbiotic relationship between death and houses can be glimpsed in the customs and superstitions still centred around screaming skulls. Several houses in different parts of Britain have such gruesome relics, which cannot be removed because they fill the place with screams and appalling disturbances and other poltergeist type activity whenever anyone attempts to do so.

Look up any index in a majority of ghost books or guides, and you will find some reference to the most curious and weirdest of all skull legends *"The Screaming Skull of Bettiscombe Manor."*

Amongst the rolling hills of the Marshwood Vale nestles the peaceful village of Bettiscombe. It is the serenity of this village which has been secured for countless years by the presence of the manor house's unusual, but sinister, occupant. Few folklore tales or superstitions are held firmly in belief for so long and in such detail as the Bettiscombe skull legend. To find out what makes this legend unique, we must dig deep into the history and the possible origins of the Bettiscombe Manor skull legend, which make it such a classic ghost story.

Bettiscombe Manor: Perhaps the most famous building in the tiny village of Bettiscombe, which nestles at the foot of the highest point in the county, Pilsdon Pen In the Marshwood Vale, six miles north west of the town of Bridport. Known to many as the 'The House of the Screaming Skull', the manor has been the ancestral home to the Pinney family for over three hundred years.

Our story begins on 30th January 1847, when a young lady by the name of Anne Marie Pinney visits the manor as a result of reading the family records known as the *"Pinney Papers"* at Somerton Erleigh, Somerset (now kept in the library of Bristol University) in 1842, that we are first introduced to the skull.

She writes in her notebook: -

> *"Mrs Groves of the farm, politely took us over the whole, and on opening a long dark cupboard upstairs, said, not very mysteriously! 'As you know Ma'am all about Bettiscombe, of course you have heard of the "Skull of Bettiscombe House", From the depths of the closet she produced a white and perfect human skull! – While this skull is kept here no ghost will ever infest Bettiscombe House", said Mrs Groves, to which I added, 'I thought it very probable', tho' I was beginning to feel myself rather being of another century in that dwelling."*

While researching the history of her family, Ann Marie learned of the dramatic events that happened in the Seventeenth Century when the Reverend John Pinney's (then owner of Bettiscombe Manor) 24-year-old son Azariah took part in the ill-fated Monmouth Rebellion (see the previous chapter). The initial sentence for his crime of treason was - along with twelve others - to be hanged. But his sister intervened, and paid a ransom of £65 and saved him from the gallows. He was exiled to the Caribbean Island of Nevis with only £15, a Bible, six gallons of sack and four of brandy.

Nevis was a new colony that was starting to prosper by sugar plantations. Azariah Pinney worked on Jerome Nipo's sugar plantation, but later became a free man, where he prospered as a merchant and sugar planter.

During Azariah's exile, his younger brother Nathaniel Pinney, in 1694 began reconstruction of the manor house, to how it looks today. It is quite possible that skull was discovered at this time, inside the Elizabethan structure, which was being dismantled, and may have been kept as some sort of curiosity.

Azariah prospered, and by 1705 he had become the co-owner of the 87-acre Charloes plantation on Nevis. He returned to England a very wealthy man, and died in London in 1719, and was buried there.

He was succeeded by his son John, who only outlived his father by a year or so. However, John's marriage in 1708 had brought the 161-acre Proctors estate into the family and this was amalgamated with Charloes and renamed Mountravers.

John's son John Frederick was brought up in England and only came to Nevis in 1739. He only stayed for three years, and thereafter refused to return, even though the estates had begun to fall into decay.

Unmarried John Frederick Pinney chose as his heir a cousin, John Pretor, on condition that the latter took his surname. John Pretor Pinney - perhaps the most successful Pinney of them all - inherited Mountravers and other estates on Nevis after John Frederick Pinney's death in 1762. He arrived on Nevis two years later at the age of 24, eventually taking over the estate in 1765. He made a religion of accounting, detested debt, and had a superb grasp of business.

John Pretor Pinney stands in front of the tiny volcanic island of Nevis – now an independent nation with neighbouring St Kitts. Nevis was once called the 'Queen of the Caribees', because of the money-spinning sugar industry that it supported.

By the time John Pretor Pinney left Nevis in 1783 to settle down in Bristol, the Mountravers plantation was one of the most successful estates in all the Caribbean. Dependent on the labour of their black slaves, the estate produced about 30,000 kg (66,000 lb) of sugar annually and 32,800 litres (7,000 gallons) of rum, and comprised of 393 acres, extending from the top of Mount Nevis on down to the sea. His combined estates had about 200 slaves; a male slave was then worth about £50, a woman £37 and children about £14 each.

John Prector Pinney's son John Frederick Pinney (the second), in 1811 begins the sale (finalised in 1816) of the estate including, Mountravers and other properties to Edward Huggins for £35,650 (about £1.75 million today). John Frederick Pinney was Anne Maria Pinney's father.

"The Pinney Papers", which Anne Maria Pinney had sorted in 1842, had remained undisturbed for ninety years. Since their rediscovery in the late 1930's, they have been extensively read and used in many publications. But no mention of the *"Skull of Bettiscombe"* has been

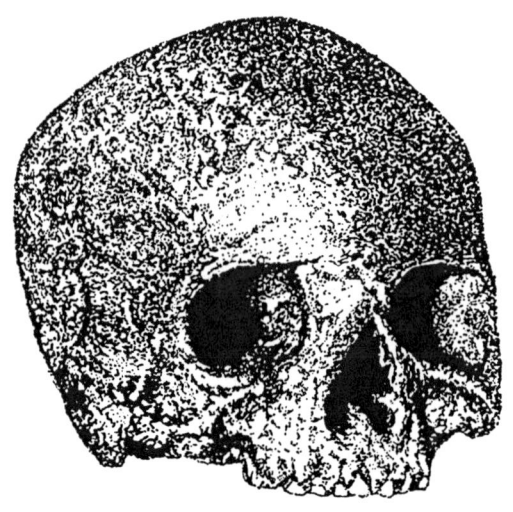

The Bettiscombe Skull

found, other than in Anne Maria's notebook. It was probably this information from the family papers, that lay the foundation which stirred Anne Maria's imagination to invent the legend of the skull.

Since Anne Maria's visit to the manor, the skull once a quiet object of curiosity in the back of the cupboard, became the legendary skull of a black slave who laid curse on the family for reneging on a promise to return his body to his native soil. Perhaps she was inspired by other ghostly manifestations associated with the house? The sounds of skittle players in the attic, footsteps along the corridors, and the legend of the coach and horses being seen near the north Courtyard. This was to later morph into the funeral procession of the skull.

In 1872, a nineteenth century Dorset antiquarian, folklorist and High Court Judge, John Symonds Udal, who later wrote *"Dorsetshire Folklore"* in 1922, first brought the skull to public attention.

In a short article published in *Notes and Queries* (Ser. IV, x, 183), he states: -

"At a farmhouse in Dorsetshire at the present time is carefully preserved a human skull, which has been there for a period long antecedent to the present tenancy. The peculiar superstition attaching to it is that if it be brought out of the house the house itself would rock to its foundations, whilst the person by whom such an act of desecration was committed would certainly die within the year. It is strangely suggestive of the power of this superstition that through many changes of tenancy and furniture the skull still holds its accustomed place 'unmoved and unremoved."

Dr. Goodford responded to this piece by writing, and enquiring whether Udal had not made a mistake as to the county, stating that there was a similar superstition attached to a house at Chilton Cantelo, in the adjoining county of Somerset.

Udal replied to this query by giving the following addition to the legend: -

"The farm-house (formerly, I believe, an old Manor House), now called Bettiscombe House, in which the skull remained, or still remains, for aught I know to the contrary, lies in the parish of Bettiscombe, about six miles from Bridport in Dorsetshire. I cannot ascertain the time when this 'ghostly tenant' took up its abode in the place, but it is tolerably certain it was some considerable time ago. It has, I understand, been pronounced to be that of a negro, and the legend runs that it belonged to a faithful black servant of an early possessor of the property, - a Pinney, - who having resided

abroad some years, brought home this memento of his humble follower. It is reported that a member of the above family, in recent years, has visited the house, but was unable to give any clue that might assist in clearing up the identity of the skull".

Once the location of the skull was established, amateur historians began to take an interest in the skull legend.

In 1883, Dr. R. Garnett of the British Museum, accompanied by his daughter and a family friend, paid a visit to the old house. At this time the attic was considered structurally unsafe, and the skull had been placed there to act as a warning.

The friend of Dr. Garnett, who was a medical student, examined the skull and came to the conclusion that it belonged to a negroid.

The manor's owner then tells them another version of the legend. Dr. Garnett's daughter writes: -

> *"The skull, we were informed, was that of a negro servant, who had lived in the service of a Roman Catholic priest; some difference arose between them, but whether the priest murdered the servant in order to conceal some crimes known to the negro; or whether the negro in a fit of passion killed his master, did not clearly appear. However, the negro had declared before his death that his spirit would not rest unless his body was taken to his native land and buried there. This was not done, he being buried in the churchyard at Bettiscombe. Then the haunting began; fearful screams proceeded from the grave; the doors and windows of the house rattled and creaked; strange sounds were heard all over the house; in short there was no rest for the inmates until the body was dug up. At different periods attempts were made to bury the body, but similar disturbances always recurred. In process of time the skeleton disappeared all save the skull which we now saw before us. We were naturally extremely anxious to bury the skull and remain in the house that night to see what would happen; but this request was indignantly refused, and we were promptly shown off the premises. Therefore the reputation of the "Screaming Skull" of Bettiscombe House remains unimpaired"*

It is in this version of the story that we first hear the mention of the skull having screamed.

Since Dr. Garnetts gave his fantastic account of the visit, we begin to find that the skull is now referred to as the `screaming skull`. In the second series of *"Haunted Homes"*, published 1844, Dr. F. A. Ingham quotes an account of the Bettiscombe Skull from an essay written by Mr. William Andrews on *"Skull Superstitions"*.

He recounts the story by Dr. R. Garnett, but embellishes it, saying that when the slave was buried in the churchyard, the haunting began; fearful screams proceeded from the grave, and strange sounds were heard all over the house, and the inmates of the house had no rest until the body was dug up. Subsequent attempts to dispose of it were allegedly followed by similar results.

Around the same time, an account published in the *Pearson's Magazine* contained a graphic description of the Screaming Skull of Burton Agnes Hall, Yorkshire; to which was appended a note to the effect that "*another 'Screaming Skull' is preserved at Bettiscombe in Dorsetshire,*"

John Symonds Udal, visited Bettiscombe Manor in 1877. He later wrote an essay in the *"Proceedings of the Dorset Natural History and Archaeological Society"* (1910). In his essay, Udal is furious to read that other writers, "had lent a somewhat heightened and conjectural aspect to the tradition." His informant had been an old lady who, in her younger days, had often visited and stayed at the manor. She resented the new versions of the story, which held the belief that the skull had been heard *"screaming"*. Udal also states that upon careful examination of the skull, he was inclined to doubt whether it was the skull of a black slave at all. This anatomical investigation goes some way to corroborate another piece of folklore, as near to the skulls traditional resting place, a niche beside the chimney-breast in the attic, there is also a priest's hole-type hiding place - a fifteen by twelve feet chamber - which is partitioned off from the rest of the attic. It is suggested that the skull belongs to a young lady who had died, or been murdered, after some long confinement in this part of the house, rather than that of a male black slave.

In 1903, John Symonds Udal went as Chief Justice to the Leeward Islands, where on duty in Nevis he stumbled upon the *"Pinney Plantation"*, and made the connection between Nevis and Bettiscombe after he was shown a memorial on the island to `John Pinney son of Azariah Pinney, formerly of Bettiscombe`.

This appeared to give Udal a satisfactory answer to the question of the origin of the skull; the assumption being that the skull was that of a black slave of the Pinney family's, brought back to Bettiscombe.

He later discovers an old *"Plantation Book"*; an inventory of slaves belonging to the Pinney estate, containing a list of slaves given the names *"Weymouth"*, *"Bridport"* and *"Bettiscombe"*. He suggests that if the skull *had* belonged to a slave, it probably belonged to the faithful servant *"Bettiscombe"*, who died at - or before - the time of transfer of the Nevis estates, and whose master had then brought to England this *"memento of his faithful follower"*, to the very place from which his trusty servant had taken his name.

The period between 1870-1920 became the golden age of the psychological and antiquarian ghost story. An era that produced many classics of horror fiction: Bram Stoker's *Dracula*, Arthur Conan Doyle's *Hound of the Baskervilles* and Robert L. Stevenson's *The Strange Case of Dr. Jekyll and Mr. Hyde.*

Amongst the famous writers of this period, Francis Marion Crawford wrote the *The Screaming Skull*. Crawford had certainly read books on hauntings and ghosts, and quite possibly Udal's article about the legend in *Notes and Queries,* as there are many references in Crawford's story to where the skull was kept, the description of it, and how the retired sea captain tried one attempt to rid of it in the pond.

"You ask me why I don't throw it into the pond--yes, but please don't call it a

"confounded bugbear"--it doesn't like being called names."

However, there are certain elements in Crawford's story that may have contributed to the skull legend.

For example the burying of the skull: -

"You thought I had fainted? No, I wish I had, for it would have stopped sooner. It's all very well to say that it's only a noise, and that a noise never hurt anybody-- you're as white as a shroud yourself. There's only one thing to be done, if we hope to close an eye tonight. We must find it and put it back into its bandbox and shut it up in the cupboard, where it likes to be I don't know how it got out, but it wants to get in again. That's why it screams so awfully tonight--it was never so bad as this-- never since I first----

Bury it? Yes, if we can find it, we'll bury it, if it takes us all night. We'll bury it six feet deep and ram down the earth over it, so that it shall never get out again, and if it screams, we shall hardly hear it so deep down. Quick, we'll get the lantern and look for it. It cannot be far away; I'm sure it's just outside--it was coming in when I shut the window, I know it."

And the skull rolling back to the house: -

"A little before dawn someone knocked at the front door. There was no mistaking that for anything else, and I opened my window and looked down, for I guessed that someone wanted the doctor, supposing that the new man had taken Luke's house. It was rather a relief to hear a human knock after that awful noise.

You cannot see the door from above, owing to the little porch. The knocking came again, and I called out, asking who was there, but nobody answered, though the knock was repeated. I sang out again, and said that the doctor did not live here any longer. There was no answer, but it occurred to me that it might be some old countryman who was stone deaf. So I took my candle and went down to open the door. Upon my word, I was not thinking of the thing yet, and I had almost forgotten the other noises. I went down convinced that I should find somebody outside, on the doorstep, with a message. I set the candle on the hall table, so that the wind should not blow it out when I opened. While I was drawing the old-fashioned bolt I heard the knocking again. It was not loud, and it had a queer, hollow sound, now that I was close to it, I remember, but I certainly thought it was made by some person who wanted to get in.

It wasn't. There was nobody there, but as I opened the door inward, standing a little on one side, so as to see out at once, something rolled across the threshold and stopped against my foot.

I drew back as I felt it, for I knew what it was before I looked down. I cannot tell

"What?...It's gone, man, the skull is gone!!"

An original illustration taken from Francis Marion Crawford's book
'Wandering Ghosts" which featured The Screaming Skull story (1911)

you how I knew, and it seemed unreasonable, for I am still quite sure that I had thrown it across the road. It's a French window, that opens wide, and I got a good swing when I flung it out. Besides, when I went out early in the morning, I found the bandbox beyond the thick hedge.

You may think it opened when I threw it, and that the skull dropped out; but that's impossible, for nobody could throw an empty cardboard box so far. It's out of the question; you might as well try to fling a ball of paper twenty-five yards, or a blown bird's egg.

To go back, I shut and bolted the hall door, picked the thing up carefully, and put it on the table beside the candle. I did that mechanically, as one instinctively does the right thing in danger without thinking at all--unless one does the opposite. It may seem odd, but I believe my first thought had been that somebody might come and find me there on the threshold while it was resting against my foot, lying a little on its side, and turning one hollow eye up at my face, as if it meant to accuse me. And the light and shadow from the candle played in the hollows of the eyes as it stood on the table, so that they seemed to open and shut at me. Then the candle went out quite unexpectedly, though the door was fastened and there was not the least draught; and I used up at least half a dozen matches before it would burn again."

It is amazing to find the striking similarities between Crawford's story and other stories about a former owner of the manor, who refused to have the skull in the house, and had it buried, before it managed to work its way up from a depth of nine feet to the surface, only to be found the next day on the manor's doorstep. In other versions, the skull of the slave was buried in the churchyard to a depth of six feet, only to work itself out of the ground, and to have rolled back to the manor to be discovered on the doorstep.

So it looks like this additional version may have been made up by someone who had read *The Screaming Skull*, as the present authors have not been able to find this version in any of the retelling of the legend, and certainly not in Udal's extensive research into the legend prior to Crawford's published story. However, this tale may have got confused with another legend in Bettiscombe, concerning a standing stone that has the ability to move. This is the *Wishing Stone*, also known as the *Sliding Stone*, located near the manor on the slopes of Sliding Hill, which is aptly named, as on Midsummer's Eve the stone is said to slide down the hill, only to return the next day.

Later, Sabine Baring-Gould, a clergyman in the Church of England in Devon, an archaeologist, folklorist, historian, and a prolific author (he is best known for writing the hymn *Onward Christian Soldiers*), in his 1913 publication *A Book of Folklore*, also makes reference to Bettiscombe and the slave legend in his chapter about Skulls. He also brings attention to another skull in Dorset, which is less well known, and which wasn't mentioned in Udal's *Dorsetshire Folklore* in 1922, "The Waddon Skull", but even here he claimed that the skull screamed when there have been no actual accounts of it having done so.

"There was a "screaming skull" at Waddon, in Dorsetshire, about fifty years ago, kept respectfully in a recess on the stairs; but as it was liable to be fractious and

cause disturbances in the house, it was given to the Dorchester Museum, where it now is. The story about it is that it was the head of a Negro, and it bore on it the mark, of a cut from a sword. The black man went to his master's room at night, and the latter, believing him to be a burglar, killed him by mistake. He was killed in the bedroom over the dining room. The owners of Waddon were the Grove family of Zeals, in Wiltshire. When Miss Chafyn Grove died some years ago, her cousin, Mr Troyte Bullock, inherited, but with the property had to take the name of Chafyn Grove.

A few miles distant from Waddon is Bettiscombe. Here also is a "screaming skull". The house was rebuilt in Queen Anne's reign, but the richly carved wainscoting and fine old oak stairs pertain to the earlier house that was pulled down when the present mansion was built. This was done by Azariah Pinney, who had joined Monmouth's forces, and was exiled to the West Indies, he being one of those who escaped sentence of death by Judge Jeffreys at the "Bloody Assizes", held at Dorchester, after the Rebellion. His life was spared through the influence of a friend at the Court of James II. He remained in the West Indies for a period of ten years, and then returned with a black servant, to whom he was much attached; and then the man died; but whether the skull be his, or, if so, why it was preserved above ground, none can say. It would seem probable, however, that it was taken along with the wainscoting out of the earlier house.

The prevailing superstition is that, if it be brought out of the house, the house itself will rock to its foundations, and the person guilty of the sacrilegious act will die within the year. The house had remained uninhabited for some years until, about 1760 or 1770, a farmer came into occupation. Finding the skull, he declared with an oath that he would not have the thing there, and he had it thrown into a pool of water. During that night and the next the farmer heard some uncanny noises, and on the third day he said he would have the skull back. He did so, and then, as the story goes, all the noises ceased. It has been carefully preserved since, and kept in a kind of loft under the roof in a cigar box."

In 1934, the Pinney family returned to Bettiscombe, when Michael Pinney purchased the freehold from the Young family, with hope of carrying on the family connection for further generations.

They discovered further stories concerning their ghostly tenant. By this time, the slave story became so popular, that when Michael Pinney first came to stay at the manor "....*the old farmer pointed out a grille at the back of the cupboard by the fireplace at the west end of the house...he said that was where they used to keep the 'black man', and he was fed by having food pushed to him through the bars of the grille.*" To add further to the confusion about the skull's origins, another popular story is that Azariah and the slave originally had a fight to the death, the skull being the only thing that remained of the loser, only nobody knows which one lost! Even the ghostly skittle players in the attic are said to use the skull in their nightly game.

Other tales that sounded more authentic were told to Michael Pinney, included one from Mr

Forsey, who, as a boy, lived at Bettiscombe Manor from 1880 to 1898. He is said to have removed the skull from the house with the help of a friend and hid it in a hayrick. Dreading that it might catch the hayrick alight, the two boys transferred the skull to the stables. That night the boys were awoken by terrible noises as if someone in the house was smashing china. So, in haste, they fetched the skull from the stables and returned it to its rightful place in the house.

A similar experience happened to a carter who worked on the farm during the 1930's. The carter took the skull from the house and threw it into the local pond, but soon raked it out when terrible screams were heard during the night, which may account for it's fossilised appearance, as this can happen very quickly if the pond water was very alkaline, but it may have possibly have been caused by the damp and moisture when the skull was in the attic and the roof was in a bad state of repair.

The Manor's duck pond, into which the skull was allegedly thrown

(Other versions of this tale have suggested that the following morning the skull was found *not* in the pond, but on the doorstep. A skull moving of its own will, is clearly an idea taken from Francis Marion Crawford's *The Screaming Skull* ghost story, more than twenty years earlier.)

They said that this incident had followed a boisterous Christmas party, just before the carter emigrated to Australia. This story was later verified some thirty years later by the arrival of five Australians who came to the house to view the skull. They claimed their father had been the carter, for he had told them of the skull, and also about the time when he threw the gruesome thing into the pond and of the strange events which followed in the night.

One of the sons claimed that his father had, indeed, died suddenly in Australia within a year of the incident, and his mother had always told him that the skull had brought a curse on them.

It may be possible that the carter may have been aware of an earlier version of the story as told by Udal, dating the event to 1760, when the farm came into occupation, and thus applying the legend to himself as some tall story to tell his children.

As Udal states in his 1891 article in the *"Somerset and Dorset Notes & Queries"*: -

> *"A former tenant of the farm once, incredulity or anger, threw the skull into the duck pond opposite the house. A few mornings afterwards he was observed stealthily returned to its old place in the house. It was said that Farmer G. had a bad time during the interval and had be much disturbed by all kinds of noises".*

Michael Pinney was disturbed to be asked by a visitor in 1939 whether the skull had *'sweated blood at the outbreak of war, as it had in 1914?'* at the start of the Great War. It would be interesting to know whether the same thing had happened in 1982 (the Falklands War), 1991 (The Gulf War), or 2003 (The Iraq War).

In the 1960s the writer, Eric Maple spent a night in the manor with the skull in the 1960's, and claimed to have not heard any screaming but was apparently plagued by nightmares. He declined an offer to stay a second night and hastily left the manor. However, he interviewed an old farm worker who said he remembered, *"hearing the skull like a trapped rat in the attic."*

In 1962, Michael Pinney asked Gilbert Causey of the Royal College of Surgeons for his expert opinion of the skull. Gilbert Causey enlisted the help of a colleague, Sir William Collins, professor of Human and Comparative Anatomy, Royal College of Surgeons, who carefully examined the skull. His conclusion of the report states that the skull is of European origin, complete except for the mandible, and was probably that of a female age between 25 and 30 years, probably nearer 30. Though no scientific dating method has been applied, it is believed to be approximately two thousand years old, and was perhaps unearthed or dug up from a prehistoric burial mound*, situated in the proximity of the house, and thus kept in the manor as some sort of curiosity or *memento mori*

Establishing that the skull is of a prehistoric woman, it would not be surprising to find such a relic in this area full of archaeological wealth.

Dr. Anne Ross, lecturer in Celtic studies at Southampton University, was involved in the excavations of an Iron Age temple inside the fortifications of Pilson Pen hillfort during the 1960's. She put forward the theory that Bettiscombe was once part of the Great Oak Wood of the Marshwood Vale, and was a place of Celtic druid worship, due to the presence of the

---

*'Burial mound', see Music Barrows & Fairy Folk

MEMENTO MORI

An object, such as a skull, intended to remind people of death. In numerous churchyards, the image of the skull and crossbones can be found on gravestones and memorials. They do not indicate the presence of a pirate's remains or plague victims! In former times the dead were placed in charnel houses, and after a decent length of time ,the skull and the thigh bones only were removed and buried or placed in a vault. In vaults or ossuaries in Europe it is common to see rows and rows of skulls, and similar rows of thigh bones - those were all that were considered necessary for bodily resurrection! Thus the image of the skull and crossbones on tombstones, perhaps surprisingly, symbolise the hope of life after death.

standing stone, located by a spring of never failing water. The forest was surrounded by hilltop tracks, and Roman legionary camp in the neighbouring parish of Stoke Abbott, which had probably been established to control the troublesome Celtic forest dwellers.

This gives credence to the suggestion that Bettiscombe is a Celtic name, meaning '*sacred place or chapel*'. This would have been a good enough reason why twelfth century monks wanted to establish a home, in order to Christianise a spot where pagan rites were still practised. Perhaps the famous skull was considered an object of power and veneration as suggested by Dr. Anne Ross. The skull may have come from the hill itself, and the shiny surface of the skull, with its fossilised appearance, may have been the result of its immersion in the

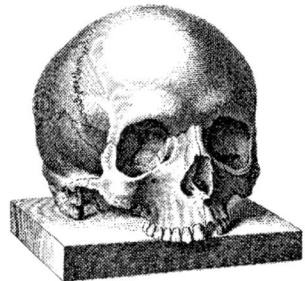

well or spring near the manor house, and the minerals contained therein. Skulls or severed heads were often used as offerings to water spirits in ancient times - they were placed in wells and ponds, and displayed outside the entrance to dwellings or homestead in hopes of protecting and dispelling evil spirits from the threshold as long as they were treated with respect. The sacred heads were feared so much that many would not even speak of where the heads lay for fear of bad luck. Stone heads were also used for guardian and luck purposes and can still be seen to this day around Britain.

This symbolic guardian to the house is carried on today in the form of the surviving Hallowe'en custom of carving images on pumpkins. This dates back to when the display of ancestral skulls, was replaced by hollowed out manglewurzels (a root vegetable fed to livestock), or turnips, as a protection from evil, on Samhein (the pagan new year); the night when it was popularly believed that the veil between the lands of the dead and the living was at its thinnest.

Generally, human bones - like blood, and some of the organs of the body - are regarded to be centers of psychic power, and to be the vehicle or dwelling-place of the soul. Life and consciousness remained in them after the death of the original owner, and it was therefore very dangerous to disturb them when they lay in the tomb. Misfortune, or even death, inevitably followed such an act, which was forbidden because of reverence for the dead, and superstitious fears of their vengeance.

Whatever may be its origin, the superstition still remains at Bettiscombe Manor, affording protection to the skull around which it clings. Anyone who sees the skull, cannot help feeling that a human skull of *any* age which has been buried and dug up, has a powerful aura of fear, melancholy, and trepidation.

For how many people do you know whose attitude would change if you told them that a person had died in the chair which they were sitting in, or the bed in which they slept? That chair or bed suddenly takes on a new meaning. It is viewed differently. It is still a chair or a bed, but it has now taken on a liminal quality; it has a symbiotic link between the living and the dead.

For the manor's tradition still stands, '*that if the skull is ever removed from the house, the house itself would rock to its foundations, whilst the person whom such an act of desecration was committed would certainly die within the year.'*

Since Michael Pinney moved to Bettiscombe, he has entertained many visitors who came to the manor for an opportunity to see the skull. The Pinney family have always treated the skull with respect, and by the time of writing, it was kept stored in a shoebox in Michael's writing bureau in his study. He told writer, Frank Smyth in 1982, that *"it is said to scream and cause agricultural disaster if taken out of the house and also causes the death, within a year, of the person who commits the deed. A photographer once carried it as far as the open doorway to take pictures of it, but my wife snatched it back indoors again without anything untowards occurring."*

In 1984, after the death of his wife, Michael Pinney decided to put the Manor up for sale. Concerned as to what might become of the skull, he was reassured that although the sale of the house contents (i.e. the furniture, etc.) would proceed by auction, whatever happened, the skull would remain at the Manor. The contents were later sold by Sotheby's for the value of £167,272. In 1986, Lady Conran became the new owner of the manor, keeping its legendary tenant undisturbed.

As the legend appears today:

"John Frederick Pinney disposed of the Nevis estates and returned to the family home of Bettiscombe Manor in the early nineteenth century, accompanied by one of the family's faithful black servants. While in his master's service, the servant was taken seriously ill with suspected tuberculosis. The servant, as he lay dying swore he would never rest unless his body was returned back to his homeland of Nevis.

When he eventually died, John Frederick Pinney refused to pay for such a expensive burial. This may have been because of the expense but is more likely to be because in the days before refrigerated ships few captains would have accepted such a cargo. So the body interred, against the servant's dying wish in the grounds of St. Stephen's Church cemetery.

After the burial, permissive ill-fortune plagued the village for many months and continuous screams and crying could be heard coming from the cemetery. Other disturbances were reported from the manor house; windows would rattle when there was no wind and doors slam of their own accord. The villagers could not take much more and went to the manor to seek advice. The body of the servant was subsequently exhumed and the body taken to the manor house and placed up in the attic where it slowly perished, and somehow only the skull remained. Some versions of this story tell of the body being shipped back to it's home in West Indies and the skull remaining behind walled up in an unobtrusive niche in the house for centuries."

THINGS THAT GO BUMP! IN THE NIGHT

*And thus I visit bodiless
Strange gloomy households often at odds,*

Thomas Hardy: *"I travel as a phantom now*

In Dorset there are many old cottages, farmhouses, and other such listed buildings that have been renovated for the purpose of holiday accommodation. People come from far and near to spend a week or two in these holiday homes, with the aim of relaxing and enjoying the atmosphere that these buildings have to offer. Some of these residences date back centuries, with a character all of their own, and a history to match. What wonderful tales and secrets lie hidden within the walls of their past?

Broomhills, a four hundred year old former farmhouse at Bridport, has seen many a satisfied holidaymaker come and go, even though it is haunted by a mysterious cloaked lady. Her `presence` has been felt many times. She has been seen by the cleaning staff, and once by a holidaymaker, who took a photo of her reflected in a mirror.

The owner's daughter, Mrs Elaine Kenway, who - as a girl - woke one night to see the ghostly grey spectre just a few feet away, witnessed the cloaked lady on another occasion. Thinking it was her mother, Elaine turned over and went back to sleep. Only in the morning, when questioning her mother, did she discover it was the resident ghost she had seen.

The Boot Inn, **one of Weymouth's oldest public houses, has many ghosts**

Many years before, when the farm belonged to `West's High Class Dairy` of South Street, Bridport, Sybil Green, then a young girl living at the farm, recalled her mother speaking of seeing the grey cloaked lady.

For the past hundred years, or possibly more, the cloaked lady has haunted the back bedroom of Broomhills without any real need for concern. However, in July of that year it all changed. A party of seven Surrey holidaymakers were staying at the thatched house for a relaxing break, but within days of arriving they fled in terror after a string of strange occurrences. They reported a strange atmosphere in the building, and that their children were frightened by an unexplainable presence they felt in one of the bedrooms. The children also began to hear strange voices and noises in the night. The family finally snapped after they were woken in the early hours of the morning by a family member; a man in his 30s, who was found screaming uncontrollably, claiming he was being choked by something - or someone - he could not see. Within minutes, the family had packed their bags and left for home.

Ghosts that are sustained by malevolence and chaotic behaviour are known as 'Poltergeists'. The word poltergeist is German for *Noisy Spirit*. Their behaviour is usually characterised by thumping, howling, hurling, and moving objects, and even bad smells.

Weymouth's seventeenth century pub, *The Boot Inn,* stands in High West Street opposite the old town hall. It has long been reputedly haunted. In November 1973, the then new licensee's,

John and Elsie Ratcliffe, who took-over the pub, were warned by the former landlord that the pub was haunted, for he had often heard the ghost singing sea shanties in the night. Neither John nor Elsie took his warning seriously, but within a week they had quite a different opinion.

On two successive nights they were woken by the sound of heavy footsteps clumping around in the bar. Mr Ratcliffe went to investigate, but saw nobody, though the heavy tramping on the floorboards could clearly be heard. The chilling incident was reported in the *Dorset Evening Echo*, saying that Mr and Mrs Ratcliffe would rather *see* the resident ghost than to continually endure the sound of his rather unnerving nightly footsteps.

In July 1977, the *Boot Inn's* poltergeist mystery came to prominence again. Ray and Gay Smith the new licensees, reported that there were probably at least *two* ghosts haunting the pub. One night they heard the spectres playing darts, - one throwing the darts, the other chalking up the score!

Mr. and Mrs. Smith had been at the pub for only two months, but in that short time had experienced a whole host of uncanny happenings, including locks being tampered with, doors opening and closing at will, wall decorations being moved, and *even* furniture being rearranged. More frightening still, was when the barmaid saw the ghostly resident as she changed a barrel in the cellar. After reporting what she had seen to Mr Smith, he went to the cellar to investigate. Suddenly he felt an intense cold come over him, he looked over his shoulder, and for a split second saw the apparition; a ghostly seaman wearing heavy sea boots.

The ghost of a former landlady haunts *The Angel Inn*, Lyme Regis

Another haunted pub is *The Angel Inn* at Lyme Regis. Among other things, doors have opened at will, strange unexplainable sounds have been heard, a glass was once seen to jump off a table, a glass cheese dish once exploded, and a cold presence has been felt.

The hauntings are blamed on the ghost of a former landlady, Lizzie Lawton, who ran the pub in the 1920's. It appears that she loved her pub *so* much, that she was reluctant to leave, but later - due to illness - was forced to. On the day she left she was reputed to have vowed to return saying: "Nobody's going to do the same here as I've done." It would seem that she has kept her word, for she has been seen on numerous occasions. She was once seen coming out of a cupboard in a bedroom by a young boy, and again by his brother, who saw her bending over his bed with a sad expression on her face. One sighting of Lizzie left a former landlord so shaken that he later died.

Bovington Camp is the home of the world famous Tank Museum, and also its resident ghost known affectionately as `Herman the German`. The ghost is believed to be that of a German officer, who has been frequently seen wandering about the museum at night and peering into a Mark II King Tiger Tank in which he is thought to have been killed. The King Tigers were the pride of the Nazi war machine and were only crewed by the most experienced of SS troops. As the war reached its bloody conclusion, many King Tigers fought in the streets of Berlin defending Hitler's bunker until the bitter end.

A poltergeist case took place at Weymouth's old museum, which was sited by the Westham Bridge, opposite the Bethany Hall, but sadly the building, (formerly Melcombe Regis School) was pulled down in December 1995 after the museum had been relocated further around the harbour.

Before its fateful demolition, in the spring of 1986, the museum staff reported a series of inexplicable events, after a Roman coffin had been moved to facilitate carpet laying. With the carpet in place, mysterious footsteps on stone could be heard Small objects, particularly keys, would disappear - only to be found in peculiar places. The electric cash till was left open at night after being emptied, but was always found closed and locked in the morning. Stranger still, an American film unit was in the area at the time making a documentary, and some filming took place within the museum. All the footage shot in the building came out blank, and the taped voiceover for the sequence contained large unexplainable gaps of silence. Subsequent checks found the equipment in perfect working order.

Another classic case of poltergeist activity took place - once again - at Weymouth, in a house on East Street, in 1861. In Stephen Newland's *Weird and Wonderful Tales of Dorset* (1982) The nightly activity of rattling crockery and knocking on walls was witnessed by many people. One night, a man fired a pistol at the spot where he heard the knocking, and was amazed when the ghost caught the bullet and threw it back at him. The poltergeist activity only stopped when an hysterical girl left the house.

According to Rodney Legg, another similar account was published in *The Times* letter page by the Rev. H Bryn. It occurred in the parish of Askerswell, four miles east of Bridport, in the latter half of the nineteenth century. Scores of people came to witness the nightly phenomenon of immense pieces of rock being hurled by invisible hands, from one room to another, all

The haunted Tiger Tank at the Bovington Museum

The old Weymouth Museum, before it was demolished in 1995

supposedly coming from the ceiling. The incidents ceased when a hysterical girl left the house for another, which was soon to be found on fire.

Could these two hysterical girls have been the same person? It is not uncommon for poltergeist activity to be focused around disturbed children, particularly pubescent girls. The details that recur in accounts of poltergeist hauntings only deepen the enigma.

One truly outstanding account of this kind, concerning two orphan girls aged thirteen and four, took place in an isolated cottage at Norton, in the village of Durweston in 1894/5. A widow woman, Mrs Best, was living alone at the cottage when on 13th December, the two girls were boarded out to her. Almost immediately, the cottage was plagued by faint knocking and scratching, which could be heard in different parts of the house. The disturbances gradually increased until the 18th December, when Anne Cleave, the elder of the two girls saw a boot come from the garden and strike the back door. Understandably this left her quite shaken, and a neighbour - Mr Newman - was called in to help calm the girl. However, as Mrs Best and the two girls, who were both in the room, told him about the strange goings on, small beads began to pelt the window. Mr Newman shouted back at the poltergeist, "You coward, why don't you throw money." Suddenly, the back door opened wide, and a number of little shells floated into the room. They entered - one at a time - at intervals varying from half-a-minute, floating so slowly that when they hit Mr Newman he could hardly feel them.

Along with the shells came two thimbles, and then a slate pencil rose up out of the copper, and a hasp* fell out of thin air into Mr Newman's lap. The boot, which was first hurled at the door and still outside in the garden, suddenly came into the room floating just off the ground. Mr Newman placed his foot on the boot to stop it moving, but the moment he took his foot away, the boot quickly rose up and knocked his hat off. Although a thorough search was made, there was no-one or anything that could account for the bizarre happenings. Due to this incident, Mrs Best and the two girls spent Christmas and the New Year at Mr Newman's cottage, but the poltergeist moved with them for the knocking continued. On the 10th January, they were visited late one evening by the rector of Durweston, Rev. W. M. Anderson, and also by the schoolmaster, Mr Sheppard. The girls were put to bed, and both the rector and schoolmaster witnessed the loud rappings on the wall of the bedroom. Rev. Anderson stayed at the house with them for a few days and later wrote:

> *'I put my ear and head to the wall, but could not detect any vibrations. But when resting my head on the rail at the bottom of the bed. I could distinctly feel a vibration varying according to the loudness of knocking. Occasionally there was noise in the wall, as if someone were scratching with their nails. When the rapping first began, I noticed that it frequently ceased when I came into the room, but after a short time it made no difference and the noise was loud and continuous.'*

Soon after, a Mr Westlake from the Society for Psychical Research [SPR], which had only been founded twelve years before, came to the house to investigate. The SPR, from their earliest days, kept meticulous records, which - together with copious reports from the *Western Gazette* at the time - is how we now know so much about the case. At one stage of the investigation, a slate and chalk was left by the windowsill in the bedroom to communicate with the

---

* *'Hasp.' A clasp or catch for fastening two parts of a garment.*

ghost. Mrs Best and the two girls waited in total darkness in the bed together, while Mr Westlake and other witnesses waited below stairs. Then at half past two in the dark of night, the silence was broken by the eerie sound of the chalk scratching on the slate. In all, this happened five times that night. - Some curves were found drawn on the slate and two words, *Mony* [sic] and *Garden*. Mrs Best said that she had held on to the girls, and no-one had left the bed, and she was prepared to take a solemn oath on the matter.

The next morning, a thorough search was made in the garden, but no money was found. The days passed and the poltergeist activity increased. The two girls were moved to another house in the village occupied by a certain Mr Cross, but once again the poltergeist travelled with them, for the noises, bangs and knocking continued in their new residence. Plaster fell from the walls and ceilings, and objects were moved mysteriously around.

Finally the girls were separated, and Anne was sent first to Iwerne Minster where these, and more, strange incidents were reported, and finally to London where she was fully examined by a doctor who pronounced her of a markedly consumptive tendency and apparently hysterical. What became of her after that is not known, but she is rumoured to have died soon after.

In 1934, Mr and Mrs Dench and their children moved to an old farmhouse called the *Iron Box Farm*, Wyke Regis, Weymouth. The farmhouse was in an isolated position; the nearest building was the *Marquis of Granby* public house, half a mile away.

One winter night, their ten-year-old son was lying in bed when he saw what he described as a dense geometric form pass across the room and disappear through the opposite wall. There were no lights outside, and therefore, this could not have been a shadow, but he thought no more of it. Some time later he was in bed again; this time the room was lit by the flames of a roaring log fire, when he distinctly felt his coverlet being forcibly pulled back, and at the same time young Master Dench felt an invisible hand smack him on his upper arm. He told his mother, and drew a picture of the strange shape he had seen previously. He was amazed when she produced another picture drawn by his brother of exactly the same ghostly shape, that he, too, had witnessed.

The most disturbing incident of all happened to their nine-year-old daughter, who was woken one night by a pair of invisible icy cold hands molesting her. At first she was too frightened to scream, but when one hand proceeded under the covers, she screamed out in terror. Her mother quickly came to her rescue, only to take part in a violent tug of war with the invisible ghost, who was pulling the girl from her bed. Many desperate moments passed, before Mrs. Dench pulled her terrified daughter away from the ghost's icy grip, dragging her back into bed, to her relief the ghost gave up by leaving the room and slamming the door.

For some nights afterwards, loud rappings were heard on the girl's headboard, and once she felt something under her bed shake her up and down. Pencils, knitting needles, and other objects would often keep disappearing until at last it all became too upsetting for the family and they sold the farmhouse and moved away. The farmhouse and the dairy was eventually demolished to make way for a residential area. The site of *Iron Box Dairy,* as it is today, is now the Lynch Lane mini-market and Alf's fish and chip shop.

Such poltergeist activity is naturally frightening, because no-one can tell where the spectres hail from, and no-one knows how to get rid of them. However, some ghosts, it would seem, are unable to rest, due to their violent and somewhat premature deaths. Often haunting the place of their death, they return to cause disruption to the living, and - in some cases - to pin the crime on their murderer, and finally see justice done.

One frosty January morning in 1748, William Light, the Squire of Baglake House at Litton Cheney, went out hunting, but after a disappointing hunt returned depressed and in a gloomy mood. He left the house again, but alone. His groom, sensing something was wrong, followed after him, only to discover his master's dead body floating in a nearby pond. Squire Light had

The geometric shape as described Master Dench of Iron Box Farm

The site of Iron Box Farm - now occupied by a mine-market and fish and chip shop

apparently committed suicide by drowning himself in the freezing water. The groom quickly set forth back to Baglake House to relay the distressing news. However, on the journey back, he was accosted by the ghost of his dead master, and thrown from his horse. The groom soon fell ill and never recovered; one of the consequences of this illness being that his skin completely peeled off before he died. (This was probably septicaemia brought on by a haemolytic streptococcus skin infection).

Not long after Squire Light's suicide, Baglake House was troubled by noisy disturbances. Some clergymen were called into exorcise the poltergeist, thought to be Squire Light himself, but they only half succeeded, only managing to confine the ghost to haunting a chimney.

Some years later the disturbances broke out again, with mysterious knockings being heard on the front door, phantom footsteps heard in the passage and on the stairs, and doors opening and closing. A rustling sound, similar to that of a ladies silk dress, was also heard in the drawing room, and in the summerhouse. The crockery would be violently moved, and on rare occasions a ghostly male figure was said to appear in the house. These extraordinary occurrences were said to have continued for many years.

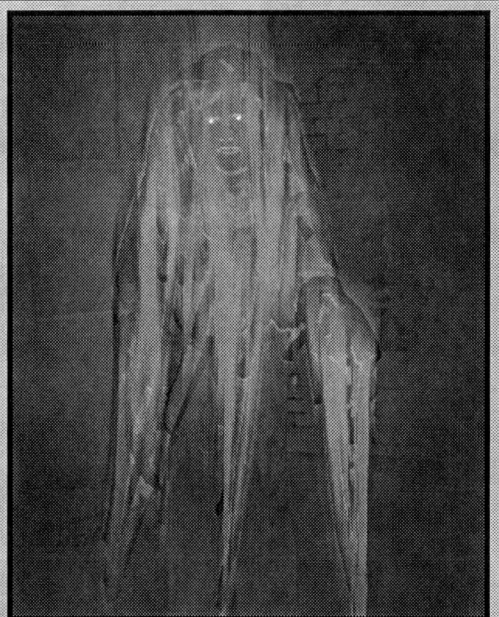

THE NOTHE FORT GHOST: The Fort is built at the head of the Nothe Peninsula, which forms one side of Weymouth Harbour. The resident ghost known as *"The Whistling Gunner"*, can sometimes be heard in the underground passages, and though somewhat frightening in appearance, up to the present, he has been harmless

Another haunting reported by Peter Underwood, the doyen of British ghost research, and that may have been contributed to by a premature death, is that of a fifteen-year-old girl called `Annie`, who is said to haunt Riverside Mews, of Mill Lane, Wimborne. The eighteenth century mill was on the River Allen where a restaurant now stands. Many years ago, Annie worked at the mill clearing the grain storage bins, and shovelling the flour into sacks ready for transport.

One day the miller took a fancy to Annie, pushed her onto the flour sacks and raped her. Annie fled out of the mill, only to trip and fall into the millstream where she hit her head on a rock, lost consciousness, and drowned. There was no positive evidence against the miller, so he was not brought to justice and perhaps because of this Annie's spirit is unable to rest. Her ghost has been seen every now and then, even up to the present day. In the early 1990s, Annie's restless spirit became particularly active. She was seen by the proprietor in the kitchen, who at first mistook her for one of the staff. The ghostly sighting was soon followed by a case of poltergeist activity. Small hand bells set on the tables would ring of their own accord, and menus would fly off the tables. Once a doll that was kept on a sideboard, was mysteriously thrown across the room just missing a member of staff, and from the kitchen a number of plates were reported hovering in the air of their own volition, before dropping to the ground and smashing. Other strange happenings included machines being turned off, and electric plugs being pulled from their sockets. One lady customer even had to leave the restaurant as she felt as if some strange presence was watching her from behind.

Like Annie of Riverside Mews, there are many more tales of tormented souls who are unable to rest until justice is done and their remains given a proper burial.

Chantmarle; ghostly voices were once heard here, in the mid 19th century

About two and a half miles north of the village of Cattistock, there is the seventeenth century mansion of *Chantmarle*, which means 'Song of the Blackbird'. In recent times the mansion served as a police-training centre, but closed in 1994. However, it has since become a Christian retreat cum health-centre, and has opened its doors for the public to enjoy. Around 1825, when the house was in its prime, a shrill piercing voice was heard every year on about the same date, mournfully crying in the hall saying. *"Search for the bones of Wat Perkins."* This was repeated three times, sending fear into the owners and servants. Word soon spread that a dreadful calamity had befallen someone. But *who* was 'Wat Perkins'?

Some years later the mystery was solved, when labourers removing a hedge near Kittwhistle, a cottage some distance from *Chantmarle*, uncovered a headless human skeleton. Kittwhistle was the home of a widow-woman who told the labourers not to tell any one else about the skeleton and to cover it over again, and she added she would give them her best cow for doing so. However, word *did* reach the authorities, and the woman was questioned. Did she know anything about the skeleton and its missing head? She said. *'If I must tell'ee, the head is under the yeath-stone,'* meaning the hearthstone. The head was found, and the woman was arrested for suspected murder. Later her confession revealed that some twenty-two years previously, a Scotsman with a fine pack of drapery had come to the cottage to buy some refreshments and had fallen asleep resting his head on the arm of the settee. The woman, wishing to steal his pack, chopped across his throat with a billhook, and killed him.

The woman's neighbours later claimed she had often said, when speaking of their clothes, that she had *'burned better things than those.'* Needless to say, the woman was later tried, found guilty - and executed - for her dreadful crime. The ghostly mournful cries of Wat Perkins were never heard again.

Kittwhistle Cottage, lies not far from where a mysterious headless skeleton was discovered in a hedgerow

Another tragic tale of murder leaving a ghostly legacy, is that of Hamworthy House, near Poole. Early in the eighteenth century, the wife of the Lord of the Manor had a steamy love affair with her husband's handsome young cousin, Bampfylde-Moore-Carew often nicknamed the *'Devil-may-care Carew'*. Whenever he wished to meet her, he would imitate the cries of birds, or give a peculiar whistle, whilst also, at times, wearing animal skins outside the house, and his lady-love would steal out and join him.

The Lord's suspicions were aroused, and one night he went in search of his wife, only to discover the pair of them making love among the bushes. In a fit of rage he shot them both! His wife's body was carried into the house, but her lover's was thrown into the pond. For many years afterwards, the cousin's eerie whistling was heard haunting the house in search of his lady-love.

The haunted *Crown Hotel*, Poole

The *Crown Hotel* in Poole, in Market Street, has been plagued by hauntings for many years. Among the many strange events reported are the sound of piano playing in a room that contained no piano, the sound of a body being dragged along the floor, phantom footsteps, and a ghost light* floating in mid-air.

In 1966 a Mr D. Browne, an Australian guest staying at the hotel, decided to conduct some experiments to disprove the hauntings. He bolted the door of the loft in the old stables and went down to the courtyard, where to his amazement he saw the door open. *"It was the most eerie feeling I have ever had in my life,"* he said.

Shortly afterwards in the same year a secret room without a door was discovered in the attic by builders. Then, in 1975 the sounds of panic stricken children rushing about screaming as if trying to escape some horrible fate were heard; it is now believed that many years ago some children were imprisoned and murdered there.

From these accounts, and others seen in previous chapters, it would appear that hauntings are most likely to occur if someone has suffered a violent or untimely death, whether by accident, battle, suicide, or murder. Stranger still, it would seem, is when a place is haunted for no explainable reason.

---

* *'Ghost light.'* See Spectral Lights.

The old branch line from Maiden Newton to Bridport was opened in 1857. On 3rd December 1962, as part of Dr Beeching's swingeing cuts of the railw network, the decision was taken to finally close the line between Bridport and West Bay for all railway traffic. On 25th August 1963, two Great Western steam locomotives hauled a special train from Bridport to West Bay. Two years later the track was lifted. The remaining branch line soon also became uneconomical and on 5th May 1975 it too had to close, exactly 120 years to the day after the passing of the Bridport Railway Act. The remaining track started to be lifted on 18th November 1975. One outcome of this was that the old stations were converted into attractive residences.

A ghost train is heard along the old disused branch line at Powerstock Common

In her book *Powerstock Station - All Change (*1996), Diana Patina Read mentions that when her family moved into the former Powerstock Station, they experienced some apparently inexplicable happenings.

None of the family smoked, but they would often smell pipe smoke in different parts of the house, particularly in the old waiting room. Stranger still, they often heard the chugging of old tank engines, similar to those which had been used when the line was in its glory. First they would hear the distant whistle of the approaching train, the crockery on the table would rattle, and then they would hear the train rushing past the building, thundering loudly over the sleepers that had long been removed.

The ghost train has never yet been seen, but on one occasion, smoke and steam from the train bellowed into the house through an open window. There are no records of a rail accident along this line so perhaps this haunting symbolises the line's untimely death.

MUSIC BARROWS & FAIRY FOLK

The Dorsetshire landscape would not be complete without its numerous ancient earthworks and barrows. In the past these burial mounds were believed to be inhabited by fairies, or as some spiritualists and theosophists would describe them, 'Etheric & Astral Elementals'*, and at Lammas Tide (1st August) they are said to rise on pillars to reveal the revelling fairies dancing inside to the sweet sound of *fairy music*.†

On Bincombe Hill, overlooking Weymouth, six such hillocks - which date back to the Bronze Age - can be seen They were known locally as 'Music Barrows,' for it was said if you put your ear to the top of one at noon, you would be able to hear the plaintive tones of music.

According to Edward Waring in his book *Ghosts and Legends of the Dorset Countryside* (1977), an unknown woman asked a Weymouth librarian whether fairies really *did* live under the bumps, and if - indeed - music could be heard. Wishing to visit the barrows, she asked for a taxi and to explain to the taxi-driver what was required. Apparently she was warned to stay well away from the barrows, but was seen going up the hill that morning, never to be seen or heard of again.

Could it be she was bewitched by the fairy music and spirited away into the hill, now a prisoner of the fairies? It is well documented by those who study such arcane matters, that fairies have the disturbing habit of kidnapping humans, particularly children, even taking babies and leaving a 'changeling'‡ in its place!

One possible reason for this is that according to legend, every seven years the land of Faerie has to pay a tithe (Teind) to Hell, and human captives are used as payment, although it is alleged that captive children can be released from a fairy barrow by burning thorns on top of it.

> *'And pleasant is the fairy land,*
> *But, an eerie tale to tell,*
> *Ay at the end of seven years*
> *We pay a tiend to hell;*

Francis James Child: *Tam Lin*

---

* *'Etheric & Astral Elementals.'* The term applied to the whole class of Nature Spirits/Elementals – ie, Dryads; wood, Sylphs; air, Salamanders; fire, Gnomes; earth, Oceanids; salt water, Undines; fresh water. When visible, they are on the 'ETHERIC' level, – a state more subtle than gaseous and when invisible they are on the 'ASTRAL' level, – a state more fine than Etheric.

† *'Fairy Music.'* Fairy music is known to be beautiful and plaintive yet wild and capricious. It has a fatal charm to mortal ears, for even just a few notes may lull the listener into a fatal sleep, while at best, they might become drawn into a melancholic forgetfulness, always yearning to hear more.

‡ *'Changeling.'* A baby or infant that has been secretly substituted by fairies, in exchange for one stolen. – Usually an old elf or sometimes a baby carved of wood, but under fairy enchantment, (Fairy Glamour) it appears to be an exact replica of the stolen child.

Bincombe Bumps where the fairy folk dwell

The Music Barrow - 'Culliford Tree' on Came Down, near Dorchester

Fairy music was heard at the outbreak of the Second World War at Colmer's Hill, Symondsbury. Members of a school field-trip reported hearing a "haunting melody of pan-pipes" coming from deep within. Perhaps this was a failed attempt by the fairies to steal the children?

Dorset children were often told to keep well clear of such fairy haunts. Wise parents protected their offspring, especially girls, by sewing bells onto their clothing, or tying red ribbons in their hair. Sometimes they were made to carry daisy chains, (the sun symbol). This custom was most commonly observed on May Day (1st May) when fairies posed the greatest risk.

Fairies often go to great pains to protect their barrows and gold. Treasure seekers digging into fairy barrows, or those choosing to build on fairy terrain, may be warned by strange voices, baleful sounds and even sudden storms. Should such warnings be ignored, ill luck, disaster and even death will be the only reward.

Not that long ago, a woman wanted to purchase a plot of land closely adjacent to the tree covered music barrow, *Culliford Tree*, at Whitcombe, for the purpose of building her house there. She was said to have visited the barrow on two occasions to make up her mind whether to buy the land or not. On both visits, she heard a sinister voice warning her to desist from her plan. After the second visit she wisely changed her mind and cancelled the project.

Opposite Culliford Tree there is a smaller barrow known as *The Singing Barrow*. It was at this barrow in 1983 that two friends heard a strange humming whining noise. It did not come from any one point in the barrow, but the so-called singing seemed to be coming from all around it.

Sadly all too often fairy warnings are ignored and their barrows are either desecrated, ploughed up or completely destroyed. There was once a barrow at *Folly Hanging Gate* in Ashmore, which was said to be inhabited by strange fairy-like spirits known as *Gappergennies*. They were often heard making uncanny noises by the villagers, but in 1840 the barrow was levelled to make a road. Some bones were found within the mound and these were buried in the churchyard. From that day to this, the strange sounds of the Gappergennies were heard no more.

Witches tend to be frequent visitors of fairy barrows, one of the many accusations made at them during the witch trials of the seventeenth century. John Walsh of Netherbury, who appeared before the Bishop of Exeter on the 20th August 1566, accused of practising witchcraft, confessed that he frequently visited fairy barrows and that he consorted with white, green and black fairies. No details survive of John Walsh's fate, but he was probably executed.

The mysterious 'Singing Barrow' on Came Down, near Dorchester

An encounter with fairies was witnessed by Mr. Foot on Okeford Hill.

Fairies tend to be very choosy as to who they let see them, but like John Walsh, others too have been privileged to glimpse the fairies of Dorset. It must be said that all fairies, whether harmful or not, enjoy dancing to music and it is in this activity they are most commonly observed.

In her article *'The Folklore of Sixpenny Handley'* featured in the Folklore Society Journal, *Folklore, vol 74 (*Autumn 1963) . Aubrey L. Parke describes a fairy encounter, which took place early on in the twentieth century, at Bottle Bush Down, which lies between Sixpenny Handley and Cranborne. The Rev. A.R.T. Bruce of Sixpenny Handley once rested on a barrow while crossing the down, and as he sat there, he was suddenly surrounded by little dancing pixies dressed in leather jerkins. They danced all around him for several minutes before disappearing, presumably into the barrow.

Sir Arthur Conan Doyle, (1859 – 1930) was a Scottish author most noted for his stories about the detective Sherlock Holmes, which are generally considered a major innovation in the field of crime fiction, and the adventures of Professor Challenger. More or less forgotten today is his involvement with spiritualism and his interest in then-contemporary faerie sightings. The following story was included in his book *The Coming of the Fairies* (1922), and one of the interesting bits of trivia surrounding this account is that Conan-Doyle, usually a meticulous journalist, got the name of the location wrong, printing it as `Oxford Hill`. This current book is the first time that the record on this particular sighting has been set straight.

In the early part of the twentieth century a Mr J. Foot Young had an encounter with fairies at Okeford Hill, Okeford Fitzpaine. He wrote to Sir Arthur Conan Doyle telling of his encounter.

"Some years ago I was one of a party invited to spend the afternoon on the lovely slopes of Oxford Hill, [sic] in the county of Dorset. The absence of both trees and hedges in this locality enables one to see without obstruction for long distances. I was walking with my companion, who lives in the locality, some little distance from the main party, when to my astonishment I saw a number of what I thought to be very small children, about a score in number, and all dressed in little gaily-coloured short skirts, their legs being bare. Their hands were joined, and all held up, as they merrily danced round in a perfect circle. We stood watching them, when in an instant they all vanished from our sight. My companion told me they were fairies, and they often came to that particular part to hold their revels. It may be our presence disturbed them."

Sometimes the names given to certain ancient monuments give a clear indication to the type of fairies that haunt them. The *Puck Stone* on Godlingston Heath; Studland, the *Puckysbury* Barrow near Winfrith Newburgh, the *Grimberry* Barrow at Corfe Castle, and the *Bug* Barrow at Bere Regis, all suggest that they are inhabited by Goblins or Bogey-beasts.

The word `Goblin` was first recorded as early as the twelfth century by Ordericus Vitalis who mentioned *Gobelinus* as a popular name of a spirit, which haunted the neighbourhood of Évreux, France. By the sixteenth century the usage of the word goblin had become widespread, and then - as today - mainly refers to the ugly, grotesque impish spirits and fairies.

There are many different goblin types, but those that are considered evil tend to go to great lengths to do harm. They are the masters of fairy glamour* and are devilishly tricky, often tempting their victims with forbidden fruit, with the avowed purpose to lead astray, or to an early grave.

Sadly, tales of goblin trickery are few and far between in Dorset, but one story concerns an eleven year old kitchen girl called Mary Marsh who - in the latter half of the nineteenth century - worked at a farm in Corscombe.

In those days it was common practice for children to be contracted out for employment, to escape the harsh reality of poverty. Like so many children of the time, Mary probably had a miserable existence, working in drudgery for long hours, and undoubtedly she was probably mistreated and underfed.

---

* *'Fairy glamour.'* Magic enchantment that deceives by appearance, hence ugliness becomes seen as beauty, and-vice-versa, or leaves as gold coins, etc.

We must not look at goblin men,
We must not but their fruits;
Who knows upon what soil they fed,
Their hungry thirsty roots?

Christina Rossetti: *Goblin Market*

One Hallowe'en night Mary was alone, working late in the kitchen, when she was startled by the sudden appearance of an ugly little goblin upon the windowsill outside. It was what most Dorset children feared – the dreaded nursery goblin called the *Spoorn!* However, Mary was unaware of this and so with curiosity asked him what he wanted. The *Spoorn* complained of the cold and begged Mary to let him inside so he could warm himself by the fire. Mary was a kind-hearted girl and taking pity on the little fellow, she opened the window and let him into the kitchen.

For sometime, the *Spoorn* warmed himself by the iron range and when he had warmed himself enough, he produced a fat juicy pear and gave it to Mary as payment for her kindness. "Take it!" said the *Spoorn*. "If you dare. It won't hurt you, I swear!" But the pear was a magic pear, for when Mary took a bite, she fell unconscious on to the floor.

It was all a wicked trick, for while Mary slept, the *Spoorn* helped himself to a tart, baked that day by the farmer's wife. The tart filled his goblin tum so much so that he decided not to eat Mary after all. The *Spoorn*, chuckling to himself, opened the window and ran away into the night.

The farmer's wife found Mary the next morning asleep on the floor, and shook the poor girl from her slumber, accusing her of eating the tart. Of course, Mary denied it, and said it was the goblin and not she. But adults know best and rarely believe in such things as goblins! And so Mary's explanation fell on deaf ears. The blame was firmly put on Mary for the Spoorn's thieving, and as such, poor Mary was severely punished with a vigorous spanking.

Shape-shifting goblins or so-called 'bogey-beasts' often appear in tales disguised as black dogs, or wild horses, and love nothing more than to scare people, and to play gruesome practical jokes, their favourite being, 'Throwing the Rider.' This they do by luring unsuspecting people to mount them, before taking them on a wild ride across the wettest and thorniest countryside, only to be thrown into a ditch or stream.

The infamous goblin Puck who William Shakespeare made so popular is renowned the world over for his mischievous tricks, and it is therefore hardly surprising that he has been blamed for numerous unpleasant fairy experiences. Even here in Dorset, Puck is believed responsible for fairy mischief. He was once encountered by the grandfather of famous Dorset poet William Barnes at Puxey Lane, Bagber near Sturminster Newton. Puck was said to have appeared as a strange, wet, fleece rolling along the ground which went under the man's horse and in that instant the animal became lame. Similar accounts from elsewhere in the country are known as `old boneless`, and a compendium of such encounters can be found in *Mystery Animals of Britain and Ireland* by Graham McEwan (1986).

Puck

Puck was also encountered down Yellow Lane at Loders, this time in the form of a phantom ball of wool which was mysteriously unwinding itself, trying in vain to bewitch the witness.

On another occasion, Puck was blamed on an uncanny haunting at Vagg Hollow not far from Yeovil. Night after night he would lie in the middle of the road in the shape of a woolpack stopping passing horses in their tracks. However, his goblin fun was soon spoiled when a brave rider struck him with his whip. Puck let out a loud shriek and instantly manifested into his true form; an ugly little cloven-hooved imp, before disappearing.

The Grey Mare and her Colts

South of Littlebredy there is a chambered megalithic tomb called, *The Grey Mare and her Colts*. This eroded long barrow probably owes its name to the goblin horses, known as *Colepexys* that are said to roam Dorset's beautiful Downs.

Some accounts say that his coat is jet black, while others claim it is grey, but whichever, he is a shape shifting bogey beast who loves nothing more than to *pixy-led* domesticated horses and travellers and to scare people - particularly children.

---

* *'Pixy-lead.'* To be misled by fairies either by light at night or by a subtle changing of landmarks and features by day.

Once a gypsy woman, who as a child lived with her family in a caravan at a site known as *Burgess Field*, Parkstone near Poole, claimed that during the light of day, her brother and herself, while in the caravan, were visited by a horse-like devil. She described the fiend as *'a black, velvety thing with wild flaming red eyes and flaring nostrils.'*

The two children sat huddled close together, terrified of the creature that was leering over the half door of the caravan. They called out for their parents in desperation, who were only just outside the caravan, but they saw nothing of the fairy creature. They searched the area, but found nothing, not even any hoof prints on the ground outside. It had simply vanished!

The mischievous Colepexy has also been known to play *Throwing the Rider*. Naughty children especially were threatened with the Colepexy so as to insure good behaviour and that they went to school as the next poetic story tells.

COLEPEXY'S COUNTRY

Seven little girls went a walking,
In the Colepexy's country,
Playing hookey from their lessons,
They thought was very funny.

Dressed smartly in white pinafores,
With bows and frills to grace,
With smiles and mischievous grins,
Upon their pretty face.

Over gates and styles they went,
Down many a winding track,
Exploring fields and pastures new,
Never once looking back.

Until they came to a hill side,
Where a shaggy grey colt they did meet,
"Hello there, pretty maidens fair!"
Was how the jade did greet.

"A talking horse, a talking horse!"
The little girls joyfully cried.
"May we get upon your back?
May we go for a ride?"

"Yes, climb up, climb up,
There's room for one and all,
Sweet little ones first,
Followed by the fair tall."

And by magic enchantment,
The colt lengthened his back,
And one by one the girls mounted,
To make the horizontal stack.
And when all were squeezed on,
Holding each other around the waist,
The fairy colt gave a wicked chuckle,

And down the hill he raced.
Galloping down into the valley,
Jumping many a dry stone wall,
The little girls held on tight,
For they did not wish to fall.

"STOP! STOP! STOP!"
The little girls frantically cried,
"We want to get off,
We don't like this ride!"

But the Colepexy just galloped on faster,
Paying no heed to their pleas,
Or their yells and cries,
Or their terrified screams.
Onward through briars and thorns he galloped,
Which tore their pinafores to shreds,
Through prickly gorse and stinging nettle,
That scratched and stung their legs.

Then at long last he threw the girls,
Head long into the River Frome,
Those bruised and scratched little girls,
Were soaked through to the bone.

And as the equine grey galloped away,
They heard him laugh, they heard him say,
"To ride upon a Pexy you must be a fool,
You seven naughty maids should be in school!"

Robert Newland

One good quality of the Colepexy is that sometimes he acts as a type of orchard guardian, protecting apple orchards from thieves.

Once in Wareham there lived an old widow who owned two fine apple orchards, which were said to produce the best cider apples in Dorset. The old lady had a jealous neighbour who often thought about stealing her prize apples to make his own cider, though the thought of meeting the Colepexy prevented him. However, he was determined to rob her orchards, and this he planned to do by hiding in a large wicker basket, which he would make move by the aid of a magic spell he had obtained from a conjuror.

One September night he decided to put his plan into action, and climbed into the basket. He said the magic words and the basket bounded down the lane and straight into the widow's orchard. Once the basket had settled, he murmured another spell, and one by one the apples flew off the branches and began pelting the basket.

Suddenly one large apple smacked him straight in the eye; he leapt up out of the basket howling in pain and as he did so, felt sharp teeth sink into his backside. Without a second thought he fled the basket and ran for his life, but the Colepexy was quicker. He tossed the apple thief into the air, and as he fell to the ground the Colepexy kicked him in the back of his neck, snapping it in two and killing him instantly.

Early the next morning, the widow found her neighbour's dead body next to his basket of apples with the imprint of a horse's hoof impressed on his neck, but the fairy colt was nowhere to be seen.

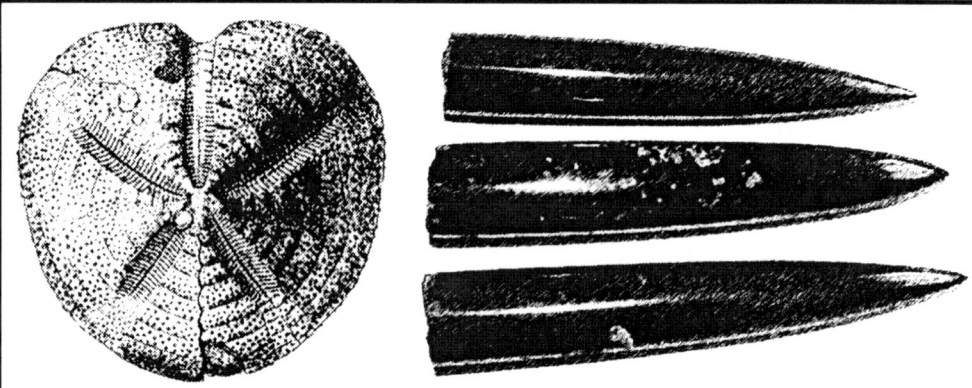

Fossil Sea Urchin   Belemnites

Fairy Loaves and Colepexies Fingers

Fossil sea urchins were known locally as Fairy Loaves, Fairy Hearts or Colepexies-heads. Also the bullet shaped fossils called Belemnites were known as Colepexies fingers. Before the knowledge of Prehistoric animals, people would often pick up these curiosities believing they were left by the fairies and were, therefore, prized as a folk charm. It was widely believed that these seventy million year old fossils prevented the evil effects of witches.

LOATHERS OF CHRISTIANITY

All fairies, whether good or evil, are the remnants of older times; living elements from when the world was young. Therefore it's no mystery then that all fairies seem to have a particular aversion to all things Christian. The crucifix or cross, The Holy Bible, holy water, holy prayers, holy bread and wine, and *even* churchyard mould, were all regarded as positive protection against fairy annoyances.

However, Christians considered the chiming of church bells twice as effective against these so-called *'People of the Toadstools'*, because not only were the bells a holy thing, but also the ringing disturbed the atmosphere in which fairies have their incorporeal being.

About a mile northwest of Evershot is the church-less village of East Chelborough. The reason exactly why a church was never built there lies hidden beneath the summit of *Castle Hill*, where a mediaeval castle was once sited.

Folklorist Jeremy Harte tells how early on in the sixteenth century, the population of East Chelborough had grown so much that a church was needed in the community for worship. After some debate a space was chosen in a field by the road at the bottom of Castle Hill, but as the residents could not afford professional stone masons they decided to undertake building the church themselves.

St James' Church, Lewcombe

No-one seemed concerned that Castle Hill was inhabited by fairies. Few even considered the matter at all, so the villagers started work on their much needed church. They began digging the foundations, and laying the first large stones of the walls, and when the first day's work was over, all the people went home pleased with how much they had done.

However, that night as the villagers slept, the fairies - in troops - came out of Castle Hill, and took great offence at what the residents of East Chelborough had done. The fairies did not want a church built at the bottom of their abode, so they picked up every stone block and with cries of *Horse and Hattock** flew northwards until they came to the parish of Lewcombe and the river there. The fairies of Castle Hill were earth beings and therefore could not cross over the river, so they dumped the blocks down in a great heap before returning back to Castle Hill.

The next morning the people of East Chelborough soon discovered what the fairies had done, but they were confident that Christianity would triumph over these soul-less beings, and would drive them away. A horse and cart was sent to fetch the blocks, and the people of East Chelborough started work on the church again. They made an enormous effort, almost building half the church that day, and when they went home, they all agreed not even the Devil himself could move so much stone in one night.

How wrong they were. For that night, the fairies came out of Castle Hill, and did exactly as before. They removed all the stone blocks and dumped them back by the river at Lewcombe.

On the third day the people of East Chelborough began to lose faith, but still they made one last half-hearted attempt to build their church, and at the end of the day went home tired and wondering if their efforts would still show in the morning. That night the fairies did the same; once more dumping the stone blocks back at Lewcombe.

The following day the people of East Chelborough gave up. They decided to build the church at Lewcombe by the river. In time the population of East Chelborough declined, and no attempt to build another church there was ever made, but the church of St. James at Lewcombe remains there to this day … and as for the fairies of Castle Hill – who knows?

The church at Holnest, and the one at Folke, (both near Sherborne) have very similar legends to that of Lewcombe. According to legend, both churches were started in Broke Wood, but that which was built during the first day was carried to their present position during the night by fairies.

**'Horse and Hattock.'* The magic words said to be used by fairies to aid the flight of Shift-horses – ie, stems of Ragwort or Rye Grass that fairies sometimes ride through the air in much the same fashion as a witch would use a broom.

SPECTRAL LIGHTS

A phosphorescent flicking light or ball of fire seen hovering or flitting over marsh land and sometimes graveyards is called *ignis fatuus*,* but more commonly known as *Will O' Wisp* or *Jack O' Lantern*.

If approached, they often recede and finally vanish, only to reappear in another direction; therefore if followed they seem to purposely mislead. This led to the popular belief that the lights were caused by a mischievous sprite or imp intent on leading travellers into pools, ditches, and quagmires.

A North Dorset tale tells of a shepherd boy who, one cold, foggy Winter's night gave chase to a strange bobbing light. Though he ran as fast as he could, he could not catch up with the light. Eventually the light led the boy knee deep into a bog, and he became stuck. Then suddenly there was an evil laugh, and the light went out! The boy then realised he had been tricked by Jack O' Lantern, and had to wait until morning to be rescued.

Another classic Jack O' Lantern encounter was printed in the *Dorset Echo*, on the 14th October 1967, The incident happened in west Dorset during the mid nineteenth century. Jonathan Albert, a labourer who worked for the Mabey family of Beaminster, would often turn up for work late in the morning saying he had seen Jack O' Lantern on his way home and had got lost.

His fear of meeting Jack O' Lantern was so very real, that on some nights he refused to go home at all, and would spend the night in the Mabey's hay loft. However, on *one* such night he felt some thing pass over him three times. He dared not open his eyes for he knew it was Jack O' Lantern trying to bewitch him. Yet, on the third time, Jonathan did open his eyes, and saw to his horror a vision of his sister holding up her hands and blood streaming down, and by her side was Jack O' Lantern. The next day he heard that she had been murdered!

Three days after his sister's funeral, Jonathan was walking home in the evening gloom when he saw Jack O' Lantern in a wood. Bewitched once again by the bobbing light he followed it, and soon fell into a water-filled ditch, but in trying to get out he only went in deeper and deeper. In his utter despair he called out into the darkness. *"Man a-lost!"* To which the doves in the wood replied. *"Who?"* To which he answered. *"Jonathan Albert, as good as man as ever bought a loaf of bread!"*, and at that he somehow managed to scramble free out from the ditch and went home.

---

* *'Ignis Fatuus.'* Caused by the spontaneous combustion of gases from decaying corpses and vegetable matter.

In old folklore, Will O' Wisp, Jack O' Lantern and other so-called spectral lights were considered to be an omen of death. People believed the lights were lost souls and often called them `dead men's light`, `ghost light`, `death fire`, `corpse lights` and `corpse candles`.

If the lights were seen in graveyards they were sometimes called *`fetch lights`* or *`fetch candles`*, for it was believed they were going to fetch the one about to die.

Where the dead go to rest, the corpse lights roam,
Among fruiting bodied fungi and upright slabs of stone.

Robert Newland: *Corpse Lights*

In the Summer of 1991, a retired baker, Mr Sidney Higgins, a resident of Weymouth, actually *saw* a fetch light. He told one of the present authors; Robert Newland, One drizzly, foggy morning Mr. Higgins was on his way to visit a friend in Cromwell Road, when, taking a short cut through the Newstead Road cemetery, he was startled to see a small, flitting, bright, white light moving swiftly on his right, from the direction of the wall. It moved in and out between the gravestones, before crossing the path, right over his boots! It eventually disappeared out of sight behind a tree a little distance away. Mr Higgins said. "It looked just like a star!"

Fetch lights, corpse lights, ghost lights, etc, are known to appear in one of four colours: white, red, yellow, and blue. The white, red, and yellow, lights were originally believed to be of an adult, while the blue were generally thought to indicate a child that had died un-baptised or a child that had been murdered and buried without a Christian funeral.

It is not unheard of for these mysterious lights to enter churches, chapels, houses and other dwellings, or indeed for them to haunt a particular location for numerous nights on end.

A red corpse candle was once seen at the remote St. Aldhelm's Chapel, sometimes known as the *'Devil's Chapel,'* which stands on the Purbeck cliffs near Worth Matravers. The light apparently entered through the door, circled the central pillar once before disappearing into the *'Wishing Hole'** located in the pillar.

---

* *'Wishing Hole.'* *It was custom for young women to wish for a husband while dropping a pin into the hole in the central pillar.*

Newstead Road Cemetery

St. Aldhelm's Chapel, sometimes known as the *'Devil's Chapel'*

Throughout the nineteenth century, the locals regarded the parish church of All Saints, Hampreston, between Wimborne and Parley with much dread. They often observed the church lit up at night by many brilliant white corpse lights that were said to be seen dancing above the pews.

Not that long ago, the *Crown Hotel* in Poole was haunted on several occasions by the uncanny appearance of a small fluorescent ghost light. It was always observed travelling from the back of the building through to the front and out of the main entrance.

Another tale of a single spectral light, which appeared on more than one occasion, was at the *Castle Inn* (formerly the *Jolly Sailor*) at Lulworth. Some time in the nineteenth century the wife of the landlord at the time was taken sick and died, but before she passed on, she said that all of her belongings were to be left to her daughter. The landlord was so upset by his wife's death and being of a tight fisted nature, he refused to give up her belongings and locked them in a large black chest.

The chest was placed at the bottom of his bed so that no-one could make off with it while he was asleep. However, that night a flitting corpse candle appeared in the room and started dancing above the chest. All night the landlord sat in bed shaking with terror, frightened to move, frightened to sleep, but as dawn approached the light suddenly disappeared as if blown out.

The next night the corpse light reappeared and just as before it started dancing above the chest and again for a second night the landlord watched in a state of abject terror.

Night after night the light reappeared until finally the landlord, at his wits end, begged his daughter to come and collect the chest.

Though his daughter wanted the belongings, she told him that if he wished her to have them he must bring them to her. The landlord was frightened to even touch the chest let alone move it, so he persuaded a neighbour to take the chest to his daughter's house. With the chest gone, the light never reappeared again.

High upon the downs of Ridgeway Hill, Bincombe there is a bowl barrow that has been given the curious name of *The Burning Barrow.* It was given this name due to an inexplicable event one night in the early 1980's. In Jeremy Harte's *Cuckoo Pounds and Singing Barrows* (1986) A woman told him in 1984, that she was riding pillion on her boyfriend's motorbike travelling along the top road of Came Down. When they were both startled to see flames shooting upward and a bright orange glow emitting from one of the many barrows upon the Ridgeway. Both the rider and the woman thought the area had some sinister air about it and didn't stop to find out what caused this unusual phenomenon.

Barrows or earthworks are often regarded as places, where hidden treasure can be found. The flames seen at the *Burning Barrow* could have been some form of *luces del dinero (*or *Money Lights)* as the are called in Mexico. Theses flames that appear to hover above the ground are said to mark the spot of treasure. A story in C. B Colby's *Strangely Enough* (1959). Told of a

All Saints Church, Hampreston

The Castle Inn (formerly the *Jolly Sailor*) at Lulworth.

Mexican who saw a *luces del dinero* and to prove that it was all a superstition. The next day he dug under the spot where it had been. He was soon proven wrong as under soil he found a rich gold deposit. In Scottish folklore too, on the eve of St. Andrew's, mysterious lights appear, hovering above the ground are also believed to be the burial site of hidden treasure.

Other spectral light sightings in our records include:

- In the Dorset Proceedings of *The Dorset Natural History and Archaeological Society* xlii (1921) In a article about *The Travels of Peter Mundy in Dorset*. The seventeenth century traveller, Peter Mundy, writes of his visit to Weymouth in 1635.

  "....My brother also told mee that neere Weymouth hee himselfe saw one of theis walking Fires called Ignis fatuus, which only Crosse his way without hurt. The natural Cawses of theis things must be left to the decision of the Learned, as also of that liaght which is reported to appear on Shipps in or after stormes, termed by the Spaniard St. Elmo, heere being of our Company that have seene them, gon to them and found a Jelly or froth, which soe shined by night, stickinge on their Mast Yards, etts."

- At the turn of the twentieth century Woodlands Farm, Sturminster Newton, was, for many nights, haunted by numerous flickering Ghost lights. Many people were said to have, night after night, visited the farm to witness this eerie show.

- A Jack O' Lantern was reported by a man walking home to Powerstock around 1910.

- A man driving past Eggardon Hill in September 1974 saw a ball of bluish light, probably a Will O' Wisp.

- On a Summer evening in 1982, an *ignis fatuus* was seen by Robert Newland, one of the present authors, at his home at Broadwey, Weymouth, described as a ball of flames about the size of a football, white and yellow in colour, about twenty feet high slowly drifting down towards the ground.

- A blue Corpse candle was seen bobbing through the coppice woodland at the hauntingly atmospheric ruins of St. Luke's Chapel, Ashley Chase in the 1960s.

Strange lights where once seen near the ruins of St. Luke's Church

BRING OUT YOUR DEAD

The picturesque and historic harbour at Weymouth has remained a working and thriving port for centuries. Fishing trawlers still regularly bring in their daily catch; ferries usher people to and fro across the channel, while freighters export and import their cargoes.

In the fourteenth century, Weymouth had strong trade links across the channel, importing goods and produce from the continent. It was this trade with the continent that first brought the spores of pestilence to England, and a history, which became known as *'The Black Death.'*

The *'Death'*, or Bubonic Plague, to give it its proper title, spread west voraciously from the orient to Europe by the aid of fleas, rats and seafarers, which carried this deadly bacillus which formed huge boils or buboes. Noted wit, author, and wartime SAS hero Sir John Verney once humorously remarked that the disease *"started under the armpits, and spread across Europe".*

The *'Death'* eventually arrived in England via Dorset in the Summer of June 1348. Two merchant ships returning from their trade with Gascony, France entered the then ports of Weymouth and Melcombe.

The Black Death arrived in England, at Weymouth Harbour, in June 1348 and quickly spread throughout medieval Britain

On board one of these ships a sailor was suffering from terrible nausea, which then developed into a fever. The sailor began to hallucinate, cough up blood and red lesions covered his body. These were the familiar signs and symptoms that were to become so firmly associated with the Bubonic Plague, the result of which would end in death! The residents of Melcombe were the first to suffer the plague as it spread throughout the confined and unsanitised conditions of the town.

Villages and hamlets on the outskirts of Weymouth, like Radipole and Came, soon fell to the plague. Many villagers abandoned their settlements seeking refuge in other parts of the county; this caused the infection to be spread over a wide area, until it eventually reached the major cities. `The Death` took a heavy toll on the people of Portland, so the quarries and fields ceased to be worked and the coastal defence was left deserted. Edward III, in 1352 ordered the movement of the islanders to be restricted.

The arrival of *'The Black Death'* to England on the 25th June 1348 was documented in the *Grey Friars Chronicle*.

> *"In this year 1348 in Melcombe, in the county of Dorset, a little before the feast of St. John the Baptist, two ships, one of them from Bristol came alongside. One of the sailors had brought with him from Gascony the seeds of the terrible pestilence and through him the men of that town of Melcombe were the first in England to be infected."*

The town of Poole was also another area hard hit by the plague. The town council bought a peninsula of land by the sea known as *The Baiter* and reserved it as a mass burial ground for the victims. The plague was so rife in Bridport that the dead were buried outside the town in plague pits at the base of Colmer's Hill, Symondsbury. The site bears no grass and is often avoided by local residents, as it is believed to be haunted.

Though the Black Death took the lives of twenty-five million European people between 1348 and 1351, outbreaks continued to occur in isolated villages, towns and cities throughout England for the next three hundred and eighteen years.

Like an outstretched hand, the pollard remains of 'The Posy Tree'

Dead Man's Lane

A lonesome sycamore tree is the only grim reminder of the terrible pestilence that occurred at Mapperton, near Bridport, some four hundred years ago.

It was common enough practice for the inhabitants of Mapperton to bury their dead at the cemetery of the neighbouring parish of Netherbury. Mapperton's cemetery was deemed unsuitable for burial because the soil was too stoney.

In 1582, this routine of burial changed due to the outbreak of bubonic plague at Mapperton. Villagers of Netherbury gathered at the parish boundary refusing to let the residents of Mapperton bury the corpses of plague victims in the cemetery. This resulted in a bitter skirmish between the villagers, but after some negotiations, it was agreed that the bodies should remain at the boundary, which the old Mapperton and Netherbury track crosses, now known as *Dead Man's Lane.*

The pollard sycamore tree known locally as the *Posy** or *Cosy Tree,* now marks the spot where the eighty dead of Mapperton were collected and buried in a mass grave within a small enclosure on the summit of South Warren Hill. After burial a copse of Beech trees was planted on the site to make sure the area was not disturbed, though after many centuries bones have been found there.

Location of the plague pits at South Warren Hill

* *'Posy.' Being the name given to the gathered wild herbs and flowers to ward off the foul odours, which emitted from the corpses of victims carrying the plague.*

THE POSY TREE

I saw the death cart carry its yield
The corpses decaying and black
Down Dead Man's Lane to South Warren Hill
And empty the cart came back

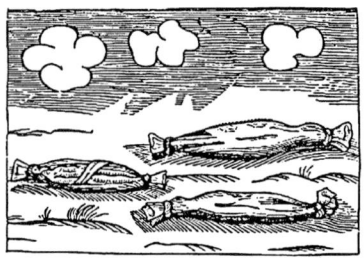

Eyes I have none, but I've seen history
History is part of me
A grim reminder of the plague
They call me... Posy tree

If I had a voice I would have screamed
With a long mournful lament
In harmony with the death bell's toll

I look more dead than alive
But my roots are deep and vast
And thus I stand firm, transfixed
To the memories of the past
I remember a dreadful time
Some four hundred years or so
I saw the Reapers scythe swing
Blow after blow after blow

My anguish I would have vent
Today I stand here empty
My heart hollow from years of pain
My limbs cruelly severed
Just my trunk now remain

I saw him plant the roses
I saw the spores of pestilence bud
I saw the sickness and the fever
The pustules and the blood

But here I am still
A reminder to you all I show
That man thou art dust
And unto dust must go

I felt the despair in the air
I heard man's dieing breath
Through every leafy pore
All I could smell was death

Robert Newland

THE WISHING WELL OF LOVE & DOOM

In the cemetery at Cerne Abbas, can be found the sacred holy well of Saint Augustine. Shaded by mature lime trees, its clear strong flow is curbed with large flat stones, where either side is a low rectangular pillar or plinth, – the one being on the south side having upon its face the carved wheel of St Catherine.

Legend says that in the sixth century, St. Augustine brought forth the spring by striking the ground with his staff in order to convert the heathens. But the pagan inhabitants of Cerne did not welcome Christianity, and drove St. Augustine out of the village by pinning cow's tails to him and his fellow monks.

Years later, when the monks returned, the well became a shrine dedicated to St. Augustine and covered by a mediaeval chapel. It was common practice for the newborn to be dipped into the well at sunrise and for the sick to drink the water in hope of a divine cure.

Henry Moule wrote in Victorian times: 'The well still works wondrous cures!'

Unmarried girls wanting a husband would go alone to the well at dawn, on either May Day, (1st May) Midsummer Day, (24th June) or St. Catherine's Day (25th November), and in a state of nudity kneel down and place her hands on *'The Wishing Stone,'* the pillar with the wheel carved upon it, and say the following rhyme:

    St. Catherine, St. Catherine
    O lend me thine aid
    And grant that I never
    May die an Old Maid
    A husband St. Catherine
    A good one St. Catherine
    But ar-a-one better than
    Nar-a-one, St. Catherine

Saint Augustine's Well as it looked in 1989

Saint Augustine's Well today

To consecrate the wish, the girl would drink and immerse herself in the water to purify her mind and body.

In the ninth century, *St. Edwold* was led to the well by a premonition after the Danes had killed his brother *St. Edmund the Martyr*, the King of East Anglia in 871A.D. A poor shepherd was at the well when St. Edwold arrived and on seeing the man's ragged clothes, St. Edwold gave him some silver coins, hence the well acquired another name, *The Silver Well*.

This legend is still remembered today, for it is customary for those visiting the well for the first time to throw some silver coins into it for good luck.

However, there is another belief associated with the well and that is it can foretell who is going to die in the forthcoming year. Those wishing to know should go to the well at sunrise on Easter Day and peer in and there reflected in the water will be the faces of those doomed to die!

Saint Augustine

From local inn signs to advertising, the image of the Cerne Abbas Giant is perhaps one of the most iconic in the world

THE FERTILITY GIANT

Carved out on the western slope of Trendle Hill at Cerne Abbas is Dorset's prize exhibit, *The Cerne Giant*. The Giant, as he is called, stands naked some hundred and eighty feet in length with a club held aloft in his right hand, his left arm outstretched.

How he came to be there and who he represents is an unsolved mystery. One old legend suggests the Giant represents a once real live giant who terrorised Cerne and the surrounding area eating cows, sheep and children. One day as he lay sleeping on the hill side, the villagers of Cerne killed him and cut out his outline in the chalk, to remind every one of their bravery.

Historians have interpreted the Giant to be a multitude of ancient Gods. From Cernunnos, Hercules and Gogmagog, to the *Green Man** or Wild Man. However, as the Giant predates Roman times he is thought most likely to represent a Celtic Fertility God.

The Celts were great headhunters. It is now thought that the giant originally held a severed head in his left hand.

One of the famous hill figures of Britain - **The Cerne Abbas Giant**

* *'The Green Man.' Representing the spirit of vegetation, he is associated with spring festivals such as May Day.*

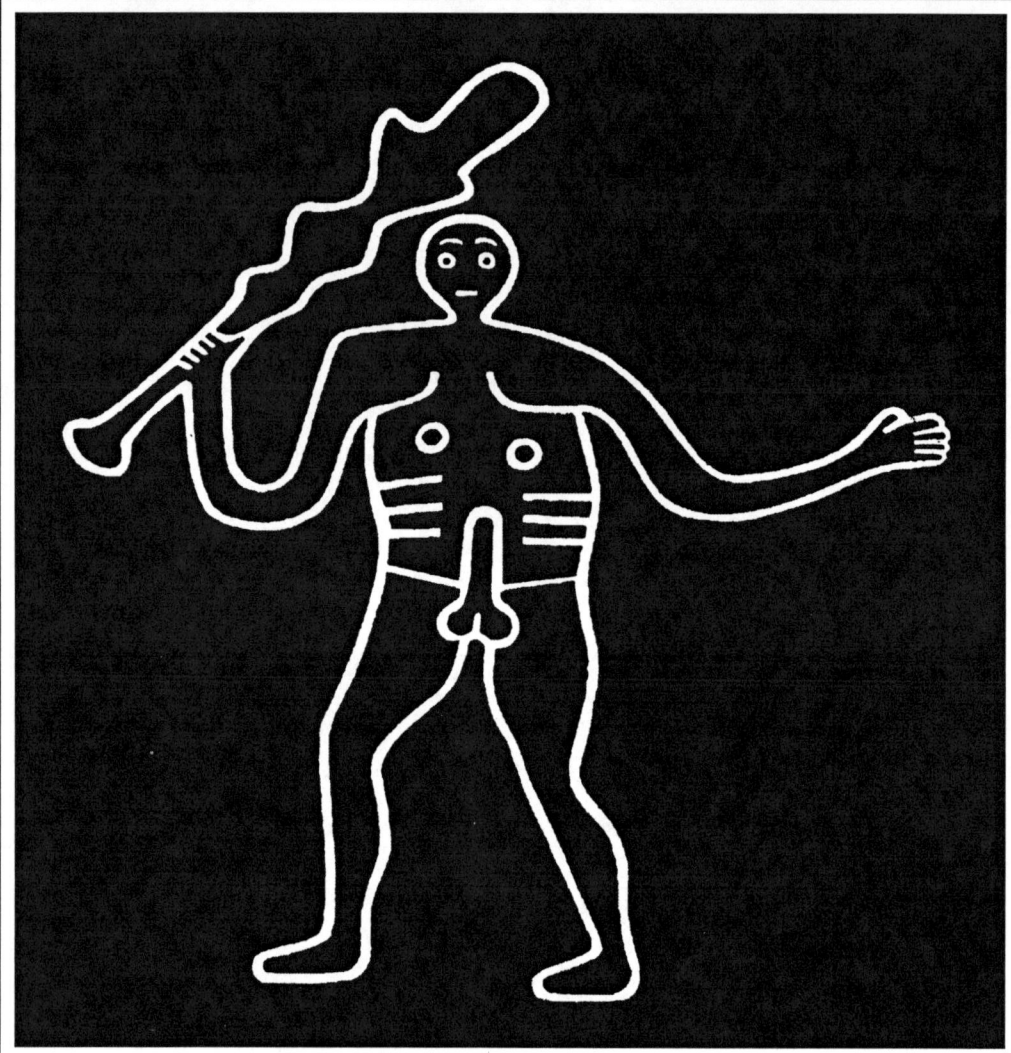

It was generally believed the Giant could cure a woman of infertility if she sat on the tip of his penis. Some accounts say that she should spend a night laying on him when there is a new moon; others say the childless couple should have actual sexual intercourse on the giant in order to conceive.

As bizarre as all this may sound, old superstitions die hard in Dorset. In 1958, the Marquis of Bath and his wife Virginia visited the site. For five years, they had tried - without success - to have children together, and then someone told them about the Giant. They laid on him, and ten months later their daughter Silvy was born. The Marquis was aware that he was in the Giant's debt: "It worked for us and in gratitude we gave Cerne as Silvy's middle name, and made G. Cerne godfather at the christening - the vicar never noticed." Until he became too old to continue his visits, the Marquis made an annual spring pilgrimage to the Giant with Silvy - now Lady Silvy Cerne McQuiston, so that she could tell her godfather what she had been up to since last they met.

As recently as 1998, Mr and Mrs Thorne, of Puddletown were pleased to announce the birth of their first child after trying for more than five years. The happy couple reported how they had heard of the Giant's mysterious power of curing infertile women and were so desperate for a child that they were willing to try anything.

After being blessed by a white witch and a midnight romp on the Giant, Mrs Thorne soon discovered she was indeed pregnant! And nine months later gave birth to a healthy baby boy.

But there is bad news for other couples wanting to test the Giant's powers. The National Trust, fearing *midnight activities* could erode the Giant's chalk form, have since erected a protective fence around the site.

Above the Giant's head is a small earthwork called the *Trendle*. In days gone by it was the custom to erect a Maypole, itself a phallic symbol, up there for May Day celebrations. But sadly this custom is no longer performed.

Apart from bringing in the tourists, the Giant plays no major role in the villagers' life today, although the Wessex Morris Men do perform Morris dancing above the Giant every May Day at sunrise (5.28a.m.).

The Wild Man of Yellowham Hill

Woodwoses were once thought to inhabit the woods of Yellowham Hill near Dorchester. They had the habit of abducting young girls from the nearby villages, many of whom fell pregnant. One such incident befell a young girl, and when questioned by magistrates, she replied. 'Please your worshipfuls, *'twere the Wild Man of Yal'ham.'* Woodwose (otherwise Wodewose, Wodewese, Woodwyse and Wuduwasa) means Wild Man, These were savage, hairy, humanoid creatures similar to the American Bigfoot that were said to inhabit the woods of pre-Christian Europe.

The Dorset Ooser

DORSET'S DEVIL

On the 1st May 1989, at the village of Cerne Abbas, a hideous horned creature, walking upright, loomed through the mist causing gasps of astonishment from the onlookers watching the Morris dancing.

Its face was one of terror, with bulging eyes, a lumpy nose and a snarling mouth. The creature, a type of hybrid, part man, part bull, was about ten feet tall and wearing a cow's skin. It walked among the crowd swiftly and silently, pausing now and again to stop. It was no doubt the very image of the Devil, it was, *The Dorset Ooser*! (Pronounced Os-ser).

However, this *Ooser* was just a replica made in 1973, designed from a photo of the original *Ooser*. The original was made of wood and had a moving snapping jaw, and a hollow head. Lucifer matches were pushed alight into the head so that smoke could bellow out from its nostrils.

The Original Dorset Ooser that was kept by the Cave Family of Melbury Osmond

The *Ooser* was for many years in the possession of the Cave family at Holt farm, Melbury Osmond, where it was kept in the tallet (hayloft) yet it mysteriously vanished in 1897. Up until its disappearance it was used for special occasions such as May Day and St. George's Day, but was mainly a Midwinter creature performing in the Mumming plays of Christmas.

In one showing around 1890, with Thomas Hurlston taking the role of the *Ooser*, he thrashed around so violently that one of its horns struck off part of a preacher's lip.

Ironically, shortly after the incident, Thomas Hurlston was at a bull-baiting when a bull struck a horn up in through Mr Hurlston's chin, up into his head, tearing his tongue from his mouth, and instantly killing him.

Sometimes the *Ooser* was used to frighten naughty children and even adults. Once it was used to frighten a young stable hand, who in sheer terror jumped through a window and accidentally killed himself.

The Skimmington Ride as portrayed in this engraving by William Hogarth

Another occasion for the *Ooser's* appearance was for the Dorset custom of *Skimmington Riding* or *The Skimmity Ride*. The villagers would often take part in punishing adulterers by leading a donkey through the streets, on which rode, face to tail, the unfaithful man and woman. The public demonstration was often accompanied by the beating of pots and pans while the *Ooser* taunted the pair of them. The scene was a symbol of the Devil leading the sinners to Hell.

> *Near whom the Amazon triumphant*
> *Bestride her beast, and, on the rump on't,*
> *Sat face to tail and bum to bum,*
> *The warrior whilom overcome,*
> *Arm'd with a spindle and a distaff,*
> *Which, as he rode, she made him twist off:*
> *And when he loiter'd, o'er her shoulder*
> *Chastis'd the reformado soldier.*
>
> Scott: *The Fortunes of Nigel*

The *Ooser* had a much darker side too! It was the stud bull of Dorset witchcraft and would have been worn by the head of the *coven*.* It was through him that female witches had intercourse with their master - the Devil, penetrating them from behind with an abnormally large artificial phallus.

Jeannette d'Abadie, a French girl who had allegedly copulated with the Devil many times while still only sixteen, claimed that he caused her intense pain with his *scaly member*, adding

---

'Coven.' A group of twelve witches and one Devil.

his semen was *'extremely cold'* and because of this she had never been made pregnant.

But the question still remains. Where is the Ooser now? The replica can be found on display in the Dorset County Museum at Dorchester. But as for the original, no-one knows. Some say it might have been taken abroad, while others believe it was used for firewood.

However, rumours persist that the theft of the Ooser may have marked it's return to a West Dorset Witch Coven where it still performs to this day!

WORK-A-DAY WITCHERY

"Claims that witchcraft is at work in West Dorset were made from the pulpit of a village church on Sunday..." - thus ran a story in a local newspaper in November 1984.

The village of Charmouth lies on the edge of the Marshwood Vale, traditionally a hotbed of witchcraft. The congregation were said to be amazed at the vicar's outburst, for it has been common knowledge that witchcraft has been practised in Dorset for centuries.

The vicar alleged that local covens were breaking up the marriages of clergymen in the area, but when asked to elaborate, he declined.

Witches were once commonplace in Dorset, and the belief in witchcraft was never stronger than in the outlying villages and hamlets - such as Hawkchurch.

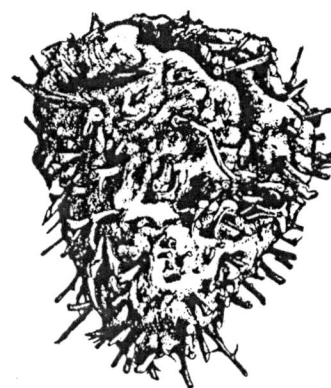

In 1884, one of its residents made an unusual discovery, for found lodged up a chimney was a stuffed bullock's heart studded with thorns, pins, and nails. It was recognised as a magic charm, and its purpose was to prevent witches gaining access to the house via the chimney.

Wise country folk took such precautions to ensure they were not `overlooked` by witches, for it was believed witches could cast spells of ill luck and misfortune, make women miscarry, and *even* brew up storms from their cauldron to destroy a neighbour's crops! What's more, witches could also fly down the chimney on their broomsticks to wreak havoc in the house!

One such account of a witch coming down a chimney, was at the village of Hilton in February 1870. A seven-year-old girl began to have disturbed nights. She screamed, and cried out that she saw a woman dressed in black come down the chimney and make faces at her. Some nights the witch pinched and prodded the girl. This only stopped when salt was scattered around the girl's bed, and a horseshoe placed over the entrance of the house.

Another popular belief was that witches could change shape, usually into hares, so they could suckle milk from cows, and leave them dry.

> I shall go into a hare,
> With sorrow and sych and meikle care;
> And I shall go in the Devil's name
> Ay while I come home again.

According to *Dorset Up Along and Down* Along by Marianne R. Dacombe (1935), In 1764, at Marnhull Common, there lived a young married couple, James and Susanna Coombes, alias 'Jimmy and Fanny.' It was said that for half-a-crown Jimmy could always find a hare for the hunters. But it was noticed the hare always doubled back to Jimmy's cottage and then seemed to vanish without a trace.

One day a hunter decided to wait at the cottage to see where the hare went. When the hare appeared it ran in through the door and changed into Fanny! Their secret was out. Witchcraft was not an easy way to riches after all.

> *Hare, hare, God send thee care,*
> *I am in a hare's likeness just now,*
> *But I shall be in a woman's likeness*
> *even now.*

A large hare was often seen frequenting the fields at Worth Matravers and drinking from the udders of cows. The farmer who owned the cows, shot at the hare time and time again, but the agile animal always bounded away unhurt as if protected by magic. His wife believed the hare was a witch, and one day instructed him to use a *silver** sixpence behind the charge. When next the farmer saw the hare, he shot it in the leg, but the hare escaped. From that day an old woman of the village had noticeably developed a limp. Was she the witch-hare?

> *Both barrels went off - that moment a cry*
> *And a horrible, sulphurous smell rose around -*
> *But neither the hare nor the witch could he spy*
> *When gladly, but firmly, he strode from the ground.*

William Smith Marriott: *Olden & Modern Times*

A similar tale happened at West Lulworth in 1789. A farmer by the name of Sam Varndell was having a terrible run of bad luck, his crops had perished and his lambs were dying. His shepherd, Jimmy Hyde, was also suffering due to his wife having contracted a mysterious sickness. Both men blamed their misfortune on an old woman who lived at Sleight, who was rumoured to practise witchcraft.

One moonlit evening, Mr. Hyde saw a huge doe hare worrying the sheep, so he loaded his gun, shot at the hare, and hit it, but the wounded animal escaped along the track leading to Sleight.

---

* *'Silver.'* A sacred metal alloy to combat evil – i.e. Lycanthropy, Vampires, Demons, etc.

Daggers Gate - scene of a gruesome murder

The next morning Mr. Hyde was fixing-up a lambing pen in the field close to the old woman's dwelling, when he discovered some of her footprints in the mud leading towards her house. Beside them was a trail of blood. He also noticed that the old crone was limping, which only fuelled his suspicions about her.

One misty morning, Mr. Hyde left his ailing wife to attend the sheep, when he saw the witch-hare once again. Without a second thought he picked up an iron bar, and threw it at the hare. There was a loud crack, and the hare slumped down upon the damp grass - its head smashed in.

Moments later, Sam Varndell came along, and saw Jimmy Hyde stooping over the dead animal. Hyde turned around with triumph in his eyes. *"I killed the witch."* He said proudly. *"And I think if you go to her hovel you will find her, no doubt with her head broken like the hare."*

Sam laughed. *"You may be right. I'm going that way to fence the rick."* he said picking up the bloodstained bar. *"I'll..... just take this bar and go and see."*

The old crone was dead! The Vicar was sent for, and the funeral arrangements were made, but there was no place for a witch in any churchyard, so she was buried at a gate by the roadside not far from her house.

With the witch dead and buried, the misfortune that plagued Sam Varndell seemed to end. Even Jimmy Hyde's wife recovered from her mystery illness, and in time all was forgotten. Some years after, Sam Varndell was returning home from Dorchester market when he saw - at the gate where the witch was buried - a woman. Drawing closer she began to shout foul ravings at him, accusing him of murdering her mother. Mr. Varndell stopped to calm the hysterical woman down, and to protest his innocence in the matter, when she suddenly drew a knife from her skirt and stabbed him in the back.

Sam Varndell died that day. The woman was tried for murder at Dorchester Assizes where she was found guilty and duly hanged. Soon after the gate was dubbed *Daggers Gate,* the name which it is still known by today, but rumours abound that the gate is haunted.

> *When swirling grey mist lingers heavy in the air,*
> *Daggers Gate opens and swings back upon its clasp,*
> *The hazy figure of the witch then does appear,*
> *Followed by her chilling scream and her dying gasp.*
>
> Robert Newland

One other account of shape-changing is that of Jinny Gould of Ulwell, near Swanage. The road that led from Ulwell to Studland had a toll gate owned by Jinny - a suspected witch. The villagers called the gate *Jinny Ghoul Gate,* for they said it opened and closed of its own accord to allow lonely night time travellers through.

One night, according to Oliver Knott in *Witches of Dorset* (1974) a traveller on approaching the gate, saw an enormous black cat sitting on top of it. Frightened by its piercing gaze, the traveller struck it violently with his stick. The cat fled for the safety of Jinny's cottage nearby.

The next day Jinny Gould was found dead in her cottage with a great wound across her back. The villager's suspicions were right. Jinny was a witch after all. Interestingly, according to Fortean zoologist Jonathan Downes, an almost identical tale is told about a gate at Morwenstowe in North Cornwall.

Jinny's name lived on for many years after her death. One story tells of a young boy called Walter Steer who visited Ulwell with his nanny. Not realising, Walter wandered into Jinny's overgrown garden* to pick a rose, but his nanny soon grabbed him and hauled him out saying that if he went in there again he would be spanked as it was a *'wicked place.'*

---

* *'Witch's Garden.'* Witches often had a garden in which they grew plants such as foxglove, hemlock, deadly nightshade, etc, for use in magic potions and ointments.

The traveller attacks the witch Jinny Gould, disguised as a large black cat

The area where the former Toll Gate once stood, know locally as Jinny Gould Gate

The road was later widened and today there is no trace of the toll gate, Jinny's cottage, or indeed her garden, which stood by the present-day water works.

Among other things, witches were believed to cause sickness and death to those who they saw as unfavourable - usually the innocent! In June 1890, at the village of Durweston, a mysterious woman in black appeared before a group of thirty school children as an omen of death. That July the parish register records the burial of five young infants, who sickened and died within days of each other.

Once at Wyke Regis, Weymouth, there lived an old woman who was suspected of practising witchcraft, for it was believed she had `over-looked` a young girl. A gypsy informed the girl's mother to hang a bullock's heart stuffed with pins inside the chimney, which in time would break the spell. The mother did this and when the heart dried out, it fell into the fire and was burnt to a cinder. Later, when her daughter recovered, the old witch was seen in a fit of rage claiming that someone had been meddling in her affairs.

PINS & NEEDLES

Wherever there were witches there were whispers and rumours, which in turn, led people to live in constant fear of being `over-looked`. People would protect themselves with all manner of magic charms. Horseshoes were often hung above doorways, and dried dead cats, witch bottles, and stuffed bull's hearts were hidden up the chimney, or in the thatch, and salt was sprinkled in the cradles.

If any of these charms failed, and one did become overlooked, it was generally believed the only effective way of removing the witch's baneful influence, was for the affected person to draw blood from the over-looker with a needle or any sharp iron object.

In some parts this was known as *Scoring Above The Breath*, which meant tearing the `over-looker's` forehead, mouth, or nose until the face became bloody. Suspicions of alleged witchery became extremely common, often reaching a stage when neighbour accused neighbour.

A case of alleged witchery was brought before the Sherborne Petty Sessions Court on 28th September 1884. The defendant, Mrs. Tamar Humphries of Cold Harbour, was accused of assaulting her eighty-three year old neighbour, Sarah Smith.

The court heard how Mrs Humphries believed her daughter was being `over-looked`, as the child had been suffering with rheumatism for some weeks. Believing her neighbour, Sarah Smith, to be the over-looker, she entered the old lady's garden and shook her violently saying. "Sal Smith, what's thee done to my child? Thou art a witch an' I'll draw the blood of thee!" And producing a stocking needle, Tamar tore it about Sarah Smith's arms and hands, making them bleed, leaving her dazed and confused.

When the defence questioned Sarah Smith, she told how she had been the Humphries' neighbour for thirty years and in that time had no cause to quarrel.

Sidney Watts, the defending lawyer said that Mrs Humphries had been given a bad name by Sarah Smith, and claimed that the violence used was nothing more than a gentle shake.

However, the bench took a serious view of the blood-letting, and considered that it amounted to a disgraceful assault on an inoffensive old woman. Tamar Humphries was fined £1 with 11s 6d costs.

A similar incident was reported from Halstock,

where a young man afflicted with scrofula, was so frustrated with the pains it caused, that he believed his neighbour's wife had bewitched him. One day in his agony, he rushed into her house, and scratched her severely about the neck and arms, drawing blood. After this the young man felt relieved of his pains.

> 'Tis now the very witching time of night,
> When churchyards yawn and Hell itself
> Breathes out
> Contagion to this world: Now could I
> Drink hot blood
> And do such bitter business as the day
> Would quake to look on.
>
> **William Shakespeare**: *Hamlet*

Another bizarre incident was reported in the *Dorset County Chronicle* of 21st July 1887. A labourer suffering a collection of mishaps, conceived the idea that his next-door neighbour was to blame, and accused her of such. She refuted the charge, whereupon the man took a reap hook, and was about to take what he considered effective means to break the spell, when he was prevented by neighbours.

According to Marianne Dacombe, John and Jane Maish, who were known as the *Wormies*, made a poor living in their old age as *spinsters** at their cottage near the church of Sturminster Newton, making rush mats and hassocks, known as 'butts'. They associated with no-one, and were avoided by all as having the evil eye. They practiced charms, hanging a bottle up the chimney with frog's entrails and a bullocks heart stuck with pins. In February 1826 they were both taken down with influenza, which they believed was caused by the village schoolmaster, so, armed with a pin, they went to meet him. But something must have gone wrong, for they were found dead in the snow by Hayden Farm near Plumber Manor.

---

* *'Spinster.'* A woman or a man who spins, especially one who practises spinning as a regular occupation.

PROTECTIVE WITCH CHARMS

Horseshoes

The belief that it is lucky to pick up a horseshoe is from the idea that it is a charm against evil forces and witchcraft. Even today it is common to see a horseshoe nailed above the door of the house with its horns pointing up, so to prevent the luck running out.

One legend of the origin of this belief, is that the Devil once asked St. Dunstan, who was noted for his skill as a farrier, to shoe his 'single hoof'. Dunstan, knowing who his customer was, tied him tightly to the wall, and proceeded with the job. However, St. Dunstan purposely put the devil through so much pain that the Devil cried for mercy. Dunstan at last agreed to release his captive on condition that he would never again enter a place where he saw a horseshoe displayed.

Witch Bottles

During the sixteenth and seventeenth Century it was common practice for those who possessed the knowledge of counteracting the effects of an evil spell or bewitchment of concealing a Bellarmine Jar (grey stoneware bottle) or a glass bottle underneath the floor boards, the hearth stone or in the cavity of walls of a dwelling.

Inside the bottle there would be placed a number of items that were believed to do harm to any witch that placed a hex upon the household. These items consisted of a number of bent iron nails, thorns, human hair and nail clippings, plus substances of blood, saliva and more commonly, urine.

A Bellarmine Jar

Once the objects and substances had been placed in the bottle, the vessel was placed near an open fire, and allowed to boil overnight. This would draw the culprit to the scene to be identified, or alternately cause the witch so much agony that he or she was obliged to lift the curse.

In the *Dorset Echo* 27th October 2005, there was a story about a historic find that was made two years previously, and was going on display at the Castle View Visitor Centre at Corfe Castle. The find was an unusual bottle discovered buried upside down on National Trust land under a wall near Langton Matravers

"Experts believe that the rare find is a 'witch bottle' used to fend off evil spirits which were thought to cause horned cattle distemper. The bottles contents was dark brown syrup and is one of only four bottles discovered in the UK with liquid still inside. Since then, a series of tests has revealed the liquid contained 30 different components including a salt solution - known as holy water at the time - covered with a layer of decayed animal fat.

National Trust archaeologist Nancy Grace, who is based at Corfe Castle, said:

"It is possible in this period that when livestock suffered ill health which was inexplicable to its owner, witchcraft was identified as the cause. "It may be that this fear led someone to fill this bottle with a mixture of animal fat and holy water to kill the evil spirit."

Parish reports of the mid-1700s show horned cattle distemper existed for 12 years in the counties around Dorset."

The Langton Matravers Witch Bottle

Ritual Protection Marks

These scratch-marks found on the timbers of the mantelpiece at Mangerton Mill, near Bridport, suggest that they were used to protect the house from the evil spirits and curses of witches. It was often regarded, that a house was always vulnerable and the tradition of apotropaic ritual was often applied to particular entry points in the house such as the chimney, windows and especially doors. The style of the marks found at Mangerton Mill are similar to other marks found elsewhere in Britain. Most that have been found date from the 16th to the 18th centuries and it has been suggested that they were used to invoke the protection of the Virgin Mary through the use of the 'V' and 'M' shapes.

Dried Cat

When renovation to an old building is undertaken, it is more often the case that a mummified cat is revealed hidden in a cavity of a wall or in the rafters of the loft or attic. Mummified cats, although the correct term is *'dried cats'.* Like the stuffed bullock's heart studded with thorns, pins, and nails found in a chimney in Hawkchurch acted as a folk charm or guardian to protect against witches gaining access or ill luck befalling to the building. In some cases the cats have been positioned, indicating that they were already dead at the time of concealment. However some weren't so lucky and were often abused and walled up alive!

These grey twisted relics have been found all over Dorset such as Corfe Mullen, Marnhull, Maiden Newton, Mangerton, Milton Abbass and Winfrith Newburgh.

In an exhibit at the Portland Museum, Easton, can be found the preserved remains of a mummified cat. The grim discovery was found in the walls of a cottage at Easton, which was reputed to have been the home of a resident wise woman.

Mangerton Mill, near Bridport contains some curious artefacts of folklore

The tearoom at Mangerton Mill with the curious scratch marks on the mantelpiece

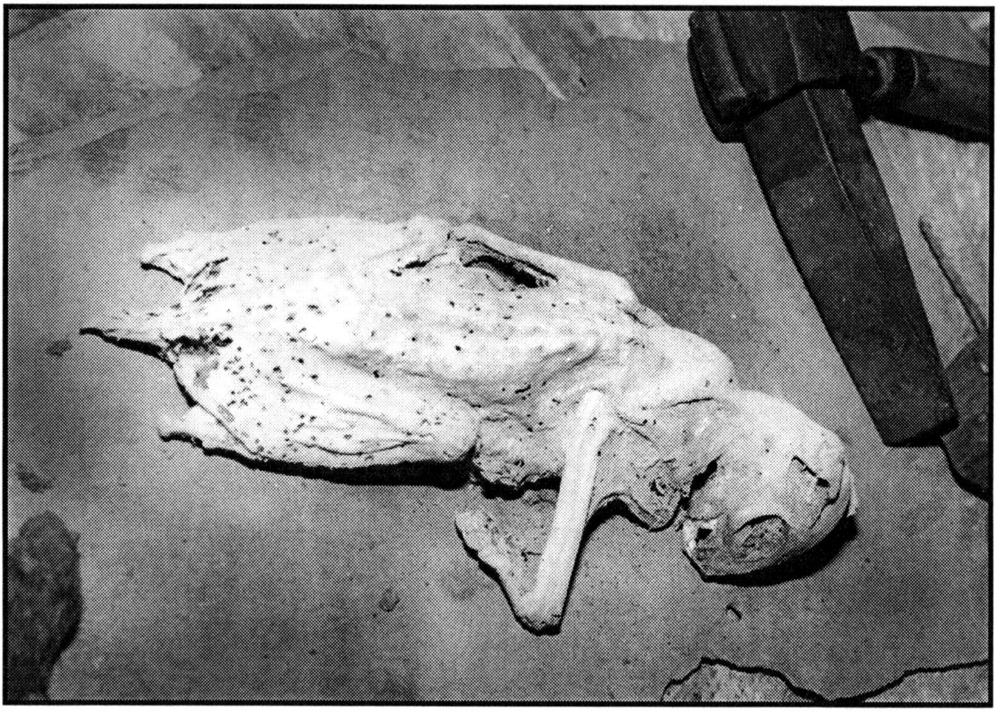

Above, the body of the cat found in the roof of Mangerton Mill and below, another dried cat found in a cottage wall cavity in Milton Abbas was probably placed there as some sort of magic charm to protect the building from the evil effects of witchcraft.

Rabbits, the Portland taboo

Many people on Portland believe the rabbit is bad luck! Even to say the word could send Portlanders into a stupour, that these creatures were often referred as, *bunny, long ears, coney, underground mutton* and *them vurry things*. The origin of the islander's fear of rabbits is based on the fact that quarry men would often see rabbits emerging from their burrows immediately before a rock fall. Such rock falls often injured and even killed quarry workers; therefore, it can be understood why rabbits became associated with bad luck. So deep was the superstition that it ruled many of the islanders lives, it was often the case that if a Portland quarryman was walking to work and observed a rabbit, he would immediately turn round and go home for the rest of the day, and if one was ever spotted when they were at work, the whole crew would down tools and go home.

West Weares Quarry, Portland. A stone bridges for emptying the stone trucks over the side of the cliff.

DIANA THE MOON GODDESS & THE MAGIC CIRCLE

Five miles northeast of Bridport is mysterious Eggardon Hill. It is by far one of the finest examples of a hillfort anywhere to be found in Wessex. It began as a Neolithic settlement, and developed through the Bronze and Iron Ages, only to be raided and captured by the Roman Second Augustan Legion in 43A.D.

Anyone who has ever spent an hour or so there on a windy day, will realise why so much superstition and folklore has grown up around the foreboding hill. It is said that Diana the Moon Goddess, leads a ghostly hunt of fairies, demons, and witches, over its summit, collecting the souls of the dead.

Witches everywhere worship and honour Diana, for it is said that witchcraft derived from her. Roman tradition says, Diana fell in love with her brother Lucifer, and as a result of their union, Diana gave birth to a daughter called Aradia. Diana took pity on the poor, rustic people of the earth, particularly gypsies, so she sent her daughter to teach them the art of witchcraft.

Aradia taught them all manner of magic, from the relatively simple spells and charms to the dark ancient magic that had existed since the dawn of time. She also taught them the art of fortune telling, astrology, and the secrets of the occult including the magic of *Fairyrings.**

> *Oh, these be Fancy's revellers by night!*
> *Stealthy companions of the downy moth–*
> *Diana's motes, that flit in her pale light,*
> *Shunners of sunbeams in diurnal sloth;–*
> *These be the feasters on night's silver cloth:–*
> *The gnat with shrilly trump is their convener,*
> *Forth from their flowery chambers, nothing loth,*
> *With lulling times to charm the air serener,*
> *Or dance upon the grass to make it greener.*
>
> **Hood:** *Plea of the Midsummer Fairies*

---

*'Fairyring.' A ring of toadstools, or a circular band of grass differing in colour from the grass around it. A phenomenon supposed in popular belief to be produced by fairies when dancing.

The magical fairyring near Eggardon Hill

The Hag Circle

Witches would often seek out fairyrings to dance with the fairies and to enhance their spells. It's no wonder then, that in Dorset fairyrings are often referred to as *Hag Tracks* or *Hag Circles*. A letter appeared in the Bournemouth Evening Echo on 28th October 1993 under the heading: *'Doing anything on Hallowe'en.'* It referred mainly to fairyrings, but it also mentioned a magic divination that could be conducted inside a fairyring:

'On Hallowe'en a maiden can find out whom she will marry by stepping naked at midnight into a fairyring and slowly turning around anti-clockwise. By doing so she should see a vision of her future lover.'

THE RIDING OF THE WITCH

All witches have some knowledge of the dark ancient magic that has been handed down from mother to daughter throughout the ages. Apart from shape-changing and casting spells of ill luck, witches were sometimes known to over-look people in other ways.

The night was the time for witches and it was then when a witch posed the most danger. Occasionally witches would take on the role of a Succubus* or Night Hag, invisibly seeking out their sleeping victims to steal their strength. They would accomplish this by squatting over their chosen victims and riding them causing unpleasant dreams and restless nights.

This was widely known as *The Riding of the Witch*, and hence their hag-ridden victims would suffer from so-called *Hag Syndrome*.

> *The witches' circle intact, charms undisturbed*
> *That raised the spirit and succubus.*
>
> **Browning:** *Ring & Book.*

Once, Mrs. Fudge of Marnhull, actually experienced *The Riding of the Witch*. She was standing in the doorway of her cottage at the foot of Church Hill when she saw a red haired young woman dressed in black coming down the hill. The young woman who was barely out of her teens, was suspected in the village of witchcraft, for it was said she had "bewitched many a handsome young man and woman."

Mrs. Fudge smiled and laughed under her breath as the young woman passed, amused at the rumours and her strange *witch-like* appearance. However, the young witch must of heard her laugh, for that night, when Mrs. Fudge was in bed, she was woken by a crushing weight on her legs that went gradually creeping upwards to her chest. Mrs. Fudge let out a loud scream that summoned her son to the room. When he opened the door, the lump jumped off, and they both heard the sound of footsteps running down the stairs and out through the front door.

Nothing was to be seen of the intruder, but the next day when Mrs. Fudge was making her bed, she found a lock of red hair, exactly matching the colour of the young witch's hair.

Such instances as this were indeed common, and people genuinely feared a visitation by a night hag; for once asleep, even the strongest was as helpless as a newborn. Knowing this, people often resorted to the age-old tried and tested magic charms to protect them through the

---

* *'Succubus.' A demon/nightmare in female form that seeks out sleeping men and women to have sexual intercourse with. Hebrew traditions tell of God creating Lilith as the first mate for Adam, but she would not obey him and lie beneath him during sexual intercourse. Therefore, she left Adam and went to the demons of Hell for her sexual pleasure. Her daughters, the Succubi,, (also known as Lilim), are much like their mother. They seek out sleeping men and steal their vigour and strength by squatting over them, reversing the male superior position.*

night. These included placing a sock under the bed, a sprig of rosemary or a knife under the pillow, or placing one's shoes under the bed so that the toes pointed outwards.

Horses also were particularly vulnerable to witchcraft, for witches had the power to bewitch them, halting them in their tracks, and keeping them rooted to the spot, although it is said that a witch's magic would not work if the rider carried a rowan whip.

> *Rowan-tree or reed*
> *Put the witches to speed.*
>
> *Old Folk Saying*

However, witches were always on the lookout for horses to hag ride. Wise horse owners would hang hag stones up in the stable and around their animal's neck, to prevent them becoming *Hagrod.** But all too often horses were left unprotected.

A Cheselbourne farmer found his horse in a terrible sweat every morning, spattered with mud and its mane all tangled. - The animal looked as if it had been ridden fast and far. The farmer put all this down to Ol' Ann Riggs, who was a suspected witch, and also blamed her for the deaths of nine other horses in the same area. No action was ever taken to stop her, so the hag-riding continued until the horse died. Another farmer refused her access to his fields to collect firewood; subsequently the death of his fine herd of cows soon followed. The local witches met in the holy road above the withy beds, to the northwest of the parish towards Melcombe Bingham. One night the witch coven was raided by the local witchhunter general, and his men. All the witches present were arrested, including Ann Riggs. They were taken to the nearest ducking stool and put to death. Ann Riggs was buried just outside Cheselbourne churchyard, but in later years the villagers gave Ann a proper Christian burial, even to the extent of knocking down and rebuilding the churchyard wall so as to include her in consecrated ground.

Like Ann Riggs, witches mainly hag-rode horses to get to and from their *sabbats*† for the besom, or broomstick, was not always their chosen transport. Some witches left their broomsticks at home, transformed to look like themselves in their beds, so to fool their innocent husbands.

They would then use their powers of *transvection*‡ to fly through the air mounted on horses and other animals, including black rams, goats, bewitched men and women, or a variety of other objects such as forks, shovels and even wisps of straw.

The magical energy that transported them came partly from a dark green ointment thickly

---

* *'Hagrod.'* Dorset for Hag Ridden.

† *'Sabbat.'* A gathering of witches for the purpose of celebrating their allegiance to the Devil and Diana the Moon Goddess and indulging in all manner of witchery such as casting spells, dancing and orgiastic sex. Sabbats were once commonly held on the following dates: Candlemas; 2nd February, The Feast of Diana; 12th February, Walpurgis Night; 30th April, Midsummer Eve; 23rd June, Lammas Day; 1st August, All Hallows Eve (Hallowe'en); 31st October, The Feast of St. Thomas (Winter Solstice); 21st December.

‡ *'Transvection.'* The action of carrying or conveying from one place to another.

smeared over their bodies, incorporating such ingredients as bat's blood, soot, hemlock, belladonna, foxglove, mandrake, and a whole host of unknown extracts in a base fat rendered from the bodies of unbaptised children.

Innocent Dorset folk lying awake in their beds at night would often hear the tell-tale whoosh of air from a passing witch in flight, or occasionally glimpse their dark shadows racing across the moon. On such nights when witches soared above the roof-tops people were naturally afraid, but the wise people of Portland had no need to fear.

Many of the old houses were built with a *Hag Seat, Witch Seat* or *Devil's Stool*

(ie, a stone protruding from the gable end of the building), so any witches flying past might rest awhile, and therefore, would not harm the occupants of the house, unlike the young girl at Hilton, seen in a previous chapter, who was molested by a witch.

A Weymouth resident, Mr. Frank Brown wrote to Edward Waring in 1975, that a house had recently been built in Weston, Portland, had such a stone purposely installed as a Witch Seat as the owner of the house wished to continue the custom.

No innocent person ever saw a *Sabbat*, but it was common knowledge that when witches converged on their chosen destination they joined a frenzied orgy of chanting, drinking and dancing where the Devil himself often provided the music.

When the revelry came to a head, all the witches present would engage in promiscuous sex with imps, fairies, demons, and each other, before finally returning to their homes in the manner in which they came to play the innocent wife or daughter once more.

Returned to their normal guises, witches would go about their everyday business - perhaps the school mistress, farm maid, shop assistant, landlady, school girl, and so on, mixing among the innocent who suspected nothing of their witchery.

Hag Stones

These naturally perforated flint stones or pebbles known locally as *Hag Stones* or *Holy Stones,* were often found along the coast - washed up by the passing tides, or disturbed by the plough in fields. In other parts of the British Isles these stones were also referred to as *witch stones*, *fairy stones*, *mare stones* and *eye stones*.

It was once quite common to see these stone baubles hanging above the doors of people's houses, for it was believed by some to prevent entry of witches and evil spirits.

It was customary on farms, to hang or nail (especially if it was made of iron as this increased the stone's power) a hag stone above the stable door, or tied around a horse's neck, to prevent them from being *hag rod*.

In some cases farmers who left their horses or other livestock unprotected would often find their animals in a sweaty and exhausted state with their manes tangled in *hag knots* (a term often used, as it was believed that a witch tied knots in horses manes to use as stirrups). The stones were also believed to protect mares at foaling time, and to protect cows from having their milk magically stolen by witches.

Along the Chesil Bank it was not uncommon for Dorset fisherman to tie, nail, or staple these stones on the bows, close beneath the gunwale of their Lerrets, in order to protect the vessel against the malevolent effects of bewitchment and so determine the outcome of their daily catch. It was once common to see the Abbotsbury fishing boats drawn up along Chesil Beach, each with a hag stone threaded upon the start-rope at the stern. Sometimes when a boat had a run of poor catches, the fishermen, believing their boat had been `over-looked`, would place a mackerel stuck with pins into the hatch to break the spell of ill-fortune.

People would also carry these stones around in their pockets as key-fobs, or tied to a length of cord and hung around their neck, both to protect themselves against the effects of the evil eye, plague, and disease, and to generally safeguard their owner's luck.

At night the hag stones would be hung on bed-posts to keep away the demons such as the night hag, nightmare or succubus, who would invisibly seek out their sleeping victims to steal their strength and cause unpleasant dreams.

At Pimperne, not far from Blandford, there was formerly a turf maze of a unique design. English antiquarian and writer, John Aubrey, writing in 1686 about the Pimperne Troytown, says it was *"much used by the young people on Holydaies and by ye Schoolboies."* The path was bounded by ridges about a foot in height. The maze was destroyed by the plough in 1730.

THE WITCH'S MIZ-MAZE

Leigh is famous for its `Miz-Maze`, sited upon a solitary hillock over-looking the village. The earthwork is a low hexagonal bank about twenty-five yards across with a mound in the centre. This maze was one of many that could be found in villages throughout England many centuries ago. There are other places in Dorset besides Leigh which had mazes. For example, Troy Town near Dorchester, and the Troy Town at Pimperne, which had the largest recorded turf maze, with a complicated and unique meandering design made up of one-foot ridges. Unfortunately this maze no longer exists, as it was ploughed up in 1730. Sometime later the site was used as a cemetery. According to Sir Frederick Treves, the old British name for mazes was *Caertroi* and that *troi* means turning or winding and not to be confused by the Greek City as often thought.

No-one really knows for certain for what reason these mazes were built. It has been suggested that it was a game played by the Romans, that it represented a form of penance or used for seasonal or religious celebrations such as May Day, Midsummer Day or Whitsuntide.

How the Leigh Miz-Maze use to look before it was neglected,

The Miz-Maze was a turf-cut maze, and due to its earth banks forming a hexagonal shape the maze was probably a complicated circular maze design very similar to mazes at Alkborough, Lincolnshire; Hilton, Cambridgeshire and also at Wing, Rutland. The complex pathways of the Miz-Maze were still in existence until the nineteenth century. The Dorset historian, Rev John Hutchins mentions in his book *History and Antiquities of the County of Dorset* in 1744, and states that it was the custom for the young men of the village of Leigh to re-cut the turf paths, and repair the earth banks once every six or seven years. After the maintenance of the maze, celebrations and festivity would take place on the site by the villagers. It would seem that the interest of the games and festivities had declined, so the maintenance of the maze was neglected.

The Leigh Miz-Maze has a connection with witchcraft, and is often referred to as *Witches' Corner* by the local residents of Leigh. William Barnes, the Dorset Dialectologist and poet submitted a short paper about the Leigh Miz-Maze to the *Dorset Field Club's proceedings* (vol. iv, p159) in 1879. In his paper he writes about a man who told him, that a corner of Leigh Common was called *Witches' Corner*. A friend of Barnes later gave him some old depositions on witchcraft taken before the Somerset magistrates during the times of 1650 to 1664. The majority of the cases were in Somerset, though some involved the county of Dorset. One of the witches of the coven said that they met at Leigh Common.

On the top of Slight Hill overlooking the village of Leigh, is the remains of the hexagonal earth banks of the former Miz Maze

However, there may have been an unfortunate mix between the Miz-Maze and Witches Corner, William Barnes may have confused the two Leigh place names from Joseph Glanvill's *Sadducismus Triumphatus* of 1681. He may have mistaken the *Witches Corner* of Leigh Common at Bayford, near Wincanton, Somerset, with the village of Leigh, linking it with the Miz-maze.

But this could be disputed, as the British Museum, London have in their possession an old map which dates back to 1620 in which the words *Witches Coven* can be found near the Miz-Maze, sixty one years before Glanvill's publication.

So whether the witches really *did* exist at Leigh, and held their midnight vigils on the maze, we shall never know, but one can easily imagine that they did, because with a little imagination, their presence can be still felt there on that solitary hill overlooking the village.

THE BELL THEIVES

Although now dominated by the ruins of a Norman Church, the ceremonial religious significance of the mysterious and magical Knowlton Rings extends well back into prehistoric times, when three late Neolithic henge monuments formed the focus of attention.

Built to Christianise what was perceived as an important pagan sanctuary, the ruined twelfth century church at Knowlton is the last surviving building of what was once a large town, which, like so many other settlements, fell victim to the plague - never to be lived in again. In time, the town fell into ruin, until finally only the church remained, with one great bell left hanging in its deserted tower.

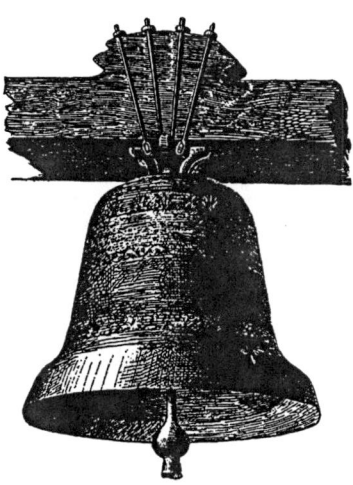

The bell was greatly admired by all the neighbouring parishes. Bell-ringers would often visit it to hear the bell's wonderful chime, but it was only a matter of time before someone thought up the idea of taking it back to their *own* village, and hang it in their *own* church tower, thus making *their* church the envy of all the neighbouring parishes.

The villagers of Sturminster Marshal came up with this idea first, and one winter's night decided to act. Under the cover of darkness, they went to Knowlton, and like thieves in the night removed the great bell. Once it was loaded on to a wagon, made off towards home and safety. A farmer who lived around Knowlton saw what the Sturminster Marshall men were up to, and quickly raised the alarm, but when the mob reached Knowlton church, the thieves were gone.

Their searches were futile in the darkness, so they went to a local witch for help. Her mother had schooled her well for, with her art, she could see *exactly* where the bell was, and where it was heading. The Sturminster Marshall men were nearly home - all they had to do was cross over White Mill Bridge that still spans the river Stour and they would be safe.

The witch acted without further delay. She uttered a magic spell, and at once the horses

The mysterious twelfth century church ruin at Knowlton Rings

White Mill Hole Bridge where the Knowlton bell was lost

pulling the wagon with the bell upon it stopped dead in their tracks, and would not budge an inch further. The Sturminster Marshall men soon realised that their horses had been bewitched. Eager to get the bell to the safety of their own parish, they decided to roll the bell over the bridge themselves.

They were half way across, when they suddenly lost their footing, and the bell rolled out of control, breaking through the stone parapet and with an almighty splash, fell into the river below. The witch smiled in her victory, and told the mob where the bell could be found.

The next day a team of horses and many willing helpers went to retrieve the bell, but no matter how hard they pulled, the bell would not budge, and so could not be recovered from the bed of the river.

> *Knowlton Bell is stole*
> *And thrown into White Mill Hole*
> *Where all the devils in hell*
> *Could never pull up Knowlton bell.*
>
> Old Dorset rhyme
> **J.S.Udal**, *Dorsetshire Folklore* (1922)

Eventually they all gave up trying, and left the bell where it was. And so the bell of Knowlton entered into legend.

MAGICAL JUSTICE

Like their female counterpart, a *Conjuror* or *Cunning Man* was also a witch, who was often respected by the local community for their advice and knowledge. Conjurors would often be willing to use their skills to cast beneficial spells, or to look into the future, for anyone who needed their services. This would often appeal to farmers who wished to be assured of a good harvest, increased milk yield, or for general predictions in weather.

Young girls too would often consult a conjuror to obtain love potions, or a spell to glimpse a future lover. Dorset maidens were often advised to sleep with a sprig of Yew under their pillow, but the girl had to pick it *herself*, at midnight, from a graveyard she had never visited before. Some conjurors stipulated that if the girl was a virgin, she had to pick the plant while entirely naked, and devoid of all body hair!

People afflicted with the palsy, the gout, or other ailments, turned to the local conjuror for advice, or a magic remedy to cure them of their suffering. This would often result in the patient performing some bizarre ritual, or being prescribed some foul-tasting medicine. These bizarre rituals or *Folk Medicine* as they are often termed, would vary from conjuror to conjuror.

A conjuror cut his wand from a tree known for its magical properties; most commonly used were hazel, rowan, or willow. Some conjurors would often mark three crosses on their wand, in order to intensify the wands magic.

Delicate though it seemed, the slender wand was by far the most formidable instrument of all the conjuror tools. With it he could summon up spirits, cast spells or wreak destruction. He could make objects disappear, or reveal to the naked eye things that were otherwise invisible.

If the conjuror was a beneficent practitioner, he might use his wand to liberate the victims of dark forces, heal the sick, test the virginity of young maidens, or identify thieves and murderers.

Powerful a wand might be, but it was *nothing* if the conjuror didn't know how to use it. Conjurors learnt their secret art from so-called *black books* of the occult and ancient lore. From these books they would make their own *grimoire,* or personal magic book. Typical contents of such compendiums described the ceremonial robes and tools to be used in magical ceremonies, the contents of

magic potions, and all manner of spellcraft.

One popular remedy to cure a headache, was for the sufferer to wear a snakeskin under his - or her - hat. For sore eyes, the sufferer was advised to drink water from a spring, rising facing due east, at the precise moment when the sun first casts its rays upon the water. One common cure sought was for warts. The sufferer was told to first pass a silver shilling over the wart and then to steal a piece of meat (usually beef) and bury it under a bramble, or gooseberry bush on the night of the full moon. As the meat decomposed, the wart would gradually disappear.

The conjurors who used their skills for evil intentions were often used by people who had a grievance with a fellow neighbour, or a member of their family, or who had been wrongly accused of a crime they had not committed. Longing for revenge, they sought out the conjuror with the blackest reputation to bring the perpetrator to justice. However, this service wasn't cheap, as it would often involve the crossing of some gold coins or even a part of one's soul.

An incident recorded in *Prodigies in Somerset and Dorset, 1661-2* reprinted in *The Somerset and Dorset Notes and Queries, 1894,* involved the use of a local conjuror in this manner. It occurred one night in the *Greyhound Inn* at Blandford in 1662.

The inn was subjected to a burglary in which the thief stole goods amounting to a considerable value. The local people of the town soon laid the blame on a servant of the house. The servant, unable to withstand these allegations and lies, turned to a conjuror outside the town for help. On meeting the conjuror, he discussed at length his dilemma, and after agreeing a price the conjuror summoned from the depths of Hell the assistance of an evil spirit to go in search of this elusive thief. It did not take long for the spiritual demon to hunt him down! Fifty miles from Blandford, in the City of Bristol, the thief was caught and dragged, by the scruff of his neck, over hills and roof tops, through hedges, ditches and rivers all the way back to Blandford, until at last he came to rest, bruised and battered, with his clothes in shreds, upon a pile of wood beside a house.

The thief lay in agony, until he was discovered by the residents of the town. The thief cried out that the Devil was on his back, and that he had fastened his claws into him. It turned out that the thief was no other than the son of the shoemaker of the town. He was quickly carried home, where laying on his bed in fits of agony he confessed to the crime he had committed. But his torment did not end there - for the demon continued to haunt him, for the stolen goods had not been returned. The poor chap lay locked in his chamber, his cries of pain echoing from his room, until one midnight on the 25th June he was taken away never to be seen again.

The Cross and Hand

THE PILLAR & THE CONJUROR

Near the centre of Dorset, situated on the edge of the Blackmore Vale, is the small village of Batcombe, where two exceptional tales of mystery and intrigue are told. Along the top road of Batcombe Hill, hidden in a verge of dense wild flora, can be found a three foot stone monolith locally known as *The Cross and Hand*.

> *Some say the spot is banned: that the pillar Cross-and-Hand*
> *Attests to a deed of hell;*
> *But of else than of bale is the mystic tale*
> *That ancient Vale-folk tell.*
>
> Thomas Hardy: *The Lost Pyx*

No-one really knows the origin or history of this ancient cross. Some suggest it marks the site where four kings agreed peace by crossing their hands, or to mark the grave of a murderer, who was tortured and put to the gallows. It is said he sold his soul to the Devil and sometimes at night you may see his gaunt, lonely spirit wandering the downs. But one story that stands out from the rest, as told by Thomas Hardy, is the tale of *'The Lost Pyx.'*

A priest from Batcombe was sent one stormy Winter's night, to assist a dying man who lived a distance of two miles away. In haste, the priest took his *pyx** which contained the blessed host and the holy book, and made his journey across the windswept hill.

The Pyx

On reaching the dying man's cottage, to his horror he discovered the pyx was missing. The priest retraced his route, believing he had lost the box on the way. Suddenly, to his amazement in the distance, a pillar of fire reached down from heaven and descended to the ground. The priest drew closer and could see a gathering of wild and domestic animals kneeling in a circle around the light, which shone upon the lost pyx. The priest picked up the casket and went straight back to the dying man. After this event the priest erected a stone pillar on Batcombe Hill in remembrance to the miracle.

Other additions to the story state that while the priest was witnessing this event, he also observed that one of the animals wasn't kneeling properly. The animal was a black stallion and when questioned by the priest, the beast replied:

---

* *'Pyx.'* A box or coffer in which the host or consecrated bread of the sacrament is reserved.

St. Mary Magdalene Church, Batcombe

Conjuring Minterne's Tomb

"Wouldn't kneel at all if I couldn't help it."
"Who then are you?" asked the priest
"The Devil."
"So why do you take the form of a horse?" asked the priest
"So that men can steal me and get hung, and I get hold of them. Got three or four already."

The church of St. Mary Magdalene is at the base of Batcombe Hill, and within the cemetery, there can be found the weather-worn tomb belonging to Squire, John Minterne. The locals nicknamed him `Conjuring Minterne`, for he was known in the village to have dealings with the Devil and the black arts.

One day Conjuring Minterne set out on horseback but had only reached the top of Batcombe Hill when he remembered he had forgotten to put away his book of spells. Afraid someone might see it and take to dabbling with the spells he called upon the aid of the Devil, and turned forthwith back to the village by making his horse take one gigantic leap from Batcombe Hill. The Conjuror glided through the sky on his horse across the village, but the horse's fiery hooves clipped one of the church pinnacles causing it to tumble to the ground.

Conjuring Minterne landed safely in a nearby field close to the church known as the *Pitching Plot* and it is said that the spot where he landed grows no grass to this day!

The pinnacle, which lay by the tower for many years after the event, was thought to bring bad luck upon the village if it was ever replaced. However, in 1906 it *was* replaced, though to this day the pinnacle can be seen leaning crooked! The story does not end there for when Conjuring Minterne died he left strict instructions that his body should be buried neither in the church nor out of it.

With the removal of the Minterne chapel, which was used to rebuild the chancel in 1864, the half tomb covered with rampant ivy looks quite out of place today.

The crooked church pinnacle

The Wandering Cross

Another interesting stone cross, is the fourteenth century Langton Herring Cross. This three foot high limestone cross can be seen from the B3157 turning to Langton Herring, below a low fence hidden in the undergrowth. It is said to make its annual one-mile journey towards the waters of the fleet at midnight on New Year's Eve, just so it can dip its hammer-shaped head into the crystal waters of the lagoon.

MEGALITHS & MONOLITHS ON THE MOVE

Large and weathered by time, ancient standing stones and stone crosses can be found erected in most isolated areas of the Dorset countryside; on open fields, exposed windswept hillsides, hidden from view in dense woodlands and on roadside verges. All have, at one time or another, been regarded by local people with some mysticism and ill omen.

Standing stones are often regarded by some folk as fairy haunts, where concealed beneath these stones lies the entrance to the *Land of Faerie*, or a place where fairy treasure is stored, hidden safe below, away from curious eyes. Fairy folk should therefore be treated with some respect and caution as when the stone casts its moonlit shadow upon the dew sodden turf, fairies are often seen to dance. Like the penalty of entering a fairy ring, however, if an unwary traveller crosses into the stone's enchanted shade, he or she is trapped and forced to revel in the fairy dance for a time spell of usually seven years.

Apart from this close association with fairies and even the Devil in Dorset, they are also regarded as a place of ill omen and sometimes a place which marked the site where a murder was committed, a criminal hanged, or the burial site of a suicide. *The Dead Woman Stone* at Affpuddle, once marked the grave of a woman who committed suicide, and was buried near a crossroads at Throop Heath, but is now thought to rest in a cottage garden at Briantspuddle. One association that is commonly shared by these megaliths and monoliths is the possession of power to move of its own `free-will`.

The parish of Melcombe Horsey, high upon Henning Hill has a long barrow called the *Giant's Grave*. Many centuries ago when Dorset had its own population of giants, there lived two giants who - whenever they confronted each other - argued constantly over who could throw the furthest. One day they decided to hold their own tournament to end this long dispute.

They met at Norden Hill, and selected their chosen missile from the large stones that littered the hillside. Each holding their precious stone, they waited in silence for the first cockerel to herald the dawn, and to signal the start of the contest.

On hearing the first cocks-crow from the nearby village of Cheselbourne, they simultaneously hurled their projectiles over the valley to their target - the summit of Henning Hill - but unfortunately, one of the Giant's stones fell short!

Ashamed of his failure, the losing giant died of a broken heart, and was buried beneath a mound beside his stone upon the western slope of Henning Hill. The stones are said to mysteriously move up to the hill's summit whenever they hear the first sound of a cockerel from Cheselbourne, only to roll back down again.

The Fordington Stone

According to Edward Waring, another stone that has the ability to move, is the large polished limestone block that is situated outside 72 High Street, Fordington, near Dorchester. During the construction of the houses in the early nineteenth century, the stone was removed by workmen and dumped near the River Frome. However, it mysteriously returned the following day!

Perhaps the most unusual tales about standing stones in Dorset are the ones that move for a purpose, as in the standing stone at Ibberton, which is said to have once rolled down from Bell Hill to the village well to drink; only to make it half way back up to a place known locally as Restongate, where it remains to this day. While at Winterborne Abbas, *The Nine Stones** are said to dance on certain days of the year, (probably Good Friday) at three o'clock in the afternoon.

**'The Nine Stones.' See The Devil's Hellstones.*

THE DEVIL'S HELLSTONES

Dorset like many other counties, has its fair share of stone monuments which have, through generations, been associated with folklore and superstition. A common theme that is often associated with them is that of his satanic majesty, the Devil.

The Hellstone or *Portesham Cromlech* is situated on a windswept down between the village of Portesham and The Hardy Monument (actually named after Nelson's captain, rather than the poet, even though they were related). The Hellstone itself is a sarsen stone cromlech*, which was probably constructed in Neolithic times (2500-2000B.C.) and consists of a large sixteen-ton capstone supported by nine uprights.

The legend associated with the Hellstone tells of the Devil who once threw the stone from Portland Pike, the northern end of the Isle of Portland, while playing quoits, a popular mediaeval pastime.

*Cromlech is a Brythonic word (Breton/Welsh) used to describe prehistoric megalithic structures, where crom means "bent" and llech means "flagstone". The term is now virtually obsolete in archaeology, but remains in use as a colloquial term for two different types of megalithic monument.

Picture The Hellstone at it was before an attempted restoration in 1866; an engraving from the first edition of Rev. John Hutchins The History and Antiquities of Dorset, 1774

The Hellstone, Portesham

About half a mile northwest of the Hellstone is a place known as *The Valley of Stones*. It is also suggested the sarsen stones that litter the valley floor were also thrown by the Devil.

Another legend that associates the Devil and standing stones can be found near the village of Winterbourne Abbas. *The Nine Stones,* or *The Devil's Nine Stones*, as they are sometimes known locally, is a stone circle that can be seen sheltered in a wood from the main A35 road.

The stones are thought to be the Devil, his wife and children, - or as another tale suggests, nine children turned into stone by the Devil while playing five-stones on the Sabbath.

The Agglestone or as some people say, The Devil's Night Cap or The Devil's Anvil

The Hoar Stones at Toller Down

The Devil's Stone, Bere Regis

The *Agglestone* or as some people say, *The Devil's Night Cap* or *The Devil's Anvil*, is a five-hundred ton lump of sandstone rock dominating Studland's Godlingston Heath. Legend says, the Devil threw the huge bolder from The Needles on the Isle of Wight in a failed attempt to destroy Corfe Castle. However, other versions of the story make Bindon Abbey and Salisbury Cathedral the target. The two stones known locally as the *Hoar Stones* at Toller Down, near the road turning to Beaminster, are said to have also been thrown by the Devil, but this time in an attempt to obstruct the road.

The Devils Armchair, Corscombe

Other standing stones named after the Devil are the *Devil's Armchair* at Corscombe and the *Devil's Stone*, which lies situated between the parish boundaries of Bere Regis and Turners Puddle on Black Hill.

The two magnificent chalk stacks that project from Studland Bay on the edge of Handfast Point are known locally as *Old Harry and Old Harry's Wif*e. The name *Harry* or *Old Harry* were once familiar names for the Devil, like the old saying, *'To play Old Harry,'* which means, 'to ruin or destroy.' Therefore Old Harry Rocks were so-called as a warning to keep shipping well clear! The land above the cliff edge, in which to view these grand chalk sentinels, is also known as *Old Nick's Ground*. This is another name for the Devil, which was in use in the seventeenth century, and is often thought to be a corrupted name from the German word *'Nickel,'* which means demon or goblin.

Old Harry Rocks, Studland

THE DEVIL'S HUNTING GROUND

To whom the Arch-enemy
(And thence in heaven called Satan).

Milton: *Paradise Lost*

Ever since the introduction of Christianity to Dorset, the Devil has played a primary role in rural folklore. We have seen in previous chapters how the Devil has been associated with the *Ooser*; blamed for the hurling of large stones around the countryside, his involvement with the feats of Squire Minterne, and his appearance in the story of the *'Lost Pyx'*.

Responsible for the evil and wickedness in the world, this supernatural being with mischievous and malevolent activities continues to haunt the imagination. We rarely believe that a horned, fork-tailed demon carrying a pitchfork will manifest itself at will, and take possession of our soul. But in the past this view would have been taken seriously.

The Devil often appeared in many disguises, so he could trick his unfortunate victims into a false sense of security before revealing his true identity. Villagers and townsfolk in North Dorset will always remember a certain incident that took place around the mid-seventeenth century at an old barn situated along a track known as *'French Mill Lane'*, between the town of Shaftesbury and the village of Cann. It was at this secret location that the local lads congregated to drink and gamble.

One Sunday a group of men from the villages decided to meet secretly there to play a game of cards. In those times it was regarded a sin to carry-out *any* leisure activity on a Sunday, and gambling was *especially* forbidden. The young men disregarded this, and once seated, they started to play. When the cards were dealt out, a stranger entered the barn, and asked if he could join in. The man was dressed in distinguished clothes, and had an air of nobility surrounding him. At first he made the young men feel uneasy, but after assessing the stranger, they decided to accept him into the game; all of them hoping to win a large amount of money from this wealthy looking gentleman.

French Mill Lane, where the Devil made an appearance

Half-way through the game it was the stranger's turn to deal. Upon shuffling the deck, he accidentally dropped one of the cards - the *Four of Clubs*.* When he bent down to pick up the card, one of the young men sitting beside him glanced down in horror to see the ebony edge of a cloven hoof. The young man jumped up and shouted to his friends what he had just discovered. The smell of brimstone quickly filled the air, and the young men soon realized who the mysterious card-player was! Terrified, they fled the barn, vowing never to return there, or to play cards again.

A similar tale, warning of the dangers of Sabbath-breaking, happened in the early part of the twentieth century within the grounds of the old priory ruins at Woodcutts, close to the Wiltshire border. Young men from the village of Sixpenny Handley would often go there to play cards, but their afternoon game was interrupted one Sunday by the presence of a large black greyhound, with no ears and saucer-shaped eyes. It dashed across the room, disappearing through one of the priory walls. Some say that this creature may have been Satan himself in disguise.

John Walsh of Netherbury, who we have met in a previous chapter, whilst consorting with fairies, claimed also to have met the Devil - seeing through his many disguises of a black dog, a crow, and a man with a cloven hoof. The Devil demanded John Walsh to bring to him two living things a year, whether they be a chicken, a cat or dog, plus a drop of freshly drawn blood.

---

* *'Four of Clubs.' Known as the 'Devil's bedpost' – the unluckiest card of the pack.*

One unusual guise the Devil has taken, is that of an age-old gorse bush known locally as the *Devil's Bush* near the hamlet of Acton, within the parish of Langton Matravers. How and why it was given this name remains a mystery, but it is possible local people regarded the area around the bush as a place of ill-omen, due to the fact many a misfortune befell anyone who passed the site, and thus blamed the Devil.

If the Devil wasn't too busy attending card games, he would often tempt an unfortunate person with an offer of a lifetime free from financial worries; the only catch would be to exchange your body and soul for it. This once happened to a poor man living at Powerstock.

One evening (but history does not relate when), the man went outside to fetch some water from his well. The night was dark and cold, so he lit a candle to aid him as he made his way down the unlit garden path.

On reaching the well, he slowly lowered the bucket into the dark abyss, and as he stood turning the handle of the crank, the idea of trading his soul to escape his poverty came to him. Suddenly, a voice boomed within the murky depths of the well. *"Have you made up your mind?"*

It was the Devil!

The man stopped cranking the handle and peered deep into the inky depths of the well, where he saw two fiery eyes. The Devil repeated his question again. The man quickly replied. *"Wait 'till I've finished drawing the water. While the candle still burns, it will give me time to think, and then I will give thee an answer."*

The Devil became impatient by the man's reply, so without giving him time for a second thought, he summoned a strong wind that toppled the candle into the well, thus extinguishing the flame. The Devil made the decision for him, and seizing the man by the throat, the Devil quickly pulled him into the mouth of the well - never to be seen again.

Upon the ancient windswept slopes of Eggardon Hill, a man who had sold his soul to the Devil was seen one night many years ago, being pursued across the down by someone whose identity was soon realised by the sparks issuing from his boots!

In the late seventeenth century, the Mayor Jones of Lyme Regis who was hated by many of the local town folk for his persecution of dissenters became the focus of a legend. He lay dying in his bed at the Great House, now known as Chatham House, when there was a sudden almighty crash. The whole gable end of the house had collapsed inwards. When the dust settled the Devil appeared and without hesitation seized the frail body of Mayor Jones.

Another version of this legend explains how after the Mayor's death, his body was taken aboard a ship by the Devil that was leaving Lyme Regis for the Mediterranean. One sailor who encountered the vessel, off the coast of Sicily while sailing back to Lyme Regis from a trading voyage, claimed he saw the ship and the Captain was no other than the Devil himself. He asked where he was bound? The Devil shouted back. *"I'm transporting the body of Old Jones to Mount Etna."* But the ship did not get far, for there was an almighty explosion as it burst into flames to leave a smell of sulphur in the air. It would seem that Mayor Jones finally got what he deserved!

John White who was the rector of Holy Trinity and St. Peter's Church, Dorchester during the seventeenth century, told his parishioners that the Devil once appeared to him when he was the rector of St. Mary's, Lambeth. The Devil appeared one night in his bedroom, and after a long pause the Reverend White told him. *"If thou hast nothing else to do, I have!"* Turning his head to one side he went back to sleep. The Devil, amazed by this remark, disappeared.

The Devil also plagues people with his mischievous pranks. The Blue Pool at Furzebrook, near Corfe Castle, was once a former clay pit, which accounts for a rare phenomenon that has attracted visitors from across the world ever since it opened to the public in 1935. Here, the hornéd one supposedly pushes people into the Blue Pool, while at Cheselbourne an unfortunate man by the name of Tom Trask had the terrible misfortune that wherever he went to bed at night the Devil would bring the ceiling down on top of him!

The Devil is said to push people into the Blue Pool at Furzebrook, near Corfe Castle

Not far from Bridport, we see the Devil has turned his hand to road building. He is said to have laid the long stretch of Roman road that begins at Dorchester, and heads west towards the ancient hillfort at Eggardon, in just one night.

The Devil has also left his mark on the landscape between Thorncombe and Marshwood. Here one can find three clumps of trees known locally as the *Devil's Jumps*. The reason for this unusual name, is that the Abbot of Forde Abbey, after a bitter argument with the Devil, gave him such a hard kick up the rear end that it sent him flying from the Abbey until he landed at the area that is now marked by the first clump of trees. The Devil hit the ground hard and he bounced twice until he finally landed at Birdsmoorgate, where these two areas are also marked by clumps of trees.

Devon people would dispute this, saying that he bounced from Dorset into Devon and then back into Dorset again. There may be truth in this, as before county boundaries were changed, Forde Abbey was in Devon. The people of Bridport would say differently as when the Devil was booted out of the Abbey, he continued to bounce from hill to hill, until he reached the coast at West Bay, where it is said the sea boiled as he plunged beneath the waves.

It's said that the Devil is also responsible for the planting of the dense Yew plantation at Hambledon Hill, which has for centuries been regarded as a place of ill-omen.

At St. Aldhelm's Head near Worth Matravers, there is a hole in a rock stack called the *Devil's Letter-box,* and it is possibly because of this, that St. Aldhelm's Chapel is sometimes known as the *Devil's Chapel.*

The entrance to Hell was once discovered, when some local men at Ibberton near Okeford Fitzpaine, went to dig up some large stones from a field close to the village. They started to dig, but the ground gave way under their feet, and plumes of smoke issued up. Quickly they abandoned their work and left the site, which although it does not exist anymore, was always called the *Devil's Chimney.*

MYSTERIOUS CREATURES

Mysterious creatures, monsters, and fabulous beasts have held a fascination for mankind ever since storytelling began. The creatures of myths and legends which inhabit the landscape of our minds, were first created from man's imagination, superstition, and fear. Despite some of these mythical creatures having being explained as *real* animals combined with an overactive imagination, even now there comes a time when an unusual creature is reported defying all explanation. This is when it becomes hard to separate what is *folklore*, from what is *fact*.

Mermaids and Water Nymphs

Dorset's spectacular coastline is a wealth of pebbles, shells, and fossils, not to mention some of the best golden sandy beaches in the whole of the country. For this reason alone, Dorset has become popular as a holiday destination. Thousands of tourists come every year, just to sunbathe on the beach and swim in the clear blue sea. However, one cannot help but wonder what creatures lie hidden *below* the waves, for the sea has been known to give up more than just the occasional bit of driftwood!

In June 1757, a strange dead creature resembling that of a mermaid was washed up on Chesil Beach at Burton Bradstock. It was seen by the Dorset Historian, Rev. John Hutchins who wrote an account of the creature in his first volume *The History and Antiquities of Dorset.* He says:

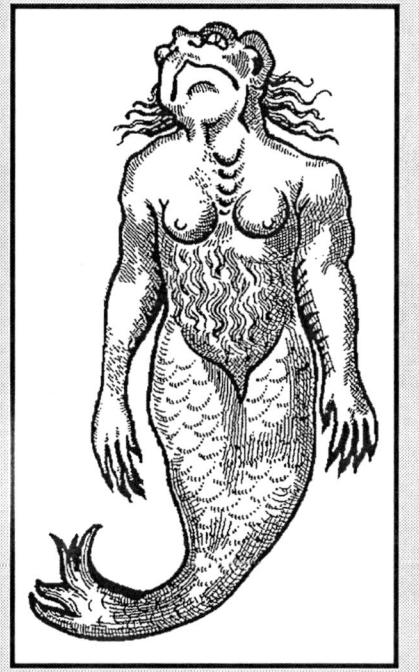

June, 1757, a mermaid was thrown up by the sea, between Burton and Swyre, thirteen feet long. The upper part of it had some resembemblance to human form, the lower was like that of a fish : the head was partly like that of a man, and partly like that of a hog. Its fins resembled hands : it had forty-eight large teeth in each jaw, not unlike those in the jaw-bone of a man.

Church Ope Cove, where once a mermaid was washed ashore

The ruined church of St. Andrew's at Church Ope Cove,
where the body of a supposed mermaid was brought.

According to ancient mythology, mermaids are the daughters of Aphrodite, the goddess of love, whose companion was Dolphin, the king of fishes. Half-woman/half-fish, mermaids traditionally lured mortal men with their beauty and seductive singing. So alluring were these sea-maidens that images of them were often depicted in churches to serve as a warning against the sensual vices.

The Mermaid Boss, Sherborne Abbey

The church at Whitcombe has one such mermaid combing her hair, and holding a mirror, incorporated in a much-faded fourteenth century wall painting. While high up among the Fan Vaults of Sherborne Abbey in the eastern bay, there is another mermaid - with a comb and mirror - carved on a beautiful coloured ceiling boss.

On the southeast side of Portland there is a beautiful little cove called Church Ope Cove. *The Mermaid Inn* above the cove commemorates a mermaid that actually once came ashore there! Some reports say she was there as the people were going to a service at St. Andrew's Church, while others suggest that she was taken up to the church and died at noon. But whatever may be, this incident must have happened many years ago, for the church was abandoned in July 1756 and now lies in ruins.

Dorset's only other mermaid was seen on *Table Rock*, off Old Harry Point, at Studland.

The River Frome starts flowing near the village of Evershot, and heads south to Maiden Newton, before turning eastward. Winding its way through the valleys and fields, it skirts Dorchester, Wool, and Wareham, before finally flowing out into Poole Harbour. However, hidden beneath the Frome's many miles of enchanting beauty, there is a dark tale.

Not far from Wool, sited on the banks of the river, is the now ruined Cistercian monastery of Bindon Abbey. Long before its dissolution, there lived a twelve-year-old boy called 'Lubberlu' who would earn extra money for his family by running errands for the monks. Sometimes, whilst on an errand, Lubberlu would walk along the banks of the river, and on hot days go swimming.

One particularly warm Summer's day Lubberlu was doing just that when out from the bullrushes appeared the most beautiful girl he had ever seen. Her blue eyes sparkled like the sunlight on the water and her silvery hair cascaded like a waterfall. She beckoned Lubberlu to come to her side and kiss her! Captivated by her beauty, Lubberlu instantly stepped forward, and kissed her on the lips, and at once became enchanted.

The River Frome, where Lubberlu met his fate with a water nymph

All that morning he laughed and talked to the girl, but eventually it was time to go. The girl kissed Lubberlu, and made him promise to return the next day and return he did. And the day after, and the day after that! Lubberlu spent many days in the company of the mysterious girl who had captured his heart, for he was head over heels in love.

Autumn approached, and Lubberlu told a monk at the abbey all about the girl, saying how one day he wished to marry her. As Lubberlu spoke more about the girl the monk soon realized that the girl was not an ordinary mortal but a nymphet* of the river - a naiad!† He knew that Lubberlu was in serious danger, for it would only be a matter of time before she revealed her true murderous nymphic nature to him and he told Lubberlu to keep away from her, there could never be any happiness!

When Lubberlu heard this he was horrified. In tears, he ran as fast as he could to the river, calling for the girl. He was never seen alive again! A few days later, Lubberlu's dead body was found tangled among the bullrushes, floating face-down in the river. He had been drowned! Dead at the hands of the nymphet!

But this was not the only encounter with water spirits that can be found within the annals of Dorset folklore.

---

*'Nymphet.' A sexually attractive young semi-divine maiden, of human height generally characterized by a morbid and uncontrollable sexual desire.

†'Naiad.' A class of water nymph inhabiting rivers. With their seductive charm they entice mortal men into their element, where in a mass orgy of carnal lust and pleasure they murder them.

Lulworth Cove is a geological marvel and a perfect natural harbour. Its circular shape, surrounded by high cliffs, is truly an impressive sight; therefore it is no wonder that Lulworth Cove has become a busy tourist attraction. One would hardly believe that this jewel of Dorset could harbour any dark tales, but indeed it does.

Lulworth Cove

Featured in the *Dorset Magazine*, Summer 1968 and article by Jill Curnock Dick. During the mid 1930s, when Lulworth was a peaceful fishing village, a retired naval commander who was sailing along the Dorset coast, sought refuge in the cove for the night. After a trip ashore for provisions, he rowed the short distance back to his converted lifeboat. With the sunlight fading, the silent, deserted, cove took on a bleak and dismal appearance.

About an hour had passed, when suddenly the peace was broken by singing. The Commander slid back the companion hatch and stood listening for a few moments, at what he thought was someone on shore with a radio. However, as he reached to close the hatch a wild crescendo of screams tore across the night air. He leapt up the companion ladder, his heart in his mouth, and desperately sought to penetrate the wall of darkness. The shrieking inferno raged all about him for what seemed like a lifetime, when - abruptly - the screaming stopped, and the cove was deathly silent once more.

Suddenly he saw from out of the water the tiny figure of a young girl walk up onto the shingle beach. The sight of her pale expressionless face and dripping body rising from the waves chilled his blood in an instant.

Once on shore she began to dance a strange jerky, macabre type of dance. Suddenly another girl appeared from out of the water, and then another, and another, until there were about a dozen willowy wraiths, all dancing an utterly joyless dance, *The Dance of Death.** His heart thumping in his chest, the commander stood frozen with fear watching this strange mournful travesty of a childhood game. Many moments passed, then without warning and all at once, the girls went still as if they had been restrained by a deathly, unheard command. Gradually they all grew faint and disappeared, leaving the curved beach just as before.

Who were these girlish nymphets? *Sea ghosts*,† perhaps, but whoever they were, they left the retired naval commander in a state of shock and shaking with terror.

---

* *'Dance of Death.'* A representation of Death, – dancing skeletons or corpses.
† *'Sea ghosts.'* The spirits that haunt the foreshore were much feared by the living, for it was believed it was the sea's sign that it wanted fresh bodies.

Sea Monsters and Strange Water Beasts

Sea monsters too have been known to come ashore! One such monster was discovered on Weymouth Sands in October 1752. It was reported to be fifty feet long and twelve feet wide, its tongue was likened to a large feather bed, and its mouth was wide enough to swallow a coach and horses. When the creature died, its belly was cut open, and over thirty thousand fish leapt out. Many thousands of people flocked daily from miles around to see the monster, and the owners expected to make 120 hogsheads (1860 gallons) of oil from it! This was presumably a whale, possibly a bowhead - a peculiar looking North Atlantic species - which would have been less familiar to the locals than other, more conventional, whales. However, the bowhead is a plankton eater, so it would be unlikely to have so many fishes in its belly, unless, of course, they were actually krill.

The golden sands of Weymouth beach, where a large creature was once washed ashore

Llewellyn Pridham in his book *The Dorset Coastline* (1954) mentions a sea monster that was once washed ashore along Chesil Beach during the nineteenth century. It was thought, at the time, to be a type of sea serpent as it had a very long neck and a snake-like head. However, the inquisitive were soon disappointed, for the monster turned out to be a camel - the animal had clearly been dead for some time!

Living monsters are rarely seen, but in 1457, documented in Raphael Holinshed's *Holinshed's Chronicles* (1577), a strange creature was witnessed emerging from the sea near Portland.

The account is as follows: -

> *"In the moneth of November 1457, in the Ile of Portland not farre from the town of Weymouth, was seen a cocke coming out of the sea, having a great creast upon its head and a red beard, and legs half a yard long: he stood on the water & crowed foure times, and everie time turned him about, and beckened with his head, toward the north, the south and the west, and was of colour like a fesant, & when he had crowed three times, he vanished awaie."*

Another mediaeval sea monster, was seen in the channel by a ship full of French monks sailing towards England. The five-headed sea dragon emerged from the sea, and flew towards Christchurch to attack the abbey with its burning sulphurous breath. So frightened by what they had witnessed, the visiting monks sought refuge in a nearby harbour. The *Laon Canons* recorded that the *"whole town had caught fire...a dragon had come out of the sea...had flown to the city, breathing fire out of it's nostrils".*

Not *all* sea monsters were sighted centuries ago. A Weymouth resident Mr. Martin Ball allegedly witnessed a strange aquatic creature off Chesil Cove, Portland one night in August 1995. On 23rd November 1995 in a Radio interview with *BBC Dorset FM* reporter Emma Clements he recounts his encounter with Chesil Beach Monster.

Chesil Cove, Portland, where a strange creature was sighted

Martin Ball: *"I was here at Chesil after Midnight sometime in August, I can't remember the exact day and was looking at Portland and suddenly I saw something. There was a little bit of moonlight, it was quite cloudy, but I saw something and thought I'm going crazy, I must be going crazy. Subsequently I was doing some research, doing some writing work in Weymouth Library and I came across two other reports of the Chesil Beach Monster, the Dorset historian Hutchins, its in his first volume. The monster according to him is supposed to be half fish half human and half hog. Now what I saw that night in August resembles that very closely. The monster or mermaid as it is sometimes called, was half fish on the bottom with some black stripes against a silver shimmery white background and the upper half of the torso, the upper half of the body was rather like a giant sea horse, I suppose you could say and then the sea horse had lots of hair and it appeared through each lock of hair that there was a hag, you know, the pebble stones you can fined on Chesil Beach with a hole in the middle".*

Emma Clement: *"So how far away was it from you?"*

Martin Ball: *"I would say that the monster was 50 metres away".*

Emma Clement: *"How big was it?"*

Martin Ball: *"Much bigger than a person. I would say three or four times the size of the average person"*

Emma Clement: *"Now some people, obviously are going to be sceptical about this, what would you say to them?"*

Martin Ball: *"So was I, I thought it was my state of mind at the time. I saw what I saw, and I was stunned, and very surprised. But now that I found that other people have seen the Chesil Beach Monster, I know for full well I saw it too."*

More recently in May 1997, the HM Coastguard reported seeing an unidentifiable large sea creature, also off Chesil Beach.

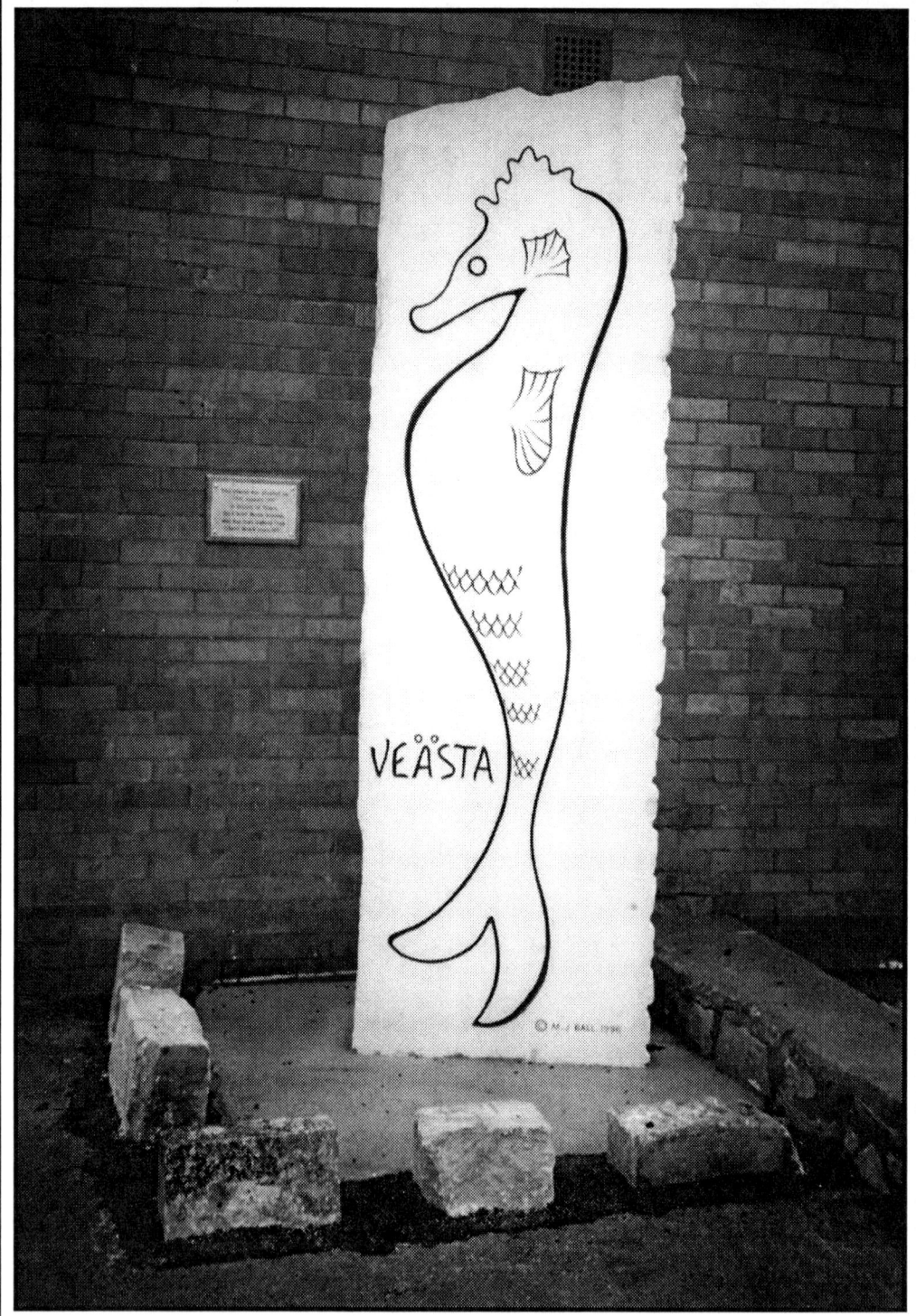

Erected in 1996, the Portland stone monument depicting the
Chesil Beach Monster stands outside the Ferry Bridge Inn, Weymouth

Apart from the famous Loch Ness Monster, there are many more tales of mysterious water creatures that haunt the lakes, lochs, and rivers, of Britain. At Poundbury, near Dorchester, tradition tells of a large lake - now long disappeared - fed by the River Frome, which was once inhabited by terrifying monsters, *'big things with fins'* as one old lady, a resident of Dorchester once said. There could well be some truth in this, as the largest fish to have been ever caught on a rod and line in British inland water, was caught by Major Charles Robert Eustace Radclyffe of Hyde House, Bere Regis, in the River Frome near Bindon Abbey in 1911. Radclyffe was a notable sportsman, who also started the breed of yellow Labrador retrievers – bred from black labradors

'big things with fins'

Here is Major Radclyffe account on how he caught the monster of the River Frome:

"Early in the season I was fishing the lower waters of the Frome for salmon with a friend. Shortly after we had started, my friend came running wildly towards me across the meadows, as if chased by a mad bull. Breathlessly he explained that he had seen the biggest salmon in the world... I reasoned with him that even a 40-pound salmon looked 'some fish' in a small river like the Frome. Whereupon he swore solemnly that this fish was a least 140lbs. As the old saying goes 'seeing is believing', so we went to the spot, and soon in the centre of the pool appeared a huge back fin shaped like that of a shark. A closer inspection showed the back of an enormous fish, which my friend had clearly underestimated at 140lbs. But this great back with scales like armour plating... was familiar to me, since I had killed sturgeon in Russia, and hence was able to say at once that my friend is a sturgeon, and a big one; but how to land him on our light tackle is more than I can say. Repeatedly the monster rolled on top of the water close between our feet, and finally we decided to borrow a gun and shoot the fish.

We waited until the fish again showed on top of the water, and then gave him both barrels in the head at a distance of five yards. The only result was to make him take a series of wild rushes across the stream... Seeing that big things required strong measures, I sent my car... home for an elephant rifle, and we waited. Just before the rifle arrived the fish disappeared in a deep pool, and although we patrolled the river, and had scouts out looking for him for days afterwards, we did not then find further traces of the fish, and decided he must have returned to the sea.

Two months later, a man arrived from Bindon Abbey with a request that I would go next morning to try and catch the biggest salmon in world, which was then in a big weir pool. From the man's description I had no difficulty in deciding that here was our long-lost sturgeon.

Early next morning, armed with the strongest rod and line I possessed, and having rigged up a grappling tackle of the largest-sized salmon flies, a party of five of us stood watching the weir pool. After an hour's waiting, there suddenly appeared the great shark-like fin, and then the back of our friend the sturgeon.

Since a sturgeon belongs to the family of bottom-feeding fish, it was obviously impossible to hook this one with any form of bait. Hence it became a problem of casting over the monster and trying to get the hooks to grapple in some soft spot. This was no means easy owing to the thickness of its skin and armour-plated scales. Finally, however, I grappled the fish under the jaw, and then the fun began. For one hour and forty five minutes I and a friend took turns at the rod, as the continuous strain on one's arms was more than one man could stand for long; and at last it felt like trying to hold or turn a motor car with a rod and line.

As a last resource we had to requisition services of a small seine net, and floating it down stream until the fish struck into it... The fish tangled itself up like a fly in a spider's web, and was thus hauled into shallow water. It took three men with two gaffs to land this leviathan, which measured no less than nine feet three inches from nose to tail; verily the largest fish ever captured with rod and line in an English river.

An amusing incident occurred as the fish was landed. A local labourer arrived with a towel on his shoulder for a morning bathe. On seeing the fish he said, 'Lord, zur, do ee think there's another of they girt brutes about, cause if 'tis I bain't agoin' to bathe in thik pool agean,' and I don't believe he has done so since."

The monster fish caught by Major Radclyffe is displayed in the Dorset County Museum

The Strange Tale of the Shapwick Monster

On October 12th 1706, in the parish of Shapwick, a travelling fishmonger from Poole, bound for Bere Regis, accidentally dropped a crab on the outskirts of the village (a farm nearby commemorates this event adeptly named *Crab Farm,* which has a celebrated wind-vane showing the crab and villagers). The villagers, strange as this might seem, had never seen a crab before, and they all believed it was some kind of Devil or monster, and so armed themselves with sticks and pitchforks in an attempt to drive away the creature.

The fishmonger, noticing the crab was gone, immediately traced his steps back to Shapwick, and on arriving back was amazed at all the commotion and disturbance the creature was causing. Amused by their ignorance, he casually picked up the crab, put it back in his basket, and continued on his journey, thus spreading the word of the dim-witted villagers of Shapwick.

Since then, the villagers of Shapwick are referred as *'Wheeloffs'* and were looked upon as a bit simple and daft. No-one from the famed village dare visit a fishmonger stall at the local markets in fear of being ridiculed. Therefore, the stigma remains today - at least that is what some may like to believe.

J. S. Udal's publication *Dorsetshire Folklore* (1922) includes a similar tale, although the monster is identified as a tortoise or lobster. Interestingly he also mentions that, as a proverbial saying, *"A Shapwick Monster"* is something too extraordinary to be explained.

Crab Farm at Shapwick commemorates where the strange incident took place

The story is best remembered in this amusing poem, which was published in 1841 accompanied with illustrations by Buscall Fox

THE SHAPWICK MONSTER

In every clime and country known,
'Tis held men most esteem their own;
Each County Town and Parish too,
Still hold tenacious to this view;
Wher'er we go, wher'er we roam,
The mind still fondly turns to home;
And though when jokes we tell of others,
There's scarce a man his laugh who smothers,
Against our birth but be the laugh
We think the jokes too bad by half;
Forgetting "unto others do
As you would have them do to you."
Thus of the Parish where befell
The tale I am about to tell,
I speak of Crabs they straight grow Crabbed,
And foam at mouth like a dog that's rabid:
Strange to take umbrage at a word
More than a century on record,
Made every Bumpkin run away.
No joking matter then but rather
A terror 'twas to son and father,
But brevity is the soul of wit,
Drop we our moralizing fit,
Against others faults no more we'll rail
But tell our plain unvarnished tale.

Once on a time, some years ago,
A Fishmonger it happened so,
His fish to sell o'er common wide,
Was forced against his will to ride,

For Blandford folk (so says my tale), he
Had like his fish found rather scaley,
And trotting on, by fortune crossed,
One of his finest Crabs he lost,
This happened on his road to Bere
Near Shapwick town, in Dorsetshire.
'Twas eve, the sun was going down.
When from his work a country clown,
Trudging along in simple nature,
By chance, trod on the crawling creature;
He found .it more with sudden start,
Against his bosom bumped his heart,
Whilst panic fear assail'd his mind
Sideways, like Crab, he crawled behind,
And horror-struck in every feature,
He gaped upon the wondrous creature.
So strange the monster did appear
He thought the devil himself was there.
His hair erect stood bolt upright,
As if he'd really seen a sprite,
He stood and viewed it at a distance,
Then thought he'd hasten for distance,
"I'll run", qoth he, "to Shapwick town,
And there I'll make the wonder known."

Away he ran, and one by one,
He told them, every mother's son,
The hirrid zite that he'd a-zeen,
Crawling upon the common green.
Enough, the country all did hie

The hideous monster to decry,
With stick and stone the silly elves
For their defence did arm themselves,
And confident in all their strength
The monster went to find a length,
But when the place in sight appears,
The scene of all poor Bumpkins fears,
Old Hobson who before had found him
Cried, "There, that's he, let's all surround him
For he's as zwift of foot, I'm zure
He's got a dozen legs or more,
With hooked claws upon his feet all,
And pinchers like a great black beetle."
The Crab a thymy bank had found,
And crawling on the fragrant ground
Still met their fearful eyes regards,

Tho' distance, at least fifty yards,
Then each to other of them swore
They'd never zeen the like before.

At length out spoke the Farmer John,
"Neighbours, I never look'd upon
So strange a zite as this afore.
And hope I never may no more;
Nobody knows from whence he came,
And not a zoul o' us knows his name.

Now Shepherd Rowe is the likeliest man
To tell his name if any can;
In Shapwick Parish there can't be
A cuter man than he can be,
But how to get him, there's my fears,
For he's been bed-ridden now six years."

However, to his house they went,
And told the sage their full intent,
Hoping their suit he'd not deny,
But go the monster to descry.
The Shepherd, struck with vast surprise,
Was first unwilling to arise,
But the recital of their fear
At length so wondrous did appear,
That he upon their earnest prayer
Consented to be carried there.

But of the joke now comes the marrow,
They wheel'd him there in a wheelbarrow
Such was the couch procured in haste,
Coaches in Shapwick ain't the taste,
And now a careful driver found,
For steady wheeling high renowned,
They in the barrow placed the sage,
Whose head was silver'd o'er with age,
And on they went, with all the town

The wind vane at 'Crab Farm' celebrates the story showing the frightened villagers in hot pursuit of the Shapwick Monster

Encircling the poor Shepherd round;
But when the Crab the Shepherd saw,
Each crooked leg, each ponderous claw,
Near thirty yards from where it stood,
The sweat of fear his face bedewed,
And knowing that he could not fly,
He feared the man might wheel too nigh,
And roar'd aloud half choked with cough,
"Tis a land monster, wheel me off!"
And terror-struck exclaim'd again,
"Wheel off, wheel off, or we're all dead men!"

Just at that time the man came back,
Who lost the Crab from his pack,
He saw the Crab you will not ask it,
Seized it and flung it in his basket.

Amazement seized the admiring crowd,
Who thus their fears expressed aloud-
"Take care, he'll bite, you've caught the Devil!"
"Pooh, Pooh," replied the man quite civil,
"If Devil he is, as I am a sinner,
I'll eat the Devil for my dinner."

But when they all perceived the man
Feared not the monster, each one ran
In haste the wondrous sight to view,

Asked how he risked to catch it too?
The Fishmonger with wide opening eyes
Expressed his sovereign surprise,
As with a sneer he thus replies-

"You silly fools, can it be true
A fish so common you don't know?
This is a Crab caught in the sea,
This morning it was lost by me,
So many fools upon the green
At one time sure was never seen."

Confounded they on each did look,
And rapidly the Down forsook,
Leaving the Fishmonger the pleasure
Of laughing at them at his leisure.

But ever since the shapwick folk,
By no means relish this same joke;
Like an old sore under scab,
They hate the very name of Crab
And each his coat is sure to doff,
At those empatic words, "Wheel me off!"
If one but speaks them as he passes,
'Tis ten to one he's mobbed by asses,
For ignorant fools all Banke's Mappick,
You'll find none can compete with Shapwick.

Creatures of the Night

Perhaps the most startling claim, is mentioned in Janet and Colin Bord *Alien Animals* (1980), of an unusual animal seen in Branksome between Bournemouth and Poole. At approximately 3.30 am on the 7th April 1974, Mrs. Joan Gilbert observed a dog-like creature loping across Western Avenue. She said: 'it had stripes, a long thin tail, and it seemed to be all grey, though it might have had some yellow on it. It was thin and definitely not a fox'. She later identified the creature from an illustrated book. The animal that best fitted her descriptions was a Tasmanian marsupial wolf, or thylacine! These are officially native only to Tasmania, and are classified as having been extinct since 1937, although continued reports suggest that they survive not only on Tasmania, but on mainland Australia, and even on the island of New Guinea. How one could have arrived in Dorset, however, is anyone's guess. The animal was most likely a fox with the distressing skin complaint mange; with a diagnostic loss of hair making its body appear dull and grey and suffering from starvation, the stripes could have been mistaken for its ribs.

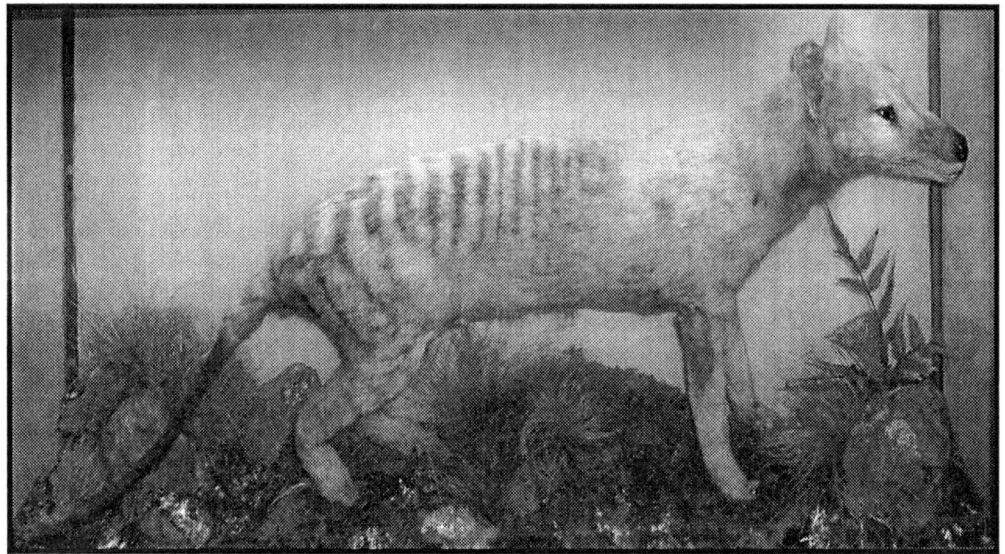

Was a Thylacine, like this stuffed specimen, seen wandering the streets of Branksome?

In her article 'The Folklore of Sixpenny Handley' featured in the Folklore Society Journal, *Folklore, vol 74 (*Autumn 1963). Aubrey L. Parke tells the story of a man making hurdles at Eastcombe in Cranborne Chase the story of a man making hurdles at Eastcombe in Cranborne Chase, who saw a great dark bird, larger than an eagle, flying towards him. It landed close by, but then seemed to disappear into a heap of brushwood. Soon other witnesses saw what they described as a massive, mystery bird of prey that was feasting on a sheep carcass. The black bird, with a three-foot wingspan, had been glimpsed in the early hours around Puncknowle. Local people believed that it was an eagle, but experts suggested that it might have been a raven.

Peter Bunyan saw the bird, while taking his dog for a walk in fields near Springfield Road.

"When I first saw it in the middle of a field, I thought it might have been a large hare or something like that but I tapped on the gate and it flew away. My first thought was perhaps it was an eagle of some sort, but you do not get eagles of that size in our neck of the woods. Sea eagles have not been spotted here for 80 or 90 years. I assume it is a bird of prey but I have no idea how it ended up in a field in Puncknowle. This is a popular spot for people in the village to walk their dogs and I would be interested to find out what it might be."

Emma Parkin, spokesman for the Royal Society for the Protection of Birds, said: "This is news to us, nobody has contacted us about this creature. It sounds like a captive bird has got out of someone's private collection. It could be a raven. They are the largest of the crow family and are solitary birds that are black all over and not commonly seen around Bridport. They are around at this time of year and might have a go at a sheep."

Wolves no longer roam wild in this country. They were hunted to extinction over two hundred hundred years ago. It's not surprising, therefore, that folk stories and tales of *lycanthropy** are particularly rare in this part of the world.

One exceptional 20th Century story in Dorset, from *Secret Dorset* by Clive Gunell *et al.* (1995) concerns a lady, and the arrival at her house of her niece, who had recently arrived back from Africa.

On one particular occasion during her stay, the niece gave strict instructions to her aunt that she should be locked in her room at night, and that it should remain locked - whatever the circumstances - until the morning. Intrigued by her niece's strange but innocent request, she agreed to do so. Around two o'clock in the morning, the aunt was woken in alarm by the terrible sounds of clawing and heavy breathing echoing from her niece's bedroom. The aunt considered whether she should go and find out what on earth was making the infernal racket, but hesitated as she glanced at the key to her niece's bedroom.

The terrifying sounds grew faint as the morning twilight arrived. The aunt, who was in a semi-doze, soon became aware of the quiet, and quickly went to her niece's bedroom. After pushing the door open, she gasped in horror to see that the room had been wrecked! Wallpaper hung in shreds from the wall, and bedclothes lay strewn about the floor; torn and ripped, while the mattress lay behind the door, with marks of long, savage, slashes in the fabric. In the debris lay her niece, naked and hunched on all fours like an animal.

After her niece had cleaned up and rested, she explained to her aunt that while in Africa she became involved in some of the native's religious ceremonies and rites. A witch doctor told her that if she left Africa, then on certain nights when the moon was full she would turn into a wolf! After that night, the niece regretting what had happened, immediately left for Africa. The problem is, that according to Richard Freeman, Zoological Director of the Centre for Fortean Zoology, the only wolf species in Africa is an extremely rare species from Ethiopia, and that was only discovered to be a wolf rather than a jackal very recently.

---

* *'lycanthropy.' From the Greek lukos; wolf, anthropos; man. The mysterious process in which a human turns into a beast namely a wolf during the night and reverts back to human form at sunrise. Other forms of Lycanthropy can be found in witchcraft. - See Work-A-Day Witchery.*

Spectral Black Dogs

Whilst investigating *zooform phenomena** in this county, I discovered that there appear to be two main types of spectral dog roaming the Dorset countryside: the pack of hounds associated with the wild hunt, and the large solitary black dog.

The black dog is perhaps the most familiar in Dorset, and appears in three distinct incarnations: as an elemental spirit, a guardian, and a harbinger of death.

Accounts of spectral black dogs turn up with extraordinary regularity in the British Isles. Devon, Somerset, East Anglia, Lincolnshire, Yorkshire, and Worcester, *all* boast of having at least one Black Dog sighting, some of which date back many centuries. The most famous is the *Black Dog of Bungay*, which appeared to a terrified congregation of St Mary's Church in 1577, during a terrific thunderstorm, killing two of them as they knelt at prayer; injuring and disfiguring another.

Though these supernatural creatures differ from county to county with their names, they all share the same qualities. They are usually distinguished from other domesticated dogs by their large appearance; usually the size of a calf, with a black shaggy coat; huge fiery saucer-shaped eyes, and their strange behaviour of vanishing at will. Black dogs are known to patrol distinct routes, which follow ancient pathways and boundaries. They can also be found *blocking* a path; barring entrances to a gate, stile, or road, to prevent travellers from proceeding further on their journey.

The black dog can take many forms, and is often regarded as the Devil, a witch, a fairy, a messenger, a guardian of buried treasure, a protector of lost travellers, a churchyard grim†, or even Death itself.

**zooform phenomena* These are not animals at all, but are entities or apparitions which adopt or seem to have animal or part-animal form. This is where we, at least partly, enter science fiction territory. In many ways, these elusive and contentious entities have plagued the science of cryptozoology since its inception - and tend to be dismissed by mainstream science as thoroughly unworthy of consideration. Zooform phenomena seem to be a mysterious blend of paranormal manifestation and mythological icons.

However Jonathan Downes, a Devon-based investigator of mystery animals who first coined the term in 1990, also maintains that many zooform phenomena are the result of complex psycho-social and sociological phenomena, and suggests that to condemn all such phenomena as being "paranormal" in origin is counter productive.

† *Churchyard Grim*. In the past it was common practice for a dog, preferably black, to be killed and buried on the north side of the churchyard so that its ghost could protect the souls of the deceased from the Devil. The term reached more people than ever in 1999, when it appeared in the third volume of the Harry Potter series by J.K. Rowling.

The last guise; the most commonly associated with the black dog, is that its pedigree can be traced as far back as ancient Egypt, to *Anubis* (pronounced *An-you-biss*), the much feared jackal-headed god of embalming. It was his task was to take the souls of the dead before the judge of the infernal regions. In Aztec mythology the god *Xolotl*, (pronounced *Show-low-tull*) is often portrayed as a man with a dog's head. He is said to have created a protector and guide for humans in the underworld in the form of the hairless dog, the Xoloitzcuintle (pronounced *show-low-its-queen-tlee*). In ancient Greek mythology, the death dog appears too, as the ferocious three-headed dog known as *Cerberus* (pronounced *Sir-ber-us*) whose task was to guard the gates of the underworld of Hades, to prevent the dead from escaping. Even in Norse mythology, we have a similar hound, *Garmr* (pronounced *Garm*) who was a huge black hound with a blood spattered breast, and eyes of burning coals. He watched over the gates of *Hel*,* where he ushered the souls of the dead into the underworld.

Looking up the words *Black Dog* in any modern English dictionary, one can find that the definition now means to become depressed or melancholy as in the expression *'The Touch of the Black Dogs'*, or in old country sayings, such as *'The Black Dog is at his heels'*, which meant that a person was about to die. Sir Winston Churchill often referred to his moods of depression as his 'black dogs'.

> **blackdog**. 1. melancholy, depression of spirits; ill humour. In some country places, when a child is sulking, it is said 'the black dog is on his back'.
>
> (Oxford English Dictionary)

In Dorset, stories of black dogs that can foretell illness or death are said to haunt the Black Down around The Hardy Monument, near Portesham, and the road between Drimpton and Broadwindsor at midnight.

However, there are two exceptional recorded incidents of a black dog appearing as a harbinger in Dorset. The first - and earliest - account, was told by an elderly lady living in Bridport in 1915. She recounted. that one Sunday, after attending church, a woman and her companion were making their way home along a quiet lane, when the woman was suddenly jolted by what she described as, *'A girt black dog so big as a donkey,'* rushing past her. Turning quickly to her friend she said. *"What's that?"* only to glimpse the creature as it disappeared, leaving the woman profoundly shaken by the experience and her friend very puzzled. It was not until the woman reached her home that she found her daughter had died during her absence. She understood the dog to have been a portent.

The second and most recent recorded account of a harbinger once appeared to a Beaminster woman in 1957. She described seeing a large black dog with long ears and large staring eyes that walked around her several times before disappearing. Within two months she was dead.

Stories of Black Dogs as portents of death have been suggested to inspire Thomas Hardy in his novel *Far from the Madding Crowd* (Chapter 40). In which the poor feeble Fanny Robins, whilst in ill health struggling towards Casterbridge (aka Dorchester) Union House, meets a

---

* *In Norse mythology, the underworld realm 'Hel' shares a name with its ruler, Hel the goddess of the dead*

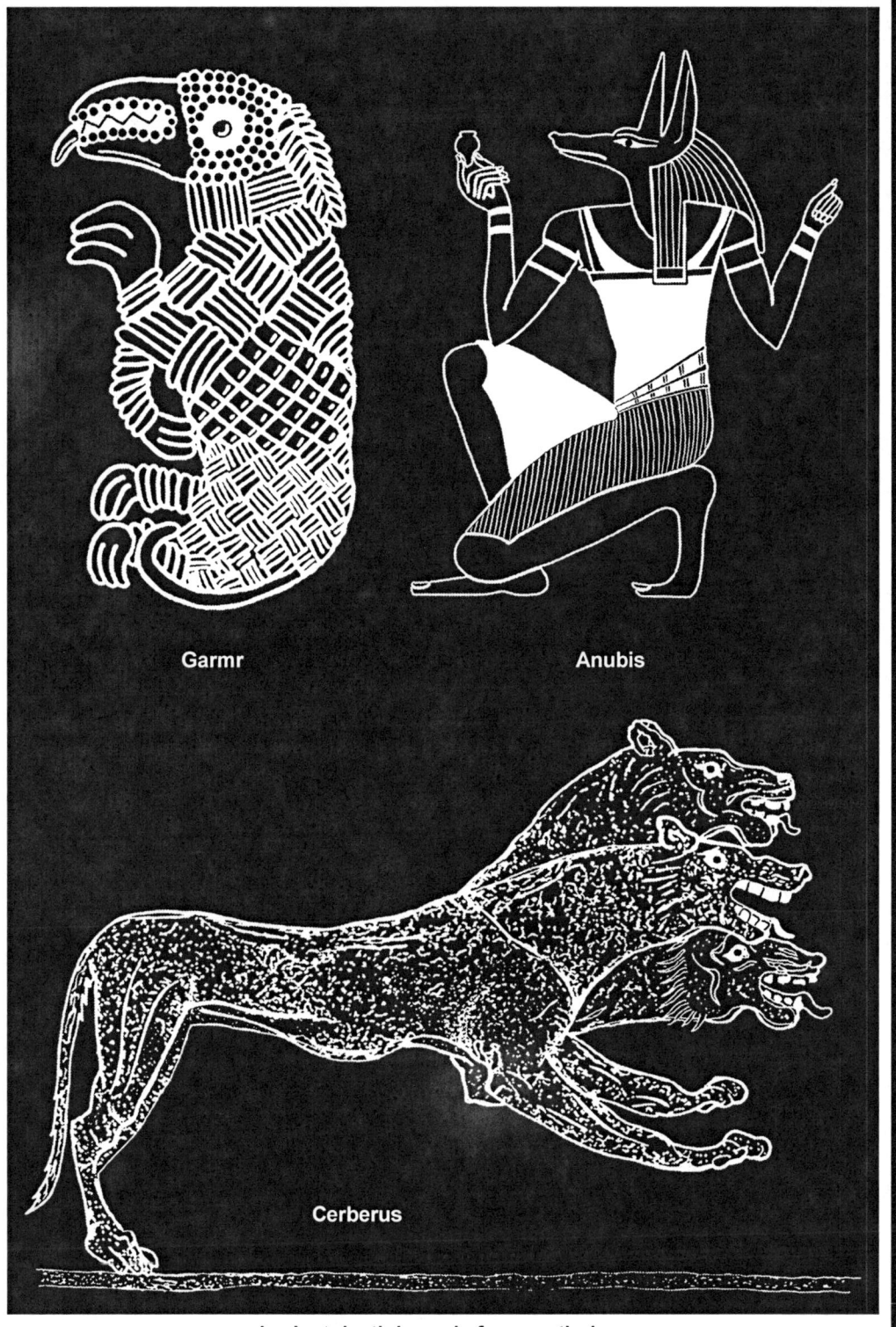

Ancient death hounds from mythology

mysterious dog at Grey's Bridge.

"From the stripe of shadow on the opposite side of the bridge a portion of shade seemed to detach itself and move into isolation upon the pale white of the road. It glided noiselessly towards the recumbent woman.

She became conscious of something touching her hand; it was softness and it was warmth. She opened her eye's, and the substance touched her face. A dog was licking her cheek.

He was a huge, heavy, and quiet creature, standing darkly against the low horizon, and at least two feet higher than the present position of her eyes. Whether Newfoundland, mastiff, bloodhound, or what not, it was impossible to say. He seemed to be of too strange and mysterious a nature to belong to any variety among those of popular nomenclature. Being thus assignable to no breed, he was the ideal embodiment of canine greatness -- a generalization from what was common to all. Night, in its sad, solemn, and benevolent aspect, apart from its stealthy and cruel side, was personified in this form. Darkness endows the small and ordinary ones among mankind with poetical power, and even the suffering woman threw her idea into figure"

The friendly dog accompanies her on her way. She reaches the door of the Union House where she suddenly collapses from exhaustion. Later someone appears and takes the pathetic figure inside. We only learn later in the next chapter of the novel that Fanny has died.

Was Hardy trying to use this dog as a metaphor for his character's impending doom? It would not be surprising, as well as a writer and poet, Hardy also collected folk tales and traditions of the county and used them extensively in his works, at a time where superstition and customs was a common part of every day of country life.

Apart from its guise of foreboding, the black dog's fame has often been greater in parts of the country where it has a name, for example the Black Shuck of East Anglia and the Gytrash of Lancashire.

At the southernmost tip of the Isle of Portland, near a place known as *'The Bill'*, there is a hole close to the cliff edge that forms a natural twenty-foot cavern known as Cave Hole. This is the lair of the *Roy Dog*, and during extreme stormy weather it is advisable to keep well away from this place as some unfortunate souls have been woofed down into his dark domain.

In one of Cecil *'Skylark'* Durston's poems from his 1987 collection *Tales from the Ragged Louse* (the `ragged louse` is - by the way - not a tatty invertebrate from the Order: Phthiraptera, but a Dorset boozer), he tells the following gruesome tale. Once, three friends - Ned, Dick and William - went fishing on the ledges near to Cave Hole, but after a full day of sport they caught nothing more than a dogfish between them.

At sunset, Ned and Dick decided to call it a day and go home, but stubborn William was defi-

The entrance to Cave Hole

The Lair of the Roy Dog, the naturally formed blowhole above Cave Hole

ant and said that he would not leave until he had caught a worthy catch.

Ned and Dick went on their way and as they crossed the common they met the lighthouse keeper. *"Be clear before dark!"* he exclaimed. *"I fear evil is a brewing tonight, for the lamp is not working right."* And he explained to Ned and Dick that he had been up and down the stair a dozen times, but he couldn't fathom out what was wrong. Ned and Dick shrugged their shoulders, and left the lighthouse keeper with his problem.

On the way home they stopped at Culverwell for a drink of water, when suddenly they were startled to see the silhouette of a huge limping black dog coming their way.

Realising it was the `Roy Dog`, Ned and Dick quickly hid behind some bushes, and watched trembling with fear as the creature bathed its injured paw before it limped off into the darkness. Both men describe the animal as if it came from a H. P. Lovecraft novel; a shaggy black dog, as high as a man, with large fiery eyes, one green, one red. Entwined in his mane of dark fur could be seen the freshly-plucked eyes of his victims. With the Roy Dog on the prowl, the two men fled for their lives, and did not stop until they were safely home.

The next morning word soon reached them that William had not returned home. Ned and Dick rushed off to Cave Hole, fearing the worst, but hoping they would find William safe and well, and still fishing. However, when they reached Cave Hole, they found William stone dead; his face all twisted in a state of abject terror as if he had seen something so horrific that it had caused him to expire. But his eyes were not there at all; for they had been plucked clean out from his head. His hands were still gripped firmly to his fishing rod, and when Ned reeled in the line they found on the hook, a sliver of flesh, and dangling from it a claw!

William had caught more than he had ever bargained for, for it seems he had hooked the Roy Dog.

The *Row Dog* of the Isle of Portland - probably another version of the name `Roy` and most likely the same creature - appears during the hours of darkness` and prowls the island without any particular purpose, though, if you encounter it, you are confronted by a huge black shaggy dog, the size of a man, with large penetrating saucer shaped eyes. His particular habit is not to attack you, but merely to obstruct your way snarling and barking aggressively.

Suggestions behind the origin of the name of the Roy Dog may lie in Anglo-Saxon myth. According to Germanic belief, the *Roggenwolf* (`Rye Wolf` or `Corn Dog`) are spirits of the fields and the movement of a swathe of ripe corn is attributed to these invisible spirit animals. During harvest time the animals would seek to escape the scythe and take refuge in whatever sheaf was left standing. This sheaf held the spirit of the corn till the following year. Therefore, we have a striking similarity in name between the Roy dog and the Rye wolf. However, the Roy Dog behaves not unlike a water fairy that hides in ponds, streams, rivers or lochs waiting to lure their victim to their watery demise.

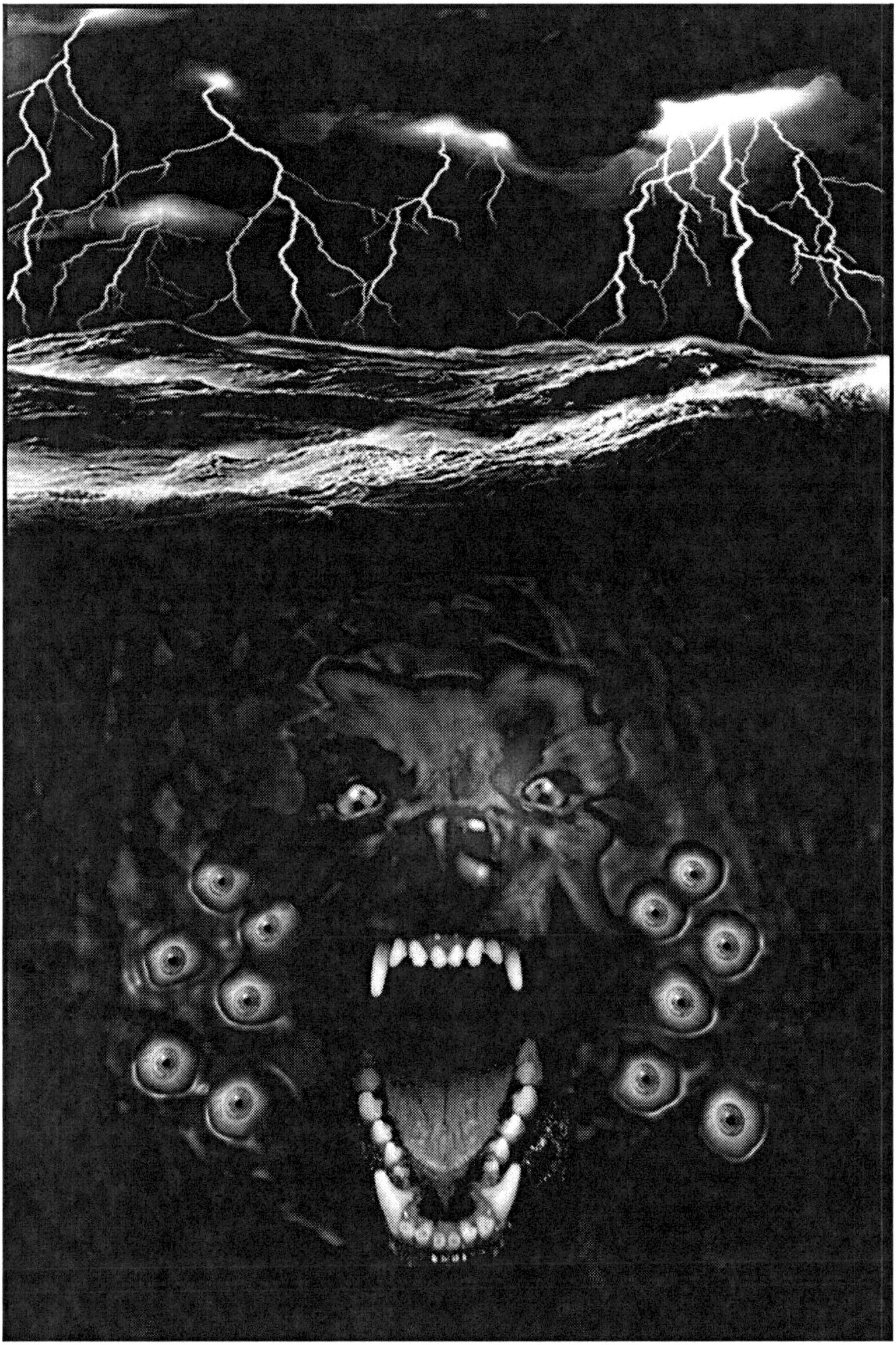

The terrifying Roy Dog of Portland

THE ROY DOG

The foghorn blasted loudly
As the sea mist suffocated the land
Warning mariners of the monster
The Isle of Portland.

I wasn't far from Cave Hole
Where a fisherman was once found dead
No marks were ever found on his body
But his eyes had been plucked from his head.

Rumours blamed his death on a spectre
A beast called the Roy Dog
That stalks in stormy weather
And roams in silent fog.

Again the Bill's voice blasted
Cutting through the ghostly grey
In the deathly silence that followed
I heard something more sinister than sea spray.

A distant soft pad, pad, padding
An eerie repetitive sound
Closer and closer towards me it came
Which made my heart pound.

I felt the colour drain from my face
As fear began to take hold
Could the legend really be true?
Just the thought of it left me cold.

As the distant padding grew ever nearer
I desperately sought to see through the fog
And emerging from the veil
Came the dreaded Roy Dog!

It was larger than a mortal dog
With sharp fangs eager to rip and tear
Flaming eyes, one red one green
And a black coat beyond compare

But what I think was worse of all
Around its neck was a trophy of fear
All seeing dead men's eyes
That never cry a tear.

The smell of decay crept up my nose
And all of a sudden I felt very cold
Something said my days were done
At this sight that I behold.

I made the sign of the cross
And closed my eyes ready to meet my fate
And like a statue there I stood
And for a long time I did wait.

At last curiosity got the better of me
And slowly I opened one eye
I found myself all alone
For the creature I could not spy.

Now why did the Roy Dog spare me?
I would really wish to know
Was it the sign of the cross I made?
Which made the creature go.

But I lived to tell you the tale
To tell you to keep out of the fog
When the Bill sounds its warning
Beware the Roy Dog!

Robert Newland

In countries like France, we find that black dogs - according to legend at least - actually *drown* people and in Belgium, a goblin called the Kludde takes the form of a winged black dog, and attacks its victims in a similar way. Thus, the `Roy Dog` may have been invented as some kind of `bogey beast` as a warning to those who venture too close to blow-holes, where air and water are forced through the natural opening by rising tides. Alternatively, perhaps a reminder of even older times when caverns or tunnels were regarded as the entrance to the infernal regions, where fierce looking dogs, like the three-headed dog `Cerberus` in Greek mythology and `Garmr` in Norse mythology, guarded the gates of Hell.

Kludde

Like the `Roy Dog`, some black dogs have appeared during bad weather, and it has been suggested that electrical storms might facilitate their appearance. There seems to be a connection with environmental phenomena, such as electromagnetic radiation and ley lines, and black dogs often have the tendency to appear near these potential sources of energy.

Water is just another one of these environmental energies with which black dogs are commonly associated; one can find rivers, streams, lakes, or the sea located close to the area in which the black dog is said to have appeared.

In Dorset, an example of this can be found along the River Stour, where a black dog is said to haunt the bridge at Blandford, and at a place not far from the bridge called Bryanston Woods. Even the dog that we discussed in Hardy's *Far from the Madding Crowd*, appeared at Grey's Bridge that crosses the River Frome.

The next two black dog stories were given to us by the Dorset paranormal researcher Catherine O'Donnell. As recently as the early 1990s, a retired teacher who was walking her elderly Labrador dog up the road that runs through the woods to Bryanston School, witnessed the black dog. Her dog started to act strangely, and tried to hide behind her legs. She looked up, and saw a large 'Alsatian-type' dog coming towards them. As the animal drew closer, she saw it was very dark in colour, and possessed no collar; so she kept hold of her dog, fearing that it may attack. When it drew level, she noticed that it was walking above the level of the road. On closer examination, the woman described its coat as 'sticking out like spikes', and that its outline was fuzzy and indistinct.

Not far from the river, is the village of Belchalwell. It was thought dangerous to go past certain gates at night because of a black dog that lurked there. This legend was supported when two men were driving along the road during the Second World War, back into the village of Belchalwell in the daytime, when they encountered a large black shaggy-coated dog which jumped from the hedgerow on to the bonnet of the car.

The weight of the creature actually caused the car to *'dip down'*. The animal glared in at the two terrified young men for a few seconds, before it leapt up and floated over the hedge on the opposite side of the road. Although they both clearly saw the dog, describing it as 'very large and very, very black', no sound was heard, and the car moved as if in a physical encounter.

I have also discovered that the *Castle Inn* at Durweston, another village that is close to the River Stour, was formerly called the *Black Dog* in the mid-19th Century, until its name was changed. One wonders whether the pub was originally named after a forgotten local legend or is it just another uncanny coincidence?

In Dorset, black dogs can be found to be as restless ghosts that haunt particular areas where they once lived. One famous example, which features in both Devon and Dorset folklore, is the legend concerning the Black Dog of Lyme.

The tale begins at Colway Manor near the town of Lyme Regis during the seventeenth century. A lonely old man once owned the manor. He lived alone, with his only companion - a loyal black dog.

One night, as he retired for bed, thieves broke into the house, and demanded his hidden valuables. But the man refused. The thieves became angry, and kicked and punched the man to death. The dog, however, was abandoned at the foot of the stairs, where he pined for his lost master, until he eventually died of starvation.

The manor was almost completely destroyed during the Civil War, and a farmhouse was built on the remaining part of the mansion. The new farmhouse retained the large original fireplace and two large antique seats, which were fixed either side of the alcove of the fireplace.

It was too these seats, every evening, the new owner, a farmer, would relax. One evening his solace was interrupted by the arrival of an eerie black dog, which came to sit on the opposite seat to him. The farmer was at first uneasy, but after a time he became accustomed to his new companion's regular appearances.

Discussing his strange visitor with neighbours, he was constantly advised to get rid of the creature. The farmer, who didn't fancy the idea of confronting the animal, jokingly replied. *"Why should I? He is the quietest and frugalest creature about the farm, neither eating, drinking, nor interfering with anyone."*

One evening while drinking with neighbours, the subject of his companion was discussed again. The farmer, who at the time was heavily drunk, got so fed up with their mockery that he stormed off back home to confront the spectral beast.

On his return, and in a terrible state of rage, he found the dog sitting at its usual place upon the chimney seat. The farmer without any hesitation seized a poker and lunged at the dog. The dog quickly jumped off the seat and fled upstairs, followed in hot pursuit by the angry farmer. He soon cornered the animal in the attic, but the dog leapt through the ceiling and disappeared. Infuriated the farmer struck a hard blow to the ceiling dislodging some of the plaster. From the hole, an old box fell to the floor. The farmer picked up the box to discover that it contained a considerable amount of gold and silver coins of the reign of Charles I. Could it be that this box contained the old mans valuables that he concealed from the thieves that broke in that night all those years ago?

The farmer later decided to buy a house a mile west of Colway Manor, and with the help of his new found fortune, converted it into a coaching inn, which in honour of his fortuitous companion named it *The Black Dog*.

The original coaching inn situated on the Devon and Dorset border remained at Uplyme until it was eventually pulled down in 1916 and a new inn, retaining The Black Dog name built in its place.

This building still remains at Uplyme, where it once had the reputation for being the first pub in Devon until its closure by the brewery in the 1990s. The property was boarded up for a while until it was bought and turned it into a refurbished bed and breakfast guesthouse. Now known as the '*The Old Black Dog*' it continues to run as a bed and breakfast business.

But the story does not end there, for when the dog ceased its haunting of the farmhouse, it took to haunting, at midnight, the lane adjacent to the inn known as '*Haye Lane*', alias '*Dog Lane*.'

One encounter with the creature appeared in volume two of the 1864 edition of the *Chambers, The Book of Days*. The contributor reported, that late one evening in 1856, a local couple, the woman whose occupation was a nurse, described the incident as follows:

"As I was returning to Lyme,' said she, one night with my husband down Dog Lane, as we reached about the middle of it, I saw an animal about the size of a dog meeting us. 'What's that?' I said to my husband. 'What?' said he, 'I see nothing.' I was so frightened I could say no more then, for the animal was within two or three yards of us, and had become as large a young calf, but had the appearance of a black, shaggy dog with fiery eyes, just like the description I had heard of the "black dog". He passed close by me, and made the air cold and dank as he passed along. Though I was afraid to speak, I could not help turning round to look after him, and I saw him growing bigger and bigger as he went along, till he was as high as the trees by the roadside, and then seeming to swell into a large cloud, he vanished in the air. As soon as I could speak, I asked my husband to look at his watch, and it was five minutes past twelve. My husband said he saw nothing but a vapour or fog coming up from the sea."

The original *Black Dog* coaching inn at Uplyme before it got demolished in 1916

The *Black Dog Inn* today in Uplyme; not a pub anymore, now run as a B&B

This account focuses attention on the very nature of the black dog phenomenon as in the incident involving a harbinger told by the Bridport Lady in 1915. One person could see the spectral creature while the companion could not.

The last reported sighting of the black dog in 1959 was seen by a family whilst on holiday in the area of Lyme Regis, after visiting *The Black Dog Inn*. The following account was documented by Devon folklorist Theo Brown, whilst visiting the inn in 1960:

'I visited the Inn on Tuesday, 17th May, 1960, and talked to Miss [X], the innkeeper's daughter. She told me the dog had been seen the previous autumn or late summer (1959) when there was a considerable coming and going of bed-and-breakfast holiday folk in transit. Sometime at the height of the season, in August or September, three people booked in one evening, a man and wife and son of about ten years old. After supper they all went for a stroll in the dimpsey [sic], down Haye Lane.

Suddenly the Black Dog appeared, very large, in mid-air about eye-level, floating from one hedge to the other, right across their path. They reported this strange event on their return to the Inn, and no-one knew quite what to make of it. Miss [X] seemed inclined to giggle at the absurdity of such a story, and only told me after some encouragement, glancing round at the customers in the pub, evidently expecting to be laughed at for passing it on. Evidently, the story had caused some embarrassment and no-one had noted the names of the witnesses or the date of their stay, and nothing further was remembered about their appearance, etc. The Visitor's Book was so crammed with entries Miss [X] considered it would be fruitless to look through it.

On this occasion, my Mother and I were eating our sandwiches in the lane behind the pub, where the wall of the Inn garden is very high, and has a curious kink in it, due to a drain or spring emerging; and from this hollow my Mother caught a glimpse of the dog emerging, a peculiarly melancholy look about it.'

Since the 1856 sighting, the legend has been elaborated from its original version like so many other folk tales. Once being a harmless ghost dog of Colway Manor, it has now become a harbinger of death.

It has been suggested if anyone encounters this apparition then death is imminent. However, if the victim can retain enough presence of mind to toss a silver coin to the dog it will disappear and the spell of ill fortune broken. A similar method also applied to killing a shape-shifting witch hare, but as there has been no recent reported encounters with this creature, there is no way of knowing whether the notion works!

Such elaboration of ghost stories as the black dog of Lyme with its unfortunate new role as a harbinger, is said to also accompany another famous ghost of the town; the notorious and infamous Judge Jeffreys, who we have met before in this book, who hanged and tortured many Monmouth rebels.

Haye Lane also known as 'Dog Lane', where the black dog of Lyme has been sighted on numerous occasions

Another popular addition to the Black Dog of Lyme myth suggests that domestic dogs should, on *no* account, be allowed to stray late at night in this neighbourhood, as there have been many cases of their disappearance in a mysterious manner. The present authors joked about this when visiting the area in 1998, as they saw a poster advertising a lost pet border collie dog pinned to a sign post at the entrance to Haye Lane.

The Black Dog of Lyme is just one of many such incidents that have been recorded, with these spectral creatures haunting stretches of roads, country lanes, archaeological sites, parish and county boundaries of Dorset.

- Around Hod Hill lurks the spirit of a black dog that was accidentally killed by a horse and cart after escaping from its cruel master. The broken chain - still tethered around its neck - can be heard as it runs through Stourpaine Village Square to Hod Hill.

- Another phantom black dog that continually haunts a quiet stretch of road was seen at *Pot Lane* in Horton near Cranborne.

- One winter's night during the 1930's, a Mr W. Armstrong and his companion were walking homeward to his cottage at Chideock along a moonlit stretch of road from

Morcombelake. They were suddenly startled by the appearance of a large black hound, which followed behind them, until they reached the cemetery north of Chideock. The two men stood transfixed, as the dark creature made its way to one of the large weathered tombstones, and - to their amazement - the dog simply vanished into thin air.

- At Shipton Gorge, near Bridport, a man walking home late one evening, was so startled by the appearance of a large black dog, that he picked up a stick, and threw it at the animal. To his amazement, the stick passed straight through the dog, which then vanished.

- At West Woodyates Manor, north of Sixpenny Handley, a similar incident happened to a farmer who was unloading hay from his cart. He noticed a black dog lying in the cart, so - with pitchfork in hand - he struck at the animal, which promptly disappeared.

- Stranger still is the appearance of a headless black dog that is said to cross *Bradford Lane* at *Dyke Head*, a junction south of Leweston, near Longburton, at midnight .

- In Pimperne. a dog that is completely *invisible,* can be heard rattling his chain, whilst running along the Salisbury road from the foot of Letton Hill. Local people who have experienced the presence of this invisible hound, talk of a soft velvety coat as it brushes past.

So, what may have contributed to these black dog legends to the county of Dorset?

People who have owned a dog do not need to be told that they can be the most obedient and affectionate of animal companions, but an encounter with a strange, vicious, dog can be one of the most terrifying experiences to be had. It is this fear that generates superstitions in isolated rural communities, and the development of the tradition of folk tales and story telling.

But, even in fear, the black dog could bring some sort of reassurance to someone in need. For the people who have lost a family member or friends through strange and sudden illnesses, it could be a comfort to say that they died because the black dog had cursed them, and thus in this strange way, these phantom creatures could help explain the inexplicable.

Since the advent of Christianity, the Devil was often the main contender for explaining the cause of any supernatural or inexplicable event. For the Devil's can change his appearance, so to trick his unfortunate victims into a false sense of security, before revealing his true identity.

One identity often portrayed by the Devil was a black dog.

One tale, warning of the dangers of Sabbath-breaking, happened in the early part of the twentieth century within the grounds of the old priory ruins at Woodcutts, close to the Wiltshire border. Young men from the village of Sixpenny Handley would often go there to play cards, but their afternoon game was interrupted one Sunday by the presence of a large black greyhound, with no ears and saucer shaped eyes. It dashed across the room disappearing through one of the priory walls.

We can say with certainty that a majority of black dog stories go back at least to the Elizabethan period, and that saucer-shaped eyes, which are often regarded as a traditional feature of the black dog, were commonly attributed to seventeenth century ghosts and demons. Obviously, also, 'tea-saucers' could not exist prior to the introduction of tea in the seventeenth century. It is also it is in this period in Dorset's history, that we find the links with the Canadian province of Newfoundland.

The county of Dorset had been trading with Newfoundland as early as the sixteenth century, when fisherman and merchants from Dorset began to exploit the rich supplies of codfish off the coast of Newfoundland. As these trading interests grew, people from the staple ports of Dorset went to work there, and eventually settled in Newfoundland.

It was probably these fishermen who worked off the coast of the eastern Canadian provinces, that first introduced two breeds of dog; the `Newfoundland` and the `St. John's Newfoundland` (or the Labrador Retriever, as it is known today) to Dorset and the rest of England. One tale regarding the first introduction the Black Dog, or Newfoundland, to this county can be found in Weymouth.

The first encounter with this breed is said to have taken place at one of Weymouth's oldest pubs. This pub which had the reputation to attract the likes of smugglers, thieves and cutthroats, was originally called *'The Dove'* until the sixteenth century, when Weymouth won the contract to trade with the newly-formed colonies of Newfoundland and Labrador.

The Black Dog Inn Sign, Weymouth, depicting the dove, the former name of the inn

The reason for the pub to have changed its name from *'The Dove'* to *'The Black Dog'*, occurred when a sea captain from Newfoundland entered the establishment accompanied by what was described as *'a great black beast of a dog'*. Both the landlord and the locals where so amazed by what they beheld.

As the captain was retiring from his seafaring days, he gave the dog as a gift to the landlord for his hospitality, thus introducing the first black dog to this part of the country. The local tale, is that the dog attracted so many sightseers from the surrounding district, that the landlord changed the name of the pub in honour of the dog, and the new-found prosperity that it had attracted for him.

Whether the Newfoundland black dog *was* a Labrador as depicted on the inn sign, is questionable. It could have well been a Newfoundland breed, which would certainly have made a dramatic impression upon the Weymouth folk at that time.

Whatever the case, it is a worthy tale to consider when researching the black dog legend in this area. As most inns called the *Black Dog* often depict the image of a Labrador as seen on the Weymouth pub. It is probable that other pubs near to the Dorset coast, such as *The Black Dog Inn* at Broadmayne and East Stoke near Wareham, adopted the animal in the same way. But unlike *The Black Dog* of Lyme, there appears to be no association with a spectral Black Dog legend.

The Newfoundland also has the traditional characteristics of the spectral Black Dog; being extremely large, with a black shaggy coat, and a well known association with water. Charlotte Brontë makes this comparison in chapter twelve of her novel *Jane Eyre*, (1847), which introduces Mr Rochester's dog, `Pilot` - also a Newfoundland - and refers to *Gytrash*, Yorkshire's Black Dog. Even more uncanny, and even more of a coincidence - at least as far as the Black dog of Lyme is concerned - is that of the dog seen by Jane Eyre on a stretch of track called 'Hay Lane'!

Both the Labrador and Newfoundland were versatile working dogs, able to rescue drifting nets and bring back shot waterfowl.

However, the Newfoundland was a much larger and much stronger breed of `retriever`, capable of rescuing a drowning man, or breaking the ice as he dove into the frigid northern ocean. The dog's lung capacity allowed the dog to swim great distances and fight ocean currents. At the end of a day's fishing, the day's catch was loaded into a cart, and the dog was hitched up to haul the load into town.

An incident in which a Newfoundland saved a drowning man is reported in volume one of the 1864 edition of the *Chambers Book of Days*:

> *"Of the aptitude of the Newfoundland dog to take to the water and courageously help drowning or endangered persons, the instances are abundant"*
>
> *"A Mr. William Phillips, while bathing at Portsmouth, ventured out too far, and was in imminent peril. Two boatmen instead of starting off to assist him, selfishly strove to make a hard bargain with some of the bystanders, who urged them. While the parley was going on, a Newfoundland dog seeing the danger, plunged into the water, and saved the struggling swimmer. It is pleasantly told that Mr. Phillips in gratitude for his deliverance, bought the dog from his owner, a butcher, and thereafter gave an annual festival, at which the dog was assigned the place of honour, with a good ration of beefsteaks."*

The origin of this working breed of the Newfoundland is disputed. Vikings and Basque fishermen visited Newfoundland as early as 1000 AD, and wrote accounts of the natives working side by side with these retrieving dogs. With the advent of European fisherman, a variety of new breeds helped to shape and re-invigorate the breed, but the essential characteristics of the Newfoundland dog remained.

Whilst Dorset was trading with Newfoundland, we also find that smuggling was rife in Dorset and other neighbouring counties, and many of them owned these dogs. It is not, therefore, too surprising to find them being noted for being black in colour, and highly agile in the sea. An example of this made the news during year of 2003. A Black Labrador named 'Todd', accidentally fell overboard from his master's boat in to the Solent near the Isle of Wight, only to swim ten miles to the mainland across cold choppy waters and a busy channel.

It would certainly have been an ideal animal to train for the illegal purposes of retrieving smuggled goods that were moored off the coast, and for plundering wrecked vessels. In fact, in Dorset, Portland had its *own* breed of Newfoundland peculiar to the island.

The Portland Newfoundland was noted for retrieving small barrels of contraband spirits hidden offshore by local smugglers. The breed has been extinct on the island since the nineteenth century. Could this be another possible candidate for the Roy/Row Dog myth?

As well as retrieving contraband, Newfoundlands or Labrador dogs may have been used as *Dog Horns*. According to Geoffrey Morley in his book *Smuggling in Hampshire and Dorset 1700-1850* (1983) As it is a known fact that further west on the Devon coast homecoming sailors were used to identifying the farms and villages onshore by the characteristic sounds made by different dogs when they barked, it has been suggested that some dogs were kept specifically for their penetrating bark, which carried well out to sea, and were even irritated on purpose to encourage them to keep up the noise when fog was about.

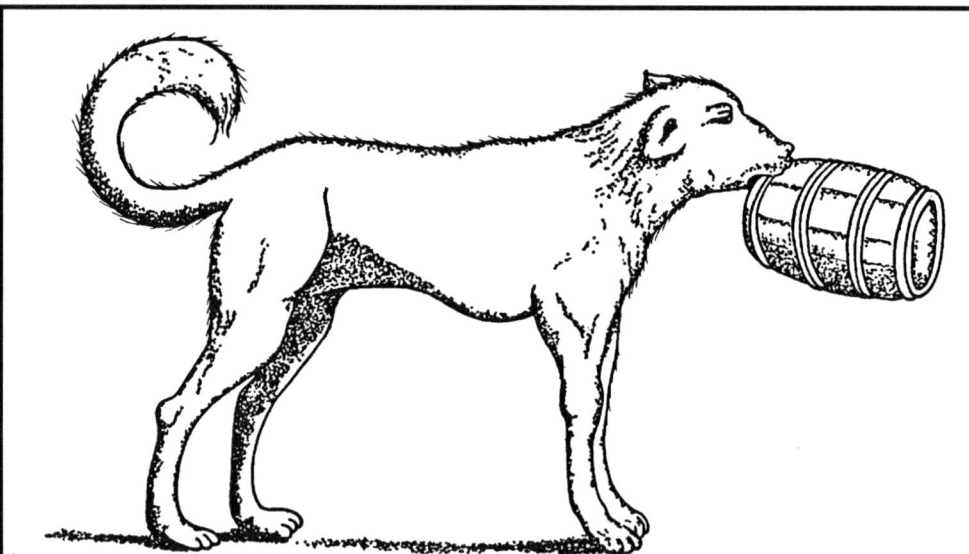

The Portland Newfoundland - Sea Dog Based on the Pen & wash drawing from Samuel Grimm's collection of illustrations of Dorset circa 1790. The picture shows a Portland Newfoundland Sea Dog or Rescue Dog. Written on the back of the original drawing: "portrait of a dog which brought three barrels of spirits out of the sea". The dogs were also trained to rescue people in danger of drowning. The breed died out on Portland in the nineteenth century.

It is logical to assume that, at some points along the Devon and Dorset coast, dogs would have been activated by fellow smugglers to signal luggers safely towards their expected rendezvous-point that night. Places known as smuggling haunts, which are also known to have black dog legends associated with them include Boatswain's Coppice, which lies between the two parishes of Lulworth and Tyneham and at Fleet. This provided the basis for John Meade Falkner's famous novel *Moonfleet*. Though a fictional story, it was based firmly on the illegal trade that flourished there.

It is easy to imagine how a lonely traveller stumbling on such an operation might have felt. Imagine that she or she saw a large black dog, possibly of an unfamiliar breed, wandering alone along the coast, or emerging from the sea at night while their masters hid out of sight. It would not take too much imagination to interpret it as some sort of demon, or spectre of doom.

The famous Dorset smuggler Issac Gulliver would often employ this very principle of deceiving the terrified locals. Gulliver once owned a farm near the mysterious Eggardon Hillfort, a Neolithic settlement, which still has a reputation of a place for its weird and inexplicable happenings, and is reputed to be the haunt of the moon goddess Diana*, who leads a ghostly pack of hunting dogs over its summit collecting the souls of the dead.

Gulliver would often use the routes that ran inland from East and West Bexington, Swyre, Burton Bradstock, and Shipton Gorge, to his farm. It was these local stories of phantom black dogs, and spectral coaches, that Gulliver and other smugglers would delight in keeping alive; embroidering and spreading them so that as few people as possible would be out on his `commercial` routes during the hours of darkness.

Gulliver is known to have used large black hounds - possibly Newfoundlands or Labradors - for poaching, and retrieving contraband. Disguised coaches and wagons that were used for smuggling, were disguised to appear ghostly. Hence, many tales were spread around the area in which he and his associates were carrying out their illegal midnight runs. For example, the tale of the headless dog reputed to cross Bredy Lane between *'Cathole Copse'* and *'Cathole Barn'* at Burton Bradstock, and the appearance of a ghostly Black Dog dragging a rattling chain, jumping over a wall on the Swyre road near Puncknowle. There is also the story of the phantom funeral procession - with four headless pallbearers - which haunts a place called `Gadger's Hole`, near Shipton Gorge, at midnight.

Of course, smuggling cannot explain *all* such encounters, although it *is* factor to consider when investigating sightings which are alleged to have been encountered around that period.

So what about the more recent sightings? It has been recently been suggested, most notably by author Di Francis in her seminal 1982 work *Cat Country,* that big cats may have played a part and been mistaken for black dogs. There is the story at Friar Waddon near Portesham, where a farm labourer was warned about a large black cat with penetrating fiery eyes and a luminous tail.

---

* *'Diana.' See chapter:' Diana the Moon Goddess & The Magic Circle.*

This link might also be possible at Sturminster Newton. There was once a terrifying creature, which ran along a track parallel to the main road at a place called *'The Hollow'*. The Rev J. B. Hirst, a local clergyman in 1965, knew of someone who spoke of it as a large black dog.

Yet there is a much older record, which shows it to have been a large cat, which appears in a 1907 manuscript *Reminiscences of Sturminster Newton* by Robin Young.

"a story was often told them of a wild and savage monstrous cat which haunted the remains of the old castle and was often seen on Newton Hill. Such horrid tales were told of this monsterous cat, with eyes as big as tea saucers, that many children were afraid to pass that way, and not only children but grown up people would be so afraid that they would walk on the main road below the hill to avoid the creature."

It is quite possible that this story supports Chris Moiser, a Devon zoologist and Big Cat investigator, who has suggested that sightings of big cats during the nineteenth century onwards might have been the result of escapes from travelling circuses and menageries. As cages that housed these creatures were extremely badly designed, and the wagons had to travel across country on poorly made roads and droves, any accident involving the toppling of the trailers might well result in whatever creature it contained escaping into the countryside. It is also

The Hollow at Sturminster Newton, where a terrible cat-like creature haunted

true that many aristocratic families kept exotic animals in private menageries. For example, as we have seen with the story of 'Martyn's Ape', in the fifteenth century the Martyn family of Athelhampton Hall, near Dorchester, kept simians as pets.

If a big cat, or any other, exotic creature was released - or escaped - from a poorly maintained facility on a family estate, it would not be surprising that local people may have mistaken it as a black dog, or another form of zooform phenomena, haunting a particular isolated area. As a result, could some of these legends and stories have grown up and become associated with these areas?

Stalkers in the Undergrowth

Phantom black dog sightings are now less frequently reported, and the tradition has been somewhat overshadowed by a *new* kind of spectral animal; the *Big Cat,* or *Beast* as it is sometimes referred too. Although there have been intermittent reports of such things for centuries, the modern era of big cat sighting started in Britain in the early 1960's, with a creature dubbed the *Surrey Puma.*

Sightings proliferated in the 1970s and 1980s, and many of these animals are thought to be the descendants of big cats that were unlawfully released by private collectors in the wake of the 1976 *Dangerous Wild Animal Act*. Similar cat-like creatures have been sighted in other parts of the country such as Cornwall, Devon, the Midlands, and Yorkshire.

Reports of large feline creatures stalking the countryside of Dorset, whether apparitional or real, continue to be seen by reliable witnesses. In 1975, a girl encountered a large phantom cat with glowing eyes in Wyke Regis, and in 1988 there were reports *the Dorset Evening Echo* of a large black cat called the *Beast of Westham* in that area around Weymouth. The creature would wreck gardens, and prey upon the Westham resident's pets, which prompted several unsuccessful attempts to catch it. The following year in June, the beast was seen on Portland by many of the islanders, who described it as a *"dark tabby feral cat about the size of a spaniel".*

It wasn't until 28th October 1998 that the black beast returned to Weymouth, when a large black cat-like creature was spotted running near the Swannery at Westham, around 2a.m. by two passengers travelling home in a taxi. Mrs. Helen Jensen told the *Dorset Evening Echo* 27th October 1998. *"It was definitely too big to be a domestic cat, it looked more like a panther."*

In August 1994 the *Motcombe Beast* began to hog the headlines of the local newspapers. Its appearance was supported by the evidence of a set of three-inch long feline pug-marks featured in the *Bournemouth Evening Echo* 1st September 1994, outside the home of Mr. and Mrs. Talbot at Motcombe near Shaftesbury. Prior to this discovery 'loud yowling noises' were heard months before.

In the same year around the Bournemouth area creatures resembling a jaguar and lynx were reported. It would seem they were moving west, for in the same year the first sighting of

Lewesdon Hill, where the 'Beast of Broadwindsor' has been sighted

'The Beast Of Broadwindsor' was reported in the *Dorset Evening Echo* 8th September 1994.

The creature was witnessed early one morning by Vincent Gavigan while he was delivering newspapers. He described the big cat as being as large as an Alsatian dog, with a head like a puma and with green eyes. The animal was within thirty to forty yards of his car; it turned its head towards him and jumped into a hedge and disappeared.

Seven days later came the second sighting of the animal was reported in the *Dorset Evening Echo* 14th September 1994. This time it was seen by Frank Smith, while driving along the B3162 road near Lewesdon Hill, Stoke Abbot. The creature was spotted around 8.30 on a bright sunny morning near Buck's Head, where he pulled off the road to watch it walking a line between fields of crops and grass, before eventually disappearing out of sight. Later described as, *'black, about the size of an Alsatian dog, and resembled a panther, with a small head and small upright ears. It had a deep chest and a long tail which appeared to be tufted at the end and it loped along like a cat.'*

Five months elapsed before another species of big cat made an appearance, this time south of Broadwindsor, on the 6th February 1995, near Miles Cross, Symondsbury. A local farmer expressing his concerns for the safety of young children, told police how he had seen a large lynx-type animal while driving to work. Mr John Turner of Highway Farm, told local newspapers that, from his van, he watched the creature amble across the road in front of him at 7.20a.m. The West Dorset farmer indicated that the animal, *'was about the size of a boxer dog, very compact with a short tail and biggish feet. It was very furry with mottled light brown, dark brown and almost black spots. It also had very pointed ears.'*

Within the next two days a woman told the Bridport police that she had seen a big, cat-like animal along Pineapple Lane, Salway Ash.

As more and more reliable witnesses reported seeing these mysterious big cats, police began to treat the reports more seriously, and issued warnings to the public that on no account should they approach these creatures. With the public now aware of dangerous creatures stalking the undergrowth, more people came forward to tell of their encounters.

One recent sighting took place on the 26th September 1998, when a Mr. Joe Tait had a gruesome encounter whilst walking his dogs at Ryeberry Hill near Symondsbury. This was first reported in the *Dorset Evening Echo* 29th September 1998. He witnessed - sixty yards away in a field - a large, black, cat-like animal, crouching over the body of a sheep. When the animal caught sight of Mr Tait, it ran off with such a speed that the dogs couldn't keep pace with it. On examining the carcass of the sheep it was found that the ribs had been crushed and torn out.

For weeks after, farmers around the Symondsbury area discovered horrific mutilations of their livestock. So much so, that evening patrols were set up to hunt down the elusive creature.

Even today big cats continued to be reported.

'Spring-Heeled Jack', the apparition with eyes of flame that leaped his way through the dark streets of London terrifying young women between 1837 and 1838, made a brief appearance in Weymouth at the turn of the twentieth century, where he was allegedly seen leaping over a cemetery wall at Wyke Regis.

STRANGE PHENOMENA

In previous chapters we have seen that the county of Dorset has a wealth of mysteries, tales, curiosities, and inexplicable events. So it seems appropriate, in the final chapter, to select an assortment of wondrous tales and *Fortean** accounts that have been reported in the county's dark past to the present day, and which don't really fit into any of the previous chapters.

However, it is not the purpose of this chapter to explore any of these phenomena at great length. Some of these are enigmas that have captured the media and public attention - UFOs, crop circles and weather phenomena. Here it is often the case that fact and fiction are so intertwined, that books have been written in vast numbers in an effort to untangle these mysteries.

Atmospheric Oddities & Mysterious Flying Objects

Spontaneous images that are produced by the effects of cloud formations can be interpreted as animals, figures, objects, cities, etc, when viewed from either the air or ground. This is perhaps one of nature's most incredible illusions, which we have *all* experienced at one time or another in our lives.

But stranger still is the appearance of a formation which is so well-defined, incredible and fantastic that it can be sometimes mistaken for the real thing.

An incident recorded in the *Prodigies in Somerset and Dorset, 1661-2* reprinted in *The Somerset and Dorset Notes and Queries, 1895,* On the 23rd April 1661, a distinguished man was out riding on a high hill between Faychurch and Lyme Regis, when at three o'clock in the afternoon, he witnessed a large dark bellowing thunder cloud drifting above the Isle of Portland. The cloud suddenly took the distinct form of a sailing ship - complete with masts, sails, rigging, bowspit and stern - which he said was 'high built'. Within the ship, he saw its occupants with their upper torsos showing. And at the head of the ship, he also saw - with great clarity - many men with pikes on their shoulders.

Within fifteen minutes, it started to rain hard with thunder and lightning. The man stood amazed and dumb-struck, as the cloud ship sailed through the air, until it eventually disappeared out of view.

---

* *'Fortean.'* A collection of curiosities, anomalies, oddities and peculiarities that have happened in the world but are outside the accepted laws of science. Derived from the name Charles Hoy Fort (1874-1932) an American journalist and author of The Book of the Damned (1919), New Lands (1923), Lo! (1931) and Wild Talents (1932) – who pioneered the study into strange phenomena.

An incident recorded in the *Prodigies in Somerset and Dorset, 1661-2* reprinted in *The Somerset and Dorset Notes and Queries, 1895,* On the morning of 6th July 1662, two people who were - at that time - residents of Forde near Thorncombe, observed a blood red sunrise, and in the sky close to the sun, they saw the perfect form of a man! Watching this, they both saw - coming from the north - a multitude of, what appeared to be, men's heads, which drew near the man, bobbing up and down earnestly. Then a large cloud, scarlet in colour, overshadowed the whole vision, and when it passed, the sky was back to normal.

On 13th July 1662, another strange sight occurred in the sky. This time it was witnessed by a man and his wife, plus several other people, at Stoke Lane, between Mappowder and Stoke Wake. One morning, they all observed the sun turn black when it was 'half-an-hour high', with a fringe of deep red that seemed, to fall to earth like streams of blood. Then, after a few moments, the black sun suddenly turned bright and then back to a shade of black again. The sun pulsated in this strange manner for two or three minutes, before it turned into several strange shapes, which the onlookers could not express, and then the parts seemed to strive with each other.

After some considerable time, seven distinct images of the sun appeared, before reuniting with each other as a whole. In the midst of this apparition, there seemed to appear a large dark cloud in the form of what the eyewitnesses described as a black glove.

The account of 'phantom suns' observed by the people of Stoke Lane may seem like a bad case of hallucinations, but if seen today, no doubt it would be reported as a U.F.O (unidentified flying object) sighting. Written accounts like this can be found throughout our history, especially towards the end of the nineteenth and start of the twentieth century, when -

due to published newspaper accounts - the awareness in mysterious flying machines increased. It wasn't until the mid-twentieth century that the media in the United States of America coined the term *flying saucer* and later the popular abbreviation *U.F.O.* - later to become the acronym *UFO*.

Thousands of people around the world have seen, or had a close encounter with, an object they are unable to identify, and every year, more and more reports recollecting their experiences are published.

A percentage of reported sightings are no doubt due to misidentification of planets, stars, meteors, satellites, re-entering space debris, aeroplanes, experimental aircraft, Ignis Fatuus, ball lightning, earthquake lights, etc. But, there remain a percentage of accounts that are inexplicable. What are they? Where do they come from? There is no immediate answer. One popular explanation is that they are vehicles piloted by visitors from outer space. Others disagree, pointing at time-travellers, ghosts, or beings from beneath the earth's surface.

Whatever the case may be, strange objects and mysterious lights continue to be seen and reported from all parts of the world, and Dorset is no exception. Here are just a few from our files:

On the 8th December 1733, a large shield-shaped object, a furlong (220 yards) in length, was seen with the sun shining on, it flying through the skies of Dorset. Many people were frightened by seeing it, as an ill omen from God.

On the same day, another witnessed of this event was a Mr. James Cracker from Fleet his account appeared in *Fate Magazine*, April 1951

> "Something in the sky which appeared in the north, but vanished from my sight, as it was intercepted by trees, from my vision. I was standing in a valley. The weather was warm, the sun shone brightly. On a sudden it re-appeared, darting in and out of my sight with an amazing coruscation. The colour of this phenomenon was like burnished, or new washed silver. It shot with speed like a star falling in the night. But it had a body much larger and a tram longer than any shooting star I have seen. . . . Next day, Mr. Edgecombe informed me that he and another gentleman had seen this strange phenomenon at the same time as I had. It was about 15 miles from where I saw it, and steering a course from E. to N."

On the 26th October 1967, a retired B.O.A.C. Comet flight-administrating officer J.B.W. 'Angus' Brooks of Owermoigne, was out walking his two dogs at 11.25 in the morning across Moigne Downs near Holworth. Taking shelter from a force eight wind, he observed a thin vapour trail in the southwestern sky over Portland. He realized the vapour trail was made by some sort of craft. It descended at a very high rate from its previous position, and - as it approached him - it decelerated fast about four hundred yards away. The craft hovered silently and motionlessly two hundred and fifty feet above the ground.

Mr Brooks describes the craft as having a central disk, twenty-five feet in diameter, and

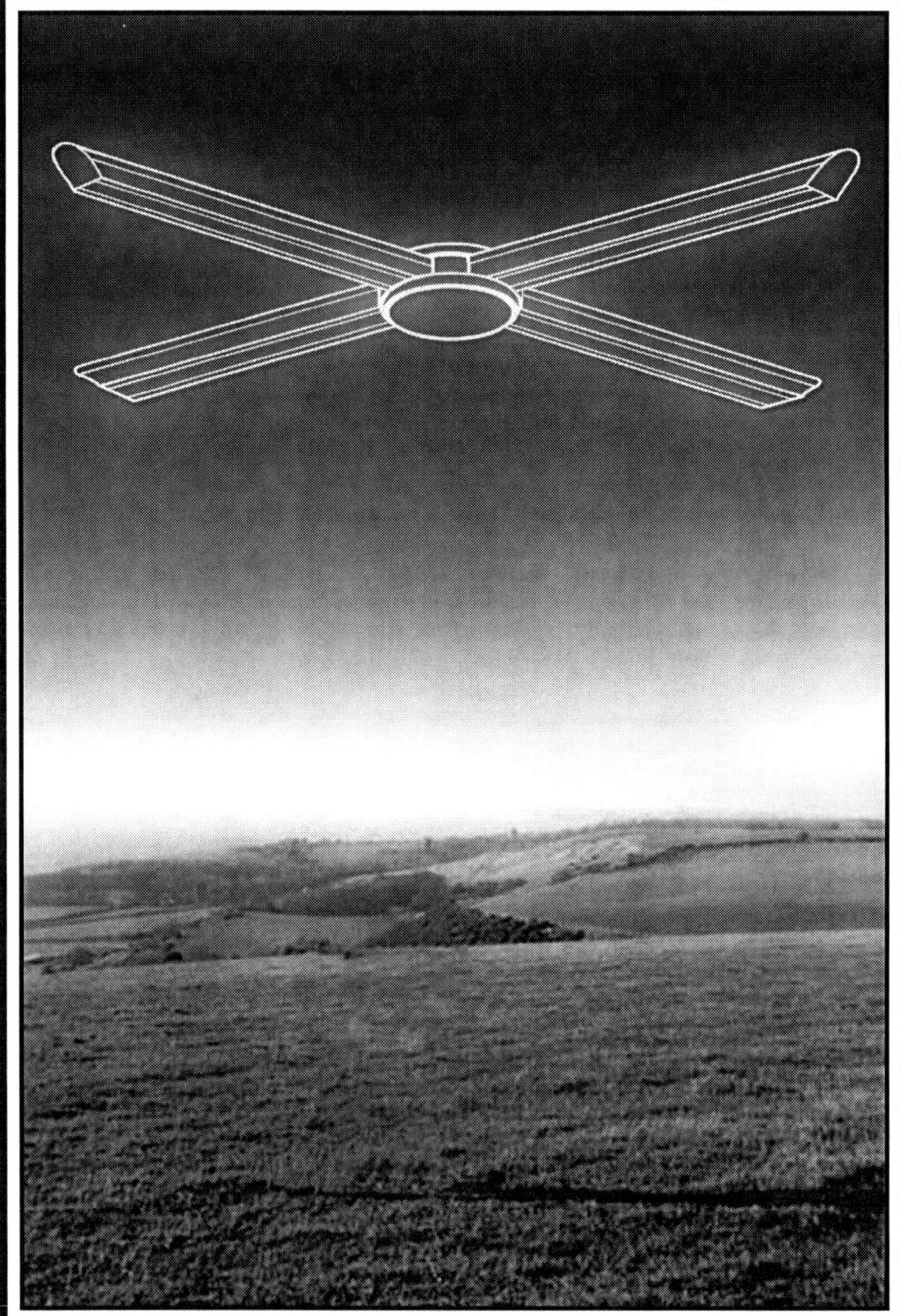

The Moigne Downs Hover Cross

twelve feet thick. Protruding forward was a girder-like *fuselage* and also three behind, parallel to each other. Their lengths were each approximately seventy-five feet, seven-feet high, and eight-feet wide, and characterised as having nose cones and groove fins. Mr Brooks noted the craft had no windows, and appeared to be constructed out of some translucent material, which changed to match the sky.

When the craft stopped, the two outer rear fuselages swung ninety degrees to form a cross with the disk at the centre. Mr. Brooks watched with amazement for nearly twenty-two minutes with his dogs, which were now very disturbed, by his side. The craft's fuselages then moved around to line up with a central, third, fuselage. The previous leading fuselage now became a different one to when it arrived. Then it suddenly turned ninety degrees clockwise and climbed at immense speed in an east-north-easterly direction towards Winfrith.

That night reports of mysterious flying lights were reported over a wide area of Southern England.

Before Mr. Brooks' encounter, it is interesting to note that printed in the *Dorset Evening Echo* 24th October 1967, that same day two policemen on routine patrol around Hatherleigh, Devon where in hot pursuit of an illuminated flying cross for twelve miles at 4.00a.m. The next day on the 25th October 1967, the *Dorset Evening Echo* reported a second sighting of cross-shaped craft, by a police cycle patrol at Halland, Sussex and other police car patrol units within the county in the early hours of the morning

In the *Western Daily Press* 14th November 2003, they printed a story of an UFO seen in Lytchett Minster by two off-duty policeman at dusk on an October day 1967. The two men saw what they describe as a large cigar-shaped spaceship, changing colour and form, hovering over the village. As they watched, it split in two, disappeared and reappeared, and then shot from view.

Two years later it was reported in the *Bournemouth Evening Echo* 22nd October 1969 of another strange flying object seen in Bournemouth. It was witnessed by Alastair Mackenzie, a manager of the Suncliff Hotel.

Whilst he was drinking coffee with his with wife and daughter, he observed something fluttering outside of the hotel window. They went out onto the veranda and saw something a resembling a jellyfish-like shape, apparently 5 inches across and glowing slightly. After about fifteen seconds, the luminous object moved out to see gathering speed as it went, at a height of 25 - 30ft.

As the object is so small it has been often suggested that it could have been ball lightning? However no storm was reported that day. Others have suggested it may be a type of animal rather than a alien spacecraft?

We asked the opinion of Richard Freeman, zoological director of the Centre for Fortean Zoology about this incident. He said:

> *"The small size of the object and the 'fluttering' that first attracted the witness suggest*

to me that this object was animate. Perhaps it was a large insect marked with some luminous substance. The distribution of the substance on the object could account for the 'jellyfish' shape. The substance could have been man-made or natural like substance such as a luminous fungus."

There is much speculation that there are organisms which could hypothetically inhabit the extreme atmosphere of our earth. Sir Arthur Conan Doyle anticipated these ideas in his classic short story *Horror in the Heights* published in *Strand Magazine* 1913. Where an airman discovers a previously unknown ecosystem of life forms in Earth's atmosphere, one of which includes a giant ethereal jellyfish.

Reported in the *Dorset Evening Echo* 4th July 1978:

On the morning of 3rd July 1978, the Mapson family from Swindon, on holiday in Weymouth, witnessed - along the Portland beach road - what appeared to be a spinning cigar-shaped object in the sky, that pulsated in colours of yellow and orange. The object, which was travelling at a great speed, remained in the sky for a length of three minutes, before eventually disappearing into the mist. Mr Morris Mapson took a couple of photographs with his instamatic camera, and when later processed, the prints showed a ball of white light in the sky.

The next day, reports of mysterious flying objects continued to be sighted. On 5th July 1978, the *Dorset Evening Echo* reported that on the afternoon of the 2nd July, Mrs Sylvia Bartlett of Weymouth, reported seeing a big white object take off from the top of Bowleaze, Weymouth. *"It looked like a big white sheet,"* she said. *"It must have been the size of a house."* On the night of the 4th July, Mr Eddie Lewis from Birmingham witnessed a bright yellow egg-shaped object passing over Portland. *"It was too big to be a helicopter,"* he said. *"It stedily got brighter and then dimmer and finally disappeared."*

Dorset Evening Echo again reported on the 22nd August 1979:

On 20th August 1979, a woman in Radipole, Weymouth reported being awoken in the early hours of the morning by a brilliant purple light. It filled her whole bedroom, along with a low persistent humming noise. She was so frightened by the presence outside her window, she remained in bed, where she could only watch the huge purple object recede past the chink in her bedroom curtains, moving off in the direction of Weymouth.

Reported in the *Dorset Evening Echo* 19th December 1984:

A daylight sighting of a flying disc happened to Mr. and Mrs. Child, residents of Weymouth, as they were driving along the main Yeovil to Dorchester Road, near the Yetminster turn-off on 15th December 1984. The object was first spotted at 4.40p.m. by the couple, who stopped to view it for ten minutes. It hovered approximately four miles over Rampisham. Andrew Childs described the object as being about the size of a medium jet plane, but being round, with a domed top and grey in colour. The couple saw no markings or any lights, but noticed it travelled slowly in a rotating motion. Other drivers stopped and shared Mr. Childs binoculars for a close view of the mysterious flying disc and all agreed it was unlike any aircraft they had seen before.

The mysterious flying disc over Rampisham

Reported in the *Weymouth and Portland Advertiser* 4th August 1994:

Holidaymakers from London, James and Pam Mullen, were camping at West Farm near Fleet in September 1990. Mr. Mullen awoke at around 2.55 a.m., to witness golden balls of light *"like sodium lamps"* manoeuvring in a strange manner in the sky. He alerted his wife who confirmed that she could see them too. After a while, his wife decided to make some tea, while Mr. Mullen went to his car to fetch his camera. Mr. Mullen recalls he was suddenly back at the tent, and telling his wife that the lights had disappeared, and they must both get some sleep. Saying this, he noticed the sun rising, and found they had both lost more than two hours of their lives, as the time was now 5.35a.m. Eight cigarette butts on the tent floor were the only evidence that prompted his wife Pam to remember that she had been sitting at the tent, smoking, awaiting her husband's return. Researchers in Ufology associate this type of episode as a classic example of `missing time` or U.F.O abduction.

Reported in the *Dorset Evening Echo* 22nd February 1992:

In the morning of 8th February 1992, two men from Bridport, Michael Sturt and Lee Brown out driving across Eggardon Hill thought they had seen about a mile in front of them, two hang gliders soaring above the hillfort. Mr. Sturt told newspapers. *"I said, look at those idiots! Because it was blowing a gale, then after a few seconds they just disappeared"*, but Mr. Sturt managed to take a photograph of the objects before their disappearance. When developed, Mr. Sturt and Mr. Brown were amazed to see not two black blobs, but three!

The following year, in March 1993, Elizabeth Dunn, a resident of West Milton, was driving along the old Roman road that runs from Dorchester to Eggardon Hill, when - after passing the turning to Compton Valence - she became aware of a huge dark object. She thought at the time that it might have been a Hercules transporter aircraft. However, she noticed it was rather larger than a previous aircraft she had seen. The mysterious craft flew parallel with her vehicle, travelling at a speed of forty-five miles per hour. The object continued to follow her slowly and silently as she approached Eggardon Hill. Then it suddenly turned sharply south-west, and sped off at great speed towards the sea. It turned, and Mrs. Dunn could make out four rows of lights along the craft, which she likened to 'windows on an ocean liner.'

Reported in the *Weymouth and Portland Advertiser* 14th July 1994:

Just after midnight on 8th June 1994, a Mr. T. Wilson of Radipole, witnessed in the sky, a large circle of tiny lights with a smaller circle of lights inside, merging in and out of each other, above his home .

On 20th August 1996, at around ten o'clock in the evening, a Dorchester family (who remained nameless) were driving on the A354 near Milborne St. Andrew, when their children noticed some strange lights in the sky. The story was featured on Dorset FM, where the mother of the family told of her encounter.

> *"We were travelling up to the Puddletown lights, turned right onto the Dorchester Road and we were approaching the bypass. When all of a sudden this appeared on our right and the boys said "It's getting closer, it's there again, it's getting closer." Don't be silly, it will be something and then they said "its over the top of the car" and it was over the car and all I saw was a lot of red, it struck me as being very red, and red lights or whatever. And I wasn't aware of the rest of the car at that point, because I couldn't tell if I was travelling or what was happening at that point, I was just aware of this redness. It wasn't frightening it wasn't scary or anything. we all drawn individual pictures of it afterwards and all of them , where all circular to begin with and as it approached and got level with us and above us it took on this triangular shape.*

When he looked out of the car's sunroof, he saw a triangular-shaped craft hovering just fifty feet above them.

The mother described seeing an intense red colour. The craft seemed to follow them for a period of time and she thought that if she had stopped the car, the craft would have stopped too.

The family didn't feel any fear, just pure curiosity in viewing the object as close as possible. They pursued the object to the Piddlehinton Road, but lost sight as it passed over a hill.

After the close encounter at Puddletown, dozens of local people of Weymouth and Portland, West Dorset and North Dorset reported seeing a similar object with flashing lights that Tuesday night. In the *Dorset Evening Echo* 22nd August 1996

- A man from Littlemoor, Weymouth claimed to have seen a collection of lights in a triangular formation, while a local woman rang Portland police station to report a strange craft just before ten o'clock in the evening.

- A farmer from Bockhampton saw an unusual craft near Tolpuddle. He first thought it was a Hercules transporter, but realized it wasn't as it just hovered motionless fifty to sixty feet above him. The farmer described it as dome-shaped with a fluorescent white glow around it.

In the *Dorset Evening Echo* 14th August 1997, a Dorchester woman reported seeing a pulsating sphere in the sky while driving up Ridgeway Hill. Mysterious spheres of light are often reported over the Ridgeway. On 12th August 1993 at 9.45p.m. a local resident of Broadwey, Weymouth, told author Mark North what he could only described as *'a glowing orange ball of light travelling fast towards Friar Waddon. The object moved erratically before disappearing.'*

On 26th July 1995, at around eleven o'clock in the evening, Southampton holidaymakers, Mr. and Mrs. Ascot, saw a large reddish pulsating light hover above the hill, quite close to the road.

In the *Dorset Evening Echo* 27th January 2000, a picture was printed showing what appeared to look like a saucer-like craft. The picture was a still from a video filmed by Dorset paranormal investigator, David Kingston. He filmed the UFO near Corfe Castle, he said in the article *"It has been confirmed that it wasn't an aircraft, weather balloon or anything else that can be explained. It must be a craft not of this world."*

In the *Dorset Evening Echo* of 1st February 2000, in response to the UFO photograph near Corfe was published many more people came forward to report similar sightings.

Mrs Laura Amor from Preston said

"I first saw an object at Chalbury Corner as I was driving home from work on my own at about 4.20pm. It was not moving and was twinkling with the sun behind it. I just thought God I've seen an UFO, but I wasn't scared. Then I saw it again on January 27th on the way to work at about 8.10am. I'd left Chalbury Corner and was driving towards Ringstead when I saw it again. My friend was in the car, but she missed it as I was trying to point it out and it disappeared. I came home and saw the picture of the saucer in the Dorset Evening Echo the same day. I told my work colleagues, husband David and son James, and they know I wouldn't make something like this up"

The next eyewitness was Peter Timmons of Wyke Regis saw a diamond-shaped object as he driving up Ridgeway Hill to Dorchester. *"It was just sitting there. There was no vapour trail and it wasn't moving. It was difficult to tell how big it was. I drove around the corner and had another look as I got to the dual carrigeway, but it was gone. It wasn't a conventional flying object. It may have been a secret new aircraft or something."*

In the Letters page of the *Dorset Evening Echo* 7th February 2000, in response to UFO reports that week, Sean Hodder from Bridport saw a ball of light rising over Vcars Farm, Bridport in 1988. *"it then shot sideways, only to vanish into thin air with a concorde-like boom. So I believe in UFOs!"*

Later the same year, the Dorset Evening Echo 14th September 2000, told the story of the Roaf family from Portland, who witnessed a strange flying object with a trail of flames, fly above Chesil Beach at 7.30 pm on 12th September 2000. Mr. Bruce Roaf claimed that the craft shot eastwards across the sky before vanishing. Mr. Roaf said

"I had just come off the phone when I looked out the window and saw it. It was a silver object like a shiny ball at the front and had plumes of the back. It was at high altitude and completely visible through binoculars. I don't know what it was but it didn't look like an aeroplane. It appeared just as the sun began to set and then disappeared in the blink of an eye. I've never seen anything like it before and there must be a logical explanation. It may have been a meteorite. We all saw it and now we just want to know if anyone else saw anything strange at the same time."

Dorset paranormal investigator, David Kingston claimed he also saw the same object that same night

"At first I thought it was a helicopter but then I saw it didn't have any of the normal lights. It was in the sky for about half an hour at about 9.30pm. Then it started behaving very erratically and zig-zagging about before it disappeared towards Swanage. It definitely wasn't an aircraft or any conventional craft."

Five days later it was reported in the *Dorset Evening Echo* 19th September 2000, another eye-witness saw a similar object that same night. Mrs. Anne Parsons of Waytown near Bridport was watching television that evening with her friend when the UFO appeared.

"It was a beautiful night when the object appeared. My son Trevor saw it first going towards Salway Ash. It was very bright and at first we thought it may have been a bright star or a planet. But then we could see that it was an object travelling upward with an upside down 'V' of flaming coming from it. Whatever it was, it was going fast."

The mystery of the UFO surfaced again, with a report in the *Dorset Evening Echo on the* 20th September 2000. This time it was seen by three cleaners; Janet McConnell, Ivy Balfour and Janet Wheatland, as they where travelling to work at a Weymouth Bay Holiday camp. Mrs. McConnell said *"we were on our way to work at 6.30am. We saw a round object in the sky with flames coming out of the back, high above the sea past Bowleaze Cove. It definitely wasn't an aeroplane as it was moving much too fast."*

The next day the *Dorset Evening Echo* reported that another two families claimed to have seen the unusual fiery V in the skies over south Dorset. The Broad family from Walditch near Bridport witnessed a silver V-shaped object as they were travelling back from Dorchester. Mr. Paul Broad said *"I am sceptical about such things. But I haven't got a clue what this was - it was very weird."* That same night, The Dowden Family saw a bright orange glow moving out to sea off Weymouth Bay. Mrs Donna Dowden *"We were dumbfounded. It definitely wasn't a firework because it disappeared and then came back again quite fast. It was in the sky and was almost golden, although it didn't have a definite shape."*

The Devil's Cryptograms

The 1980's were the time when crop circles were first brought to the media's attention, and the growing interest in the phenomena continues to capture the public's curiosity. The term *crop circle* is given to complex patterns, usually circular, but sometimes complicatedly geometric in design, which appear mysteriously in arable crops and dense grassland, often near ancient landmarks, though in recent reports around the world strange circles have appeared in woodlands, swamps, paddy fields, and even snow! They can vary in measurement from several feet to a thousand feet in diameter.

The condition of an arable crop, after a circle has appeared, is usually found as delicately-layered flattened corn or grass, with the stalks neatly swirled in a clockwise, or anti-clockwise, direction without being damaged, or broken in any way, at the stem of the plant. Samples of seeds and plants from *certain* crop circles, have often revealed altered cell structure, which have left scientists baffled.

The phenomenon of crop circles is far from being a modern one. In past centuries, people have written accounts, and drawn pictures of, unusually flattened circle formations in the field; often attributing them to the work of demons and fairies. Other folk say they are the result of some natural causes, such as crop diseases, feeding birds, rutting deer, and even rampant hedgehogs!

Some of the circles have been created as practical jokes by hoaxers, but they often fail to get the same effect; resulting in broken stems, dead plants, and debris left behind. There still remain a number, that some pundits believe to be genuine. Although there is no real definitive answer on how a circle is formed, past popular theories have included whirlwinds, plasma vortexes and earth energies. A much more modern theory is that they have been made by some cosmic influence, namely extra terrestrial's and UFOs. This idea has been fuelled by many sightings of mysterious lights, strange humming noises in the air and unusual craft seen in the vicinity before, during and after a crop circle has been formed.

Crop circles formed in Dorset first caught media attention in the summer of 1991, with the discovery of a flattened circle with a single outer ring measuring ten metres in a field at Knights-in-the-Bottom, Langton Herring. Local farm workers claimed they never saw or heard anything strange before the formation appeared.

From then circles have appeared all over the county's fields: Bincombe, Corfe Castle, Dorchester, Gussage All Saints, Maiden Castle, Milton Abbas, Puddletown, Ridgeway Hill (Weymouth), Shaftesbury, Sixpenny Handley, Sutton Poyntz, Winfrith Newburgh, Winterbourne Herringston, and Whitcombe.

Reported in the *Weymouth and Portland Advertiser* 19th August 1993.:

On the night of 15th August 1993, a strange mysterious light was seen by a lady, flying close to her home near Dorchester. Other witnesses included Mr. R. Peacocke of Dorchester, who saw a bright orange light flit extremely fast from one cloud to another as he travelled along

This ringed crop circles made its appearance in this field at
Knights in the Bottom, Langton Herring in the August 1991

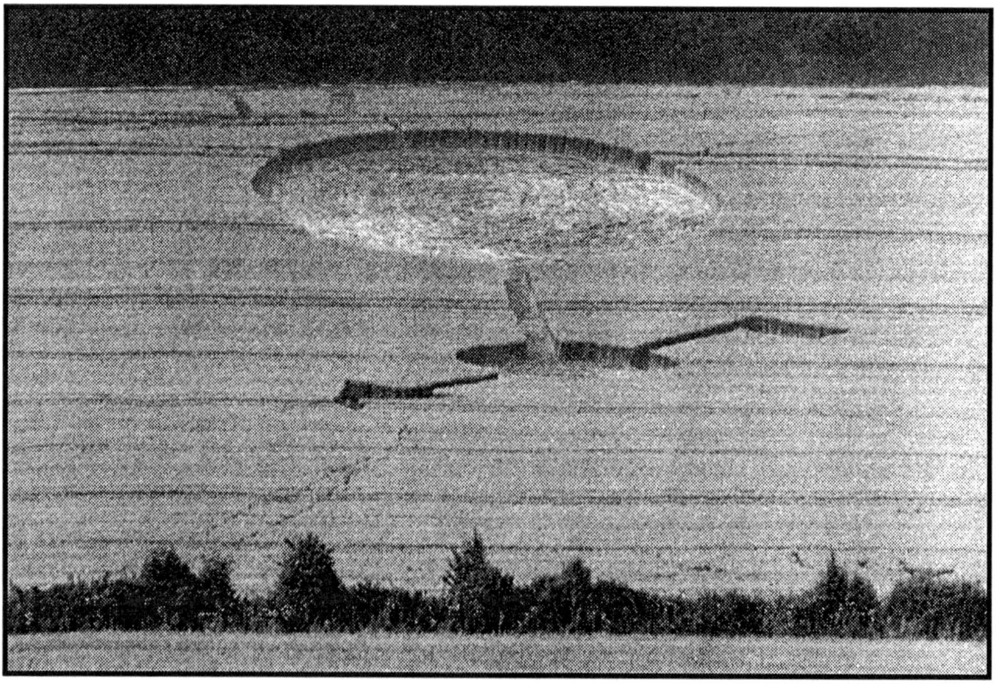

This crop circle with a 'Weather Vane' design was discovered at
Came Park, near Dorchester, in July 1995

Verne Common Road, Portland.

Both sightings coincided at 9.20 that night, but the next day brought an even *more* bizarre coincidence. In a field by the Ridgeway between Dorchester and Weymouth, a crop circle formation was discovered, measuring just over forty-two feet in diameter, with a ring of three foot six inches or so wide. Separating the two was a ring of corn, eight foot six inches wide. Both formations had flattened corn swirling in a clockwise direction.

The Bincombe landowner couldn't understand how anyone could have made the formation, which was only a hundred and nine yards from his home, without alerting his dogs or without trampling the corn to gain entry to make the design. It is true the formation crossed two sets of *tram lines*,* which could enable someone to walk along to make the formation, but it would have been an awfully long detour to get to the site without making themselves known. A hoaxer would have had to be very quick, as the night was very short and clear, and therefore he would have been seen from the road below.

Could it be possible that the mysterious lights seen the previous night were responsible for the creation of this circle?

On 26th June 1994, six crop circles were discovered in fields around the town of Dorchester. The largest corn circle to appear that weekend was in a field on the slopes of Conygar Hill, west of Herringston Dairy House, Winterbourne Herringston. The circle measured a hundred and thirty-one feet in diameter, with a unique pattern of eight inner circles ranging in thickness from two feet to thirty feet. All formations around the town appeared to be in perfect alignment. The appearance of these designs came after reports of strange lights seen in the sky the night before by two local witnesses. The first to see them was a nineteen-year-old man travelling alone on his way back from Poole. He was startled to see a sphere of reddish light the size of a beach ball go from side to side across the dual carriageway in front of him. The glowing orb continued to follow him in this manner from Bere Regis roundabout until he reached his home at Castle Park, Dorchester. The experience quite unnerved him. Meanwhile, a woman from Radipole, who was travelling by car, reported seeing two large circles of light in the sky. The two lights began to rotate, and then converged into a single ball of light, before taking off ,and then doubling back on themselves towards Puddletown. Later investigation showed no reports of helicopters or planes flying in the vicinity at that time. The crop circles that were discovered the next day appeared in perfect alignment and, it is thought, reflected the flight path taken by the spheres of light.

---

* *'tram lines.'* A term used to describe a pair of long parallel lines used by farm labourers to allow access to the crops for tractors.

Phenomenal Falls

Fafrotskies* or *Sky Falls* are the popular terms for occurrences in which objects other than those applicable to ordinary weather conditions, such as rain, snow, etc, descend without warning from the heavens, sometimes when the sky is completely clear, and for which there seems to be no logical explanation.

For many centuries, from all parts of the world, there have been reports of peculiar sky falls including frogs, fish, snails, rocks, stones, straw, and various types of seed and grain.

Though there have been many theories about these phenomenal falls, the most popular explanation is that they are caused by freak whirlwinds and waterspouts. Indeed, these must be very unusual winds to enable them to draw up living organisms, whether on land, rivers, lakes or sea, and to select and reject the surrounding environment in which they live, like sediment, weeds, rocks, plus various small animals, and carry them into the atmosphere only to deposit them many miles away.

This still does not explain how objects have fallen from clear skies or rain down continuously or repeatedly on one specific area of land for a period of time. American journalist, Charles Hoy Fort, imagined within the outer limits of our atmosphere there is some kind of *Super Sargasso Sea* where things are raised to this region by some mysterious force, only to be trapped until disturbed by passing storms.

However, there seems to be no rational explanation forthcoming to account for the percentage of really odd showers: coins, bank notes, wooden crosses, blobs of jelly, meat and even blood. Perhaps the answer lies beyond the physical aspect and in the realm of the supernatural!

In the Dorset Proceedings of *The Dorset Natural History and Archaeological Society* xlii (1921) In a article about *The Travels of Peter Mundy in Dorset.* The seventeenth century traveller, Peter Mundy, writes of his visit to Weymouth in 1635.

"When I came over to Weymouth side, I found there on the grass a multitude of small coulord shell snailes, ½ as bigg as pease. The people report they dropp out of the Ayre, findeing them on their hatts as they walke the fields. The like is reported of the raineing of small froggs in the Isle of Jersy (where I had formerly bene)."

***Fafrotskies**, condensation of **FAll FROm The SKIES**, term coined by cryptozoologist Ivan T Sanderson. Precipitation of objects from the sky that are not normally expected e.g. frogs, fish, coins etc.

Around the same time, this unusual storm of gastropods fell on Portland, where they were subsequently eaten by the grazing sheep. It was later said the consumption of shells gave the Portland mutton extra flavour!

An incident recorded in the *Prodigies in Somerset and Dorset, 1661-2* reprinted in *The Somerset and Dorset Notes and Queries, 1895,* In 1661 during the month of March, raining wheat was recorded in several parts of the county, a quantity of which was taken to Dorchester for inspection.

In Janet and Colin Bord's *Modern Mysteries of Britain* (1987), they refer to an incident that happerned in Bournemouth in 1821.

'One day we had a violent thunderstorm. Having no shelter, I was wet to the skin in a few minutes, and saw small yellow frogs, about the size of a florin or half-crown, dashed on the ground all around me...Thousands were impaled on furze bushes on the common close by, and days afterwards the stench from decomposing bodies was very noticeble'

A huge volume of water fell on the village of Chetnole in the 19th century. Charles Hoy Fort wrote in his book *LO!* (1931). With reference to an article that appeared in the Meteorological Magazine

"One of these bodies of water that were not rain fell at Chetnole, Dorsetshire, England. The people, hearing crashes, looked up at a hill, and saw it frilled with billows. Watery ruffs, from eight to ten feet high heaved on the hill. The village was tossed in a surf. "The cause of this remarkable occurrence was for sometime unknown but it has now been ascertained that a waterspout burst on Batcombe Hill". So wrote Mr. Symons, in whose brains there was no more consciousness of all that was going on in the world about him than there was in any other pair of scissors

It was not ascertained that a waterspout had burst on Batcombe Hill. No waterspout was seen. What was ascertained was the columns of water of unknown origin had fallen high on the Hill, gouging holes, some of the eight or nine feet deep. Though Mr. Symons gave the waterspout-explanation, it did occur to him to note that there was no statement that the water was salty

People reported hearing the sound of rumbling thunder and looking towards Batcombe Hill. They saw a great wave, swollen to a height of eight to ten feet upon it. The unusual volume of water came crashing down the hillside engulfing the village in a large surf."

In the *Dorset Echo*, 26th October 2000, there was a report of a mystery explosion which sent a huge column of water into the air near the Cobb at Lyme Regis. Several people are said to have witnessed a water spout 100 metres from the Cobb Gate Jetty, and reported it to the harbour master. Lyme Regis inshore lifeboat searched the area but found nothing, and Portland Coastguard said the explosion could have been caused by an old piece of ordnance.

In an article about frogs that fell in South London, *The Daily Mail* 5th March 1988 mentions

that in 1948, a shower of herring interrupted some surprised golfers while playing a round of golf at Bournemouth.

In issue 26 of the *Fortean Times* it was reported that in the *Daily Express 9th August 1977*, there was a report that on 8th August 1977, a shower of rain fell at Poole, which developed into an unusual cocktail of falling hay and grass clumps with roots and soil. According to witness John Kay, who was holidaying with his family at Rockly Sands caravan site. *" I am not crazy. It did happen. Grass fell on me! There had been a shower of rain... Then suddenly it began to rain grass. There was a large rain-cloud about 1000ft above us and it was coming from that."* said Mr. Kay.

The Dorset Weather Book by Mark Ching and Ian Currie (Nov 1997) tells how Poole and Bournemouth were bombarded by a severe hailstorm on 5th June 1983. Some of the hail that fell was compared to the average size of a hen's egg. One resident collected up to 92 pieces, but what was curious still, is that embedded in these pellets of ice were lumps of coal! Meanwhile, further along the River Frome, this mixture of hail and coke caused a herd of cattle to stampede, and nearby, a lady was bruised trying to rescue a tortoise from her garden.

On 19th October 1988, a substance resembling white paint was seen falling from the heavens, spattering houses in Bournemouth, leaving their occupants amazed, and the police - who were called to the scene - baffled.

In issue 51 of the *Fortean Times* it was reported that in the *Daily Mirror* 20th October 1998, there was a story telling how, on 19th October 1988, a substance resembling white paint was seen falling from the heavens spattering houses in Bournemouth, leaving their occupants amazed, and the police, who were called to the scene, baffled. Eleven days later it was reported in the *Daily Mirror* 29th October 1988. An even more unusual substances fell from the sky on 25th October 1988. Police and emergency services were alerted after a member of a trawler crew off the Dorset coast reported their boat was engulfed in a sticky white cobweb that had descended from the sky. With night drawing in, the mysterious cloud that rained sticky threads, and was estimated to be thirty square miles across was now drifting over the area of Christchurch. Later a coastguard spokesman told newspapers. *"We have no idea what it is or where it comes from."*

This phenomena which has been frequently reported around the world is often termed 'Angel Hair.' Witnesses usually describe this substance as being not unlike a spider's web, cotton wool, or candy floss. But it disintegrates when attempts are made to analyse it. On occasions when this white gossamer has been seen falling, witnesses have also sighted UFO activity.

Another account was reported in the *Dorset Echo* 7th December 1994 of freak weather phenomena which happened on 3rd December 1994. Mr. S. Clark, a resident of King's Road, Radipole, Weymouth reported that small red and blue stones fell from the sky, littering the pavement outside his home. A frightened neighbour was the first to alert Mr. Clark, having witnessed this phenonenon from a car outside his home.

Strange Storms and Ball Lightning

Fierce and spectacular storms, have from time immemorial been regarded as something other than being mere natural phenomena. In ancient mythology, it was often thought thunder, lightning, and strong winds, were manifestations of vengeful gods. In other parts of the world, a person killed or struck down by lightning, was deemed to have been directly overwhelmed by the divine wrath.

During the Middle Ages, and especially the seventeenth and eighteenth centuries, there was a strong belief that particular bad or strange storms were conjured up by the Devil and his disciples; namely witches.

In those dark times, many a supposed witch was tried and condemned for their participation in summoning a storm, to wreck ships at sea, damage property, crops or livestock, on land and also for using their skills to manipulate storms, to avenge themselves against certain individuals.

An incident recorded in the *Prodigies in Somerset and Dorset, 1661-2* reprinted in *The Somerset and Dorset Notes and Queries, 1896*, tells how on 3rd May 1662, a violent thunderstorm erupted above the village of Purse Caundle. A woman by the name of Dorothy Chapman, who had a reputation for cursing, was struck down by a bolt of lightning that burst through the front door of her house, throwing her three children to the floor, and striking her dead, as she sat before the hearth. Her clothes were ripped and torn above her waist, and her hair was stripped from her head, and scattered about the house. The house had literally turned upside down, and - in the air - hung a thick layer of smoke and the distinct odour of brimstone.

Her husband, Leonard Chapman, came back to witness this terrible devastation, but soon left the house with his eldest son, vowing never to return, fearing that he too would be struck down by this malevolent force.

An incident recorded in the *Prodigies in Somerset and Dorset, 1661-2* reprinted in *The Somerset and Dorset Notes and Queries, 1895, tells the story of a* sheet of lightning struck the town of Shaftsbury in the early part of June 1662, which caused several people to be thrown to the ground in the street. It also smashed down the door and entered the home of a godly minister, throwing him, his two daughters, and young child, down hard on the floor. Luckily none were injured. The lightning then left the house by breaking through a glass window, leaving behind a smoke-filled room. The pewter dishes kept in the minister's kitchen were all found to be melted.

In the seventeenth century, another unusual thunderstorm visited the town of Shaftsbury. Local residents were praying at one of the town's churches when the storm struck. Many of the congregation fell to their knees. It was later said that the sign of the cross appeared on their bodies after the storm had passed.

Spontaneous images of the crucifix imprinted on the Shaftesbury congregation are just one of

many accounts of this strange phenomena. In their book *Phenomena - A Book of Wonders*, John Michell and Robert J.M Rickard tell of similar incidents that were found during a Summer storm at Wells Cathedral, Somerset in 1596, and also during the eruption of Vesuvius, Italy in 1660. One theory for this effect is the exposure to intense light from lightning that can transfer an image of local scenery or an object on to bodies, garments or any other object. Similar to the effects when the atomic bomb was dropped half a mile away in Nagasaki, Japan, in 1945, the flash from the blast produced *'nuclear shadows'* to be cast onto objects and buildings.

It was this idea of *Lightning Photography* that caused much debate among serious nineteenth century scientists. They named the subject *keraunography*, but some images found in impossible places, for example, imprinted on the skin beneath garments or on a wall behind wardrobes, remain unexplained.

Featured in the *Dorset Echo* 29th May 1999, weatherman Mark Ching talks about some very unusual weather phenomena that were witnessed by Mrs. and Miss Warry, as they were walking near Ringstead Bay in 1887, when, due to an approaching thunderstorm, they had to take shelter in the disused quarry, near Ringstead Dairy. On entering the quarry, they were astonished - and somewhat frightened - to see all around them, a vast number of strange lights, the size of billiard balls, all moving up and down and hovering at different heights, from inches off the ground to three feet above their heads. The storm soon passed, and the two women - not wishing to remain in the quarry any longer - hurried away. What Mrs. and Miss Warry had witnessed was probably the phenomena of Ball Lightning.

Ball lightning is relatively short lived, occasionally lasting up to 20 seconds, and is most often seen floating through the air in the shape of a glowing red, orange or yellow ball , 10cm to 40cm in diameter. Sometimes it appears blue, with spokes or rays, like a luminous cornflower, and sometimes a hissing or buzzing sound may be heard. The exact nature of ball lightning isn't clearly understood, through theorists believe it consists of a mixture of ionised gas and electromagnetic field energy. It tends to form after an initial flash of lighting, and sometimes seems to be guided by metal conductors. As a rule, ball lightning vanishes silently, but in about 30% of cases it explodes.

On 30th January 1922, Mrs Richardson wrote about a ball of fire that was witnessed by her gardener. She writes:

> *"Thomas Issacs (my gardener) was outside the potting shed at 7.30 - 7.40am when he saw a ball of fire about the size of two fists come out of the clouds and move away in the general direction of Chickerall, till it was lost to view behind the shed in front of which he was standing. No noise was heard; it was perhaps a meteor but more likely that it was globular lightning."*

Reported in the *Dorset Echo* 30th October 2000, Weymouth had been hitting the weather headlines at the Meteorological office with a chain of reports about ball lightning. One of them was made by Mr. Graeme McQuilkin, who saw the phenomenon opposite his home in The Finches Road, Littlemoor on Friday 28th October 2000.

> *"I got up, looked out and saw a white bright ball of light almost hovering on the roof of a house opposite It moved up towards the top of the roof and then changed direc-*

tion and came back down again before disappearing. I have never seen anything like this before. I thought it was ball lightning and I rang the Met Office up to tell them so. They told me that I was the fifth person to ring up about it in 20 minutes."

It was reported in the *Western Gazette* 31st August 2006, that on Saturday 19th August at 5.15pm, Dorset historian and Author Rodney Legg was walking up a flight of steps from the bottom of his garden at his home in Mapperton, near Beaminster with his two cats after a sudden downpour. Mr Legg was suddenly confronted by a bright flash and a simultaneous crack of thunder. He believes he witnessed a rare incident of ball lightning.

"Ten feet in front of us was a dense oval of blue flame which burst from something not much bigger than a rugby ball," he said.

"It rolled over the site of a bonfire and disappeared through the fence into the garden of Fairview."

His neighbour, Julie Paniccia was sorting through a box of bric-a-brac and looking out across her garden into the valley. She said:

"I was frightened out of my wits. I have never seen anything like it in my life. A big red and orange flame, pointed at the front end, flashed across the window and went into the hedge behind the chicken run."

On the other side of the hedge at East Cottage, Lorraine and Nick Allison and their family were indoors watching television. The electricity cut out and a car alarm was set off but there was no sign of any damage inside or out. Mr. Legg, said:

"There was no other thunder or lightning either before or after the phenomena.

"Ball lightning is such a rarity that it was not properly described until a few years ago.

"It must come in various sizes as it has been described as resembling golf or tennis balls when it has appeared in mid-flight and rolled down the aisle of airliners during electrical storms.

"The energy from my fireball appeared to come up from the ground rather than down from the sky."

Spontaneous Combustion

Often, when there is a sudden outbreak of fire, either in a building, or on land, the cause is usually explained by carelessness, arson, or natural causes. For example, a lightning strike, or when heat is generated during fermentation, produced by moisture contained in plants. A similar effect can also be found in other organic matter: bird droppings that have accumulated over a period of time on roofs, but fires that mysteriously appear without any explanation have always been a puzzling enigma.

In April 1827, the east cliff at Ringstead Bay, near Weymouth, once caught fire. The cause was once thought to be the effects of a lightning strike igniting the oil shale, but geologists' later discovered heat generated by the decomposition of iron pyrites ignited the bituminous shale, and black stone. Once alight, the cliff was said to have continued to burn for several days, until it exhausted itself; hence the name of this area - *'Burning Cliff'*.

People visited from miles around to witness the fiery phenomena near Ringstead

Another outbreak of spontaneous combustion ,similar to that of Burning Cliff, also occurred on the landslips known as the *'Spittles'*, between Charmouth and Lyme Regis in 1751 and again in 1908, when it was nick-named the *'Burning Volcano'* or *'Burning Mountain'*.

It was reported in the *News of the World* 21st July 1996, that an unusual blast of heat was experienced by Laraine Davis from Poole, as she opened her back door on a cold night to retrieve washing from her line.

> *"It was like opening an oven door when your face is too close to it. It was eerie and silent as well. The hair rose on the back of my neck."*

Days later Laraine heard from her neighbour that the contents of there greenhouse had been incinerated - yet the structure itself was untouched. She said.

"the heat was so fierce it destroyed tools. Only two lumps of molten plastic - once a garden table and a wheelbarrow - proved there had been anything in there at all. The glass was not cracked and shrubs alongside were untouched. Even a small fire would have lit up the area and been visible to us all. But no one saw anything."

So what this mysterious heat was remains a mystery to the residents of Poole.

Dreams of the Future

Throughout the ages, many people have had an unexpected vision or glimpse of the future, and a majority have become very famous for their prophecies.

Precognition usually occurs in dreams, or during times when we daydream. These are more visual and precise in detail than premonitions, which are unfocused sensations, that occur when in a conscious state, or as remembrance of a semi-forgotten dream. These precognitions of the future are likely remembered for their accuracy. Some of the famous prophets express their prophecies in a vague way, mainly in the form of riddles. It is because of this, that people, when reciting premonitions, precognitions, and predictions, tend to interpret them into whatever they believe the prophecy tells them - *some* of which seem to have come true!

In Marianne. R. Dacombe's *Dorset Up Long and Down Along* (1935) she tales the story that one night during the seventeenth century, Baron Ryves lived near the town of Blandford. Once while he was asleep, he dreamt that he was walking in his garden, when the ground shook beneath him, and a sound of rumbling filled the air. He looked up in horror, to see before him, a huge monster with fire seeming to usher out of its nostrils. The monster approached with great speed, and he quickly hid from it among bushes. He watched with curiosity, as the beast continued its journey. Passing before him, he was taken aback with astonishment to see a multitude of heads of human beings illuminated by light, looking out of holes, which ran the full length of the monster's body. The dream abruptly ended after the monster had been consumed by the earth. Did Baron Ryves dream foretell the arrival of the Somerset and Dorset Railway that opened two hundred years later?

The Stalbridge Cross once had a carved Latin inscription upon it, which is said to have contained a prophecy that, if the inscription was ever erased, the Greek island of Rhodes would fall to invaders. The prophecy came to a *Hospitaller** knight of Malta called Galfridius de Mervin in 1309, as he laid in bed, recovering from terrible wounds received in a victorious battle over the Saracens. Recovering in bed, a vision of St. John suddenly appeared. The saint was clutching a bottle of ointment, which miraculously healed his wounds. The vision of St. John ordered him to erect a pillar, which was to be removed into several countries, where he might in future times set his mind to live. He also told him that an inscription should be en-

---

* *'Hospitaller.'* Members of the religious and military Order of the Hospital of St. John of Jerusalem founded in 1100.

graved on the pillar. The Saint prophesied the Knights of Malta should possess the island of Rhodes without interruption, until the time should come when the said inscription on the pillar should suddenly be obliterated. After many years of carrying out St. John's instructions and obtaining great wealth, Galfridius de Mervin reached England bringing the pillar with him. He stayed at the Dorset town of Stalbridge, where his sister Elfrida married the Lord of the manor of Stalbridge. It was here that he decided to erect the pillar, where it remains to this day.

In January 1522 during the reign of Henry VIII the inscription was erased, and the fated island of Rhodes was conquered by Solomon the Magnificent, thus fulfilling the prophecy of St. John.

In Harry Ludlam's *The Restless Ghosts of Ladye Place, and Other True Hauntings* (1967). In 1924 a Somerset gentleman by the name of Percy Newport had to retire from his butchery business due to ailing health, and because of this, he came to Dorset to be cared for by his daughter and her husband (Mr. and Mrs. Faulkener), who lived at Leigh.

On 27th January 1925, Mrs. Faulkener was busy cleaning in the kitchen, when she heard her father upstairs in his bedroom shouting and bellowing. Leaving her work, she rushed to her father's aid, and found him sitting up in bed staring vacantly into space. *"Look, look. That nurse. She has a black pot with hot steaming stuff in it. And a card, the ten of diamonds. She is threatening me, she will empty it over my head if you don't take the card away."* Mrs Faulkener looked around the room, but could not see anyone, and after calming her father down went back to the kitchen.

Later that day, Mr Newport dressed, and went downstairs. Spying a pack of playing cards on a shelf, he told his daughter to remove the ten of diamonds and throw it into the fire. However, she refused to do it, as the playing cards would then be useless.

The next day Mr. Newport had to return to Somerset to go into the Victoria Hospital for an operation, but he didn't recover, and died *TEN* days later.

The funeral started at his brother's house in the Somerset town of Frome. The coffin was carried out of the house and placed on a bier* in the garden. The dead man's brother, together with Mr. Faulkener, was leading the funeral procession on foot when, glancing down, both men saw on the path at the head of the coffin a playing card - the ten of diamonds. Anxious not to disturb the procession, they left it where it was, but after the funeral went back to retrieve it. However, it had vanished.

A few days later, Newport's brother visited the Faulkener's at Leigh, and after dinner they all decided to play a game of cards. A brand new pack was brought to the table and slit open. But before they started the game, all the cards were checked. Just one card was missing - the TEN OF DIAMONDS! Was Percy Newport's vision a precognition of his own death? Or was it all an uncanny coincidence?

---

* *'Bier.'* *The movable stand on which a coffin is placed before burial and which it is carried to the grave by bearers on foot.*

Strange Disappearances

It is no coincidence that the first line of Robert Newland's poem *Beware!* says, *'Beware of that lonely forest pool.'* The warning echoed in these words has, through the ages, been impressed upon the minds of people everywhere. Ponds and pools have always had an air of mystery about them, and wise folk know all too well of the sinister beings, (monsters, nymphs and water demons), that lurk in their hidden depths. Children and unwary travellers are particularly at risk, for not only do these isolated pools have one or more sinister inhabitants, but also many are believed to be bottomless! Thus we find that we are constantly reminded of the unfortunate soul whose name is forever associated with the forbidden place in which they have met their untimely death, whether by lure or accident.

BEWARE!

Beware! Of that lonely forest pool,
For shameless beings live there,
Maidens so beautiful to see,
Maidens so sweet to hear,
Beckoning you to caress and kiss,
Invitations to do what you wish.

But! Beware! Human they are not,
For they are water nymphs, a treacherous lot,
Cold webbed hands with an iron grip,
Will drag you down into the water pit,
Under the water and into the gloom,
Down and down to meet your doom!

Robert Newland

Dangerous water nymphs are said to inhabit the lonely forest pool known as Rushy Pond at Thorncombe Woods, Higher Bockhampton

A quarter of a mile southeast of Hardy's cottage at Higher Bockhampton, near Dorchester, there is a circular pool called Rushy Pond. The pool is said to be inhabited by beautiful water nymphs that lure unwary travellers into the pool, never to be seen again.

Near Pine Lodge Farm at Higher Bockhampton, less than half a mile south of the farm, below Duddle Hill opposite the former Pond House, there is a spring-fed pond known as *Heedless William's Pond*. It acquired this name due to an unfortunate accident, which occurred one Winters night.

It was probably during either the seventeenth or eighteenth century, that a coachman by the name of `Heedless William` ('Heedless' being the nickname given, due to his reckless driving), had his misfortune.

One cold December night, (Christmas Eve or New Year's Eve) William, in a drunken state, set off with his coach-and-four full of passengers. He careered recklessly around the country lanes with his passengers clinging on for dear life. Approaching Duddle Hill, William turned the corner too fast, and came off the road, rolling the coach headlong into the pond. William and the passengers lay unconscious, their fate of drowning imminent, as the coach quickly submerged into the dark icy depths.

The muddy waters completely covered the victims of this accident; the only item to remain visible was William's ground-ash whip stick. It is said the mature ash tree, that stands to this day at the edge of the pond, is the whip; which took root, and later budded.

Obscured by trees the bottomless pool know as Heedless William's Pond, the large ash tree in the centre is reputed to be the whip staff that took root

The bottomless 'Heedless William's Pond'

A similar incident is said to have taken place at a large pool of water adjacent to the turning to Winterborne Monkton, near Dorchester. One night a coach-and-four careered off the Dorchester Road into this muddy pool, and is said to have disappeared without a trace.

Located at Bryants Puddle Heath, Affpuddle, there is another reputedly bottomless pool called Rimsmoor Pond where another coach once disappeared. One dark stormy night, a coach and horses was travelling at great speed along the byway between Cheselbourne and Melcombe Bingham, when suddenly the coachman took the double bend in the road below Highdon Hill too sharply, and lost control of both horses. The coach went headlong into the withy beds, where it slowly submerged, never to be seen again.

In a similar tale, a large pool of water fed by the River Stour at Durweston, near Blandford, is said to be the home for a horse and cart that once disappeared there.

BIBLIOGRAPHY

▶ *The following books were very helpful in the creation of Dark Dorset and we are particularly indebted to them.*

Ashley, Harry:	*Dorset Inns*, 1987.
Ashley, Harry:	*The Dorset Coast - History, Lore and Legend*, 1992.
Baring-Gould, Sabine:	*A Book of Folklore*, 1913.
Bickley, Francis L	*Where Dorset meets Devon*, 1911.
Bord, Janet and Colin:	*Alien Animals*, 1980.
Bord, Janet and Colin:	*Modern Mysteries of Britain*, 1987.
Boswell, Babara:	*Leigh: A Dorset Village*, 1988.
Brown, Christopher:	*Haunted Sherborne.* 1975.
Brown, Mary:	*Dorset: Customs, Curiosities and Country-lore*, 1990.
Brown, Theo:	*Devon Ghosts*, 1982.
Cooper, J.C:	*Brewer's Book of Myth and Legend*, 1992.
Crawford, F. M:	*Wandering Ghosts*, 1911.
Dewar, H.S.L:	*The Dorset Osser*, 1968.
Dewar, H.S.L:	*The Giant of Cerne Abbas*, 1968.
Dacombe, Marianne. R:	*Dorset Up Along and Down Along*, 1935.
Davies, Glanville. J:	*Touchyng Witchcrafte and Sorcerye*, 1985.
Downe, Jonathan	*The Rising of the Moon - The Devonshire UFO Triangle* 2005 ed.
Doyle, Arthur Coanan:	*The Coming of the Fairies*, 1922.
Dudridge, M:	*Superstition and Folklore of the West Country*, 1984.
Durston, Cecil. A:	*Tales from the Ragged Louse*, 1987.
Chambers	*The Book of Days*, 1888.
Ching, Mark and Currie, Ian:	*The Dorset Weather Book.* 1997.
Colby, C.B:	*Strangely Enough*, 1959.
Eedle, Marie de G :	*A History of Beaminster*, 1984.
Eedle, Marie de G and Paul, Raymond E.	*The Death and Times of John Daniel*, 1987.
Ellis Chris and Owens, Andy:	*Haunted Dorset*, 2004.
Emerson, William R:	*Monmouth's Rebellion*, 1951.
Farquharson-Coe, A:	*Hants and Dorset's Ghost's*, 1975.
Fraser, Mark:	*Big Cats in Britain Yearbook 2006*, 2006
Fort, Charles. Hoy:	*The Book of the Damned*, 1919.
	New Lands, 1923.
	Lo!, 1931.
	Wild Talents, 1932.
Guttridge, Roger:	*Ten Dorset Mysteries*, 1989.
Goldsworthy, Margaret:	*The Dorset Bedside Anthology*, 1951.
Gunnel, Clive, *et al*:	*Secret Dorset*, 1995.
Grinsell, Leslie	*Dorset Barrows*, 1952.
Harte, Jeremy:	*Cuckoo Pounds and Singing Barrows*, 1986.
Harte, Jeremy:	*Discover Dorset - Legends*, 1998.
Hartland, Edwin Sidney	*English Fairy and Other Folk Tales*, 1890.
Hine, Richard:	*History of Beaminster*, 1914.
Hole, Christina:	*Haunted England*, 1940.
Hutchins, John:	*The History and Antiquities of the County of Dorset, Vol 1 – 4*, 1774.
Hutchings, Monica:	*Inside Dorset*, 1965.

Howard, Nesta and Underwood, Spencer:	*Penguin Guide - Wilts and Dorset*, 1949.
Hopkins, R. Thurston	*Thomas Hardy's Dorset*, 1922.
Hymas, Maureen:	*Dorset Folklore*, 1981.
Knott, Olive:	*Witches of Dorset*, 1974.
Lea, Hermann:	*Some Dorset Superstitions*, 1969.
Lea, Hermann:	*Thomas Hardy's Wessex*, 1966.
Legg, Rodney	*A Guide to Dorset Ghosts*, 1969.
Legg, Rodney:	*Mysterious Dorset*, 1987.
Lloyd, Polly	*Legends of Dorset,* 1988.
Ludlam, Harry:	*The Restless Ghosts of Ladye Place, and Other True Hauntings*, 1967.
McEwan, Graham. J:	*Mystery Animals of Britain and Ireland*, 1986.
Moiser. Chris.	*Mystery Cats of Devon and Cornwall*, 2001.
Michell, John and Rickard, Robert J.M:	*Phenomena - A Book of Wonders*, 1977.
Morley Geoffrey:	*Smuggling in Hampshire and Dorset 1700-1850*, 1983.
Newland, Stephen:	*Weird and Wonderful Tales of Dorset*, 1982.
Knight, Peter:	*Ancient Stones of Dorset*, 1996.
Knight, Peter:	*Sacred Dorset*, 1998.
Osborn, George:	*Dorset Curiosities*, 1986.
Perrott, Tom, *et al*:	*Strange Dorset Stories*, 1991.
Pinney, Michael:	*Bettiscombe,* 1988.
Pridham, Llewellyn:	*The Dorset Coastline*, 1954.
Readers Digest:	*Folklore, Myths and Legends of Britain*, 1973.
Roots, Ivan:	*The Monmouth Rising*, 1986.
Street, Sean:	*Tales of Old Dorset*, 1985.
Turner, James:	*Ghosts in the South West*, 1973
Treves, Frederick:	*Highways and Byways in Dorset*, 1906.
Trubshaw Bob:	*Explore Phantom Black Dogs*, 2005.
Udal, John. Symonds:	*Dorsetshire Folklore,* 1922.
Underwood, Peter:	*Ghosts of Dorset*, 1988.
Underwood, Peter:	*Ghostly Encounters*, 1992.
Waring, Edward:	*Ghosts and Legends of the Dorset Countryside*, 1977.
Whitlock, Ralph:	*In Search of Lost Gods*, 1979.
Wilnecker, Patricia M:	*Ghostly Tales of Wessex*, 1995.
Wood, G. Bernard:	*Smugglers Britain*, 1966.

▶ *Other articles and accounts on Fortean phenomena, Legends and Folklore related subjects were also found in the following, magazines and periodicals:*

Animals & Men - The Journal of The Centre for Fortean Zoology
Bournemouth Evening Echo
Bridport News
The Daily Mail
Dorset Evening Echo
Dorset life
Dorset: The County Magazine
Dorset Year Book
Devon Association
Fate - True Reports of the Strange Unknown
Fortean Times - The Journal of Strange Phenomena
Notes and Queries of Somerset and Dorset
Proceedings of the Dorset Natural History and Archaeological Society
The Western Gazette
The Weymouth and Portland Advertiser

ABOUT THE AUTHORS

Robert Newland was born in London in 1969, and moved to Dorset in 1979. A keen writer, artist, and published poet, he has a strong passion for the Dorset countryside, which he loves to explore. He has a broad band of interests that range from photography, legends and folklore, to history, astronomy and nature. As well as having his works published in *The Countryman*, *Dorset Life* and the *Dorset Echo*, he has also published '*Dark Dorset: Fairies*'

Mark North was born in Dorset in 1975. He has long been fascinated by local legends, folklore and Fortean phenomena, and has built up an extensive collection of data and images on the subjects. Apart from collecting legends and folklore, other pastimes include drawing cartoons and illustrating magazines, and also he reads horror and science fiction, especially the works of H.G. Wells and Eric Frank Russell, whom he admires. He is also Assistant Director, and Design Manager for the Centre for Fortean Zoology.

ACKNOWLEDGEMENTS

We wish to express our gratitude to all those who have helped us during the creation of Dark Dorset:

Tina Askew, Jonathan Downes, Jo Draper, Richard Freeman, Merrily Harpur, Jeremy Harte, Sid Higgins, Graham Inglis, Corinna James, Derek Johnson, Audrey 'Stiv' Johnson, Peter Knight, Chris Moiser, Stephen Newland, Jonathan North, Catherine O'Donnell, David Phillips, The staff of the Dorset County Record Office, The staff of the Dorchester and Weymouth Public Library, The Dorset County Museum, The Wessex Morris Men and the readers who emailed us stories and information via our website.

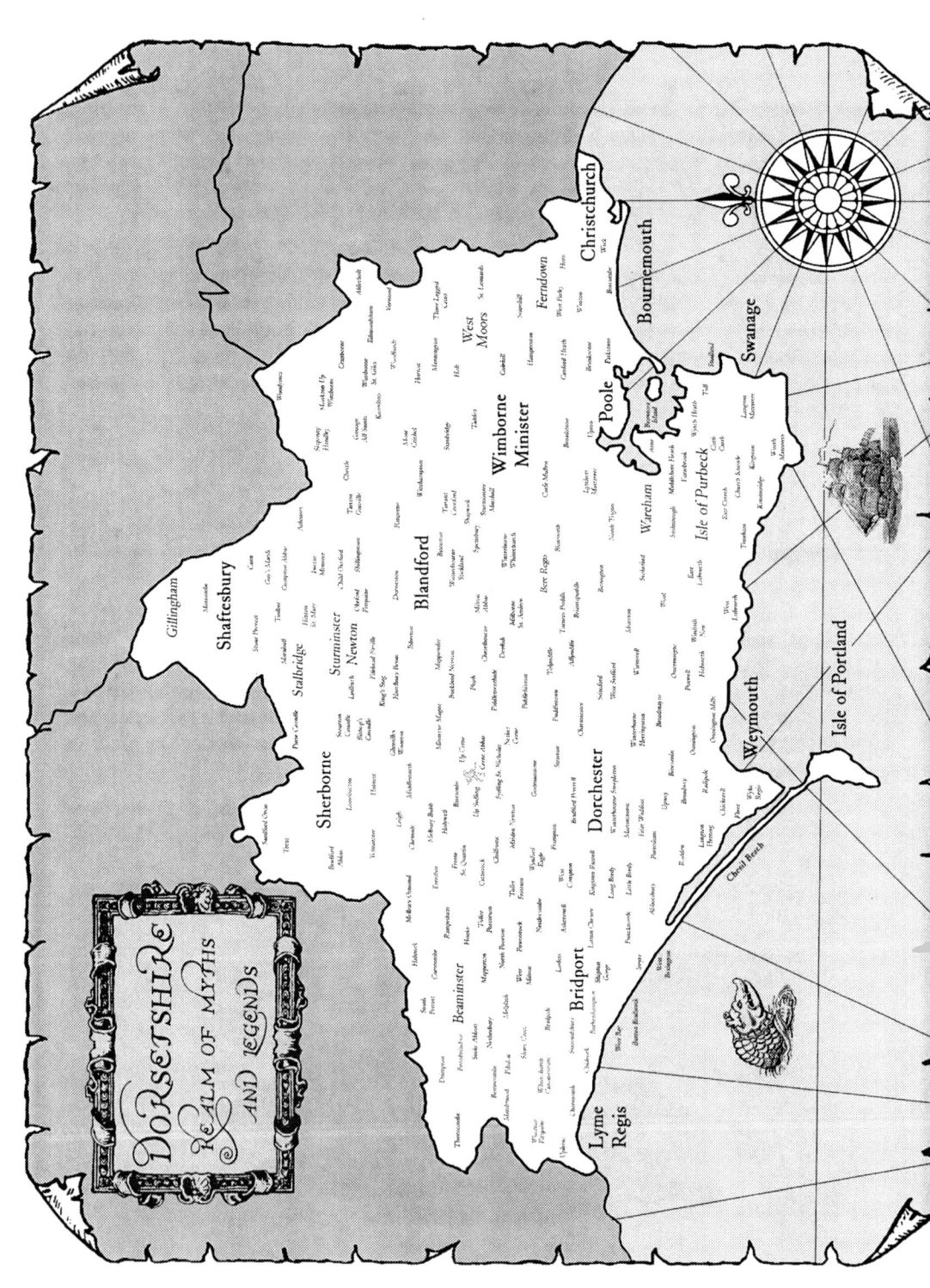

INDEX

This index acts as a guide for the curious traveller, to folklore and mysteries that can be found in locations all over Dorset. They are identified as Towns, Village parishes, Earthworks, Coastline, and Borders, with a category of interests that may be found there giving quick reference to the visitor

- Dorset Towns and Villages -

Abbotsbury

Customs	166
Ghosts	41

Acton

Devil	193

Affpuddle

Stone	183
Strange Event	264

Ashley Chase

Will O' Wisp	126

Ashmore

Fairies	108

Askerswell

Ghosts	61

Batcombe

Devil	179, 181
Stone	179
Strange Event	179, 253
Witchcraft	179, 181

Beaminster

Dark History	67
Ghosts	17, 63-68
Mysterious Creatures	216
Stone	189
Will O'Wisp	121

Belchalwell

Mysterious Creatures	223

Bere Regis

Devil/Stone	189
Fairies	110
Ghosts	15, 16
Mysterious Creatures	207, 209
Strange Event	251

Bettiscombe

Dark History	76

Ghosts	17, 73-89	**Broadwindsor**	
Stone	83		
		Ghosts	18
Birdsmoorgate		*Mysterious Creatures*	216, 236
Devil	196	**Burton Bradstock**	
Bincombe		*Mysterious Creatures*	197, 233
Fairies	105	**Came**	
Strange Event	249, 251		
Will O' Wisp	124	*Dark History*	131
		Ghost	41
Blandford		*Will O' Wisps*	124
Ghosts	52	**Cann**	
Mysterious Creatures	223		
Strange Event	259, 264	*Devil*	191
Witchcraft	177		
		Cattistock	
Bournemouth			
		Ghosts	101
Ghosts	23		
Mysterious Creatures	213, 235	**Cerne Abbas**	
Strange Event	243, 253, 254		
		Customs	135 - 137, 139 - 141
Bovington		*Dark History*	144
		Giants	139
Ghosts	25, 94	*Saints*	135
Bradford Peverell		**Charmouth**	
Ghosts	15	*Strange Event*	258
		Witchcraft	147
Briantspuddle			
		Cheselbourne	
Ghosts	18		
Stone	183	*Devil*	194
		Giants	183
Bridport		*Stone*	184
		Witchcraft	164
Customs	156		
Dark History	71, 131	**Chetnole**	
Ghosts	14, 23, 91, 92, 104		
Mysterious Creatures	214, 216	*Strange Event*	253
Strange Event	247, 248		

Chideock

Mysterious Creatures	228

Christchurch

Mysterious Creatures	204
Strange Event	254

Church Knowle

Ghosts	40

Colehill

Dark History	20

Corfe

Devil/Stone	189
Strange Event	136, 247, 249
Fairies	110
Witchcraft/Customs	155
Ghosts	22

Corfe Mullen

Ghosts	43
Witchcraft/Customs	156

Corscombe

Devil/Stone	189
Fairies	110

Cranborne

Fairies	109
Ghosts	15
Mysterious Creatures	213, 228

Dorchester

Customs	145, 169
Dark History	20, 27, 29, 65, 69, 71, 84, 150
Devil	127, 128, 194
Ghosts	11, 37, 41, 43, 45, 46, 49, 50, 51
Mysterious Creatures	207, 216
Strange Event	246, 247, 248, 249, 251, 253, 262, 265
Stone	184
Witchcraft	150

Drimpton

Ghosts	18
Black Dogs	216

Durweston

Dark History	152
Mysterious Creatures	224
Strange Event	264
Witchcraft	152

East Chelborough

Fairies	117, 119

Evershot

Dark History	28, 29
Ghosts	22, 28

Fleet

Mysterious Creatures	233
Strange Event	241, 245

Folke

Fairies	119

Forde

Devil	196
Ghosts	57
Strange Event	240

Fordington

Stone	184

Friar Waddon

Dark History	83, 84
Mysterious Creatures	233
Strange Event	247

Furzebrook

Devil	194

Gillingham

Ghosts	20

Gussage All Saints

Strange Event	249

Halstock

Ghosts	13, 14
Saints	12
Witchcraft	153

Hampreston

Will O' Wisp	124

Hamworthy

Ghosts	102
Dark History	43

Hawkchurch

Witchcraft	147, 156

Higher Bockhampton

Ghosts	45
Fairies	262
Strange Event	262

Hilton

Witchcraft	147

Hinton Parva

Dark History	20

Holnest

Fairies	119
Ghosts	15

Holworth

Strange Event	241

Horton

Ghosts	23
Mysterious Creatures	228

Ibberton

Stone	184

Kingston Russell

Ghosts	14

Langton Herring

Stone	182
Strange Event	249

Langton Matravers

Devil	193
Witchcraft	155

Leigh

Customs	169
Strange Event	260
Witchcraft	169, 170

Lewcombe

Fairies	117, 119

Littlebredy

Fairies/Stone	113

Litton Cheney

Ghosts   98

Loders

Ghosts   14
Fairies   112

Lulworth

Ghosts   14, 20, 41, 124
Mysterious Creatures   202, 233
Will O' Wisp   124
Witchcraft   148

Lyme Regis

Dark History   69, 71
Devil   194
Ghosts   72, 94
Mysterious Creatures   224, 227
Strange Event   239, 253, 258

Lytchett Matravers

Ghosts   17

Lytchett Minster

Ghosts   18
Strange Event   243

Mapperton

Dark History   133
Strange Event   257

Mappowder

Strange Event   240

Marnhull

Customs   156
Ghosts   18
Witchcraft   148, 156, 163

Marshwood

Devil   194

Melbury Bubb

Dark History   27-29
Ghosts   30

Melbury Osmond

Customs   143

Melcombe Bingham

Witchcraft   164
Strange Event   264

Melcombe Horsey

Stone   183

Milborne St. Andrew

Ghosts   18, 35
Strange Event   246

Milton Abbas

Witchcraft/Customs   156
Strange Event   249

Morcombelake

Mysterious Creatures   229

Muckleford

Ghosts   15

Netherbury

Dark History   108, 133
Devil   192
Fairies   108
Witchcraft   108

North Poorton

Ghosts	19

Okeford Fitzpaine

Devil	196
Fairies	109

Pimperne

Customs	168, 169
Ghosts	20, 21
Mysterious Creatures	229

Poole

Dark History	13
Fairies	114
Ghosts	18, 43, 102, 103
Mysterious Creatures	213
Strange Event	251, 254, 258
Will O' Wisp	103, 124

Portesham

Devil/Stone	185, 186
Ghosts	23
Mysterious Creatures	216, 233

Portland

Customs	156, 159, 165
Dark History	131
Devil/Stone	185
Mysterious Creatures	199, 204, 205, 206, 218 - 222, 232, 235
Strange Event	239, 241, 244, 251, 253
Witchcraft	156, 165

Powerstock

Devil	193
Ghosts	18, 19, 104
Will O' Wisp	126

Puddletown

Ghosts	54
Strange Event	246, 249, 251

Puncknowle

Mysterious Creatures	213, 214, 233

Purse Caundle

Ghosts	56, 57
Strange Event	255

Salway Ash

Mysterious Creatures	237
Strange Event	248

Shaftesbury

Devil	191
Mysterious Creatures	235
Strange Event	249, 255

Sherborne

Dark History	153
Ghosts	14, 41, 57
Mysterious Creatures	199
Witchcraft	153

Shipton Gorge

Mysterious Creatures	229, 233
Ghosts	13

Sixpenny Handley

Devil	192
Strange Event	249
Mysterious Creatures	213, 229

Sleight

Witchcraft	148

Stalbridge

Ghosts	47, 48, 49
Strange Event	259, 260

Stoke Abbot

Dark History	88
Mysterious Creatures	236
Ghosts	17

Stourpaine

Mysterious Creatures	228

Studland

Devil/Stone	189
Fairies/Stone	110
Ghosts	46
Mysterious Creatures	199

Sturminster Newton

Mysterious Creatures	234
Ghosts	57
Fairies	112
Will O' Wisp	126
Witchcraft	154

Sutton Poyntz

Strange Event	249

Swanage

Ghosts	41
Strange Event	248

Symondsbury

Dark History	131
Fairies	107
Ghosts	23
Mysterious Creatures	236, 237

Tarrant Gunville

Ghosts	51 - 53

Thorncombe

Devil	194
Strange Event	240

Todber

Dark History	18

Toller Down

Devil/Stone	189

Tolpuddle

Strange Event	247

Trent

Ghosts	15
Strange Event	15

Turners Puddle

Devil	189

Tyneham

Dark History	31 - 35
Ghosts	31 - 35
Mysterious Creatures	233

Ulwell

Witchcraft	150

Wareham

Fairies	115
Ghosts	15, 37, 38, 39

West Bay

Devil	196

West Milton

Ghosts	18

Weymouth

Dark History	129, 131
Witchcraft	152
Ghosts	41, 46, 92, 94, 97, 98, 99, 100
Mysterious Creatures	203, 230, 231,

Strange Event	235, 244, 246, 247, 248, 249, 251, 252, 254, 256, 258	**Wool**	
		Ghosts	15, 16, 17
		Mysterious Creatures	199
Will O' Wisp	122, 126	**Worth Matravers**	

Whitcombe

		Customs	122
		Devil	196
Fairies	107	*Ghosts*	40
Mysterious Creatures	199	*Will O' Wisp*	122
Strange Event	136	*Witchcraft*	148

Yetminster

Strange Event	244

Wimborne

Ghosts	43, 100

Winfrith Newburgh

Fairies	110
Witchcraft/Customs	156
Strange Event	249

Winterborne Abbas

Devil/Stone	187
Ghosts	37
Stone	184

Winterborne Herringston

Strange Event	249

Winterborne Monkton

Ghosts	41
Strange Event	264

Woodcutts

Devil	192
Mysterious Creatures	229

Woodyates

Dark History	69
Mysterious Creatures	229

- Ancient Hillforts -

Badbury Rings

Ghosts 43

Dudsbury Camp

Ghosts 96

Eggardon

Devil	193
Ghosts	37, 161
Mysterious Creatures	233
Strange Event	245, 246
Will O' Wisp	126

Hambledon Hill

Devil	196
Ghosts	46

Hod Hill

Ghosts	46
Mysterious Creatures	228

Maiden Castle

Ghosts	43
Strange Event	249

- Coastline -

Chapman's Pool

Ghosts 40

Chesil Beach

Customs	166
Mysterious Creatures	197, 204, 205
Strange Event	248

Ringstead†
Strange Event 247, 256, 258

Worbarrow Bay

Ghosts 35

- Dorset/Devon Border -

Uplyme

Ghosts	72
Mysterious Creatures	224, 225, 227, 228

THE CENTRE FOR FORTEAN ZOOLOGY

The Centre for Fortean Zoology is the world's only professional and scientific organisation dedicated to research into unknown animals. Although we work all over the world, we carry out regular work in the United Kingdom and abroad, investigating accounts of strange creatures.

THAILAND 2000
An expedition to investigate the legendary creature known as the Naga

SUMATRA 2003
'Project Kerinci'
In search of the bipedal ape Orang Pendek

MONGOLIA 2005
'Operation Death Worm'
An expedition to track the fabled 'Allghoi Khorkhoi' or Death Worm

Led by scientists, the CFZ is staffed by volunteers and is always looking for new members.

To apply for a <u>FREE</u> information pack about the organisation and details of how to join, plus information on current and future projects, expeditions and events.

Send a stamped, addressed envelope to:

THE CENTRE FOR FORTEAN ZOOLOGY
MYRTLE COTTAGE, WOOLSERY,
BIDEFORD, DEVON, EX39 5QR.

or alternatively visit our website at: www.cfz.org.uk

Other books available from
CFZ PRESS

THE OWLMAN AND OTHERS - 30th Anniversary Edition
Jonathan Downes - ISBN 978-1-905723-02-7

£14.99

EASTER 1976 - Two young girls playing in the churchyard of Mawnan Old Church in southern Cornwall were frightened by what they described as a "nasty bird-man". These sightings have continued to the present day. These grotesque and frightening episodes have fascinated researchers for three decades now, and one man has spent years collecting all the available evidence into a book. To mark the 30th anniversary of these sightings, Jonathan Downes, has published a special edition of his book.

DRAGONS - More than a myth?
Richard Freeman - ISBN 0-9512872-9-X

£14.99

First scientific look at dragons since 1884. It looks at dragon legends worldwide, and examines modern sightings of dragon-like creatures, as well as some of the more esoteric theories surrounding dragonkind. Dragons are discussed from a folkloric, historical and cryptozoological perspective, and Richard Freeman concludes that: *"When your parents told you that dragons don't exist - they lied!"*

MONSTER HUNTER
Jonathan Downes - ISBN 0-9512872-7-3

£14.99

Jonathan Downes' long-awaited autobiography, *Monster Hunter*... Written with refreshing candour, it is the extraordinary story of an extraordinary life, in which the author crosses paths with wizards, rock stars, terrorists, and a bewildering array of mythical and not so mythical monsters, and still just about manages to emerge with his sanity intact.......

MONSTER OF THE MERE
Jonathan Downes - ISBN 0-9512872-2-2

£12.50

It all starts on Valentine's Day 2002, when a Lancashire newspaper announces that "Something" has been attacking swans at a nature reserve in Lancashire. Eyewitnesses have reported that a giant unknown creature has been dragging fully grown swans beneath the water at Martin Mere. An intrepid team from the Exeter based Centre for Fortean Zoology, led by the author, make two trips – each of a week – to the lake and its surrounding marshlands. During their investigations they uncover a thrilling and complex web of historical fact and fancy, quasi Fortean occurrences, strange animals and even human sacrifice.

CFZ PRESS, MYRTLE COTTAGE,
WOOLFARDISWORTHY BIDEFORD,
NORTH DEVON, EX39 5QR
w w w . c f z . o r g . u k

Other books available from
CFZ PRESS

ONLY FOOLS AND GOATSUCKERS
Jonathan Downes - ISBN 0-9512872-3-0

£12.50

In January and February 1998 Jonathan Downes and Graham Inglis of the Centre for Fortean Zoology spent three and a half weeks in Puerto Rico, Mexico and Florida, accompanied by a film crew from UK Channel 4 TV. Their aim was to make a documentary about the terrifying chupacabra - a vampiric creature that exists somewhere in the grey area between folklore and reality. This remarkable book tells the gripping, sometimes scary, and often hilariously funny, story of how the boys from the CFZ did their best to subvert the medium of contemporary TV documentary making, and actually do their job.

WHILE THE CAT'S AWAY
Chris Moiser - ISBN: 0-9512872-1-4

£7.99

Over the past thirty years or so, there have been numerous sightings of large exotic cats, including black leopards, pumas and lynx, in the South West of England. Former Rhodesian soldier Sam McCall moved to North Devon and became a farmer and pub owner when Rhodesia became Zimbabwe in 1980. Over the years despite many of his pub regulars having seen the "Beast of Exmoor" Sam wasn't at all sure that it existed. Then a series of happenings made him change his mind. Chris Moiser - a zoologist - is well known for his research into the mystery cats of the westcountry. This is his first novel.

CFZ EXPEDITION REPORT 2006 - GAMBIA
ISBN 1905723032

£12.50

In July 2006, The J.T.Downes memorial Gambia Expedition - a six-person team - Chris Moiser, Richard Freeman, Chris Clarke, Oll Lewis, Lisa Dowley and Suzi Marsh went to the Gambia, West Africa. They went in search of a dragon-like creature, known to the natives as `Ninki Nanka`, which has terrorized the tiny African state for generations, and has reportedly killed people as recently as the 1990s. They also went to dig up part of a beach where an amateur naturalist claims to have buried the carcass of a mysterious fifteen foot sea monster named 'Gambo', and they sought to find the Armitage's Skink (Chalcides armitagei) - a tiny lizard first described in 1922 and only rediscovered in 1989. Here, for the first time, is their story.... With an foreword by Dr. Karl Shuker and introduction by Jonathan Downes.

BIG CATS IN BRITAIN YEARBOOK 2006
Edited by Mark Fraser - ISBN 978-1905723-01-0

£10.00

Big cats are said to roam the British Isles and Ireland even now, as you are sitting and reading this. People from all walks of life encounter these mysterious felines on a daily basis, in every nook and cranny of these two countries. Most are jet-black, some are white, some are brown; in fact big cats of every description and colour are seen by some unsuspecting person while on his or her daily business. 'Big Cats in Britain' are the largest and most active research group in the British Isles and Ireland This is their first book. It contains a run-down of every known big cat sighting in the UK during 2005, together with essays by various luminaries of the British big cat research community which place the phenomenon into scientific, cultural, and historical perspective.

CFZ PRESS, MYRTLE COTTAGE, WOOLFARDISWORTHY BIDEFORD, NORTH DEVON, EX39 5QR
www.cfz.org.uk

Other books available from
CFZ PRESS

THE SMALLER MYSTERY CARNIVORES OF THE WESTCOUNTRY
Jonathan Downes - ISBN 978-1-905723-05-8

£7.99

Although much has been written in recent years about the mystery big cats which have been reported stalking Westcountry moorlands, little has been written on the subject of the smaller British mystery carnivores. This unique book redresses the balance and examines the current status in the Westcountry of three species thought to be extinct: the Wildcat, the Pine Marten, and the Polecat, finding that the truth is far more exciting than the currently held scientific dogma. This book also uncovers evidence suggesting that even more exotic species of small mammal may lurk hitherto unsuspected in the countryside of Devon, Cornwall, Somerset and Dorset.

THE BLACKDOWN MYSTERY
Jonathan Downes - ISBN 978-1-905723-00-3

£7.99

This is the soft underbelly of ufology, rife with unsavoury characters, plenty of drugs and booze." That sums it up quite well, we think. A new edition of the classic 1999 book by legendary fortean author Jonathan Downes.

In this remarkable book, Jon weaves a complex tale of conspiracy, anti-conspiracy, quasi-conspiracy and downright lies surrounding an air-crash and alleged UFO incident in Somerset during 1996. However the story is much stranger than that. This excellent and amusing book lifts the lid off much of contemporary forteana and explains far more than it initially promises.

GRANFER'S BIBLE STORIES
John Downes - ISBN 0-9512872-8-1

£7.99

Bible stories in the Devonshire vernacular, each story being told by an old Devon Grandfather - 'Granfer'. These stories are now collected together in a remarkable book presenting selected parts of the Bible as one more-or-less continuous tale in short 'bite sized' stories intended for dipping into or even for bed-time reading. `Granfer` treats the biblical characters as if they were simple country folk living in the next village. Many of the stories are treated with a degree of bucolic humour and kindly irreverence, which not only gives the reader an opportunity to re-evaluate familiar tales in a new light, but do so in both an entertaining and a spiritually uplifting manner.

FRAGRANT HARBOURS DISTANT RIVERS
John Downes - ISBN 0-9512872-5-7

£12.50

Many excellent books have been written about Africa during the second half of the 19th Century, but this one is unique in that it presents the stories of a dozen different people, whose interlinked lives and achievements have as many nuances as any contemporary soap opera. It explains how the events in China and Hong Kong which surrounded the Opium Wars, intimately effected the events in Africa which take up the majority of this book. The author served in the Colonial Service in Nigeria and Hong Kong, during which he found himself following in the footsteps of one of the main characters in this book; Frederick Lugard – the architect of modern Nigeria.

CFZ PRESS, MYRTLE COTTAGE,
WOOLFARDISWORTHY BIDEFORD,
NORTH DEVON, EX39 5QR
www.cfz.org.uk

Other books available from
CFZ PRESS

ANIMALS & MEN - Issues 1 - 5 - In the Beginning
Edited by Jonathan Downes - ISBN 0-9512872-6-5

£12.50

At the beginning of the 21st Century monsters still roam the remote, and sometimes not so remote, corners of our planet. It is our job to search for them. The Centre for Fortean Zoology [CFZ] is the only professional, scientific and full-time organisation in the world dedicated to cryptozoology - the study of unknown animals. Since 1992 the CFZ has carried out an unparalleled programme of research and investigation all over the world. We have carried out expeditions to Sumatra (2003 and 2004), Mongolia (2005), Puerto Rico (1998 and 2004), Mexico (1998), Thailand (2000), Florida (1998), Nevada (1999 and 2003), Texas (2003 and 2004), and Illinois (2004). An introductory essay by Jonathan Downes, notes putting each issue into a historical perspective, and a history of the CFZ.

ANIMALS & MEN - Issues 6 - 10 - The Number of the Beast
Edited by Jonathan Downes - ISBN 978-1-905723-06-5

£12.50

At the beginning of the 21st Century monsters still roam the remote, and sometimes not so remote, corners of our planet. It is our job to search for them. The Centre for Fortean Zoology [CFZ] is the only professional, scientific and full-time organisation in the world dedicated to cryptozoology - the study of unknown animals. Since 1992 the CFZ has carried out an unparalleled programme of research and investigation all over the world. We have carried out expeditions to Sumatra (2003 and 2004), Mongolia (2005), Puerto Rico (1998 and 2004), Mexico (1998), Thailand (2000), Florida (1998), Nevada (1999 and 2003), Texas (2003 and 2004), and Illinois (2004). Preface by Mark North and an introductory essay by Jonathan Downes, notes putting each issue into a historical perspective, and a history of the CFZ.

BIG BIRD! Modern Sightings of Flying Monsters

Ken Gerhard - ISBN 978-1-905723-08-9

£7.99

Today, from all over the dusty U.S. / Mexican border, come hair-raising stories of modern day encounters with winged monsters of immense size and terrifying appearance. Further field sightings of similar creatures are recorded from all around the globe: The Kongamato of Africa, the Ropen of New Guinea and many others. What lies behind these weird tales? Ken Gerhard is in pole position to find out. A native Texan, he lives in the homeland of the monster some call 'Big Bird'. Cryptozoologist, author, adventurer, and gothic musician, Ken is a larger than life character as amazing as the Big Bird itself. Ken's scholarly work is the first of its kind. The research and fieldwork involved are indeed impressive. On the track of the monster, Ken uncovers cases of animal mutilations, attacks on humans, and mounting evidence of a stunning zoological discovery ignored by mainstream science. Something incredible awaits us on the broad desert horizon. Keep watching the skies!

STRENGTH THROUGH KOI
They saved Hitler's Koi and other stories

Jonathan Downes - ISBN 978-1-905723-04-1

£7.99

Strength through Koi is a book of short stories - some of them true, some of them less so - by noted cryptozoologist and raconteur Jonathan Downes. Very funny in parts, this book is highly recommended for anyone with even a passing interest in aquaculture.

**CFZ PRESS, MYRTLE COTTAGE,
WOOLFARDISWORTHY BIDEFORD,
NORTH DEVON, EX39 5QR
w w w . c f z . o r g . u k**

Other books available from
CFZ PRESS

BIG CATS IN BRITAIN YEARBOOK 2007
Edited by Mark Fraser - ISBN 978-1-905723-09-6

£12.50

Big cats are said to roam the British Isles and Ireland even now as you are sitting and reading this. People from all walks of life encounter these mysterious felines on a daily basis in every nook and cranny of these two countries. Most are jet-black, some are white, some are brown, in fact big cats of every description and colour are seen by some unsuspecting person while on his or her daily business. 'Big Cats in Britain' are the largest and most active group in the British Isles and Ireland This is their first book. It contains a run-down of every known big cat sighting in the UK during 2006, together with essays by various luminaries of the British big cat research community which place the phenomenon into scientific, cultural, and historical perspective.

CAT FLAPS! Northern Mystery Cats
Andy Roberts - ISBN 978-1-905723-11-9

£6.99

Of all Britain's mystery beasts, the alien big cats are the most renowned. In recent years the notoriety of these uncatchable, out-of-place predators have eclipsed even the Loch Ness Monster. They slink from the shadows to terrorise a community, and then, as often as not, vanish like ghosts. But now film, photographs, livestock kills, and paw prints show that we can no longer deny the existence of these once-legendary beasts. Here then is a case-study, a true lost classic of Fortean research by one of the country's most respected researchers; Andy Roberts. Cat Flaps! is the product of many years of research and field work in the 1970s and 80s, an odyssey through the phantom felids of the North East of England. Follow Andy on his flat cap safari as he trails such creatures as the 'Whitby lynx', the 'Harrogate panther', and the 'Durham puma'. Written with humour, intelligence, and a healthy dose of scepticism, Cat Flaps! is a book that deserves a place on the bookshelf of every cryptozoologist.

CENTRE FOR FORTEAN ZOOLOGY 2007 YEARBOOK
Edited by Jonathan Downes and Richard Freeman
ISBN 978-1-905723-14-0

£12.50

The Centre For Fortean Zoology Yearbook is a collection of papers and essays too long and detailed for publication in the CFZ Journal Animals & Men. With contributions from both well-known researchers, and relative newcomers to the field, the Yearbook provides a forum where new theories can be expounded, and work on little-known cryptids discussed.

MONSTER! THE A-Z OF ZOOFORM PHENOMENA
Neil Arnold
ISBN 978-1-905723-10-2

£14.99

Zooform Phenomena are the most elusive, and least understood, mystery `animals`. Indeed, they are not animals at all, and are not even animate in the accepted terms of the word, but entities or apparitions which adopt, or seem to have (quasi) animal form.

These arcane and contentious entities have plagued cryptozoology - the study of unknown animals - since its inception, and tend to be dismissed by mainstream science as thoroughly unworthy of consideration. But they continue to be seen, and Jonathan Downes - the Director of the Centre for Fortean Zoology - who first coined the term in 1990, maintains that many zooforms result from a synergy of complex psychosocial and sociological issues, and suggests that to classify all such phenomena as "paranormal" in origin is counterproductive, and for researchers to dismiss them out of hand is thoroughly unscientific.

Author and researcher Neil Arnold is to be commended for a groundbreaking piece of work, and has provided the world's first alphabetical listing of zooforms from around the world.

CFZ PRESS, MYRTLE COTTAGE, WOOLFARDISWORTHY BIDEFORD, NORTH DEVON, EX39 5QR
w w w . c f z . o r g . u k

Printed in the United Kingdom
by Lightning Source UK Ltd.
123808UK00001B/464/A